The Ten Word Game

a&b

The Ten Word Game
JONATHAN GASH

Acknowledgements

The QE2, P&O Line, and the Curators of the Hermitage Museum, St Petersburg, Russia

Thanks: **Ta, Susan**

This edition published in Great Britain in 2004 by
Allison & Busby Limited
Bon Marche Centre
241-251 Ferndale Road
London SW9 8BJ
http://www.allisonandbusby.com

A catalogue record for this book is available from
the British Library.

ISBN 0 7490 8321 2

Printed and bound in Great Britain by
Bookmarque Ltd, Croydon, Surrey.

Jackie with love

They are like strawberry wives, that laid two or three great strawberries at the mouth of their pot, and all the rest are little ones.

Queen Elizabeth the First (1533-1603)

Chapter One

The woman beside me slept. I thought, is she the one?

Years ago, I invented the Ten Word Game. It's simple: put any problem into ten words. No extras. You can describe the Olympics, America, or the entire universe in ten words. Try it.

You can also describe a woman. I'm not saying it's easy, just that it teaches you.

Like this: A young engaged couple met as usual. "I've found another," she told him. "He's a go-getter so I'm leaving you. Goodbye."

He said, "I've just won the lottery. I'm a multi-millionaire. Bye!"

True story, thank God. Nobody would believe you if you made that up.

In the ten words, though? Here goes: Two lovers; she dumps him; he scoops lottery.

See? It's all there, so you've won the Ten Word Game. I looked along the pillow at the lovely woman. She was so tired after her journey.

We'd come together when I was forced to rob the Hermitage Museum in beautiful St Petersburg, Russia. Ever since I'd arrived back, astonished to find her in my lonely cottage, I'd been trying to express her in ten words. But women and antiques are the Ten Word Game I can never win.

I didn't even know how she'd got there. Course, I was relieved, delighted, thrilled. Worn out after everything we'd been through, I gave up, pulled her close and slept.

* * *

The great ocean liner's funnel was just visible. I'd been staring at the thing ever since it hoved in (note the nautical term) at eight o'clock that morning.

"Work!" Benjo boomed. "No idlings!"

"Right, boss."

"No staring at ships." He gave me a glare. "Work! Make this place no mess!"

"Right, boss."

Meanwhile, his gorgeous wife Gloria was making her entrance, the minute I arrived. It was a performance. First, down the steep stairs her high-heeled white shoes would appear. Then her lovely legs. Then the trim skirt, the exquisite shape, the frilly blouse, the voluptuous figure and the dazzling bracelets, emerald-littered watch, the eight-tiered necklace that dulled the vision, the looped diamond earrings, and the blinding blonde hair adorned with diamond slides.

Finally reaching land, Gloria examined her reflection in a phoney antique cheval mirror. This needed tutted exclamations and a handbag bulging with cosmetics. She applied lipstick thickly to a lurid scarlet mouth, plastered her cheeks with layers of creams, rouge, did her eyes with those gruesome black brushes, layered on more unguents, preened her hair – a gleaming array – and smoothed her hands down her hips. After more posturing, she did a slick pivot and said, "Well, I'll just have to do!" The galaxy could relax.

Gloria was hypnotic. I admire beauty.

Her labour consisted of lighting a cigarette while perched on her stool at the shop counter. For an hour she would sit there, dealing with no customers and repeatedly checking her face in a diamond hand mirror. Tennish, she would sigh and say, "God, it's been one of those mornings!" and depart for coffee in the Barter Mart.

This busy schedule called for an absence of three hours, after which she would return laden with boxes from Bright Flight or Hex Pecks, shops famed for expensive designer apparel, and announce, eyes fluttering, "I think I deserve a lie down. Call me if there's a rush." And upstairs she would go. Not a single one of us – me especially not – ever noticed her exquisite legs receding step by seductive step upstairs to her well-deserved slumber. Thoughts of Gloria reclining in abandon didn't cross anyone's mind. I mean that most sincerely.

Benjo was her husband, a squat man of enormous girth, sweating continually in a string singlet. Black hair fungated above his straining belt. Think of a wheezing mattress coming unstuffed, and you have Benjo. He bawled continually into two or three cell phones at a time, breathing garlic fumes through a mat of stubble and giving out abuse in sundry Middle-Eastern languages interspersed with threatening phrases from American gangster films. "I keel you bizniz total!" was one favourite, with "I mek offer no refuse!" his ultimate screamed menace. Our importers seemed unfazed and always sent their goods in days late.

There were three employees. One was Frollie, an indispensable lady who hated Gloria, and a van driver called Tez who'd once worked the Cunard Ocean Liners as a steward. Frollie had a husband who operated Southampton's football turnstiles. Tez had a wife who did school dinners. Each lunch-hour Frollie and Tez retired to a store-room, locking the door until their silent withdrawal, so to speak, was up. They emerged never to look at each other for the rest of the day. They had been at Benjo's fifteen years. Benjo and his missus Gloria lived above the Emporium.

Then there was me. I'd joined three days before.

By way of introduction Frollie shot me the usual woman's questions whenever Benjo was screeching into his phones and no massive throngs were queuing for our desirable tatty produce. She had a habit of answering her own questions. Like, "You don't live local," or "Divorce, I'll bet." And, "It was women who ruined you. I can always tell." Tez made me help with the loading. I asked him about ships.

"Don't work the cruises," he told me. "Run you ragged." And the grimmest warning of all, "More intrigue on board than anywhere." The third time I asked him about getting a job aboard he appraised me, fag smoke wrinkling his eyes.

"You on the run, mate?"

"Me?" I was indignant.

"You're edgy as a frog in a pot, mate. Eyes everywhere, and you jump a mile when a customer comes in. Don't worry. Me and Frollie never says nothing to nobody not nohow."

"Not me, Tez," I said, innocently.

"Half the crews are illicit. Trouble is, there's the parade – that's the shipping union, see?"

"Oh."

My heart sank. No escape on there, then.

The shop was untidy with unlabelled boxes and goods stacked between grimy windows. Nobody knew what they contained except Tez, and he only guessed. Our shop front proclaimed to the waiting world "Benjo Diamond's Mail Order Emporium". On show were indescribable heaps of frocks – packed or unpacked made no difference – fake jewellery, dolls, toys, dud cameras (I'd tried one) and plastic anythings. There was also Today's Great Free Gift Prize for the next lucky shopper. The one customer who dared to ask if she'd won the Great Free Gift after buying a ten-penny packet of elastic bands received a tirade of invective. Benjo threw her out, raising his hands and saying people wanted blood. He actually sobbed.

He paid me half the official minimum wage, though I was logged for over fifty hours a week. The previous Monday I'd spotted a postcard in his window saying

JOB VACANCY GOOD PAY. I went in, ready with a pack of lies to explain how a postal strike in East Anglia delayed my employment cards, the usual claptrap. Benjo looked me up and down. A knowing smile lit his eye. He said, "Start now." He paid me cash at five-thirty, deducting whatever he wanted. He knew I'd not complain. Frollie and Tez took me in their stride, and Gloria didn't even notice I was there.

Tez's news about the ships was grim. I'd have to scarper some other way. Cruise ships had seemed so easy – go aboard, and the engines would do the rest, whisk you off somewhere untraceable. Hunters don't think of luxury liners as a bolt-hole. I wondered about being a bus driver, but you're stuck behind a wheel for everyone to see. They'd catch me in an hour. Still, I was safe in Benjo's.

Until Thursday, when the world changed.

*　*　*

It rained Thursday worse than anything. I was early. Tez said there was a new cruise liner coming in at noon and I wanted to see it. She would berth in the great passenger terminal opposite. Even as I entered by the loading door – Benjo left a key under a brick, secret as the TV News – motor cars of passengers and dignitaries were thronging the dock gates. Camera crews were getting background footage. Some personage was going to re-enact the commissioning ceremony of the brand new white *Melissa*, so deserving of a rich clientele. I did my envious gape, longing to embark to safety.

"It's only me," I bawled up the stairs. "Good morning."

"Oke-kay, Lovejoy," Benjo called down. "Start end bay."

"Right, boss."

The rule was, first in got free coffee. Benjo kept a tin for money, the prices marked on the wall by the kettle. Six leaning stacks of cardboard containers blocked the loading bay. Tez wasn't in yet, so I'd have to move them to the exit bay. I switched the kettle on and stepped to the window, wistfully eyeing the passenger terminal, when two luscious arms extended round my middle and clasped tight.

"Isn't it time you saw to me?" a husky voice said in my ear.

"Gloria?" She'd never spoken to me before. She hadn't yet made her glamorous entrance.

"Benjo does his bank today. Come upstairs at five-past twelve. Tez and Frollie will be doing their thing."

And she was gone. I looked round, but this time I didn't even see her disappearing heels. No Gloria, just a faint perfume.

I swallowed. In the two months I'd been on the lam I'd had a score of jobs, all of them neff, all underpaid and some frighteningly risky. Like this. I knew Benjo would marmalise me if I so much as looked at Gloria. Women can be highly worrying. Time to leave?

If I scorned Gloria she might bubble me to Benjo, and that would be that. If I didn't, she might scream blue murder, yell I was Jack the Ripper. It's hard being a bloke, because you've nobody to call on if things go ballistic, and the only safety is miles away.

How people start courting these days I'll never know.

"Work! No starings!"

Sharply I came to. "Right, boss."

Benjo had come down. Hurriedly I started shifting the boxes of heavy toys, allegedly from Taiwan. Benjo composed labels for this crud on some machine he kept in his office. It was always a two-cigar job, fumes enveloping him as he tapped, yakking into sundry phones. I was sure he made the labels up, putting any old guesswork on each. It was Tez's task to drive them to Benjo's discerning customers.

Tez arrived, thin and cachectic, hanging up his jacket, flat cap on his peg and spitting on his hands. The van was in the loading bay. As I carried the boxes, I wondered about the nature of true love. Passion is strange stuff. I mean, Tez looked like a dried prune, face of a walnut and spindly limbs. Fifty, fifty-fivish? Decent bloke, but still something out of a cartoon. Frollie was a florid matronly figure, quite dumpy and getting on a bit, though age doesn't matter with women simply because they are what matters. Life can't go on without them. Every woman is interesting and has appeal, though women don't know this. They think that being young is everything, when in fact it's hardly anything to do with anything.

Even so, this hard-working couple ensconced in the locked storeroom every noon, presumably for supportive psychotherapy or other activities. I was glad for them, and so were they.

While hefting the boxes a queer thing happened. I fell over. Now, I gave up serious drink after Cissie left – she lived on doughnuts and olive oil and kept squirrels – so it couldn't be that, and I'd felt well until I picked up a box and humped it to the van's tail-board. Tez, with the extraordinary power of the wiry, picked me up.

"You okay?"

"Fine."

"He's shaking," Frollie said. "Hot sweet tea and a lie down."

"I'm fine." I stared at the box. It hadn't been heavy, just a wooden crated thing. The instant I stepped near it, I went dizzy. Only one sort of thing ever does that, so I knew it contained some genuine antique. "What's in these, Tez?"

He shrugged. "Just toys." He squinted at the label, invented seconds before by Benjo, and read it like gospel. "Father Christmas devices."

"You'd better lift that one. I'll bring the rest."

The van got loaded without any more ado.

Benjo announced he was going to the bank. I served a few customers. Benjo left. Tez drove the van away, brought it back empty. A woman came in asking for a set of toy Easter bunnies. I served her. She was pleasant, chatty, didn't want to go. Youngish, smart in a yellowish suit, hem expensively cut, specs and bright hair, she kept on saying, "I'll just have another glance round. Might find something. Have you worked here long?" I felt she was phoney. And I didn't like the look of a bloke hanging about outside. He'd parked his car in an illegal spot, and a strolling policeman simply got the nod and walked on. I gulped. Had they caught up with me? I judged the distance to the rear exit.

"You all right, mate?" Tez asked me.

"Women," Frollie said comfortably. "That's his trouble."

No such luck. It wasn't yet noon, when Gloria's tryst was due. I wondered even more about scarpering.

"Where do most of your imports come from?" the customer asked, smiling. "West Africa?"

"Dunno, miss," I said, uneasy. "The boss is out."

"Shall I wait? I'd like a talk with him."

Now, I'd already wrapped up her set of Nodding Easter Rabbits In Dazzling Colours (Batteries Not Provided). If she was so interested, she could read our brochure. I offered her one. She declined. Maybe its misspellings offended her aesthetic sensibility. ("You will enoff satisfy with our ranje and varietis!" and so on).

"We close at twelve, " I promised her, "and reopen at one. He'll be here then." But would I? "Can I say who asked for him?"

"My card. He's expecting us."

Us? She was alone. The bad feeling returned treble strength. I remembered the box that had felt so odd, and grew nervous. She looked directly into my eyes.

"I'll be back," she said, smiling in threat. Beautiful lady, spoke like a gun. I thought, you're Customs and Excise, love, that's who you are.

"Wait!" I called as she reached the door. Frollie gasped. Tez froze. I hurried after, carrying her Easter Rabbits. "You forgot these."

She actually laughed.

"Thank you. Mustn't forget those. Not at the prices you charge."

Her card said Miss Lacy Trimble, *Advisor*. I closed the door so it didn't clonk. The front entrance's Chiming Cowbell – another bargain line – really annoyed Gloria when she was having her lie down. She was always thumping on the floor for us to stop it.

Frollie and Tez looked over my shoulder to read the card.

"What does she advise on?" Frollie asked.

"Law," Tez and me said together.

"Advise who?"

We both stayed silent. The police, that's who.

"Tez? There's a bloke out there."

Tez went to the window, but the man and his motor had vanished as Miss Trimble left. Tez looked worried. Frollie looked worse.

"Just shift that last box, mate." There was one by the loading bay. "Stick it in the van. We'll shut early."

He and Frollie locked the front door and went into the store-room. Alone, I went to lift the box. My chest went thick and hurting, my breathing slowed and damned near stopped altogether. I recoiled a few paces, and instantly felt right as rain. My giddiness ended, the shop straightened. I felt normal. It was the box. Same one, or different? I turned. Tez was standing watching.

"You okay, pal?"

"Fine, Tez, ta."

He went back in and I heard the lock go. They went quiet. Well, it was only a partition wall.

For a second I hesitated, then drew breath and rushed the box, lifted it and almost hurled it in the van. As if in a dream, I saw my knuckles whiten as they gripped one of Tez's crowbars from the van's rack, and prised the wood. I'd done it often enough. The rule is, never disturb the slats, then they look untouched after you shove them back in place. I lifted one slat then another, and moved the packing. Sweat started pouring off me. My hands shook like an old man's and my vision swam. I stared at the single object inside. It took only half a second for me to know.

Trembling and aching, dizzy as a bat, my legs shaking as if my malaria was back, I pressed the slats down, risked one thump of the nails with the crowbar, and went back inside.

Gloria was on the stairs. "What time did I say?" she asked, smiling.

"Noon, missus."

She looked at the clock. It was a minute to. "Come on, then." I followed her heels upstairs, politely trying to look anywhere else and failing. I'm good at that.

Chapter Two

"Was I all right?"

Here's a basic truth: I can't understand women. How come they all wonder the same thing? Gloria had been ecstasy, bliss, paradise. Yet there she lay, head on the pillow, frowning and giving me was she all right. Can you believe it?

"Perfect. Heaven."

She propped herself up on an elbow, took hold of my face so I couldn't look away with any sincerity.

"Honestly?"

"As God's my judge. You were wondrous."

Her brow cleared. "I've never heard anybody tell me that before. Wondrous!"

Like I say, this passion business is beyond me. What on earth did other blokes tell her? That she'd been so-so? Say to her, well, Gloria, you were really pretty average, something like that? I could see I'd have to be tactful.

"You're off your frigging trolley, love. If you're stunning, what else is there?"

She wouldn't give in. "As good as the rest?"

What rest? I worried for a second. Did she know anybody I knew? I finally guessed she was still anxious. "Blinding, love."

"Tez said you were taken poorly in the loading bay." She smiled to herself.

"Eh? Oh, just dizzy. Lifting the crates."

She drew a pattern in the sweat on my chest.

"I like a man who sweats. It's rewarding."

"What does Benjo say?" I was more worried than she. This job was protective colouration. If Benjo found out about me and Gloria, I'd have to vanish sharpish.

"Benjo does as I say." She glanced at the clock and

lay back. "Time for more?"

Where's the choice? Women rule. It's their world. We blokes only get by. It was definitely love, but listening for the warning clonk of the downstairs door's Chiming Cowbell was frightening. Benjo was a giant.

* * *

I woke with my heart thumping, thinking I'd heard something. Gloria was in the bathroom. I tried to calm myself. My hair was drenched as usual afterwards. I thought of the crate that made me keel over in the loading bay.

Antiques are all the rage nowadays. That's because stocks and shares change with the weather. Hour by hour, something in Kyoto causes the dollar's value to evaporate or double. There's no escaping the evil erosion of gold prices or land investments, even the value of your own house for God's sake. Everything is a shifting sand.

Except antiques.

Think of your Great-Aunt Faith's alexandrite pendant, the one her spouse George brought home after the First World War. Its setting is now so unfashionable that youngsters wouldn't touch it with a bargepole, right? The wretched thing is hardly worth a light, and no lady would wear it for a gold clock. The jeweller you take it to sneers (they're really good at sneers) "There's no call for this old Moscow jewellery, love. Too dated." And he'll offer a groat for it, to "take it off your hands."

Don't believe a word. Here's why:

Once upon a time, there was no such thing as alexandrite. Okay, we all know it's a gemstone and was there lurking in the ground these gillion years, but until Tzar Alexander the First lent his name to the lovely greenish stone it was never seen. Therefore an early Russian setting is valuable, simply by definition. Therefore the jeweller is fibbing, hoping you'll sell it him for a song. The lesson is this: unless you're a drug-pusher or a gun-runner or a Stock Exchange insider trader, you have no way of beating the system except honest work and frugality.

But one magic wand outdoes Savings and Loan systems the world over. It leaves government Blue-Chip stocks standing. It outstrips gold, junk bonds, and investment corporations. Everybody knows it.

It is a blindingly brilliant world in microcosm called antiques.

Now, I've always had a flaw – two, if you count women. Antiques send me strange, very like a sudden attack of early flu. I've only to stop near a genuine Rembrandt and my breathing goes funny. My vision flickers and shifts, like seeing things underwater. A doctor I know says my blood pressure must fall like a stone, but much he knows. If I step away a minute or two I'm right as rain. Stand near an exquisite cabinet by Hepplewhite, a Sheraton desk or Chippendale bureau, and over I go again. In the antiques trade a person who does this is called a divvy.

It doesn't happen with fakes, frauds, forgeries, or anything modern. Because all things modern are crud and gunge, a divvy like me is a vital commodity. A divvy can tell if your antique is antique, or (horror of horrors) isn't.

When I opened that crate and shifted the packing – those expanded polystyrene squiggles nobody ever knows the name of – I saw instantly. It had looked like a strange wooden doll. (Incidentally, I'm not being blasphemous here, just trying to describe.) It resembled a squat truncated figure with its feet in a puddle. Its hair was swept in a racing-helmet shape. Its legs were shorter than legs have a right to be, and its arms were almost unshaped. Brass rings on its wrists, deltoids and neck, and no features to speak of. It stood on a little plinth.

Worthless, right? Wrong. It was an ancient reliquary statuette, and worth three times your house plus your most valuable car plus all the clothes you stand up in. I'd guess it was the sort anthropologists call Fang Byeri, from Gabon. The little figure stood no taller than, say, ten inches (26cm if you're a metric maniac) and shone with a black patina. Modern fakes are imported by the hundred, but they're great tall things almost up to your shoulder – skilfully carved, but not worth a light. They're what the trade calls firewood.

Now, the brass on this little doll thing was merely brass, and the wood was only wood. But to an antique dealer it was money in the bank, *especially if imported illegally*. I gulped, remembering that smart Miss Lacy Trimble who'd bought some Bargain Line crud. Benjo was working an illegal scam, and the Excise plod were onto him. Definitely time to go.

Something made me look up. Benjo was standing in the – *his* – bedroom doorway. I yelped, sweated more.

"Iss okeh," he said soothingly. "You okeh?"

"Yes!" I whimpered, lying, because my last hour had come.

"No!" he thundered. "Stay still! Get water. Water iss good, no?"

"Yes!" I whined, crazy about water.

"He fell over, Benjo," Gloria said over his shoulder in that accusing tone women use when somebody's not well. She was fully dressed, thank God. I wished I was. "He's not been eating properly."

"Why you no eatings?" Benjo boomed, jabbing a finger at me.

"I…" Why wasn't I eating?

I'm like a gannet. I'd had some fried eggs and toast

in the doss-house that morning, two bananas, stale left-over cake and some sardines in chip paper. I couldn't admit to Benjo I was a divvy, and had rumbled his smuggling scam just as the Customs woman had come a-hunting, could I? Actually I was hungry as hell. Making smiles with Gloria had left me famished. I could hardly tell him that, either.

"Feedings!" Benjo yelled. "He iss on run, no?"

Gloria gave that smile-without-smiling only women can do, and said, "Go downstairs, Benjo. I'll get him back on his feet. Give me an hour."

"Good! I yev eem new job."

Gloria smiled and locked the door after him. We were alone.

She came over and stood looking down. She undid the belt of her skirt, her eyes on mine. I honestly don't know how women do it. They're cool. If I tried to get away with half the things they do, I'd go to pieces. I suppose that's why the best spies are female.

I should have remembered that.

* * *

I wasn't put out by Benjo's machinations. I'm as honest as the next person (joke), and everybody's at it, selling daftness as value. I know a lass called Nina in Southwold who sells psychic powers. She says she can tell if your dog is a born hypnotist. Truly. She calls herself Queen of Hypno-Dogs, and charges you a week's wage per dog, plus travelling expenses. She looks into your dog's eyes, and gives you a certificate stating your dog is (or is not; I don't know her figures) a hypnotherapist. Naturally, the dog hasn't a clue, just wanting some tasty morsel. She dreamt the idea up two years ago and hasn't done a day's work since. And, just like Mr Cruft (yes, him) she hates dogs, loves cats.

And a dealer who lives off a similar con trick. He's called Aussie, lives in Brixton, and markets antique statues of the Virgin Mary. They're made in Taiwan, cost eight zlotniks plus p&p. On Good Friday they're supposed to weep tears, but only if you, the proud owner worshipping her on the mantelpiece, have been good during the previous year. Work out the chances of *that* in the average household. A sort of morals barometer, they sell like hot cakes. They never work. If the Virgin fails to weep, whose fault is that? You've been bad, see?

Kellon's another. He's a Norfolk ticket tout at boxing arenas. On the side, he fakes (and sells and sells) Sir John Suckling's one and only prototype cribbage board. It is Kellon's only antique forgery, yet he makes a decent living. He turns out one every three months and advertises them on the internet. When that brave and elegant Cavalier poet Suckling invented cribbage ("the world's greatest card game") in the early 17th century, it took all England by storm, then Europe and the world. There are a million other scams, so many it makes you wonder if all money isn't scammified. I like scams, as long as consters don't con me.

Ho Chi Minh's flatmate's private diary is another regular fake, very common in London this year. As a young bloke, that esteemed leader had digs in London, being a humble assistant pastry cook at the Carlton. Several of HCM's mythical flatmate's diaries come to the market every now and then, full of revealing details about his early years. People always buy them even though everyone knows they're duds. Fake diaries aren't all Hitler's, Churchill's, Shakespeare's, or Queen Victoria's. One I particularly like is the vaunted *Diary of a Young Lady of Fashion, 1764-1765*, published in 1926. Back then it rattled through nine editions in a few weeks, to critical acclaim. It was in fact the fake dreamery of Magdalen, the Irish teenage daughter of Admiral Sir George King-Hall of the Royal Navy. Collectors still hunt first editions.

In East Anglia alone, we are offered Jimi Hendrix's last guitar at least once a month, properly smashed and burnt – fake, of course. The star destroyed his instruments, to the delight of all, on stage during performances. Most of these forgeries are pathetic travesties. I can't understand fakers who go to endless lengths to buy and smash the correct make of guitar (*Stratocaster*, if you're going for it) and even engrave it with his paratrooper's red parachute and 101st Airborne, his mob, then mess the forgery up by offering you a manufacturer's bill-of-sale dated 1971, when Hendrix actually died the year before. Crazy not to check details. The library's free, for God's sake. I hate sloppiness.

If you're a forger, at least get it wrong right, right?

Cheapest and, I think, cruellest of all are the mysticism scams. Pottle Bott and his woman – in Archway, London – market "mystic triangles", actually simple pieces of job-lot black silk. You buy one, put it on your forehead facing north-east (or any other way, I suppose) and it foretells your future. Unbelievably, Pottle sells over 1,000 every year, and there's their next Mediterranean holiday.

The laughable, weepable, thing is, when fakers get collared and clinked up for misleading the honest old public, they instantly pitify themselves. Indignant to the end, they always claim they were innocent, and say things like, "People are glad to be diddled, so where's harm?" Most breathtaking fib of all, they claim the goods were genuine at the time they were sold, so must have been replaced by fakes – corrupt police in court, you understand.

The problem is, where is the honest person who can

swear blind they've never deceived a single soul in their lives? Not me, nor anyone else I know, either.

* * *

That afternoon – me even hungrier – Benjo outlined my new job.

"I wann you go place," he told me.

I'd forgotten it was his sausage time. Three o'clock, he sent Frollie for some hot sausages as long as your arm. These he scoffed, slurping and belching, with the weirdest shaped pickles on earth. I don't mind what people eat, honest, but I wished he'd wash his fingers instead of wiping them down his singlet.

"Anywhere, Benjo. I'll do anything."

The customer door clonked. I went to serve an elderly lady. She tottered in on crutches, breathing hard. I placed a chair for her and she subsided, smiling. Lot of smiling women today. I've no sense, so didn't heed the warning signs.

"I want two Giant Bonanza Garden Illuminators," she said.

Pleased at hearing I was being sent out to somewhere safe, I felt full of myself and said jauntily, "Say please, like a good girl."

"What?"

She was astonished, then chuckled. Her spectacles wobbled and almost fell. They were the rimless sort pensioners get, and she had the dense grey hair that comes with old age. Her skin was fine, though, and you could tell she'd once been gorgeous. Her feet were narrow and neat, though I can't for the life of me understand why old folk wear such thick material. This lady had on a dozen jumpers and a hat with a miniature lavender forest. You couldn't see the old dear for warm clothes.

"Please, then!"

"Right." Her glare made me grin. I liked her. "Hang on."

Benjo had no compunction about extortion. Instinctively I hated the thought of asking her Benjo's price for the tat we sold. The Giant Bonanza Garden Illuminators were only garden lights on sticks. I was ashamed. Rubbish has its place, I know, but in a shop?

"Oh, dear," she said, dismayed at the price. "It's my grandbaby's birthday party."

She thought a second, then rummaged in her handbag. It was the size of a tram. Out came bundles of newspaper. She unwrapped a small porcelain and laid it on the counter.

"Can I have them for this, dear?"

"No, love. The boss says no exchanges. I'm sorry."

"But it's valuable. I have three. Let me show you."

"They're all fake, love," I said sadly.

"You haven't even seen the other two!" She delved more, but I stayed her hand.

"Look, love." I felt really sorry for her. "Have the two Illuminators for your grandbab's party on the house. I'll pay."

"Then you shall have this Early Worcester jug as a gift!"

I glanced about. I was alone with the old dear. "No, love. Take it back." I shoved our G.B.G.I. dross into a bag and re-wrapped her fake porcelain.

"Aren't they genuine?" She was visibly upset. "Great-Aunt Bertha said they were her mother's."

"They're new, love. Some crook must have swapped them when you weren't looking." I didn't tell her that crooks are often close relatives, so beware.

"That can't be true!" Her lips quivered. I sighed.

"You want proof? Early Worcester has a scaggy unglazed ring round its underneath rim, see?" I inverted the little sauce jug and showed her. "They used wooden pegs to scrape the glaze off before they fired it. This hasn't any." I explained how she would sometimes see antique dealers run a sharpened pencil round, to see the graphite mark.

"Is that good?"

"No. Bad. Genuine Early Worcesters were all pegged that way. Just look at the damned thing, for God's sake." I held it up. "See the stuff it's made of? Should be sort of greenish. It's not."

Odd, but her eyes were shining as if she was pleased as Punch, thrilled by trade secrets. "You might be wrong."

Wearily I said, "I'm never wrong, love." I could tell her the truth, because she was an old crone I'd never see again. "There are a good few markers to tell genuine Early Worcester. That means before 1774." I held the jug against the window light. "If it were real, there'd be small patches of what resemble pinpricks, by transmitted light. This has none. The trade calls it Worcester pepper."

"You're very kind, young man."

She let me stow her gunge back into her voluminous handbag. I rescued her crutches and got her to the door.

"One thing," she said as I clonked the door ajar. "How did you know they were *all* fake?" I looked blankly at her. She had the old-age head-shake of Parkinsonism. Maybe she was deaf as well.

"I just told you, love."

"No. You only saw one. I never showed you the other two. Yet you knew they were forgeries as well. I distinctly remember."

"Eh? Oh, just guessed."

"*Au revoir*," she said, hobbling off down the pavement.

"Tara, love. Don't run!"

I went back in, and reluctantly paid into the till the extortionate cost of the two Giant Illuminators I'd given the old crone, just as Frollie came back. Tez reappeared, slamming the loading bay door. Benjo emerged from the office, beaming. I was sure he'd been listening, no harm in it I suppose. Gloria was having another lie down. Tired from some exertion, I shouldn't wonder.

"Now!" Benjo said. "New job, yeh?"

"Great," I said. "Where?" I wondered if he'd let me use his motor. It was an old beat-up Hawker, but when the devil drives...

"Sheep," he said, guffawing as I gaped.

"Ship? Me?" I looked across at the giant cruise vessel. It dwarfed Southampton.

For one mad minute I hoped, before common sense flooded back. He must mean some glug-and-hop-it party on board, the cruise line ingratiating itself with local traders. I'd been on the run too long for false hopes. I'd have needed money, tickets, clothes...

"It's okay," Tez said, grinning. "The boss gets temporary passes."

Such trouble for a wine-and-wad do? Why should I have to go?

"You takings customer to boarding party, ess?"

A boarding party storms a ship intending to slaughter everybody and sink her. I made allowances for language and asked why me.

Tez said, "It'll get the boss off the hook with Customs, see?"

"I need to kit Lovejoy out first, a complete set of clothes," Gloria called down.

"Feex eem cloves," Benjo commanded.

Frollie cooed, "I'll take him! I love a good shop! You'll need shirts, shoes, suits..."

Gloria descended from the clouds and swept in,

beckoning me. She wafted past Frollie with poisonous sweetness.

"I rather think this requires someone with taste, dear. You stay and work. Come on, Lovejoy. We've hardly time."

Frollie gnashed her teeth. I trailed dismally after. We left the Emporium and headed for the shopping mall. I wondered how things had suddenly changed. Why was I going to a party on the new ship? To do what? Help some old customer aboard, yes, but was I to arrange some last-minute fiddle for Benjo's dodgy import business? I've always been a duckegg, and never see the obvious. As we reached the mall, I'm sure I noticed the lurking motor across the road with Miss Trimble at the wheel.

Humbly I followed Gloria, hoping she'd explain.

I thought I was getting away with murder, which was something I'd yet to do.

Chapter Three

Women and shopping have a weird relationship. It's symbiosis, and I don't get it.

If I have the money to buy some shoes, I go and do it, end of message. If some shoe shop nerk shows me different shoelaces, colours, styles, shape and decoration, I immediately know I'm in the wrong shop. I simply try a shoe on and if it fits I say, "These, please." I pay, don the shoes, and exit leaving my worn-out pair. Time? Six minutes flat. Women, though, want their sisters, cousins, and at least eleven friends in a posse who hunt, suggest, disagree, exclaim. This tribe surges round shopping precincts, all for one measly pair. Time? An entire day. Imagine how joyous I was, traipsing after Gloria.

Those three hours were purgatory. She was in her element, spending money like water. I kept saying, "All this for a sail-away party?" until she told me to shut it.

I had to be furtive, hiding my face, stoically looking into windows, in case the people hunting me had spies out. She had me measured for shirts. Did you ever hear such? *Measured* for *shirts*. Daft, because a shirt doesn't count as real clothes. Socks, a dozen pairs. Ties, handkerchiefs, three casual suits, two blazers, five pairs of trousers, and shoes. A dinner jacket. When I asked what on earth, she said with a face of stone, "My brother Cal sails on the *Melissa* tomorrow. You're exactly his size. He can't come to choose for himself."

Faintly, I began to see. Her brother was maybe coming out of gaol, or was he too on the run? Maybe he was being sent abroad in disgrace, I thought knowingly, banished to a far-flung shore never to be heard of again. It happened in Victorian heart-throbbers –

I'd been brought up on those, my gran and me reading Marie Corelli by candlelight, stumbling over difficult words after Gran's old eyes began to go.

"How long did he do?" I asked in a whisper.

She looked at me. "Mind your own business."

Fear silenced me after that. He had my sympathy. I'd never done long in clink. I stopped complaining, and even pretended to take an interest. Gloria had just chosen two pairs of cufflinks for her brother when I noticed a small antiques shop at the far end of the mall.

"Gloria. These are modern clag. We could find cheaper antique ones."

"Really?" She judged me, and we crossed to the antiques window.

The shop's name was unfamiliar, or I wouldn't have made the suggestion. I glanced in as a customer left. An elderly lady behind the counter I'd never seen before. My spirits rose. The last thing I wanted was to be recognised by some antiques dealer. There aren't many divvies. In fact I only knew of two, and the French one had passed away years ago, *requiescat in pace*. Cheered, I entered with Gloria.

The creaky old bird smilingly showed us two velvet-covered trays of what she called sleeve furniture. She meant cufflinks. This is typical antiques trade, to call everything furniture so you'll be impressed and reach for your purse. Earrings, nose rings, and silver tongue studs (ugh!) become "Our special collection of face furniture, madam!" Dealers are less forthcoming about nipple rings and penis rings – both were popular in Victorian times, though it isn't true that Prince Albert started the fashion in 1851. Trendy dealers sometimes claim that, wanting a royal connection at any price.

We dithered over some silver Art Deco cufflinks (I

hate Art Deco, all those stark shapes, like nobody could be bothered doing a decent design), and a pair of Edwardian onyx efforts in gold. The really good pair looked like ancient Egyptian scarabs mounted on London gold, 1930 or so. I always carry a loupe, but didn't use it to examine the hallmark in case it set Gloria wondering. The old dear knew what she was selling, and smiled when I picked them off the tray.

"They're very expensive, young man," she warned. "I can tell you like them. Are you all right?"

I felt a bit queer and had to sit for a second on the customer chair. I pointed to a set of six enamelled stud things.

"D'you think those could be made into cufflinks?" I asked innocently. "They're shirt-front things, aren't they?"

"I don't like them," from Gloria. I could have clouted her, stupid cow.

"Yes, dear, old shirt studs. My husband could change the style for you. I think they're maybe gold, but don't have a hallmark."

"Not bad," I said casually to Gloria. "Why not get them for Cal? Can you afford them?"

The studs were small, blue enamel on gold stems, set in a phoney modern leatherette case.

Gloria hardly glanced at the price tag. It was only pencilled in.

"A lady brought them in late yesterday," the proprietress said. "I really should wait until my husband gets back, but I'd hate you to be disappointed and miss a good buy. I think they're lovely."

A real antique dealer's wife, she put it the right way round. Not, note, that she would be disappointed missing a sale. She probably bought them from some old dear "for a bite and a button" as the antiques trade says enviously of anything cheaply got. Most dealers never, never ever, use the expression "going for a song". Dunno why.

"Look at the time." I tottered to my feet hoping I'd make it to the door. "I'll start the car."

Outside I stood against the wall to recover from the divvy giddiness as people thronged past. A bloke playing a mouth-organ came along. I gave him a coin. He gambolled on. An infant clutched my leg shouting, "Dad-da! Dad-da!" until its embarrassed mother hauled it away and strapped it in its push-chair, apologising profusely. Some students clowning in fancy dress frolicked by. It was all happening in Southampton. I checked inside where Gloria was still at it. I sat in a nosh bar a few shops down, eyes closed. I had a headache. This is what happens, like in Benjo's shop with the illicitly imported African tribal antique.

Shirt studs mostly came in sets of six, and were sold in cases five inches or so long, always round at the corners. Very highly sought by collectors, and are copied by modern (meaning rubbishy) designers lacking ideas of their own. The ones Gloria was haggling over were made by Lalique, enamel on gold. A genuine set, even not in their original case, will buy a new family motor car. If I'd time, I would have bought a fake original case – they'd cost only an average day's wage – and have a Lalique label forged by Sally Salva in Long Melford. They would look superb.

"Hello, Lovejoy."

"Wotcher," I said mechanically, then started and squinted up. "Er, no, afraid you're mistaken." I invented in a panic, "My name is, er …"

"Don't come it, Lovejoy. It's only me, Pennel."

"You have me at a disadvantage, sir. I'm a stranger." I went into an abysmal French accent, and tried to move off.

Pennel answered in perfect French, something

about wishing me well. I said feebly, "Lovejoy's my cousin, lives in East Anglia."

"Hungry, Lovejoy?"

I surrendered. "I'm starving, Penno." So much for principle. He bought me a plate of chips, three eggs, a slab of madeira cake, a stack of bread and butter, a pint of tea, a couple of pasties for afters and a whimberry tart. I wolfed them in random order. He sat opposite and watched.

"You always did love your grub, Lovejoy. Good to see somebody eat." Pennel has four daughters, two of them trying for anorexia. "Been in Dumbo's?"

That halted me in mid nosh.

"That antiques shop belongs to Dumbo Chesterton?" The sign said Hartwellson Antiques.

"You're safe, lad. He's at Weller and Dufty's antique sales in the Midlands. Not back till tomorrow."

Thank God for that. I resumed scoffing. Pennel weighed me up. He's a pleasant oldish bloke with false teeth that keep clicking together when he doesn't want them to do anything of the kind. You can get sticky stuff for that. He used to be a buyer for Gimbert the auctioneer. Like most antique buyers he can't keep secrets, so my safe sojourn in Southampton was doomed. Pennel collects car mascots, those ugly figures on radiator bonnets of motor cars. I'd once done him a favour, showing where he could find a Spirit of Ecstasy, that gorgeous flying lady Charles Sykes designed for Rolls Royces in 1910. He's not a bad bloke, sticks to honesty. It's a saying in antiques: *stick to honesty – should all else fail.*

"Who is the pretty bird, Lovejoy?"

"A shop lady. Her brother's done porridge, just out. She's buying him posh gear."

"They haven't caught up with you, then."

"Would I be sitting here if they had?"

He sighed. "I'm glad I'm old, Lovejoy. All this aggro, no sense anywhere. People don't think antiques, only gelt. I blame money. Everything changed when ram raiders came in." He eyed me, rheumy old eyes wise and woeful. "My advice, Lovejoy? Do a moonlight. Bad enough having the trade hunting you without the Old Bill after you too. One or the other's bound to catch you."

"You going to tell on me, Penno?"

"Sorry, son. You know the game. If they heard I'd clocked you and not bubbled you to them, they'd come down on me. So would the plod."

"Does that mean yes?"

"Sorry, Lovejoy. I'll give you a week. Okay?" He stood. "Last week I bought a Vulcan Motor Company mascot, genuine 1903. Mint. Best and first of them all!"

He'd bought cleverly, and most expensively. (Tip: never, never ever, buy automobilia gadgets if they've been repaired. It's throwing money away.) Pennel must be doing all right, spending such large sums. I wondered who his friends were, and why he was here in Southampton, gateway to the world. He comes from Luton, a long way off. Was he hunting me? I ate faster.

"Anyway I can help, Lovejoy?"

You can always tell when betrayal comes to a friend's mind. Their eyes focus on some distant advantage.

"Aye, Penno. Tell me what you've heard."

He grimaced, glanced round as if at spy school.

"Common gossip, that's all. You robbed the Marquis of Gotham's place in Northamptonshire." He raised his hands when I looked up, narked. "Not saying you did, Lovejoy. It's just what folk say. The marquis and two other lords hired David Buddy to hunt you down. The bounty hunter."

"They say that, do they?"

"Lord Featherstonehaugh and the Marquis of Wells. They're paying David Buddy a third each for your capture. And the police want you too."

"Is that all?" My joke fell flat.

"Christ, Lovejoy, isn't that enough?" He tapped his nose, to show he was speaking about prison. "Dave Buddy did nine years of porridge in Durham clink for nicking Rembrandts. He knows the trade."

"Nothing else?"

"No. Wish you good luck, son. So-long."

"Cheers, Penno. Ta for the nosh."

Off he went with his satchel slung over his shoulders. Pennel is a typical collector, and would sell his wife for a trinket. I've nothing against them. I really do admire a bloke who'll steal, beg and borrow to complete a collection of antique chimney pots, porcelain fingernails, old *Vogue* posters, or specimens of dinosaur dung. I've met them all. But morals, who collects those? Penno had promised me a week. I divided that by my truth factor, which ranges from three to ten depending on the degree of terror, and judged that he'd give me until the day after next unless there was something in it for him. So I had to leave today. I was tired of running, but not when it's the only way to stay alive. Time to go. I melted among the shops, checking I wasn't being followed.

* * *

I'm like every antiques dealer on earth. We look grotty, but we harbour a dream. It's the dream of miracles. In truth, one miracle in particular. Every antiques dealer calls it The Epic. It's the big one, that truly world-shattering discovery – an Old Master on a street barrow, the long-lost Diary of Will Shakespeare, the burial place of Christ, or the Grail – that will make their moniker a household name for ever and ever. Then (the dream goes) will come the knighthoods, presentation at Court, fanfares, sexy harems and riches beyond imagination. And, as dreamers say as we wake to bitterness, all that jazz.

The trouble with dreams is that they really do happen – to someone else. Like those workmen in Cambodia who started repairing that old temple in 2002. They discovered thirty-one statuettes of the Compassionate Buddha. No big deal? Well, yes, because twenty-seven were solid gold, three were pure silver, and one bronze. And that's when greed – yours, mine – hits the fan. All an antiques dealer needs is a pencil drawing of some miraculous find, plus a vague idea of scale (if pushed, he'll do without either) and he'll create a dozen fakes to flog to collectors.

Of course, it doesn't matter if his forgeries don't look genuine antiques, because who's seen them except forgotten labourers in some deep jungle? As he sells them, he invariably mutters that his are the *real* Cambodian statuettes. And, nudge-nudge, he begs you to keep quiet about them because Interpol is everywhere... He'll swear he smuggled them out of Cambodia before the United Nations tore in, et fictional cetera.

In the trade, dealers call this by the impossible term "the Not-A-Word-To-Betsy", after some famous old radio catch-phrase. The most exalted instances are the Portrait of the Duke of Wellington, once stolen and ever since reproduced for secret sale by a zillion fakers ("Honest, guv, *this* is the original, but not a word, eh?"). And the long-vanished Stone of Scone – I've seen nineteen of them sold to tourists, and that's only in East Anglia. You could rebuild Edinburgh with the number of Scotland's Genuine Unique Coronation

Stone of Scone fakes sold off lorries on our motorways, all with sworn guarantees. And practically every Corot painting, and Modigliani sculpture . . .

For any forger, the great risk is forgetting what fakes you've made. Once, I came close to bidding for one of my own forgeries at an auction, would you believe, and made myself a laughing stock. I almost fell for Yank Impressionist pointillism paintings by Shaw, who was said to be a friend of Vincent's, no less. It was at Gimbert's Auction Rooms (why is a single room always plural?) and only drew back when I recognised the frame. I'd painted, and framed, the Japanese garden scene a year previously. It was a different forgery that had set me running for my life.

* * *

We'd left Gloria's purchases at the mall's security desk. The service is free to shoppers. Gloria still hadn't emerged so I went to collect our shopping. I didn't intend to vanish with the expensive clothes Gloria'd bought, honest. But thoughts of escape were on my mind. If I hopped it, I'd save on sad goodbyes. I was hurrying out to the taxi stand when Gloria caught me up.

"Leaving so soon?" she asked sweetly.

"Just being useful," I lied. "Taxis are hard to find at this hour."

Gloria looked at the eighteen taxis queuing for custom. "And you found one! What were the chances of that?"

"Lucky me," I said weakly.

We loaded up. As we left the mall, I was sure Miss Lacy Trimble was walking casually along the pavement, a blue saloon car drawing alongside. She was wearing dark sunglasses – in drizzle? – and smiling to herself. Pennel was by the public telephones fumbling for a coin. Nice place, Southampton, but goodbye.

On the way back Gloria made the driver pause at a leather place, and bought her brother a set of suitcases and a travelling satchel. I envied him. At least he'd look legit even if he was an ex-con. I wondered what he'd been in for.

The *Melissa* was still boarding. I'd heard Tez say she sailed later today, something to do with tides. I wouldn't be here to wave her off. I'd be over the hills and far away like in the song. Except, I remembered uneasily, that ancient ditty was about lads leaving for some impossible wars where they were to die. I carried Gloria's shopping upstairs, and went to help Tez with his loading. The blue saloon parked across the road, Miss Trimble inside talking into a mobile phone while her bloke stood on the kerb looking at the weather. As secret as Derby Day.

We stopped work for a cup of tea. I worked out how much money I'd got. I had digs round the corner, but it would be daft to nip back there. I only had an old raincoat, one extra pair of underpants and a plastic razor-blade. I usually nick soaps and shampoos from bed-and-breakfast places. This time I'd have to go without, in the interests of speed. I'd left my lonely cottage with my passport, little money and no credit.

Half-three, Gloria called me. I shouted up that I was loading with Tez, ready in a sec. She was evidently on the phone. I heard her say, "Yes, well, our new man can wheel you on board. Are you there now?"

Frollie came to me, Tez in his lorry ticking the documents. She embraced me round my middle. Frollie could have gone into a pint pot. "Look after yourself, Lovejoy."

"Thanks, love." Was it so obvious I was leaving?

"If you'd asked me, I'd have . . . well, you know?

Maybe another time, eh?"

Gloria called down, "Ready, Lovejoy? That old lady wants you to wheel her aboard. She's in the Terminal."

"Why me?" I called, trying to disengage Frollie.

"Do as you're told!"

Women make you respond to orders. "I'd best get over there," I told Frollie.

"One thing."

"Yes?"

She looked so sad. "Here." She gave me a piece of paper with a phone number. "Nine o'clock, any evening. My chap's always at the pub. I know I'm nothing to look at, but I'll help if I can."

What could I tell her? I couldn't say I was going to keep on running in case they left me floating in some dark canal, could I? Maybe I'd shacked up with the wrong woman, Gloria instead of Frollie? Except Tez was tougher than I'd ever be. Look at the way he shifted crates. Mistakes about women can never be altered. I've learned that.

"Ta, Frollie."

"Just push her through the Terminal," Gloria was shouting.

"What about your brother's things?" I called back.

"Tez will bring them on board."

So her brother was actually going on a cruise? I didn't blame him.

"Right." I stepped to the door and lied half-heartedly, "Be back in a minute."

"Tara, love," Frollie said, sorrow in her voice.

Hurrying across to the Terminal I joined the throng. I don't know if you've ever been among passengers boarding a cruise, but it's a rugby scrum. I'd never seen so many different shapes and sizes. One or two were already swigging hard at the bar, some definitely reeling, the rest greeting friends with

"Remember the last cruise when we...?" to shrieks of laughter. I found my old lady attended by a squat annoyed nurse of cuboidal shape.

"You're late!" the nurse snapped. She shoved me at the wheelchair and marched ahead.

"You?" I said to the old dear in the wheelchair. It was the lady who'd bought the garden illuminators from Benjo's Bargain Emporium. "You're going on a sail?"

"Be quick or I shall miss the boat." This set her off into peals of laughter. "Did you follow my pun? Miss the boat?"

"Very humorous." I shoved her to the gate.

"Just give the officers the folder. Follow the nurse."

I complied. Embarkation is a grubby, shop-soiled business. You've to mob successive desks while uniformed aristocrats, very snooty, talk of luggage and tickets. The nurse did all that, thank God, while we were waved through. They wanted my passport. I obliged, some security thing I supposed. I was honestly glad to leave the hubbub of the departure lounge.

A uniformed officer greeted the old lady, obsequious and smart. He gave her priority. It actually crossed my mind, but very fleetingly, that if the old lady had so many people willing to shepherd her through the various gauntlets and barriers, why on earth was I there? I was too thick to realise something was wrong.

"I can't," I explained when this officer geezer gestured me through the gate. "I'm waiting for someone." Gloria hadn't got here yet. I'd done exactly as she said.

"Good to see you, Lady Veronica," he said to the crone, taking the folder. I asked after my passport. "Returned when you leave the ship, sir," he said. "Go through."

I pushed the wheelchair under an arch thing. There

was a lass with a camera, just my luck.

"Smile, please!" In time, I looked to one side and hurried on past. However Miss Veronica's snap came out, my photo would be a blur.

"This way, please!" A stewardess wafted us through a corridor and into a lift. We seemed to be priority.

"Have I got long?" I asked nervously. "I'm due back any minute. When does this thing sail?" The previous day I'd imagined escaping on this very ship. Now I had visions of my picture on TV News At Nine with zany newspaper headlines, *Stowaway Forger Caught in Typhoon At Sea*. I stood a better chance back where I belonged, in towns with railways stations and cars where I knew my way about.

"Very soon, sir." The stewardess couldn't help glancing at my dishevelled appearance, which narked me because I'm always clean underneath, even if Benjo's Emporium smudged me up a bit. She could keep her rotten ship and her posh white outfit.

"State Room 1133," Lady Veronica chirped.

"Here it is, your ladyship."

We made a door that opened onto a spacious room with an unbelievable spiral staircase and a balcony overlooking, it seemed to me in that instant, the whole of Southampton's docklands. A piano, a lounge, a dining area leading off, and three other doors standing ajar. I was surprised. I'd thought ship's cabins were just closets with a bunk bed and a shared loo. I noticed a beautiful pair of pedestal vases, each as large as a breakfast bowl. Only decorative, but the most gorgeous pair of Blue John rarities I'd ever seen. The two together would buy a sizeable freehold house or a Grosvenor Square rental for life. Fourteen types of Blue John exist, eight of them from Derbyshire, although not all kinds are gem quality. Blue John is called that from the anglicized old French for blue-yellow, *bleu-jaune*, its principal colours, the best from the Castleton mines if you're feeling lucky.

My palms itched. The thought didn't honestly cross my mind, of nicking them and scarpering ashore. I tore my eyes away. Posh ship, this.

"Now, young man, you deserve a drink!"

"I am Marie," said a small uniformed lass, taking over from the welcome party who dashed away to bring yet more folk aboard. "Drink, your ladyship?"

"Cocktail of the day, Marie, please, and a beer for this restless soul." Lady Veronica's bright eyes gleamed up at me. "Isn't that what you require?"

"Haven't time, I'm afraid." I was supposed to be helping Gloria's brother with suitcases. "Ta, though. Have a pleasant, er …" French bits in our lingo always sound pompous when I try to say them. I can manage cul-de-sac, but "*Bon voyage*!" sounds made up, and names of wines are death. I always go red and never believe what I'm saying. I nearly told the old dear to have a pleasant flight. "A pleasant sailing," I finished weakly.

She twittered, "We always have a drink on arrival. It's tradition, isn't it, Marie?"

"It is, m'lady," carolled the slim lass, busy with drinks at a grand-looking bar. I guessed Filipino, maybe Indian.

"I've not got long," I said. "They've still got my passport."

"Gloria will call for you here. You like our Blue John vases?"

"Er, yes." Cunning as ever, I added casually, "Is that what they're called, Blue John?"

"Castleton stone," Lady Veronica said. "Especially rare. Do you like this suite, Marie?"

"Yes, m'lady."

"Close the curtains." Lady Vee accepted her frosted

glass. "I can't stand brightness."

Brightness? It was still grey and wet out there. I could hear a band. The old dear told me to be seated so I perched somewhere while tons of luggage arrived. Marie sent the cases through into a bedroom. No tips, I saw with awe, stewards smiling and cheery. Well, going on a cruise they would be happy.

Music drifted from hidden speakers. I sipped at the beer to be friendly though it gives me a headache. I'd have murdered a cup of tea. Marie fetched little cakes, the sort that barely fill a tooth. I wolfed them all except for a coconut thing Lady Vee got to first.

She began to speak wistfully of cruises she had known, ships she loved, parties and dances in tropic climes. The band outside played on. I felt lulled and safe. That should have warned me. A stupid they'd-never-find-me-here conviction seeped into my mind. I tried hatching plans to ditch Gloria on the way back to the Emporium, saying I needed the loo, dart to a taxi to reach the motorway, maybe get a lift north . . .

Lady Veronica was still yakking. I felt she ship rumble slightly. I caught myself almost humming along to the tune the band was playing.

"Champagne, m'lady? Sir?"

"Not for me, thanks." I stood, placed my drink on Marie's tray. "Better be away. Bon trip, love."

"It's traditional," the old dear told me, accepting a champagne flute and raising it.

Lots of tradition on these ships. It came to me of a sudden. Too much, maybe? I walked to the curtain and pulled it aside.

The ship was rumbling all right. The shore was twenty yards away and gliding. People on the top deck of the departure building were waving, throwing coloured streamers and filling up with tears, like you do when a ship leaves harbour.

I swallowed, turned, looked back at Lady Veronica.

"Here," I said, in a voice that tried to strangle. "The ship's moving. I can't ..."

"Don't be silly. What's to keep you at that terrible old shop? Your cabin is F188, Lovejoy," Lady Vee said, smiling. "I'm told it is quite acceptable. Not a suite like this, of course, but it's best if appearances are maintained, don't you think?"

"Cabin?" I looked outside, opened the balcony window and stepped out. The cabin's height was ridiculous, miles in the air. I could see whole roofs below me, cars below and people waving. The band was hard at it, playing *Sailing, We Are Sailing* ... Like the duckegg I am, I'd hummed along. I always miss clues.

For a lunatic moment I imagined leaping off the balcony, swinging from one of the derricks to a gangplank and making it to some night-running lorry on a fast run into Salford. For a mad instant I thought I saw Miss Trimble among the crowd, but surely that must have been imagination.

"You'll find it all quite pleasant," the old woman said amiably. "Never been on a cruise before, I take it?"

"Not really." Hong Kong's Star Ferry didn't count.

"You'll love it. Everyone does." She smiled, enjoying herself, one up on the male of the species while that male sweated in fear.

My face felt grey and my skin prickled in terror. The ship was a floating prison. I could see that now. What had seemed a brilliant mode of escape was nothing more than a trap. Had she worked it with Gloria? Was Gloria on board? Who'd run the Emporium? And I'd been abducted.

"Will they put me ashore? Look, Lady Vee, this isn't my fault. Will I get fined? Does the boat stop anywhere?"

"No more of those thoughts, if you please," she said blithely. She was thrilled with herself. "We have to go to the lecture on life-jackets and ship safety. They will remind us never to jump overboard. Attendance is compulsory, isn't that so, Marie?"

"Yes, m'lady."

"Did Cal get left behind, then?" I knew pilots went ashore in a little boat once big ships got clear of, what, coral atolls, sand bars? My nautical lore came from pirate ship stories in *Boys Own* Annuals.

Or was Cal a copper, also after me? I realised you could easily lose a person overboard, if that person wasn't very, very careful. I moaned aloud.

"You're really not very bright, are you, Lovejoy?" Lady Veronica said testily. "There is no such person as Cal. It was a ruse. Please go to your cabin. I'll send for you. How long do we have, Marie?"

"Thirty minutes, m'lady. Your steward and luggage are in your cabin, sir."

"Thank you," I said mechanically, then thought, here, hang on. Luggage? Cabin? Steward, for God's sake?

"Please remember your life-jacket. F Deck is down, centre lifts." Marie handed me a card for Cabin F 188.

I found myself saying thanks, like I was here for the duration and everybody wanting to make me welcome. I could hardly feel movement, but when I looked out of the window – was it a porthole now? – it seemed to be going at a hell of a lick. I blundered about a staircase, quite lost, until a steward ushered me into a cabin.

"I'm Emil. Anything you want, sir, it's that button on the phone. Life-jacket talk in twenty minutes."

The cabin was a mere nook compared with Lady Veronica's. Shower, bed, cupboards, drawers, a little television, a miniature armchair, a place to write, and a safe. No Blue John fruit bowls here. I wondered about

Embarkation. I hadn't seen the forms or documents in that folder. The grim nurse had done it all.

"Champagne, sir?" Emil beamed at me. "It's traditional."

Them and their bloody tradition. "No, ta." I sat on the bed. The suitcases I'd seen Gloria buy stood there, rainbow ties on them labelled F 188.

He handed me an orange life-jacket, telling me he'd wait outside to take me to the muster station for safety practice.

They'd finally caught me. Fright made me feel queasy. It wasn't from bobbing on the briny. Some tannoy system made the ship quiver, warning about life-jacket practice. I took my orange thing and trooped among a cast of millions to a lounge. There, pretty stewardesses taught us to strap ourselves into the cumbersome things and told us to blow a whistle if the ship sank. Everybody in the crowd was laughing. I felt silly. No sign of Gloria.

After the talk, we dispersed. I went to the cabin and fell on the bed and slept. I dreamed horrors.

Chapter Four

The worst dreams are real ones, dreams of what's actually happened. I knew I was dreaming, even felt the ship thrumming slightly, but couldn't stop.

* * *

Dawn broke over the Fenland. I was dangling from a gargoyle praying the night would last until I got clear. Robberies always make me sweat. I hate doing them. Other blokes in antiques never feel half as frightened.

In the gloaming below, I could just make out Belle's huge four-by-four vehicle, a toy with a glittery roof from this height. The sky's early pallor reflected in the ornamental pond, showing me which way to run if I ever made it down. I had tied the stolen painting round me. In theory, women should be the best burglars because they have a waist. I'm basically cylindrical. The painting had started to slip.

Belle's pale face looked up from in the box-hedge maze. She never shuts up. She was endlessly whispering on a cell phone.

"You okay?" she kept saying. I should have lobbed her damned phone into the Koi carp pool. It kept pinging like a death knell.

The painting belonged to the Marquis of Gotham. (Please don't write and complain; it's a real place in Nottinghamshire, not just Batman's nickname for New York.) It wasn't an Old Master, simply a forgery done by my own lily-whites. A superb work of art, though I say it myself. I shouldn't have been in this mess. It was not fair.

I clung on. The Marquis's mansion was an enormous baronial hall, with barmy Tudor brickwork chimneys, really a mini-Hampton Court, all parapets

and mullioned windows. Skeggie, a night-stealing cat
burglar, had walked the building for me on a Public
Open Day, taking photos, pretending to be a mature
student from Norwich. Skeggie mapped out every
inch. In these lord-of-the-manor places there's no real
security. They can't afford it. Trouble is, cranky old
retainers tend to have old-fashioned notions of right
and wrong, and use double-barrelled shotguns before
asking burglars to please vacate the premises. I'd taken
advice from night-stealers before. I was ready. Forging
antiques isn't half so much trouble.

The reason I was in peril was Drogue. A drogue is
actually a sea anchor, a canvas thing you throw overboard to keep your boat from drifting. Drogue's nickname is a joke. He maims people with a walking stick he
carries. Friends say there's a sword inside, but if you're
near enough to worry about such things it's too late. I've
seen Drogue batter a bloke senseless. It's got gold and
silver mounts.

Once a boxer, he looks a real gent and wears a mon-
ocle, very Brigade of Guards, waistcoated, suit,
George boots, a toff. He hires thugs, never keeps a
bodyguard, and trusts no one. He said he'd pay me if
I stole my forgery back, and punish me if I didn't.
Different words, of course.

The pub was crowded, football night.

Drogue rents his smiles out to women of a particular
character. At me, he frowns.

"Break in tonight, Lovejoy. The Marquis is at a
London premier. Two old retainers, no gamekeepers,
it'll be a doddle. Off-season, see?"

"I'll take Belle." She had a Land Ranger, good on
rustic roads.

"Best time's four in the morning, Lovejoy. Do it
right."

"Okay, Drogey. You paid Skeggie? He did a good

job, maps and everything."

"Use the cran in Dragonsdale."

A cran is a place – hole in a wall, hollow tree, a disused bell-tower in some old church – where thieves leave stolen goods until fuss has died down. It's common practice among people of low repute. (I don't mean me, or even you, only everybody else.) The lady at Dragonsdale runs an Olde Englishe Tea Shoppe. She lets the antiques dealers use her chicken coop for a small fee. I like Hyacinth because she gives me bags of tomatoes when I'm short of money. She offers me chickens too, but I haven't the nerve. You have to throttle a hen to eat it, and who can do that?

"Fingers crossed, Drogey."

"No, Lovejoy. Fingers *broken*!"

He left, chuckling at his clever play on words. I chuckled along because I'm an ingrate. Women smiled at him all the way to the door. If he'd beckoned, any of them would have brushed off their skirts and made after him.

Blind Elsie came over to finish Drogue's drink. She empties glasses from one end of Suffolk to the other but is never tipsy. She runs antiques from here to the Kent coast. Ugly as sin, heart of gold, she's not really blind, just pretends because the myth helps her to sell mystic fortunes with the assistance of a toad in a bottle called Ape (the toad, not the bottle). She feeds it flies if it has a good run of clairvoyance. I can't watch her do this. She carries Ape and a tube of bluebottles in her handbag. I think she's a fraud, but other people say she's a mystic who really Has The Eye. Claptrap, of course, though 60% of people believe in psychics.

"Find Belle for me, Elsie."

"Is your robbery tonight?"

Everybody knows my business but me. I nodded. "I need wheels."

"She's just back from Llandeilo. Her cousin Stephen's boy's been ill."

Gossip in the Eastern Hundreds is like weather, everybody shares. I sighed. If word had got round this quickly the police would be forming a queue at the Marquis's gate revving their Black Maria.

"Lovejoy." Blind Elsie took my hand. "Watch Drogue. He's dicey. It's one of your own forgeries, isn't it?"

See? Gossip weather. "Aye. I've to nick it."

Vincent Van Gogh's *L'Hiver* is simply a bloke shovelling snow in a rural garden. You honestly wouldn't look at it twice. It's one of his dour pictures – worth a king's ransom, of course. I can see why nobody wanted it when he was alive. Poor bloke only sold one painting in his lifetime, and that was to his brother Theo. Now, the real *L'Hiver* is in the Norton Simon Museum of Art, Inc. because Americans are all millionaires and buy everything.

Some clever girl took an X-ray of it, and found underneath an obscured painting of a woman spinning thread. (This was common, to paint over old canvases. Impoverished artists used one canvas over and over, and nobody was poorer than Van Gogh.) The lady in the picture has bobbed hair, is concentrating on her spinning, treadling away.

This is where I came in, because once I'd seen that mysterious lady in the X-ray I couldn't get her out of my mind. I like women, so I painted her in Van Gogh style. When forging, I always use the same materials and canvas as the original artist. We have a strange woman who weaves superb canvas in the old style, lives with a cobbler in Southwold.

By the time I finished Van Gogh's *Spinning Woman* I was strapped for food, rent, money. A dealer gave me a meal and some paints for it: Rose Madder, Yellow

Ochre, Burnt and Raw Umbers, and (apologies to any honest forgers reading this) an ounce of Rowney's Flesh Tint that real artists hate. I love portraits, and those are the basic colours. I'd just parted from a weird lass who had moved in to my thatched cottage. She was crazy about a racing-car driver, and listened all night to recordings, literally, of his Formula One engine revving up, daft loon. I didn't get a wink of sleep, what with making smiles with Clara while listening to those bloody pistons.

She also ran the Mighty Shrew Rescue Service, which rescued shrews from death and destruction. My cottage was full of the damned things in cages. She finally left, when a lady from the local farm complained that Clara's shrews were nothing less than rodents and should be shot. Clara went berserk and stormed out saying my friends were fascist oppressors of Mother Nature. I slept for three days. The trouble was, Clara was very wealthy – benefactors funded her shrew hospital – and kept me in grub and passion. Shrew-less, I didn't eat the following week, so I painted *Spinning Woman* in a hurry. The dealer took it.

Later, Skeggie reported it was in the Marquis of Gotham's mansion, listed as a genuine Van Gogh. I was proud but, famished and threadbare, I moaned about it at the Treble Tile. Drogue overheard. He insisted I steal it back. Drogue would then sell it as a genuine Van Gogh. This happens more often than you dare think. I'd eeled in (easy, after Skeggie's research), sliced the canvas from the frame (ten seconds with every art thief's favourite tool, the black-handled Swiss serrated-bladed chef's knife) and dangled away. Three minutes flat. The lads in the Marquis of Granby on North Hill would have a laugh, me taking so long. Dusty Malton robbed Oxford University on millennium New Year's Eve and took only forty-one seconds. I knew he'd never let me forget it.

For clarity, here's a vital question: What percentage of "genuine antiques" are *truly* genuine? Answer: three – that's 3 – per cent. It means that 97% of "genuine antiques" are forgeries, fakes, duff, dud, Sexton Blakes, sham, lookalikes, replicates, all meaning worthless. And that's on a good day.

Where was I? Hanging on this mansion wall in the lantern hours, hoping I wouldn't be seen, while Belle whispered into her cell phone from the box-hedged garden maze below. I heard some oldie come creaking along a passage. I wanted to shut Belle's tinny voice up but she kept on hissing "Lovejoy? You okay?" like a gnat in my ear. I didn't want a chat. My gran used to say, "Lord, save me from mine helpers!" Mostly she meant me. I knew how she'd felt.

The steps came closer. I tried to flatten myself against the ivy-covered wall. A crone's voice warbled, "Is anybody there?" A leaded window opened and an old dear's head poked out into the gloom. She wore a mob cap and held out a Norfolk lantern. It's really only a candle in a perforated cup. For a second I thought she looked directly at me, but her eyes must have been bad. She withdrew. My hands had gone dead. Slowly I started down.

That night me and Belle delivered the painting – my stolen *Spinning Woman* forgery – to Drogue. He sold it for a fortune to some Dutch geezer. The Marquis claimed on the insurance, saying he'd had a genuine Vincent V. G. stolen, and received another fortune. The underwriters paid up, barely enough to buy two holiday villas in the south of France and another yacht. Everybody rejoiced except me, because Drogue welshed, didn't pay me a farthing. See what I mean? Where is justice when you need her? A forger does a brilliant job, sells his superb work for a meal and a few tubes of paint, and everybody else gets everything. I don't think it's fair. Quite honestly, it's dishonest.

Belle's a kindly soul and I like her. She lives in a trailer home, what used to be called a caravan, out on the Peldon Marshes. Ghosts of Roman soldiers rise out of the sea mists there every high tide, so I don't visit unless it's a bright sunny day and the tide's out. Not that I'm scared, really not, because ghosts are only primitive superstition. It's just that I don't like taking chances.

She loves our town's mayor, a happily married father of two. She lives with an accountant called Vernon who keeps proposing marriage. She turns Vernon down because she's in love with … Join the dots and make sense of women. She has this dream of discovering some enormous scam – robbery, smuggling racket, bomb threat, whatever. She'll unmask them with one bound, and the mayor will sweep her up and they'll ride into the sunset. It will never happen.

Vernon is decent, plays bowls for the county, writes for church magazines and helps in the Hospice. He cares for old folks, and every weekend visits Belle. Don't get me wrong. They aren't saintly and celibate, just oddly matched. Between times I fill in Belle's aching void of loneliness, so to speak, and educate her in the world's wicked ways. She feeds me pasta and goat's cheese she creates from two nanny-goats on Peldon's shore line. I don't complain. I've lived among forty caged shrews, and count my blessings. She lends me a groat now and then, in payment for teaching her about antique jewellery.

After my theft, three nobs got together. The Marquis of Wells, his pal Lord Featherstonehaugh (pronounce it Fanshaw to be classy) and the Marquis of Gotham were sick of their Old Masters being stolen. One had had his prize Titian nicked. Another lost an

Oudry painting, about 1753 give or take a yard, of a duck – no kidding; it doesn't sound much, but it's worth enough to stand for parliament, and maybe get elected. The last was the Marquis of Gotham, who waxed eloquent about his stolen Van Gogh. He actually sobbed on TV, the lying swine. He knew it was a fake, and where the original was in the USA. I watched him on the six o'clock news, the night before I went on the run.

"I know there are allegations about its attribution," he blubbed before the nation's cameras. "But experts say it is genuine Vincent. I'll pay seven million to get it back…" et lying cetera. I swear my paint was hardly dry. The pig had used phenolformaldehyde to harden it up, plus French craquelure varnishes. See how corrupt folk are?

Then came the fatal words. The TV presenter smiled into the camera and said, "And here's the man who will lead the noble lord's bounty hunters. You're just out of gaol, David, aren't you?"

This heavily built geezer sat there with a face devoid of expression. I'd never seen him before, but I knew instantly he was the David Buddy who'd got nine years in Durham for nicking Rembrandts.

"Yes," David said evenly. "The police don't like it, but is it my fault if they can't hack it? I'll catch him."

And he looked at the camera. I actually shivered. *He meant me.* They say in the antiques trade that every dealer knows everything and newspapers know nothing. A uniformed Northumbrian plod came on and said it was morally wrong for criminals to make money out of crime – like the police don't? What really frightened me was the bounty hunter's final remark.

He said, "Fine. Then let's see who catches the bloke who stole *Spinning Woman*. Want a bet?"

The lads in the antiques trade were already be lay-ing odds on how soon David would collar me. He was a class act. I'm not.

That night I had one last maul with Belle in my cold damp cottage, and lit out. She dropped me on the A12. I got a lift from an all-night wagon heading for the Channel Ports. I was in Southampton by midnight, complete with passport. With the police and a bounty hunter after me, I'd no choice. I had to keep going.

* * *

I dreamt on, reliving the terrible fright of the footsteps, me clinging to the ivy, the crone shuffling closer with her lantern. A bell began to ring. It bonged closer. I woke in a sweat, pleading for everybody not to catch me.

"Dinner is served, ladies and gentlemen," a loudspeaker voice said. Somebody knocked and called, "Dinner."

My heart was going like a hammer. I woke with a yelp and sank back in relief as I remembered. I'd got away, sort of, and couldn't quite understand how. Memories crept in, the old lady I wheeled aboard, Benjo's Emporium of rubbish, the supercool Miss Trimble who was stalking Benjo for tax revenue. Shakily, I showered and undid a suitcase, donned Cal's new clothes and left the cabin. Emil directed me to the restaurant, cutting labels off me every step of the way.

Chapter Five

I'd assumed I was shanghaied in a derelict tub, doomed to sea-sickness until I could jump ship. I'd also thought I'd have to queue with a tray for grub that would cost the earth. I'm never right, and was wrong again.

* * *

The dining room was reached through a warren of plush staircases. The entire ship was unbelievably elegant. I hated the paintings along the corridor walls, except for some August Macke prints – in richer days, I'd travelled to Berlin to see the originals. Huge flower arrangements flanked the dining room entrance. Waiters in uniform, head geezers in dinner jackets, smiles everywhere like they were really, truly, glad to see shoals of hungry passengers arriving for nosh. The stylish restaurant was better than in any city.

"Table One-Five-Four, sir!" cried some serf, really delighted I'd turned up. He ushered me through the mob and seated me at a table.

"I am Jude, your waiter for the cruise, ladies and gentlemen!" said another, beaming. I'd never seen so many sincere smiles since my friend Jean, a rival antiques dealer, went down for embezzlement. Other stewards, mostly Indians from Goa, seemed equally thrilled, rushing about with serviettes, water carafes, menus.

The other passengers at Table 154 did those wary introductions that might mean anything: "Hello, I'm Ivy, this is my husband Billy. We're from the Wirral," and all that. I said I was Lovejoy and yes, it was my only name, when some pleasant lady wearing genuine diamonds asked.

"They still call me Billy the Kid down at the station house!"

Billy guffawed, showing teeth like tombstones. His hair was all flowing silvery locks. He obviously groomed himself as a Western hero, lantern-jawed and tall, gold studs in his ears. Ivy, a mousy lady, watched her husband anxiously and shut up whenever he spoke. The prat wore a black string tie and had cheroots sticking from his pocket. She looked cowed.

Down at the station house, though? Only cops and railway men used that term, station house. This extravert, with his diamond cufflinks and commanding pose, was no humble signalman. Copper.

No prices on the menu. I gulped. In my circles that means a new mortgage, always assuming you'd paid off your old one. It promised umpteen courses I'd never heard of. I wondered if I could afford a decent meal before the money in my pocket ran out.

"Er, look, mate," I said to the next diner, "where do we pay?"

"Pay?" The bloke who said he was Kevin laughed, telling everybody round the table, "Lovejoy wants to pay twice! He thinks meals are extra!"

That broke the ice. They didn't know if I was putting it on or not. I laughed along, feeling a duckegg. Conversation moved to prices they'd paid for the cruise. It seemed to be a challenge, who paid least. Like, book your cruise through those people in Cumbria and you get a third off, but in St Helens it's even cheaper. Scared somebody would ask me how come I was on an expensive cruise, I put in that I'd paid the full price. They were instantly full of concern for my sanity, and gave me guidance on how to handle rascally travel agents.

"You'd never survive in the antiques import business, Lovejoy," Kevin said bluntly. "We can't be timid about money."

"Use the Internet, old boy," said a crusty bloke called Jim Akehurst. He was with Millicent, a shimmering lady with diamonds. "Book at the last minute. Prices go down."

"They do!" twittered Ivy, still anxious. I liked her. She wore black, trying to vanish I suppose in her loud-mouthed husband's presence. "A girl in the Wirral books for us. She knows a hairdresser on board."

"Kevin always bests me," said a woman in casual fawns. No jewellery, no rings, a hard glint in her eye. "Hello, Lovejoy. I'm Holly. Kevin here's my partner. Hotel decoration and antiques import-export." Kevin waggled his eyebrows roguishly. He had painted fingernails. "Watch out for Kevin. He's nothing but trouble. I gamble, and Kevin practically lives in the ship's casinos."

Kevin tittered shyly. "We cohabit in sin," he announced loudly, causing heads to turn at nearby tables. "The hotels we decorate are sheer horror. Especially," he added with a glance of pure malice at Holly, "if some cow gets *colours* disastrously *wrong!*"

"Now, darling, don't start." Holly smiled, cool.

Every relationship is like being in a row-boat full of cakes and ale, where each person claims to do all the oar work while the other only noshes and idles. Neither they, nor anybody watching, knows the truth, about who does what.

"Millicent loves the swimming pool," Jim Akehurst boomed. "Every morning and afternoon."

"I'm into shows," Ivy remarked. "So is Billy. The glamour!"

"And films," her husband added. "I doze off in the cinema when I'm worn out from boozing. Ha-ha!" He laughed shotgun style, long pauses between. I could see he might unnerve me.

Everybody paused expectantly. I went for it, risking derision. "Pool? Casino? Cinema? Are there...?"

"The poor poppet!" Kevin exclaimed as Jude came to take our orders. Just in case, I felt my few notes in my pocket, and asked for one of everything. I was starving. "He really is new, isn't he?" Kevin tapped Holly's knuckles. "Holly, you must take Lovejoy in hand! Show him the ropes."

"Never seen the adverts on TV?" Billy demanded. "All holidays are cruises nowadays."

"They have everything," his wife Ivy said quickly when he looked at her, as if prompted. "Library, a computer room. Didn't you get a ship's plan? Your steward should have given you one. Call at the purser's office."

"I'll manage, ta."

The reminder made me glance warily round the dining room looking for anybody I might know from a previous existence. Too many people to take in at one glance. Balloons bobbed at tables where waiters were singing somebody a happy birthday. This wasn't merely a ship; it was sheer luxury in a floating town. You couldn't tell we were moving.

As the first course arrived – melon, somebody choosing poached eggs with a French name, others a prawn and apple cocktail – they started exploratory chat. It was friendly, nobody wanting to be left out, all telling of exhausting travels to join the ship at Southampton. It became competitive: my journey was more tiring than yours, et exhausting cetera. You had to get up at six this morning? Well, *I* got up at *five*, so there! It was all good-natured. I vaguely claimed I'd stayed in Southampton at a cousin's, deliberately getting the streets wrong. Only Jim Akehurst was a problem. He and Millicent went into Southampton shopping every week.

"Our trouble is finding a time," glitzy Millicent

said. "Every morning it's tons of legal paperwork."

Her husband agreed. "I keep trying to retire, but I've never worked as hard."

A lawyer? Which explained Millicent's diamonds.

"Conveyancing's the problem," she said. "Can you imagine, we own three antiques shops in that new shopping precinct?"

Lots of antiques people about, I thought.

"Sign of the times," everybody said. I muttered edgy agreement.

"I hope they're good," Kevin gushed. "The speakers, I mean. Nothing worse than bores talking about old pots, unless it's big money."

"Old pots?" I said.

"The cruise theme, dear. Antiques. Antiques talks, TV antiques personalities. Didn't you know?"

Antiques? I must have looked suddenly apprehensive. They reassured me: nothing was compulsory, you didn't need to attend.

Talks, antiques demonstrations, they were all entirely voluntary. They laughed about getting lost on board. The ship had no Deck Thirteen from superstition, but a fourteenth. Listening, my spirits gradually rose. I could tolerate this luxury, for the brief time it would take the *Melissa* to reach some landfall. They told me we would soon reach Holland.

They waded into the first course, saying that my travel agents had given me atrocious service, not telling me about the entertainment, talks, celebrities travelling with us.

"Don't book through them again, Lovejoy!" Holly commanded, easily into anger. "Those young girls only sit there doing their nails. It isn't good enough!"

And so on, through steamed lemon sole with sauce vierge, whatever that is, roast loin of pork, stuffed breast of chicken on lentil mousse, stilton quiche and coriander something. The one job I'll never try, I resolved during that first gargantuan meal of a zillion calories, is travel agent. They get the short end of the stick from everybody. They can't win. I mean, here they all were on elegant Table 154, stuffing our faces in a floating Valhalla, slurping their way through mounds of superb grub to a final shoot-out with fresh strawberries steeped in drambuie and rum chocolate slices under orange sauce, and all they did was grumble about the travel agents who'd rescued them from humdrum lives and got them here? Give me a frigging break.

"I hope the comedian's good," they eventually got round to.

"The magician's not up to much," somebody else said, replete.

"I want to hear the classical pianist."

"I like the Stadium Theatre Company. Brilliant. They were on *Oceana* in Barbados."

"No, Kevin. You're mistaken…"

"Are the shops better here than on *Aurora*?"

"I'm going to play golf, really slim in the gym this cruise."

I listened, taking it all in. Somebody showed me the ship's daily newspaper, *Melissa Today*. Blue headlines told of delights to come, singers, dancing shows, dining hours in sundry restaurants, pools and bars galore, forty-odd events going on all over the ship every single day. Everything was free, except drinks.

On cue, sinking under the weight of food, I asked for a glass of wine, having the presence of mind to make my signature an illegible squiggle. A waiter wanted to see my card. I produced a little maroon plastic the cabin steward had given me. As we wobbled out, bloated, Kevin asked me what I did for a living.

"I'm here to establish more contacts for my antiques import business," he told me affably. "An underdog, but I'm happy."

"That's the main thing, Kevin."

"You?"

"Oh, er, a driver. For the town council."

Lots of grey hair about, but women always look superb so it never matters if they get older. They don't know this, thinking for some reason that all sexual attraction depends on being twenty-three years old. Barmy. They talk themselves into despond. Even Gloria did, but I've already told you that.

For a while I wandered the ship, up staircases, along corridors, passing several bars with bands and singers and merry drinkers, a cinema announcing feature films, the Palladium Theatre with tonight's show about to start.

"Good evening, Lovejoy."

The familiar voice pulled me up short. I looked down at Lady Vee in her wheelchair.

"Wotcher."

"I shall expect you for drinks in my state room after the evening show. Ten o'clock exactly. You must meet some people."

"Er, ta, but – "

"Ten," she ordered sharply.

"Lady Veronica!" Billy and Ivy came to greet her. "How marvellous! You're on the ship too!"

They exchanged pleasantries about the last world cruise, d'you remember that dreadful girl in Mombasa and the malarkey over the Customs, while I wondered about coincidences and Billy Sands being an ex-cop. I muttered an excuse, and went to the Atrium. This seemed to be the centre of social life, where grand staircases swept down to a dance-floor from the bar balconies and tiers of elegant shops. A long ornate counter called Reception was staffed with a galaxy of assistant pursers. Like a hotel? I went and asked to see the passenger list.

Michelle, a bonny girl, raised her eyes. "We no longer publish those, sir."

"How can I find out where, er, my friends are? We want to talk over old times. The last world cruise," I explained helpfully. "That dreadful girl in Mombasa and everything!"

Michelle didn't quite giggle, but came close. "Wasn't it terrible? Look, write a note and I'll see it gets to them, okay? Enjoy the show, sir."

Stumped, I went to the performance. Two entrances to the theatre, rows of seats for eight hundred of us. Lovely dancers, an aggressive songstress, a comedian called Les Renown everybody recognised except me, a magician, more show-stopping dancers, and I was first out, lurking in the hallway by the lifts as the crowds emerged. Nobody I knew. I was relieved. No more coincidences.

As people strolled on deck for a breath of maritime smog, I tried to work out exactly what I was doing on the *Melissa*. I'd been tricked aboard, ostensibly to help some old dear I didn't really know. My tricksters – Gloria and Benjo – ran a tatty import-surplus shop where I'd worked. They imported priceless ethnic rarities, illegally. They'd deceived me, got me ticketed, carded, and on up the gangplank. They were helped by the fact that I'm thick half the time and daydreaming the rest. But why on a ship? Particularly, on *this* ship. If they'd wanted me to do something for them, I could have done it in Southampton.

Looking for clues, I searched the notices and listened to bar chatter. The ship's themes were antiques and music. I learned about a string quartet, a pianist in the Curzon Lounge, and operatics. Okay, fine, if that's what you like. But to me opera is a long bore separating four beautiful arias. I lived with a woman once who dragged me from one opera to another for three months. She sobbed through every single one and played hell if I as much as hummed along. I think operas ought to cut the chat and get on with the songs. Still, I told myself repeatedly, I'd last out until we docked in Amsterdam.

The answer must lie in antiques.

※　※　※

Now, antiques aren't classical music. They are like women, the breath of life. Take away antiques and women, the world vanishes. Take away one of the two, existence becomes pretty pointless, because I am obsessed by both. Folk think you need only one. They're wrong, because with only one, you're into the mad world of delusion. Give you an instance:

Spring is a woman I know. She bought a High Street holiday firm, and for three years was a lone operator. The only thing she couldn't do for a tired traveller was change currencies, but the rest – book you to Thailand, sir, with a stop-over in Malta? – she could do. Fortune smiled, she made a stash of gelt, and one holiday season took on a young bloke to help. She was nearing forty, and Handsome Joe twenty-nine. He'd been a trainee auctioneer.

When Handsome Joe joined Spring's travel agency, I was seeing Spring. She was merry as a carnival and full of stories, never stopped talking and wore colours that blinded me. She occasionally got tipsy, but so?

Well, before long I got the sailor's elbow – nudge, splash – and I was banned from her second-floor Camden Town flat once Handsome Joe came to live, so to speak, under Spring. Soon after, I began to hear rumours. Handsome had been involved in auctioneering frauds in Norfolk. Nothing spectacular, such as

Sotheby's and Christie's might be proud of in their time-honoured way, just the old familiar milk-drop.

This simple fraud, incidentally, will defraud you sooner or later, so I'll mention it. It's where an auctioneer accepts bids "off the chandelier" or "off the wall", as auctioneers say – meaning phoney non-existent bids – then knocks an antique down to some joker who's really there but who afterwards raises trouble, claiming *never to have made a bid at all*. The trade calls it the milk-drop. The joker then goes spare in the auctioneer's office afterwards, tearing his hair and storming out with, "Go on, then, sue me!", etc, etc. Luckily, there's a casual customer nearby who overhears this, and who instantly offers to buy the antique at a knock-down price. What a stroke of luck! The firm is only too glad to get rid of the item, unsold items being every auctioneer's nightmare. Nothing damages their reputations more than having items left on their hands. Sotheby's will tell you.

The auctioneer is then secretly paid the difference between the actual price and the estimate, or a third of the antique's value, whichever is most. The accomplice is usually a woman who oh-so-casually visits the auctioneer's office. She buys the antique. Her cut is the antique, which she gets for a few groats. Seems fair? Yes, except some poor soul loses out. It's you, the person who sent the antique in, to be sold for an honest price. You really did hope for a fair honest auction. Handsome Joe worked the scam a dozen times with various women, until finally some jealous Norfolk colleague installed auto-video CCTV and had him arrested, fired, fined, gaoled, and drummed out of the Brownies.

Whereupon he leeched on Spring, and I was shown the door with the usual, "Don't think this is goodbye, Lovejoy. We'll still be friends..." while I said,

"Doowerlink, it's been wonderful..." et dismal cetera. It's always a laugh, especially when I'd slaved for years – well, three weeks – helping her to amass a collection of advertising and packaging collectibles. They weren't really old, but I'd assembled a hundred of the things, which are everywhere and usually pretty cheap. Think tin trays marked Coca-Cola, boxes for Kellogg cereals, old cigarette posters of Players Weights and Robin Starch, those things we all keep meaning to throw out but can't be bothered. I'd gone to some trouble to find her a 1930s Morris Trucks enamel advert. Spring's reward was making smiles with me for a weekend because she was over the moon about it; and well she should be, because one of these enamel posters, if mint, will buy your family a month's holiday in the Maldives. Later Handsome Joe scarpered with her entire collection. I went to see her, from sympathy.

"Don't worry, Lovejoy," she said, smiling with fondness. "I had him for three whole months. He really loved me, so I've known true love. How many women can say that? Okay, I lost a few trophies. It was worth everything."

She even said the same when she got evicted because Handsome Joe had sold her travel agency and her flat using false documents. Spring went to the bankruptcy court smiling and content. End of story.

See what I mean? Paradise is women and antiques together. Women fix on one, and forget the other. It's called delusion. The self-deception women like Spring operate, is a sort of trickery they seem able to manage quite well, thank you very much. I don't understand how, but when it happens they're unabashed. Spring blithely told the court, "I won't press charges, Your Worship, because my Joe is really nice deep down." This, note, about a gorilla who'd stolen her business, antiques, assets, and the house she lived in. Can you credit it? I gave up on Spring after that, but still like her. I couldn't say what I'd do if she came knocking, because women are the only gateway to heaven, and that's also not my fault either.

❊ ❊ ❊

No sign of any familiar face except for Marie, Veronica's uniformed stewardess, ascending a staircase near the Crystal Pool on Deck Twelve. I watched a musical group perform under strung lights. The night air was warm, people were friendly, the bars hard at it and the cruise taking off in style. I could see why folk loved the life.

A few got into conversation but I made little response. I kept imagining I saw people I knew, finally concluding it was just me being worried sick. I couldn't wait to get back to solid land. I don't know why I was so scared. I'd been desperate to escape – on this very ship, in fact – and here I was, yet still spooked. If anybody wanted me nicked, they could have done the deed days ago.

Somebody offered me the ship's newspaper for tomorrow's entertainment. I read it through. A morning lecture, "Antiquities in Amsterdam", caught my eye. A talk was listed, "Things to See in Holland". Passengers were urged to book early for shore excursions. The headline was, *Welcome to Amsterdam!* I smiled, the first time since I'd left East Anglia. As soon as the ship stopped, I'd be off like a whippet.

Spirits rising, I left the wassailing swimmers and dancers to their jollity, and went to Suite 1133 to see Lady Veronica.

Chapter Six

Marie opened the cabin door, the sturdy nurse Inga glowering in the background. Lady Veronica was clearly there on the sofa, in spite of which Marie went through the formalities.

"An assistant wishes to enter, Lady Veronica."

Humbly I waited until her ladyship beckoned to any interloping serf. I felt I should be on my knees. Inga left, emanating hatred and slamming the door.

"Wotcher, m'lady."

"Wotcher, Lovejoy. Did I say it correctly?" She smiled and gestured to an armchair. I crossed the plush carpet and sank into more luxury, looking round. The suite was superb.

The balcony windows were open. Summer night and music wafted in, the curtains stirring gently. We could have been on a garden terrace. Outside, darkness and starlight, with a gibbous moon drifting along, formed a setting for romance. Maybe this astral influence made me notice Lady Vee's appearance. Every time I saw her she'd lost a few more years. Tonight she looked even younger. Women can do this dramatically: a lighter touch to the hair, more stylish dress, shoes, cosmetics, and suddenly a new woman meets your eye. This one was two decades younger, slimmer, active, certainly not in need of a wheelchair. She wore a long brocaded dress of midnight blue, and an amethyst necklace in gold. A huge zircon ring was her choice this evening. She was no longer the elderly worn-out invalid. Deception was afoot. I was pleased, because deception's my game. It makes me feel at home.

She caught me staring and smiled, thinking admiration.

"What is it?"

"You silly cow," I said.

Her face changed from beauty to savagery. "*What* did you say?"

"I suppose you use sun-ray lamps?" I pointed to her zircon ring. "It was once a lovely blue. You've ruined it. It's gone muddy. I bet you leave it on a window-sill. Poor old zircon always gets shambled by daft mares like you, with more money than sense. UV light, direct sunshine, those glamorous tan-your-skin lamps, they all cause even the best zircons to revert to a horrible soiled brown. Yours is on the turn. See how it fails to pick up the light? You've killed it dead, silly bitch."

She stared at her ring. "Gemstones can't change, Lovejoy. They are millions of years old."

"That doesn't mean you can treat them like dirt." This kind of ignorance really narks me. "And your amethyst is on its last legs, poor little sod."

"My necklace?" She fingered it.

"Just because a woman's gorgeous doesn't give her the right to ruin an Edwardian necklace a jeweller created a century ago."

She said faintly, "But I'm always most careful."

"Balls, m'lady. It's bleached at one side. I'll bet you have it in an illuminated display cabinet, so the peasants can ogle it when your estate is thrown open to the paying public on summer weekends. Does some ignoramus clean it in a jeweller's dip-bath, hoping it'll sparkle more?"

She coloured slightly. She was the culprit.

"Honest to God, you women nark me." I went really bitter, because antique gems can't answer back for themselves and somebody has to do it for them. "You go mad for jewels, then ruin them. Your grandma wouldn't have made those mistakes, love. Grandmas knew hell of a sight better. You take care of frocks, shoes, jumpers, then insult your antique jewellery. Your pearls must be worthless."

Involuntarily she glanced at a bureau. I guessed her safe was in there. "You are appallingly rude."

"I'll be Beau Brummell if you behave."

A knock on the door made Marie revert to ceremonial mode. A uniformed man, his breast tag labelled Executive Purser, entered.

For the most part, I'm easy going. I mean, of the two genders women are preferable, and blokes come second, so when meeting someone I try to help. If they say hello and smile, I do the same. Does no harm, costs nothing. I don't understand people who come in like gunfighters into a Western saloon ready to spill blood. This chap was smart and aggressive, looking destined at least for monarchy status. He was boss. Lady Veronica was instant attention, not quite fawning but willing to go further if he insisted. He wore insignia, black letters on gold, like a campaign medal and didn't shake hands. Take that, oaf. I withdrew my hand. Take that, pompous nerk.

"You're the one in trouble," he announced at me in a precise rasp.

Which was me done with. I watched them go through their hello-again rituals, and guessed they made secret smiles in the lantern hours. Well, so would I if this new, younger Lady Vee gave me half a chance. Brenda, a woman I know who runs a boutique in Sudbury, swears she can always tell when people are lovers. She also claims to be able to say exactly how long they've been at it, just by seeing them buy a packet of Maltesers. I've found no way of checking her accuracy.

"This is Purser Mangot, Lovejoy."

"Is she here?" He ignored me, signalling to Marie who leapt to obey. She made him a drink, ice in last, and fetched it at a swift grovel. She'd done it before. She offered me none. He glanced at his watch, gave it a curt nod that spared its life. Somebody could still make it on time, but the world had better watch out.

"They'll all be here, darling, if the show tidies up."

His head rose angrily at the conditional. As if on cue another arrival brightened the evening. Marie went through her admission process for a young uniformed lass I vaguely remembered as one of the dancers. She bubbled merrily in, greeted everybody – Mangot with discreet awe – and told me she was Amy the dancer, instantly demanding if I'd seen the show. I said it was the best I'd ever seen. It's the only way with performers. Less than total adulation sends them suicidal. Mangot sipped, coldly inspected Amy as if he'd have her shot for crooked seams. She seated herself, guardedly thinking seams, but shone at my praise.

"We're doing a new routine," she offered. "Rehearsal time is difficult because – "

"Because of disorganisation." Mangot quelled her. "The *Melissa* runs smoothly unless people get sloppy."

So there. Amy quickly agreed that everything wrong was her fault. Lady Vee smiled to placate us, while Marie let in and announced the comic who'd entertained us in the theatre, the nearly-famed Les Renown. He wore brash plus-fours and yellow tartan jacket and looked ready for a summer season on the pier. He too got a drink, unquestioned. Me, none.

"Thank you, Marie." The dismissal worked instantly, Marie silently leaving to the kitchen. "Now," Lady Veronica began amiably. "We all know why we're here, except Lovejoy. We should start by telling him how we shall proceed."

"Proceed with what?" I cleared my throat in the silence.

"I think we get rid of him," Purser Mangot said.

"He's a sham."

"Okay," I offered helpfully. "I'll get off at Amsterdam."

"No." Astonishingly it was Les who spoke so decisively. No chuckles and one-liners now. "Lovejoy's essential. We all know why."

Except me. I said out loud, "Except me." They looked at each other, eyebrows raised in silent question like parents used to when you were an infant hearing things Not For Little Ears. Lady Veronica kindly relented.

"The robbery, dear. We need you for it."

"Why would you need me?" I was asking in a the voice of reason, when her words struck home. I stood up and screeched, *"Robbery*? A frigging robbery?" Sending a careless postcard would get me cemented under some new motorway, and they were going to involve me in a robbery. The whole world would know immediately where I was.

"Of course, dear." She smiled. If I'd been nearer she'd have patted my head, there, there. "Stop shaking."

"Lady, I'm in enough trouble."

"Sit," Purser Mangot commanded. I sat. I'm pathetic. "There's no way out, not for you, not for any of us. This theft is going down, or the game is up and the thieves will get away with everything. It will be the costliest robbery since the Brinx-Matt." He seemed proud.

"Lovejoy," Lady Vee gushed, openly worshipping the odious creep, "we are the good people, not the bad. Don't you see?"

"No."

"Let me explain. I am what is known as cover." She tittered shyly. "Who would suspect me? Purser Mangot is our legitimate authority. Amy is our talented stage artiste – as such, she can go anywhere, and serves as a registered courier when passenger tours go ashore. That's vital. And Les Renown is our charming scamp whom everybody loves." She leant to me and whispered, "He's really a policeman. Amy is only sort of police, more Fraud Squad."

Amy was enjoying this, secrets unmasked and me thunderstruck.

"She has degrees from the Courtauld, you see. Fine Art and antiques. The pity is," Lady Veronica said wistfully, "it isn't as exciting as I'd hoped. So far it's been quite mundane, apart from enticing you on board. I *loved* your kindness over Mr Benjo's silly garden candles."

"That's the last time I ever show anyone kindness," I said. "Charity gets you in trouble. You don't need me."

"You're the crook," Mangot grunted, irritably swigging the rest of his drink and tilting his glass in mute command. Her ladyship herself rose and brought more hooch for the pig, confirming my suspicions. He bully, she Jane. Whatever turns you on, I suppose, but I couldn't help feeling envious. I swallowed the insult because I'm not really a crook. I just manage life the best way I can. Amy's gaze stayed on me, wanting me to react with violence as women do. I stayed cool.

"Why do you need a crook?"

"To be the one they watch, stupid." Mangot swigged, grimaced.

Now, hang on, I thought, suddenly more alert. Good people don't need a crook unless *they want somebody to blame afterwards*. It happens in corporate business, in big-firm scandals on the financial news, and in august antiques auction houses like Sotheby's and Christie's. It happens in governments. Classical case: When some duckegg is promoted to Cabinet

Minister, they want somebody to blame for things going wrong. It's the blame game. They simply wanted me there to get arrested while they looked squeaky clean.

"In Amsterdam?" I asked.

"No," a new voice said.

We all turned. A woman came from the second bedroom of the suite and headed for the drinks cabinet to pour her own. I recognised her, and my heart sank. It all fell into place, my abduction and the planned robbery. I'd known her. She was June Milestone from television, she of the long hair and dicey crook of a husband who was awaiting trial for embezzlement. She'd started the Antique Trackers Hour twenty years since, and it was still going on Channel Tee, highest trunk-junk show in the ratings. Was she staying with Lady Veronica? June was more elegant than I remembered. I usually watched her TV show for old time's sake. She'd become more slender, shapely, and dressed with style. On telly she looked stouter. Actors always say TV adds ten pounds in the wrong places.

"No, not in Amsterdam." She brought her glass, smiling. "Lovejoy, isn't it? I'm June Milestone."

"Where, then?" I would have risen to say hello, but gallantry was having a hard time of it in Suite 1133.

"St Petersburg," she said easily.

"That's torn it," Les Renown grumbled. "He'll have it all over the ship."

"I thought we weren't to tell him until we got there," Amy said.

"St Petersburg?" I said, voice on the wobble. "Isn't that – ?"

"Where the Hermitage Museum is?" June said affably, seating herself next to Lady Veronica. "Yes, when last I heard."

"Rob the Hermitage?" I bleated. It took me three

goes to get the words out. "The world's biggest art gallery? Over three million works of art? In 322 suites of rooms along thirteen miles of corridors? And you want me for *that*?"

June tutted. "You've gone quite pale. *We* are not robbing. We are *preventing*. You will come out of this like a knight in shining armour."

"And you lot?" I said.

"We shall simply be doing our job."

"Er, one thing. Who is doing the robbery, exactly? Are they on board the boat?"

"Boat!" James Mangot said with disgust. "Ship, you ignorant cretin."

"Why don't you arrest them now, then?" I asked doggedly, mind still fixed on Amsterdam, where we were to dock in the morning and I could leap off with a glad cry of farewell. I shivered, not acting. "I've heard about Russian gaols. They're all snow and Gulags. They chuck away the keys and leave you to rot."

"We are the good people," someone repeated.

I thought, oh, aye, is that right? Then why do I always finish up hunted across our creaking old kingdom while everybody else gets the blondes, Monaco villas and yachts in the Caribbean? My expression must have given these thoughts away because Lady Veronica called the gathering to an end.

"Well, that has served our purpose!" she trilled. "We've all met, and explained our purpose on the *Melissa*." She leant confidingly to me. "You'll love St Petersburg! It captivates the interested traveller!"

"And no questions," Mangot growled. "No gambling. No involvements, no stunts."

"Don't make waves," Les Renown put in. "Don't get drunk And don't yak your head off."

"We've put you with a quiet table," June pointed out. "They'll do quizzes and shuffleboard, maybe bingo and go to our antiques talks."

"I told them I'm a driver for some town council."

Cried Lady Veronica, "How clever!"

"One's a retired ploddite, dunno what rank."

"Uniformed branch, ex-sergeant," Les said with a sneer.

We rose to leave. I ached to escape, feeling stultified. Lady Veronica conjured up Marie to show us out. I got the feeling the stewardess had sussed the corridor, making sure nobody was around to see us leave. I found myself walking with June Milestone and adjusted my pace to her slow stroll. The others went on without a word.

"This way," she said.

"Er, look, Mrs Milestone. I'd better turn in, because – "

"Cut it out, Lovejoy," she said quietly, and drew me into a corner of the Century lounge. She waved a stewardess off and sat in an armchair, me opposite. The place was quiet, just a few groups chatting and laughing, a pianist playing selections from some operetta. "Now, Lovejoy, a few rules to be getting on with."

I slumped. "I thought you'd forgotten."

"Forget you, you bastard?" She didn't laugh. "My only chance to possess a genuine Thomas Saint sewing machine, and you tricked me out of it."

"It wasn't like that!" I said indignantly.

"You were ogling that tart, Lovejoy. I wasn't taken in for a single minute. You told her the truth, that it wasn't a Singer but a Saint. I'd have made a fortune..."

She spat venom while I sat there and took it. The only time she paused was when an elderly couple paused to say how much they were looking forward to her talks. Instantly she was all sweetness and light.

"Oh, I'm so pleased!" she carolled. "Weren't you on

the *Oceana* cruise to Venice…?" and similar gunge.

Our spat truly hadn't been my fault. An Englishman, Thomas Saint, patented the first sewing machine in 1790, having worked on the design for yonks. Find a genuine one and you've a fortune on your hands, though early Singers also cost. I'd been doing a sweep through the Midlands, where June lived with a mad penniless poet who believed he was a reincarnation of Chaucer. I visited an auction. June was in. A bonny woman carrying a babe was listening to the auctioneers. Most items were dross – wardrobes from the Utility period of World War Two, faded books, pock-marked mirrors that would cost the earth to restore, a few derelict chairs, fly-specked etchings. I was on the point of leaving when something bonged within my chest. I could hardly breathe, and homed in on this small gadget that shone into my eyes. It was a little sewing machine, almost mint. A genuine Thomas Saint. Don't laugh. It would keep the buyer in holidays for a lifetime. I gaped at it. Someone plucked at my arm. It was the lass with the bab.

"Excuse me," she whispered. "Would you please do me a favour?"

"What?" I gasped, strangled.

"Could you bid for it, please? Just to maybe make people think it was worth something? Only, I heard those dealers over there asking you about the antiques." She reddened. "People have been laughing at it."

"Is it yours?"

"Yes. Well, my gran's. It was her grandma's, and I know it's not automatic … What's the matter? You've gone white as a sheet."

I picked the Saint up and took her arm. The baby goggled. "Take it home, love. It's worth a new pram and holidays all over the USA."

"Here, Lovejoy!" One of the whifflers – blokes who move the gunge about in auction rooms and (sometimes) remain honest while doing so – came and hissed angrily, "What the – ?"

"Lady's grandma's changed her mind," I whispered back and dragged the woman outside.

We rang Bondi from the Welcome Sailor pub at East Gates, and he drove over from Frinton. By eight o'clock that evening Bondi had sold the little sewing machine on commission (10% isn't too bad, when you think what Christie's and Sotheby's do you for) to a collector in Leeds. I checked next day to make sure she'd banked the gelt. I honestly got nothing out of it. I just hate the lads doing that. "The circus", we call the Brighton and Solihull teams of dealers who come trolling round country auctions. They jeer at anything that takes their fancy, just to put genuine bidders off. Now, why the lass with the bab hadn't gone to the library and looked up old sewing machines, to check whether her gran's was valuable or not, God only knows, but she hadn't. If I hadn't happened along, she'd have thrown away enough money to put down on a new house.

People say virtue is and has and must be its own reward, but it isn't and it hasn't so it can't. To prove it, here I was getting hate from Mrs June Milestone, the most influential antiques TV personality on earth, just for being virtuous. Holiness isn't worth it; I'm always holy, and I know.

Meanwhile the old couple passed on their way, and La Milestone reverted to viperish spite. "Don't come the innocent with me, Lovejoy. That harlot rewarded you in kind, you sordid reptile…" and so on.

All because June had been there, laughing with her antiques dealer pals, sure she was going to make a fortune by cheating a poor woman with a babe. I'd noticed her stormy glance at me and the lass as we'd left the auction. Wearily I let June's rage wash over me. I've been detested by experts. One more wouldn't make me lose any sleep.

"Five rules, Lovejoy," she said finally when she stopped seething. "In this enterprise, you do as I say. Obey me, and you'll escape unscathed. Capeesh?"

More rules? I'd already had a dozen from Executive Purser James Mangot and our secret ploddite Les Renown, ship's comedian. "Aye."

"Rules two, three, four and five are – "

"Same as Rule One?" I guessed. I'd had this before from warders in clink.

She smiled a wintry smile. It was like sleet. She included me in its chilly radiance. "Agreement at last! Here's my cabin number. Never ring, never visit. One last caution."

"What?"

"No revelations, or I shall have you packaged home to the Marquis of Gotham and his band of hunters. And …" She hesitated, having difficulty phrasing the last command. "And no mention of how you once tried to … well, be friendly towards me."

Which was a load of tat. "As I remember it," I said, now seriously narked, "we made smiles at that big Midlands Antiques Expo just after you left that lunatic airline pilot. You even wanted me to –"

"That will do!" she ground out. I quietened as she accepted yet more tributes from passing folk who just *loved* her TV work. Her smile for them was warm affection. When they'd left she turned with a snarl of pure malice. "You and I are strangers, Lovejoy. D'you hear? You will attend my antiques talks and report to James Mangot every morning, noon and evening. We need you solely because you are a divvy, for no other reason. Obey, and I shall let you escape on conclusion of the scheme. Disobey, and you will be handed over to the authorities."

"Right," I said miserably. It actually meant *not* being handed over to the authorities, because the hunters would intervene and I would be disappeared in a phoney escape bid. Crooks call it doing an Argentina, from the methods of disappearing undesirables over there. I wondered if a ship this big usually had police on board, legitimate ones I mean.

"What are we nicking from the Hermitage?"

"Not a single thing." She beckoned the stewardess and ordered a drink. None for me. "It's crooks who're doing that. I thought I'd explained."

"Sorry. I quite forgot." I meant it really sincerely.

She let me go. I turned and looked back. She was watching me with calculating eyes. I felt like you do at the doctor's when he says good morning when he's wondering where to stick his needles.

There was a midnight buffet – soups, sandwiches, cakes, drinks, merriment. I went for a fresh load of calories in case we sank in the night, then went to my cabin. They'd folded down the coverlet and put chocolates on the pillow. I watched the TV until twoish, playing my Ten Word Game and trying to describe the mess I was in. I failed.

When I woke the ship had stopped moving. We were in Amsterdam. I felt better. Time to go.

Chapter Seven

Amsterdam.

Saying the word calls to mind diamonds, drugs, songs about mice in windmills, tulips, painters like Rembrandt and Van Gogh plus a few similar amateurs (joke). I thought these thoughts, leaning on the Promenade Deck rail looking out at Holland. So near, and here was me stuck on board.

Remarkable city. The world's first ever lottery was run by a Dutch artist's widow, Mrs Jan Van Eyck, to help the poor of Bruges in Belgium, kind lass. And now it's the Dutch, not the Scotch, who claim to have invented golf long before St Andrews got weaving. (Leave me out of the argument. I don't take sides.) They also say Amsterdam invented modern banks in 1609, so the Dutch have a lot to answer for. I hate golf, and do banks ever help?

I'd had breakfast. Passengers booked on city tours were disembarking. It's the sort of thing that can make you sad. For a start, there seemed to be only two avenues off the ship. Each was a narrow gangway leading down from Decks Four and Five to the quayside. One person at a time, every single person showing their maroon plastic I.D. folder. Ghurka ex-soldiers checked everybody with electronic bleeper gadgets, and again when they reached the wharf. I felt bitter. As if anyone could vanish from the middle of an open gangway in broad daylight. I ask you. How petty can people get?

Uniformed crew met jaunters at the wharf, and away they went in coaches for canal trips and visits to the Rijksmuseum and the Van Gogh Exhibition. Meticulous. They weren't going to lose some old dear on a foreign wharf, not the *Melissa*. The coaches were labelled. Passengers wore stickers. Ghurkas tallied passenger. In case you don't know about Ghurkas, they are the most cheery soldiery in existence. They are also the most bloodthirsty. They hail from the Kingdom of Nepal, and by ancient treaty form regiments in Britain. When they retire, they take up security duties on ships, in banks and august firms in the City. Sounds okay? Sure, if you're honest. Horrible if you're a crook, because in action they're the most loyal and savage warriors in existence. They're famed for it. Once their killing knife is drawn, it's never sheathed until ... I won't go on.

Six Ghurkas on gangway duty. In the eight minutes I watched, they made no fewer than eleven checks, totting up passengers, ticking lists, talking into cell phones and only letting buses leave when their counts matched the requisite numbers. They did a lot of signalling to their compatriots on the shipboard end. Accuracy gets me down.

Depressed, I wandered to the front of the ship – bows, we nautical types say – and then the rear end, to examine the ropes fastening us to the dockside. No way down. A squirrel would have a hard time jumping ship that way. I walked round the entire ship. The other side faced only water. It seemed hell of a way down. I gave up thoughts of swimming.

Below, though, was one place the Ghurkas seemed to shun. A doorway in the ship's side let out directly onto the wharf, where fruit and other victuals seemed to be loading. A fuel pipe, if that's what it was, was attached to the hull by Dutch workmen wearing harbour logos. Our crew was busy. Water, maybe? Fuel? Sucking out ship's waste? I suppose all that goes on, and I was simply seeing the business bits of a ship's operation. Just in case, I got my jacket from my cabin and my I.D. folder. I went downstairs, and met Table 154's Diamond Lil making her way on Deck Five among a crowd.

"Going ashore, Millicent?" I asked, judging the throng queuing at the gangway.

"Yes, are you? Poor Jim," she said. "He had far too much last night. He always does. Headache city."

"Can't he come?" I saw she had two tickets. I'd seen the Tours Office in the Atrium printing them out. "Look. Could I have his ticket, pay you back later? Only I'm desperate to see the, er…" God, where were they going?

"The Rijksmuseum? Certainly!"

I gave her hand a friendly squeeze, in my eyes the sincere love I always feel for any woman who falls for a con trick. I'd miss her, once I reached dry land.

We shuffled down the gangway. Only one heart-stopping moment, when I forgot to show my I.D. plastic, but after that it was plain sailing. We boarded a coach and rolled grandly into Amsterdam. I was free.

* * *

Dry land? Not so you'd notice. Canals were every-where, but not like Venice. Amsterdam's waterways are alongside streets, not instead of. On the coach we chatted, a happy band of oglers. Ivy sat in the seat next to me, silent as ever. No Billy the Kid, I noticed. She just looked out of the window.

Tourists aren't good news nowadays, what with pollution and crowds adding to problems. East Anglia villages – Dedham, East Bergholt – are leaving official tourist trails, unable to cope with the numbers who overwhelm their hamlets. Except, what's a city to do if it has Rembrandt and Co? Van Gogh too has his own museum, so people flock and bring money galore. Tourists spend, spend, spend, so fierce arguments begin, conservationists versus developers. Even at this early hour Amsterdam was awash with visitors thronging coffee shops.

Millicent was so considerate when I admitted I'd left my money behind. She lent me a small bundle of Euros. I loved her even more.

"Make sure he pays you, dear!" some old crone wheezed.

Another blue-rinse chipped in, "But not in kind!" I added a grave ha-ha to the riot, and we disgorged at the Rijksmuseum.

There are two other museums that matter, the Van Gogh and the Stedelijk Modern Art place. I ignored the latter, of course, and managed to dawdle and lose myself. I simply sat on the grass and became part of a crowd watching some jugglers, a fire-eater and unicyclists who banged drums in noisy procession. My *Melissa* mob trundled on without me. I thought I heard Millicent call, "Now where's he got to?" I lurked for ten minutes, and saw the last of them entering the museum.

It was Ivy. She paused on the top step, and saw me. Then she walked in. Not a word, not a sign. I thought, why on earth didn't she tell the others, shout, beckon? She did none of those. If I ever saw meek little Ivy again, I owed her one for keeping shtum. I was at liberty, with gelt and time to think.

The urge was too great for idleness. Two paintings were recently nicked from the Van Gogh Museum. Interested, I walked round its walls. The thieves had used a simple ladder, which they left against the brickwork after owffing Vincent's *View of the Sea at Scheveningen* and the dour *Congregation leaving the Reformed Church in Neunen*. Got away scotage free. I gazed at the wall, guiltily trying not to feel that twinge of admiration, then went back to sit and ponder among the frolickers.

* * *

Antiques is a truly desperate business. Nobody knows that better. I often joke that antiques is a war in search of a wardrobe, but it really can be blood-curdling mayhem. You can't stay pure. I've seen all sorts, even murder, for a few sticks of furniture. I saw two sisters stab each other in a terrible fight over an old auntie's breadbin in which they imagined, quite wrongly, there was a hidden fortune. God's truth. And I've seen a dealer top himself, deliberately crashing his car because he missed buying a rare and valuable silver epergne made by the brilliant, dazzling mid-eighteenth century Edward Wakelin. (Epergne? Think of an impossibly ornate silver table-centre, fashioned as a central basket attached to either four or six smaller baskets, sometimes so extravagantly shaped you can hardly tell what it is trying to be.) The dealer, R.I.P., was Veen, an old bloke from Hamburg who arrived late at a country auction, first time I'd ever seen him suicidal. And last.

Misery and despair abound in antiques, and so does crime. I've done a few robberies – always from the undeserving, mind you, because I'm straight – and helped in others when I'd no way out. So I know methods. And I know famous exalted robbers who are household names. My experience as a divvy has rubbed most of my corners off, so I *know* when some scam carries the whiff of doom. On the other hand, I can also spot the truly golden rarity that emits the fragrance of success.

This St Petersburg gambado? It stank. Rob the Hermitage, join this gaggle of duckeggs enacting a crazy Priscilla-of-the-Lower-Third dream? It wasn't even silly, and would end in catastrophe. I might as well have chosen a team from some Women's Guild – in fact, the Women's Guild would get organised. From what I'd seen of Lady Veronica, Amy, Purser Mangot, Les Renown and June Milestone, they'd as much chance of stealing Russia's priceless treasures as of winning the Lottery. Less, in fact, the Lottery is 1 in 14 million; better odds.

It was a hot day. How long did I have before they emerged to return to the ship? Not even tourists could do the Rijksmuseum in less than an hour. I'd never felt such relief. Dozily I rested on the greensward. The clowns clowned, youths aped, girls laughed and the fire-eaters spewed flame. Children played improvised volleyball, and a couple on a nearby bench made enthusiastic groping love ignored by all. I sat under a tree looking at a nearby phone box. Tempting, but phone who?

Back home I had Jane Markham – posh magistrate's wife who was willing but full of deep suspicions. She wasn't speaking to me because I went to Leicester with her cousin Agatha who had a collection of eight Staffordshire spill-holders. These valuable mid-Victorian ceramics go in pairs, one for each side of the fireplace, and held waxed rush-piths so the lady of the house could light her nocturnal candles or touch her husband's pipe to a gentle smoke. Agatha's were leopards prowling near a hollowed-out tree (to hold the spills) the boles of which were coloured an exotic orange. They are unbelievably ugly, but you'd have to sell your best car to buy an undamaged pair of these utterly useless, unbelievably rare, ornaments. Before Agatha, I'd only ever seen one such pair, and that was in a car boot sale. Agatha had four pairs, all mint.

I made smiles with her in a despairing attempt to woo them off her. I failed. Full of the information I'd given her about the Staffordshire pieces, she sold them by phone while I slept, which only shows how cruelly insincere women are. They lack trust. I'm glad I'm not like that. Mrs Markham ignores me now. She lacks basic loyalty.

Then there was Mortimer, my teenage youngster. It

had been a shock discovering I had offspring. Barely out of the egg, he lives wild in Suffolk though he owns an ancient manor house and an estate, from his adoptive father Arthur now deceased. Like me, he's a divvy – the only other one I know – but has a serious ailment called honesty, which puts him out of reach. I couldn't very well ring Mortimer and tell him I'd been kidnapped to thieve Russia's wealth – he would simply write to the Prime Minister giving a succinct account of crooks in general, naming me in particular. Honesty's a pest.

Elise also crossed my mind. I like Elise. She plays the clarinet, lives with a double-bass player in Feltham. I'd been seeing her for a fortnight. She unnerves me because she tells her bloke everything. Hopeless, though, because Elise's always on a gig in Luton. I think she's got other blokes. She's enormously rich, so is the sort I should stay friendly with. The chances of reaching her were remote – you have to ring her agent or her husband, who is a policeman.

Any others? Tinker is my barker. A barker is a fetch-and-carry bloke who helps an antique dealer. I pay him when I can. He is loyal (always), thick (always), drunk (usually) and filthy (most of the time). He has a police record. Still, you can't chose your friends, or have I got that wrong? I found I'd dozed off, wasting half an hour. I decided to move away in case I was spotted by marauding tribes of *Melissa* passengers.

One thing I didn't want was to get killed hang-gliding into St Petersburg's Hermitage Museum or spending life in a Siberian salt mine. I'd done the right thing to escape. If conscience plagued me in later life, I could quell it – I'm good with guilt – by posting Millicent a few zlotniks to repay her loan.

When in doubt, return to your roots. I rose, dusted

myself off and plodded into sunny Amsterdam in a hunt for antiques.

* * *

Odd what things surprise you in a strange place. I had a cup of coffee and was astonished. It was good! I thought only Yanks could brew coffee, but here was some perfect stuff in Holland. I felt I'd invented the wheel. How do people do it? I used to make coffee in my cottage, but gave up. My coffee's horrible, like all other coffee in England. I honestly don't know what I, we, do wrong. I tried watching an American woman brew coffee for me, and slavishly copied her every action only to be told, "What *have* you done, Lovejoy? It's dreadful!" et shaming cetera. Now here was little old Holland among the coffee-making big guns. Well, well.

The cafe was in a square. I'd walked for an hour, twice crossing streets I'd already been through. They served me cake of unspeakable sweetness – therefore inedible – but I didn't mind, seeing they'd scooped the European coffee-making championship. I was offered some tobacco, oddly scented. Startled, I recognised the aroma of ganja, hash, and almost panicked until I saw some police stroll by. They were quite unconcerned that here was a caff peddling marijuana. When in Rome.

Pretty squares abounded, with trees and shops round the edges and people already starting midday nosh. On canals you could hire a kind of water bicycle or board a water-bus. Long canal boats were already hard at it, one with a jazz band aboard. I looked closely, but no Elise, presumably still parping in Luton. I was tempted to drift towards Amsterdam's famed Spiegel Quarter, but was uneasy. That was the one place they'd hunt for me when they realised I'd legged it. I sat in a church for a long while because it felt old and friendly. I haven't got much of an eye for architecture – Early English, fan-tracery, Norman buttresses and all that – but antiques huge and small always have the same effect.

They're warm, genuinely responsive, like meeting someone you just know you're going to get along with. I really do believe that buildings, even houses, have feelings. They look at us as we look at them. This church felt welcoming. I stayed in the gloaming while shoals of tourists trooped in and out. I almost laughed aloud, though, when a courier guide came through saying, "Count Floris the Fifth stormed Amsterdam in 1274, so repairs on this Oude Kerk were temporarily discontinued!" A lull happened about noon. I went to stand a moment by the grave of Saskia, Rembrandt's beloved missus, just to say hello and tell her I admired her old chap. A brownish skinned miniature bloke came to stand beside me.

"This Mr Rembrandt's wife?" he asked in stilted words.

"Aye." He was dapper, busy, eyes everywhere.

"She nice woman?"

"Everybody should be so lucky."

"I am Mr Moses Duploy."

"Er, wotcher." I left him to it. A tourist hustler, offering to show stray visitors the sights, the best night-clubs, the red light districts, for a fee and percentage of the drinks.

Twice I had to duck from sight when a tour mob from our ship passed to photograph and sight-see, but they didn't stay. They trailed after a guide carrying a pole surmounted by the *Melissa*'s rainbow logo went into the sunlight. I felt safe again. The ship, I knew, sailed today. I only had to bat out the afternoon. Easy.

Except, I knew Amsterdam was famous for its flea market in Waterloo Square. The temptation was too much, and anyway, what were the chances of being seen in a major capital city like this? I strolled out, walked the red lines of my Amsterdam map, and entered Waterlooplein's open-air market with a sense of relief. I decided I'd do a quick once-round then wave the *Melissa* off from the harbour wall. As ever, my legend didn't fit my reality.

Flea markets are never up to much. Old clothes, a scatter of books, old pots and new pots, plastic everythings, imitation Delft ceramics, religious emblems, rusting bits from motor bikes, toys, and one barrow would you believe selling worn shoes. I always look at trinket stalls. The offerings mostly consist of trinkets masquerading as jewellery, and priced as such. I look for jewels masquerading as trinkets, and priced as such. Find one, and you've got your next holiday, plus that excellent fitted kitchen you've always wanted. The Waterlooplein flea market disappointed me, though folk were buying stuff in cart-loads.

Mr Moses Duploy bumped into me while I examined some wood carvings (modern fake Indonesian). He tried to get into conversation with dreadful pedantic slang straight out of a 1930s *Boys Own* Annual, "Ho, there, sir! We meetings anew, no?" I smiled distantly and wandered on. No harm trying, and I don't suppose I could speak a single word of his language, but I was at risk here and couldn't risk chatting to a Cling-On, as I call chisellers like him.

Yet in any auction, boot sale, village market, junk fair, there's always pure gold somewhere. I almost wept when the familiar distressing clanging started up in my chest, and edged my way through the press. A couple were running a stall. They looked off the road, and had an eleven-month bab strapped to an improvised cot. They smoked a strangely scented cigarette, which they shared turn and turn about. I stood looking. So far in the flea market I'd seen nothing, except a collection of brass oil lamps about ninety years old. For once common sense prevailed. I'd not the money to buy them, and I'd need a van to ship them to a dealer who'd buy them as a job lot. I'd make a week's survival money on it, and still owe for the truck. Nope.

"Want anything?" the girl said in English.

"That cot. How much?"

"The cot?" She looked at her infant. It was warbling some invented ditty and grappling its foot towards its mouth. "You want the cot?"

The singing babe was lying on a cane recliner, the cause of my chest ache. About the middle of Victoria's century, fashions changed. We think we've invented fashion, but we're mere beginners. The Victorians, those superb go-getters, have us beaten to a frazzle for inventiveness. They poured into the world new materials, new textiles, paints, machines, styles. Okay, enormous damage was done, and some say the world was utterly ruined back then, but you have to hand it to them. They really did give life a go. One brilliant style was simple bentwood furniture, like the reclining cane chair the baby thought was its cot.

It was the particular style of a German called Michael Thonet. He used pale woods like birch, so different from the mahoganies then in favour. His recliners look all scroll, deceptively simple. Try to draw a seaside rocking chair without taking your pen off the paper, so it becomes all loops, and there you have the Thonet style. I'm not describing it very well, but to me it still seems terrifically modern. This one was about 150 years old. Canework seating is the best kind, since Thonet's laminated seats don't stand the test of time. You can sprawl on it and rock or doze. Thonet curved the wood (hence "bentwood") in his steam workshop, which paradoxically makes its points enormously strong. My tip to spot one of Thonet's masterpieces: the recliner/rocker chair is curved in every plane. Look at it with a flat piece of wood in your hand as reminder, you can't go wrong.

"You are smiling," the girl said seriously.

"Why are you smiling?" her bloke asked, also seriously.

"It's beautiful," I told them.

"Thank you." The girl smiled with pride at her offspring.

"I mean the chair." No hopes of buying it, no reason to, seeing I was on the run. I lifted the infant out to see the recliner beneath. "Excuse me, master," I told it. "I want a gander at your cot, okay? Won't be a sec."

"You are so serious," the girl said, coming to see. She said to her bloke, "He smiles, but is so grave."

I told her about Thonet. "Nothing like Sheraton or Hepplewhite, but it's only half a century later. What stupid moron painted it green?"

"Ah," the bloke said.

"Oh. Sorry, mate." I went red. "Er, it's better if furniture is left untouched."

"Is it worth anything?"

They stood gazing down at the Thonet. I got an earful of dribble from his lordship, a real performer still entertaining the universe. I find babs really heavy after a minute or two. Women are creased in the middle, so they have a ledge on which to lodge a babe. We males have to exert a constant muscular effort. I was worn out just standing there.

"How much do you make in a week?" They told me, and I said, "Treble it. You'll find details of Thonet in any decent library. For God's sake don't scrape that hideous green off. Get some paint man to do it, but

don't let the recliner out of your sight until it's finished because thieves," I added piously, "are known to
nick valuable antiques like this. Thonet's chairs are
highly sought by rich artists..." and so on. I returned
their infant.

I was embarrassed when they said thanks. "I'd best
get on. Good luck."

They tried pressing some of their queer tobacco on
me but I drifted off among the crowd.

* * *

Like a fool, I'd forgotten the address of Predgel. I
knew his shop was near a bridge, but Amsterdam was
a city of canals, and guess what canals have a-plenty. A
phone operator said there was nobody of that name;
several months before I'd posted off two antiques to
him. He'd paid on the nail, a rarity. Something-Strasse,
or was that German? I stood in the traffic.

Then I remembered he'd sent me a photo. His
daughter had just graduated. He, his girl and his missus were standing proudly on a canal bridge. He'd
inked an arrow on the picture to show a shop with
steps and the thinnest shop window you would ever
wish to see. He'd written, "Any time you're in
Amsterdam!" Behind, a little theatre advertising a re-
run of *Cabaret*.

In a market square I found a Tourist Information
booth. Open! This is remarkable, because in East
Anglia they're built already permanently shut. In
Holland they function. I hope this strange custom will
spread. A lady, speaking better English than I ever
would, knew exactly where *Cabaret* had been revived.
It hadn't been particularly well reviewed, she mentioned, like it was a hanging offence. I thanked her,
and followed the lines she inked on a city map. Great

inkers, the Dutch.

Hubert Predgel was there. I could see him moving. The window was painted up to head height, so no contents were visible. I went in and introduced myself. Hubert was delighted. He'd have come round the counter in greeting but there wasn't room. Like I say, thin shops.

"Lovejoy! Welcome to Amsterdam!"

He shook my hand. Tall, stooping, older and greyer than I'd expected, but his shop had a few decent antiques. They were in cabinets, with expanding grilles of meshed iron on runners to lock after hours.

We spoke of the things I'd sent him.

"It is not often I receive three genuine antiques in one delivery, Lovejoy. You have more?"

"I'm travelling light," was as near truth as I could offer just then. "I might have some things for you before long."

"The quintal is beautiful."

He nodded to the wall. I recognised my 1850s Copeland wall bracket in bone china. It looked smashing, and I was really proud. "Copeland means Spode" is the antique dealer's joke, because Copeland took over the sales of the Spode output when Josiah Spode ("the Second") died in 1797, but the firm ploughs on to this very day. Leaving aside their troubles, and Josiah ("the First") Spode's failed experiments, they went on and on. I admire those old blokes, faithful potters all. And why? Because Spode marks, right from the first day Josiah walked into a little-known pottery firm in Stoke-on-Trent, were plain and straightforward. Spode and Copeland and their descendants *stayed honest*! I pause for breath when I think of it, because potters of the world play a neff little game. Some rotten swine had (and have) this terrible habit of making their marks resemble Meissen, or

Chelsea, or Wedgwood, etc, etc, in the hope that buyers will be conned and snap their goods up for an inflated price. So let's hear it for the Spodes and Copelands of this world – they're few and far betwist. Great experimenters, and makers of style.

"Did you like the quintal?"

"Beautiful. Sold in a trice!"

Two wall brackets – cornucopias, really, for flowers on the wall of a lady's with-drawing room – and a quintal had been my shipment. It doesn't sound much, but I was pleased. A quintal is a five-stemmed pot for standing on a table, a little flower in each. Five of anything was an auspicious number for a lady, signifying the opened hand offering feminine attributes of charity, honesty and loyalty, all things handsome visitors might admire. I got it from a car-boot sale in Coggeshall one Sunday in torrential rain for a groat, and offered it to Jacintha, a toothy lady who competes at point-to-point races and frightens you to death by insisting you pat her gigantic horses. She didn't turn up one afternoon, and a bloke has to eat so I put the quintal in Predgel's parcel. By seven o'clock two days later the money came through and I was able to eat. I tried explaining this to Jacintha. She walked out and started up with Conti on East Hill, who has a penny-farthing bike. I saw them out together, him pedalling like a dolt and Jacintha on a giant mare. A mad artist in Horkesley gave them free meals for a week just so he could paint the two of them together. Is life fair?

"I have never met a divvy before. Did you know the Frenchman, Lovejoy?"

"No. I heard he was a nice chap."

"Ya. Such a pity."

We talked prices. Antique dealers the world over speak in a lower register when mentioning money, never higher than baritone. We go all sepulchral, like talking of the dead. I think it's grief, because a dealer thinks of money out, never money in.

"There's an English ship in port, ya? To St Petersburg, ya?"

"Is there?" I said, offhand. "You've got a bonny warming pan there, Hubert."

It was rightly an ember pan, with the usual three-legged joints for the lid. No design on the lid, in lovely reddish brass, so Dutch. Later versions were copper. I don't know why everybody nowadays thinks warming pans – they came in during Elizabeth the First's time – are always copper, but originally they were brass. Heavy English brass preceded the lighter Dutch metal, then copper. The ember pan's copper is simple plate one-six-teenth of an inch thick. I think they're unattractive things, always reminding me of the time my gran set her bed on fire trying to get it warm. (You shovelled red coals from the dying fire with a small fire-dog, and put the covered pan between the sheets.) Oddly, you still find a zillion warming pans in every boot sale, but never, never ever, the knitted woollen pan-cosy into which it slotted when actually in use. Funny, that.

"It's London, after 1660 – heavier English brass was a pig to work. Rotten stuff for a metalworker. Brass and iron handle, with ebony. Too heavy for the lighter brass things. They're 1720 or so. Okay?"

I went round his shop, into the sanctum of his back room, sussing his antiques. Lots of fakes and later things, but enjoyable. Like good old times, before I ran for my life.

"Are you expecting anyone?" he asked a few times.

Telling him no, I went on picking things up, putting things down, smiling and frowning. He made tea – Dutch aren't any good at tea. I drank it from politeness.

An hour later I put the question, heart in my

mouth.

"I've a few things from local excavations. Metal-detector finds, that sort of thing, Hubert. Interested?"

I detailed seven finds, including an Ancient British torc – that's a twisted gold neck adornment made for a tribal king. I added a couple of Saxon gold-and-garnet rings, a brooch and a cape clasp, and two or three pilgrim tokens from devout wanderers of the AD 700 period, give or take a yard. I had to be vague about their number and dates, because I hadn't any antiques at all.

"Ah," he said, thoughtful. "You haven't got them here?"

"Not yet. I'm going home by train this evening," I said, wilder still. Truth has to suffer, so why not extinguish it completely? "I'll send them to you when I get back. Only, I can't bring them myself because…"

Why couldn't I? I halted, flummoxed.

"Because you might be recognised?" he completed for me. Kind bloke, Hubert Predgel.

"That's it!" I said, pleased. "Customs and Excise, see? Only, I'd need a deposit if I was going to consign them to you."

"How much deposit?" he asked gravely. "I don't keep much money around – thieves are everywhere, ya?"

We settled on a wodge of Euros. I thanked him, signed a receipt, then noticed the time with theatrical surprise.

"Leave the back way, Lovejoy," he said politely. "It will save you walking all the way round to the railway."

"Ah." I didn't know what to say after that.

"Pleased doing business with you, Lovejoy." He opened the door and looked out before stepping aside. "Just checking for traffic. Youngsters come down here at such speed."

I dithered on the step. "Er, ta, Hubert." I wanted to say much more, but couldn't find words. "You're... Thanks."

"Not at all, Lovejoy. Come again to Amsterdam..." He paused, thinking. "When time is less pressing, shall we say."

"I shall."

He told me a long telephone number and shrugged. "It's my cell phone, constantly switched on. For night calls from overseas." I had more sense than write it down.

No more to say. He let me out, smiling, and I walked away. It was only then that I realised we hadn't agreed a price for my imagined antiques, and he hadn't demanded details of them.

Nice folks, some antique dealers. I added Mr Predgel to my list of three decent ones, out of the 583 I know well, and went furtively into the city.

※　※　※

About three o'clock I entered a nosh bar called the Cassa Rosso, a pub of sorts along a place unbelievably named Oudezijds Achterburgwal. I got a tonic water and watched the world with suspicion. I admit I was scared, feeling that David Buddy or one of his hunters, or anyone of my country's forty-three separate police forces, might tap me on the shoulder. I'd no illusions. A trio of youngsters nearby were arguing heatedly about petitioning the Dutch parliament to abolish the Dutch language. They asked my opinion. I said dunno, always safest with politics.

"We are students!" the girl said angrily. I already knew that because they were furious about irrelevances. Never having been an official student of anything, I don't even know how it must feel to wake up each day in a permanent apoplexy against this or that, and set to sawing placards.

"The world speaks English!" said her mate, a male hunched under a mass of dreadlocks. "You must agree!"

"Don't answer!" the other girl told me angrily. "There is no *must*, or where is democracy?" I nodded sagely while they went at it. Others joined them to differ violently, democracy being one of their prompt words. I edged away and bought a London-edition newspaper I could read by a nearby canal.

"This," said Mr Moses Duploy, sitting himself down beside me, "is Amsterdam red-light district. You like it, sir? I providing tour of every kinds for lost tourist."

"No, thank you."

"Amsterdam is world's first red-light district!"

"No." I was fed up with him. What was Dutch for no? "Dodge City in 1870 had a lady called Big-Nose Kate, I think. She ran a red-light house – painted her windows red. Chinese wine-houses in the Sung Dynasty covered their lanterns with red silk from AD 980 on. Folk still argue."

I was narked with myself for getting drawn in. I read my paper, a load of claptrap. I never buy newspapers because I finished with comics when I was nine. Every news item is made up. I don't even believe the date.

"You see antique chair under babba! You magic eye! With Mr Moses Duploy we make money-money, yes!"

"No, ta. I got lucky." I thought bitterly, this is lucky?

"I providings excellent service, sir! Cheapo!"

"I have no money."

"Ah, but you owings, no? Givings I.O.U. to Mr Predgel! Englishman's word is moneys in banks, no?"

I eyed the fidgety little git. "Well, no."

Think of the world's greatest crooks, and a fair sprinkling were Englishmen, all of whom gave their word to go straight. From the romantic backwoodsman Grey Owl – actually plain old Archibald Belaney from Hastings – to the many breathtaking modern fraudsters of international money markets, a fair old chunk have been true-blue Englishmen with tongues of silver and a dishonest eye for the main chance.

"I personal service, sir! You for ever gratitude!"

I rose, leaving my newspaper. Nothing in it about me. He stayed there, feet dangling over the canal.

"I stop followings person, sir!"

"Eh?" That halted me. I looked about, saw only tourists on a nearby bridge, and the arguing students now surrounded by a mob of others all smoking, gesticulating, proving points. "Following who?"

"Small-small fee is deal, no?"

"No." The little bloke was making me nervous.

He rose and came with me. "Follow-person near Rijksmuseum. I see you try … "

Short of words, he hunched, peered right and left, a graphic picture of a hunted man in a crowd. Was I that obvious?

"Who is he? Where?"

"Small-small fee deal?" He indicated the bridge full of tourists. "That bridge Deutsche Brucke, German Bridge. Prostitutes sell heroin in night-time. This red light district! No cameras, sir!" He became a melodrama expressing ineffable horror. "Cameras, no! Red-light girls stab camera tourist!" He tittered, hand in front of his mouth, eyes crinkling in humour at the thought of people getting stabbed for taking snapshots. "Blood on straat! Blood in canal, yes yes!"

My throat wouldn't let me respond. I looked back, forward, around. A guide came onto the German

Bridge carrying a furled umbrella topped by silvery strands and the P&O logo. A crocodile of passengers followed. Quickly I turned down a small lane.

"Cassa Rosso best Amsterdam pub, sir! You buy Mr Moses Duploy fine beer, I stop follow-person, sir!"

"Is he still there?" I asked, breathless.

He trotted alongside. "Small-small fee deal?"

I wished he'd stop saying that. I'd only Hubert's escape money. If I hadn't the gelt to buy a genuine antique, how the hell could I afford to hire somebody? I reached the junction of three lanes and a canal bridge. Across the other side was a broad square full of people, lined by elegant shops, caffs everywhere. Trams pinged and whirred. A grand theatre advertised the latest musical. I felt really down.

"Is he still behind?" I asked Mr Moses humbly, lost.

"No, sir!" he exclaimed jovially. "Follow-person now ahead waitings."

I gazed at the mob, the crowded cafes, the shops, the leafy canal walk, and miserably asked him how much. He mentioned three times what I'd got. I promised him that much for every half-day he kept me safe from follow-person. Small-small fee deal, as we Europeans say. I didn't shake hands. He was over-joyed, and we walked towards the Spiegel Quarter where antiques abound. I still smarted over the Thonet antique recliner. I could have bought it on a promise, and made enough profit to clear out of Amsterdam. I'm too soft, but what can you do?

"We partners!" Mr Moses explained in his foghorn voice. "I safings you from follow-person, yes! Where hiding tree? In forest yes yes!"

He fell about at his quip. I said ha-ha. Come five o'clock I'd ditch the blighter and cut out, leaving him with my I.O.U. What was one more debt? I judged the time. Four o'clock now. In one hour I'd be safe. Except I'd been telling myself that every ten minutes for days, and was still scared out of my wits.

We headed for the Spiegel Quarter, where seventy antique shops of great reputation waited for me.

Chapter Eight

My gadfly was often nowhere to be seen. I simply got directions from him to the Spiegel Quarter, and walked. He occasionally reappeared and trotted beside me, once nodding at a narrow lane I should take as a short cut, then vanishing.

The Spiegel Quarter is decidedly moneyed. You only shopped here if you needn't worry how many noughts were on the price.

"This it?" I asked Mr Moses.

"Yes yes, Spiegel Quarter. You want diamond quarter?"

"Here's fine. Watch out for follow-person, okay?"

"Indeed indeed."

"Here. Is it a woman or a man?"

"Quick doorway!" he hissed, and thrust me into a furniture place. An elegant lady was just entering so I didn't have to buzz. She held the door for me. Not having had much luck lately with such suave creatures, I went red and just muttered "Ta, lady." She smiled at my embarrassment. The antiques places had control panels on their doors. I found myself in a tasteful antiques place where assistants mingled with customers.

The place was double pricy, ethnic trappings and furniture, most of them Far Eastern. Actually, you aren't allowed to say Far East nowadays because "equalists" say it's imperialist or fascist or whatnot. I mean Indonesian, Indonesia being once a Dutch colony. Textiles abounded, though most were sorry substitutes and replicas – poor Indonesia's original textiles and styles are vanishing because of Western commerce. A number of kris knives, some truly old but others dross, were decoratively arranged on the walls. I smiled to show innocence, and moved in. The elegant lady had evidently come to inspect three large bronze drums, magnificent musical pieces obviously set out for her inspection.

"They are genuine original Indonesian bronzes, madam," a splendid grey-haired gent was giving it. "Just like the great 'Moon of Bali', known to be the largest ceremonial bronze drum in the whole world. Such brilliant skill, and truly ancient! These are the only matched trio known. They came to us at enormous expense from Bali, where they were recorded almost two hundred years ago."

They lapsed into Dutch. I drifted, but lingered. I love listening to lies. Truth is the bricks in the wall of civilisation, but lies are the mortar holding society together. Nothing wrong with a good lie, of course, because some lies are worth having. A woman uses make-up so she looks dynamite, and might tint her hair to look even more fetching. Cosmetics aren't lies, just simple tricks, though some religious sombre-sides damned all cosmetics – St Jerome, for instance, though that didn't stop him from leading his troop of virgins to Palestine in A.D. 389 in, of course, a thoroughly saintly manner. I like to see women making their lips redder, their hair shinier, their teeth more dazzling, their faces bonnier…

"Yes, sir?" a smoothie enquired. I showed interest in a miniature temple carving with eleven floors and balconies. The more storeys, the greater the deity.

"Very apotropaic, those representations, sir," he gushed. I was too embarrassed to ask what the word meant. He was tall, toothy, in a suit that could have bought my cottage. "Typical Indonesian. Our speciality!"

"I'll come back to you in a minute," I lied, moving on.

The antiques were a mixture of antiques and gunge. Nothing wrong with copies, fakes, forgeries, like two of the massive bronze drums the pleasant lady was buying. But actually selling them as antiques when it's only for money puts a bad taste in my mouth.

"Excuse me." I turned back. "Do you provide certificates of authenticity?"

"Yes, sir!" He wrung his hands in ecstasy. "With every single purchase! Our entire stock is original and genuine. We are of course well known in England, and can provide references and provenance for everything in our emporium..."

I only pretended to listen while I watched the pleasant lady open her handbag and take out a cascade of credit cards and a cheque book encased in gold. She was going to buy the three massive bronzes.

"I was actually fascinated by your ceremonial religious bronzes," I told my groveller. "Would they still be for sale?"

He looked stricken, led me to join the lady and the head geezer and explained my query, politely switching to English.

"I'm afraid I am just about to buy them," the lady said. "Are you a collector? My husband works at the Hague, and I am decorating our entrance hall. We loved Indonesia. Don't you think they will look absolutely superb?"

"Only one is genuine, lady."

The world stopped. She glanced at the salesmen, back to me, the credit cards, cheque book, her elegant fountain pen.

"One? But I am persuaded..."

The lead man smiled with disdain. Nobody can show disdain like a con man in pursuit of money.

"I promise you, sir, we have these items authenticated by the best international experts. Genuine provenance – "

Provenance is the paper trail proving where an

antique comes from, legitimising every step of its journey from olden days into the modern world. Once, provenance was taken for granted. Now, it has become the biggest factor in authenticating an antique ever since forgeries became the modern epidemic. Provenance is a simple thing, but hard to establish. If you have your great-grandmother's oil portrait showing her wearing her Wedgwood gold-mounted cameo necklace, made unique by her addition of a briolette (a drop-shaped gemstone covered with triangular facets for brilliance, and often added as a pendant), then antique auctioneers will fight at your door for the privilege of handling the sale. It would be virtually cast-iron provenance. Otherwise you'd need documents, bills of sales, perhaps even early letters describing your necklace, all to attest its authencity. Without it, the money you'll make falls like a stone.

The lady was listening to the salesman. She started to write the cheque. I ahemed.

"Forged documents are everywhere these days, lady."

"We do not use unattested documentation," he said frostily. I felt somebody take my elbow. They were going to evict me.

"Don't, missus," I said to the lady. "The middle one's genuinely old. The others aren't."

"How can you tell?"

"It's the truth. I'll prove it."

She pursed her lips, judging the bronzes. "How?"

That stopped me. I could prove it to myself, easy. But how could I tell these strangers I was a divvy? Most dealers think divvies are a myth, until they meet one. The middle bronze was already making me feel decidedly queer. I wondered if the odd figures and the weird geometrical designs made it worse. I've heard that ancient Egyptian tomb drawings send lots of people dizzy. Sweat was on my forehead and my knees were starting to go. Soon I'd keel over.

"Bring an industrial chemist to take samples. Hire him. The middle one will have the right trace elements of ancient Indonesian bronzes. The other two will give modern readings."

"Out!" In a babble of Dutch I was ejected into the street. The door slammed behind me, its buzzer frantic.

So much for honesty. No follow-person seemed to be hanging about, and no Mr Moses Duploy. So much for loyalty, and I was paying him a fortune in hiring fees – well, promising him, which was nearly almost virtually practically the same thing. It had been a mistake to speak to the lady. Try to help someone, see what happens.

Darting from doorway to doorway like a cartoon cat, I made it to the corner – and bumped into the elegant lady.

"Do come," she said, smiling. "My car is at the end of the straat."

Dutch folk are always a yard taller. She however was tastefully kitted out, exuding wealth.

"Er, look, lady," I stammered. "I'm kind of busy. I have an appointment."

"No. Thank *you*. May I introduce myself? I am Inga Van Rijn. I own hotels. My husband is a diplomat. I ought to at least give you a lift, in return."

"Well…" Not a bad idea. Who'd think of looking for me in a posh car? "Thank you."

Walking with such a stylish woman, I felt so proud. She moved with grace, like all women, but she was specially wafty, never making way for anyone else. Even street hooligans and riff-raff edged out of her path. Traffic stopped to let her go even when the lights weren't in her favour. Women have that effect. I sailed along, basking in her reflection. I wish this happened more often.

A Bentley stood at the intersection, a uniformed driver leaping out to open the door. She beckoned me in as I hesitated. I joined her, and we drove off.

"Where to?" she asked.

"To the, er... you know the railway station, please?"

She told the driver in Dutch, and we sat back in luxury.

"You knew the genuine one," she said.

"Yes." No harm in admitting it to Mrs Van Rijn. I'd never see her again.

"Divvy, is it not?"

"Yes." Her eyes were flecked with a sort of gold in the iris, her pupils the blackest on earth. I always like to think how I'd paint a woman's face. The right light is vital.

"It is a gift, something born within, is it not?"

"Yes." I'd have to use oblique lighting, cast from her left side. Painting a lady's portrait by candlelight was "corny", Tom Keating the great forger used to tell me, but I think he was wrong. Some faces scream out for a muted golden glow. This lady's features were made for it.

"You study my face?"

"Yes, Mrs Van Rijn. It's just that ... Hang on. Your name. Are you related to...?"

"Rembrandt Van Rijn? You guessed!" She laughed and clapped her hands softly. She wore genuine Berlin lace gloves, older than many of the streets. "Yes! He was my husband's ancestor."

It took six deep breaths to say it. "I'm honoured, Mrs Van Rijn."

"Artists are always overcome," she said. Her smile dazzled. "I am actually a descendant of another artist, a minor Impressionist, I'm afraid. You must be a portraitist yourself?"

"Yes, when I'm…" What, free? Not being hunted? Not wanted for robbery, theft, forgery, by New Scotland Yard and David Buddy the bounty hunter? "When I'm home."

"You can paint me," she suggested, "when you get back."

The massive saloon car had stopped. We were on the wharf, alongside a massive white ship. It was the *Melissa*. I looked at Mrs Van Rijn. She was smiling with a fondness that would normally have melted my heart. She made a sign. The door opened.

"Greetings!" cried Mr Moses Duploy. He was wriggling in ecstasy, like a hound obeying orders. "Just in times! Sailings on seventeen hour!"

Stupidly I looked from him to Mrs Van Rijn. If I didn't know different, she seemed rather sad. I didn't move for a second, then worked it out. Mr Moses Duploy had shoved me into the shop where Mrs Van Rijn and the three bronzes were.

"You?" I said to him.

He fell about laughing. It was a pantomime of a laugh. "Ho, ho, ho," he went, literally holding his sides. "Yes yes! Follow-person is Mr Moses Duploy himself!"

"Good luck, Lovejoy," the lady said, still with that look of faint sorrow, but this time I wasn't taken in.

"With what?"

"St Petersburg. I shall be thinking of you."

The words fell on me like hammer blows. The only people within earshot were Mr Moses, the driver, Mrs Van Rijn, and myself. I looked up at the rail. There was Lady Vee and June Milestone at their balcony, smiling and tapping their wrist watches as if to say hurry, hurry.

I got out my I.D. plastic and showed it to the Ghurka on gangway duty. He waved me through, and

I climbed the gangplank. Historians now say that, in the two-and-a-half centuries of sea-faring piracy, and despite all the stories about walking the plank, only one captive ever suffered that terrible punishment.

Make that two.

* * *

On the good ship *Melissa* you could eat and drink all day. Worn out by Dutch treachery, I went up to the Lido Deck where the vast cafeteria called the Conservatory offered eternal tea, coffee and nosh. I sat at table looking out as the ship sailed from Amsterdam. I thought of robberies I had known and some I admired.

Fashions change (otherwise they wouldn't be fashions, right?). Nothing has altered as much as theft. Think of it. If you wanted to nick a king's ransom *and get away*, you'd not filch your neighbour's motor. You'd not raid the nearest railway station's ticket office or hot-wire the SAS's wages van. You'd do what the really big thieves do these days – you'd steal stocks and shares, from within. Or you'd get yourself appointed Chief Executive Officer of some multinational corporation and fiddle away until, finally unmasked, you'd glide away in your valuable yacht to live the life of Riley. It's the modern way, to steal so much money you could buy the best lawyers, plus the law, and get away scotage free.

Think of it: exactly how many city gents ever serve time? Hardly any. And how much do they get away with? Millions, and all the marshmallows they can eat in their megabuck complexes in Bahamian suntraps, while the innocent investors languish in poverty. The TV news is full of them. Make no mistake: catching them is like knitting fog. Can't be done. And if you somehow manage to find them, they're still somehow immune from Law. Watch any news, and you'll see.

The trouble is, theft on such a scale is the privilege of those who dwell in grand offices and share titles like Vice-President or C.E.O. and have secretaries. It's not for the likes of you or me. Like, Alfred Taubman, a Sotheby's boss, got done for a $290 million price-fixing scam which almost ruined the world's entire art/antiques system. The guilty bloke got gaoled for a year and a day. See? The posher you are, the less your punishment. I know pals who got longer terms of imprisonment for eating with their elbows on the table.

So here we were, assembled to pull off a great scam, with no giant firm to smokescreen our sinister doings. Suppose it was just you and me up against it, and we were broke. What then?

Here's a fact: the easiest objects to steal are antiques. I include all art works. For a start, they are everywhere – country houses, museums, galleries, town halls, government offices, shops, auction houses, schools and old universities. Another fact: you can inspect most of them quite legitimately. In other words, you can suss the security, literally check the lie of the land exactly as I'd had my mate Skeggie suss out the Marquis of Gotham's stately home before me and Belle did our stuff that landed me in this mess.

A third vital point: the full value of the items is known to the whole wide world. Ask at your public library, and they'll tell you quite openly, "Yes, madam, the cost of Lord Nerk's silver collection is 13.9 millions, based on the pro-estimate of 2016. Do you want photographs? Unfortunately, the book is on loan this week, but next Friday…" and so on. Your only anxiety is that the other borrower might be some wicked thief nurturing the same idea as you. See what I mean?

Now, the antiques trade has a series of maxims about stealing antiques/art. One goes like this: Nine-tenths of all stolen art/antiques that get returned are fakes, false, replicates, *because the stolen originals don't come back.* The most famous is the *Mona Lisa*, of course, nicked before the Great War, later found in a railway Lost Property Office. The suspicion lingers yet: *is the Louvre's Mona Lisa the original?* Legend says not.

Another maxim: The greatest stimulus to art/antiques forgery is the theft of some famous antique. So a stolen Old Master will be copied a hundred times the instant the news breaks, and the replicas sold before the day's out. Like, the *Mona Lisa* was copied and the fakes secretly sold to millionaire art collectors umpteen times – people say nine, others thirteen – before the "original" came to light and returned in triumph from Italy.

Theft spawns illicit money. Rightly or wrongly, money grows, flows and shows when antiques are nicked, but you have to be careful and steal only the right thing. The Enigma code machine is an example of filching the wrongest thing imaginable. This encryption device was invented by several countries, including Germany, for use in World War Two. Their proto-Enigma was owffed by brave Poles and smuggled to London, saving countless lives. There are two Enigma machines. One was stolen from Bletchley Park and a ransom demanded. It was actually returned intact, and they say not a groat was paid over. The warning here is, don't steal something of national importance unless you've got nerves of steel – and somebody to sell it to. This last point is vital, because where is the multitude of rich collectors who'd really want an Enigma machine? Nowhere.

But where is the multitude of rich collectors who'd want a priceless Old Master? Answer: everywhere.

They're in London, New York clubs, in presidential mansions, in the World's List of Moneyed Mavens. Immediately Rubens' missing masterpiece *The Massacre of the Innocents* came to light, it became a candidate for greed of a different kind than the actual purchaser's lust. An Austrian monastery had thought their old oil painting was by Jan van den Hoecke and worth a meagre ten million, until Sotheby's decided it wasn't quite so trivial and bragged it was Rubens at his 1610 best. I was at the auction, breaking my heart when it went to an undeserving billionaire.

In the Top Ten paintings – scored by money, not merit – Picasso leads currently with four; Van Gogh has three, Cézanne one, Renoir one, and now that Rubens has joined this pricy elite. The whereabouts of all ten is precisely known. That means the identity of the guards, curators, visitors, the manufacturers of the electronic CCTV and alarm systems is instantly traceable. And that means crooks know everything too. If the paintings slumber in a gallery or museum, they can be visited and the invigilators sussed, just as Skeggie did for me before I robbed the Marquis's humble abode. If a new owner selfishly gloats over his Old Master in some remote mountain castle or a Home Counties lair, ask yourself what on earth is *Who's Who* published for? And it's off to the public library again. They're so helpful, when you're planning anything from fraud to hijacking a new cruise liner.

Rich honest people – if there are such – believe that thieves are thick idiots with the insight of a yak. Wrong, because robbers are often experts in chronbiology. Example: Theft has certain inflexible rules. A distinguished doctor at the Royal Society of Medicine in 2002 proved the human biological clock doesn't adapt to night-shift work. Proof? Night dangers include Chernobyl's nuclear catastrophe, Three Mile Island, the *Exxon Valdez* calamity, Apollo 13's tribulations – all of which happened in the lantern hours. The biological trough occurs almost *exactly at 3.30 a.m.*, which is when your John Constable heirloom will vanish.

I don't mean it's easy to rob anyone of anything. Famous paintings are simply money in the bank, because everybody knows you can't get a Turner oil for a few cents, not any more. And what's easier to carry home in the dark hours than a picture sliced out of its frame and concealed round your middle with a string? Sometimes I think it's strange that thieves don't steal more successfully more often. Except thieves can go wrong.

Like the couple of blokes who wanted to steal the wealth of a social club. They got a boat, crossed a lake, and hauled up the oxyacetylene gadget they'd pur-loined to cut open the clubhouse safe. After hours of hard labour they found that they'd absent-mindedly stolen a welding device instead, and had spent the whole night welding the steel safe more secure. Or like the Millennium Raiders, that famed London gang who tried to steal the giant Millennium Star, a dazzler on show in London's ugly Dome. They're supposed to have had ammonia sprays, smoke grenades, gas masks, sledge-hammers, body armour, scanners and other gadgets, and driven a great bulldozer thing inside to smash through to the Star and its attendant eleven blue diamonds. The police were everywhere, and took the prisoners to the Old Bailey.

My point is this: the gang bought a farm, a speed-boat – bobbing on the Thames to make a getaway – plus massive excavation gear, sundry fancy equipment. These things don't come cheap. Robbery this grand needs multo blokes and training. Another antiques maxim is: *You can always get enough backers to fund a heist.* Secrecy is more uncertain, but if you plan a superb robbery and do your homework, you can get enough backers (wallets, the trade calls them) for your robbery in a fortnight, and that's just in dozy East Anglia. Imagine how quick it can be in the speedier areas of the kingdom.

Manchester's the fastest; they'll fix up a robbery in a day. London comes second, with Glasgow and Leeds tying for joint third-quickest at about five days, though Glaswegians always want a deposit of a tenth of the expected moneys up front, and robbers don't like leaving calling cards around town before pulling a job. And this, note, is to rob anywhere – Hallam House, Dublin's art museums, or even your (that's *your*) house.

"Where'd you meet this lot, June?" I asked, still looking out of the window at the shifting seas and receding land. I saw her reflection in the glass. Her scent was the same. I'd known her so well, so I could be frank.

"Hello." I could tell she was smiling. "Whose limo *was* that?"

"Mine," I said rudely. "The coach was uncomfortable."

"And such a pretty lady!"

"Whatever scam you're on, it's doomed, June. You know that."

"You don't know the details."

The Conservatory was emptying now, folk drifting to prepare for dinner, the cinemas, casino, the vaudeville theatre. It seemed safe.

"They don't know we knew each other, right?"

She was as bonny as before. She started to take out her gold cigarette case, then looked casually about and replaced it. We were on the wrong side of the ship, smoking only permitted on the port side. "I was the one who suggested you might be needed."

Might? I almost bleated it out. *Might*? I was abducted for a might, an if, or a maybe?

"Look, June." I felt insulted, and prepared to beg.
"I'm in trouble back home. I was on the run. I'll help
you to pull a money scam, if you'll drop me off somewhere. Okay?"

"What money scam?"

Infants do it all the time. Most women can still do
it when they're grown. It's like their eyes wallop you
across the bonce and send you dizzy. Her eyes met
mine. I felt it. It isn't passion, merely a sensation of
another person's eyes shafting into your skull and taking a quick shufti, checking round.

"You want one? I'll offer you two, you'll make a
fortune."

She sat back. "Go on, then."

She wore a plain blue dress, with a Fair Isle cardigan
in the thinnest wool. Her pearls were genuine, of
course, earrings simple drop shapes. June Milestone
always did scrub up well, as Cockneys joke, and look
top cutlery. Her hair was different. I could remember
when it had been sweat-soaked in a tent on an Oxford
lawn – her lawn, of course, in the early morning. Her
maid-servant brought us breakfast at half-seven. It had
been raining, and it was our third-from-last encounter,
but I'd forgotten all that, and I'm definitely never
going to remember it.

"You've heard of the Vinland Map? Proved Vikings
discovered the Americas before Columbus? Priceless,
right?"

"Go on." She was amused, doing that woman's
laugh-non-laugh that comes with the set.

"Yale University's map, worth a mint. Well, I'll do
you one better. You could sell it."

"Wasn't it a forgery, though?"

"Course it was!"

I went over the facts. It was faked up by the Reverend (not quite so reverend) Joseph Fischer, a Jesuit from Austria who, mesmerised into forgery by political right-wingery in mid-1930s Germany, scrawled his Vinland Map to show it wasn't slothful old Latins like Columbus but noble flaxen Aryans who discovered the Americas. Some folks claim Fischer was moved by nobler motives. Yeah, right. He used its "discovery" to add to his reputation as an exalted mediaeval scholar. Somehow, though, it came into dealers' hands for less than US$4,000. They offered it to the British Museum in 1957, then a charitable Yank – the sort every antique dealer except me seems to know – bought it and gave it to Yale University. Sensation! Believers multiplied, and Bjarni Herjolfsson is famed in song and story for his A.D.985 landfall there. I don't disbelieve in random intrepid Norsemen, or in Leif Eriksson who went touristing along in A.D.1002. I just disbelieve the map. The antiques trade calls such trifles crappy-mappy, and thinks them too good to be true. The trade's right. Dealers make up comical poems.

"Fischer's long gone," I finished. "He used a parchment page from an old book, authentically 1440s or so, so it would test right under a microscope. Except the ink let him down. It contained some stuff called anatase, whatever that is, only in use since 1923."

"And you?"

"I'd buy authentic parchment. But I'd have inks specially made, and work in a Class 100 laminar-flow laboratory. I'd invent a Portuguese navigator, pre-1300. Or an ancient Chinese bamboo book – they're easier, and cheaper to get – and old Chinese inks, and depict the Californian coast as far as Oregon. You'll have to find American buyers, just to shut the international press up. The media in USA would create mayhem, saying China could claim Mexico to Vancouver as China's first colony."

"You're a scream, Lovejoy." She glanced about first, those eyes of hers, to check nobody was within earshot. "The second?"

"I'd fake Vicari, that modern painter. Money for jam, and the scam'd be dirt cheap. Cost a day's wages, no more. Anybody could do it."

"Are you joking?" She scanned the vast cafeteria, still wondering if she could get away with lighting a fag.

"He's a modern artist, lives somewhere in Monte Carlo, probably owns the damned place by now. Charges the earth to paint your portrait, but only if you're mega-famous, like kings, moguls, frightening dictators, untouchable gangsters."

"And do what?"

"Paint what he would have painted. A collection of august royals, or some movie mighties, film stars."

I was starting to get enthusiastic, the way ideas take hold when you're on a roll.

"A load of fake Vicari paintings, and you'd pay journalists to talk them up as original?"

I remembered her smile like from yesterday, and found myself smiling back.

"I'd get some lads to nick the paintings in transit, then go to the mogul's friends, movie studios, the royal house, the dictator's hoods, whoever, and offer to rescue them unharmed, saving face all round and preventing scandal. Tah-tah-tah!" I made a fanfare of imagined success.

"Hasn't that sort of thing been done?"

"Everything's been done before, June." I wanted to reach for her hand, but two of the ship's officers were passing on their way to the Crystal Pool. Anyway, she probably still hated me, or she wouldn't have landed me in this mess.

"You always get one essential thing wrong, Lovejoy."

"What?" I'd promised her an easy fortune.

"You forget, Lovejoy. We're the good gang. The actual robbers, who we don't yet know, are the perpetrators."

"I only wanted to – "

She rose, smiling hard. "That will do." She moved away and gracefully joined the officers. One was the purser girl from Reception. Neither smiled my way.

It wasn't too hopeless a meeting. I'd discovered a few things. First, I didn't believe in her, or her good troupe. Who prepares a fake robbery to prevent one? June wasn't just in it for the money alone. For another, I was expendable once we reached St Petersburg, but for some reason absolutely vital until then. And a third thing: she wasn't the king wallet, the scam's principal backer. Wealthy as she was, she was only along for some other reason, and that reason was probably me. I knew now I would have to die somewhere in Russia's old capital city, once I'd served their task.

There's only one thing I'm good at. June knew this, and the others had reason to believe her. If I suddenly pretended otherwise – that I'd lost the divvy gift, or maybe faked some illness – they might change their plans, but they wouldn't fly me home in a first-class aeroplane. They'd just lob me into the Baltic.

No, I was down to me. I went to find out where the ship would stop next.

Chapter Nine

The table buzzed at dinner. I got the "Where did you get to? We looked high and low." I said I'd decided to get lost and managed to get a lift from a lady. They were thrilled. Millicent laughed, "Anything to get out of repaying me for that ticket!"

I began to suss out nearby tables. I'm hopeless at seduction, because women are always ahead of me, but they're sometimes kind and gullible. Chat up someone with whatever line would convince, I might be in with a chance.

Somebody mentioned the cost of sending a fax. I listened, heard there was e-mail available.

"Telephoning's expensive once we're out of port," Jim grumbled, "but at least you can do it from your cabin."

On the whole they were good company. I felt fond of them. So far, they had provided me with the one opportunity of escape, and here they were almost guiding my next steps. If we were in prison, they'd be offering me files, and shovels to start a tunnel. I began to think what nice people they were. And when Kevin chipped in about going to the morning session on antiques, I brightened more. Today he wore a shiny eye-shadow and loop earrings.

"Come with us, Lovejoy." Holly Sago perked up. Until then she'd been pretty morose. I'd glimpsed her in the Conservatory when June was trying to convince me I was in clover. I was about to say no when she said, "I mean to the Casino. Help me control Kevin's gambling fever."

"That bingo session was a disaster!" Kevin brought out several coloured cards in proof. "Every game, I only needed one number!"

Holly tapped my hand. "He wastes hundreds every

cruise. Never wins."

Kevin pouted. "That's not true! On the Venice cruise I won a tenner!"

"And lost seven hundred." Holly confided to the table, leaning forward. "He brings three thousand for gambling money, and goes home with less than a fiver. Can you imagine?"

The table rejoiced at hearing people's foibles. A chat began about risks.

"Antiques are the worst," Ivy from the Wirral put in. "They're coming round with one now."

"Eh? Where?" I looked, but couldn't see what she meant. The restaurant waiters thronged and passengers were wading into their dinners. I'd never seen so many crooked little fingers. We were so posh.

"See Mr Semper? He runs a competition, brings round an antique. Whoever guesses the right value wins one!"

I'd seen Henry Semper on TV, the Sunday night favourite show, *Antiques on the Road*. June Milestone was a frequent visitor on it. The idea was simple: take along some treasure from your attic, experts prove it's worth a gillion and you can spit in your boss's eye on Monday. Or, as sometimes happens, not.

"He's here now."

Laughter from other tables clued me in, and here came the great Henry Semper accompanied by a plain specky lass in a severe suit. Mr Semper limped, a short bulky man with a stick.

"Evening, all! It's an antique coffee pot tonight." He spoke in that gravelly voice now known to the world. "Lauren, show them."

"This is a wonderful coffee pot by one of the six greatest silversmiths ever." The girl was in raptures, trying to keep out of the way of the waiters as she lowered her tray so we could inspect the object. "Paul de

Lamerie, eighteenth century!"

The tray was glass-bottomed, with cushioned sides. Innocently I dropped my serviette and beat the waiter to picking it up. The coffee pot was beautifully engraved sterling silver. The spout had a small hinged lid, the handle at right angles to the spout.

"It is exceedingly rare," Lauren said earnestly. "Note the finial on the hinged cover, and the maker's marks in a line by the handle?"

"Values, please." Henry Semper placed blank cards on the tablecloth. His smile was his hallmark, they said of him on TV. "Hand in your guesses as you leave, with your cabin numbers!"

"What's the prize tonight, Henry?" Billy and Kevin asked together, causing a laugh.

"That'll be telling!" Henry said, limping on with his gravelly laughter rattling crockery round the place.

"Let's all enter!" Millicent breathlessly filled in her card while Holly tried to peek. "We'll keep score, shall we? See who wins most by the end of the cruise?"

"They take a small sum from your account," Ivy explained, seeing me hesitate. "For charity."

"It's all in a good cause," they all agreed. Except me.

We finished the meal. I wanted to see tonight's film. When I was little, cinema was my only culture apart from books. The difference was, I had to nig in to see a picture, and libraries were free. Civilisation, I always think, is free libraries and pavements. The rest is just window dressing.

On the way out, everybody comparing what they'd written on their guessing cards, I was stopped.

"Lovejoy hasn't done one!" Millicent said loudly.

"Hasn't he?" Kevin and Holly handed theirs in to Lauren, who was waiting proudly beside her splendid eighteenth century Paul de Lamerie silver.

"You have to!" Millicent decided. "We agreed!"

"Here, Lovejoy." Ivy found a blank card and a pencil. The waiters were all smiling as I wrote. I shouldn't have let my temper get the better of me. Lauren took it with the others, glancing at it as she placed it on the pile. I saw her face change.

There was always a new flower arrangement at the restaurant entrance. I tried to join in conversation when two ladies paused to admire them. I failed, because Lauren, with my card in her hand, quickly attracted the attention of the indefatigable Henry Semper, who was belly-laughing with a nearby coterie of admirers. I had to scarper. People are mesmerised by screen fame and Henry basked in worship. He'd even brought a group of antiques enthusiasts on board to revel in his glory. Get your face on TV, you're a celebrity, even if like Henry Semper you were running a nasty little crooked scam.

Moving quickly on among the evening crowd, I found myself in the Atrium. Open staircases swept down to a dance-floor where a small band played, with bars and people lounging and chatting. It was affluent serenity. On the first tier of balconies was another lounge bar with shops rimming the walls. Above that, yet another tier with the library, jewellery shops and clothing places. To make sure I'd dodged my fellow-diners, I slipped into the a garment place and gaped at the clothes, tee shirts with embroidered *Melissa* logos, anoraks, evening dresses, shoes.

"They do a sale after the second sea day," a lady told me. She was looking through a rack of blouses. I recognised her as one who'd been admiring the flowers by the Pacific restaurant. She'd cold-shouldered me when I wanted to get into conversation. I didn't need spurning again. I usually find that once does it.

"Right." I peered about until the coast was clear, and went to the cinema.

The film was sparsely attended. I liked it. Mostly I read American thrillers and Victorian English writers, then anything else I can get hold of. As for films, anything goes. It was late when the film ended. By the time the credits rolled, I'd worked out where to direct my pleas for help. I decided to write a letter, envelope and stamp in the old-fashioned way – "snail mail" as folk now call it – and to post off a fax. Then I'd speak to the captain, who sometimes held cocktail parties. They couldn't stop me telling him with everybody there, could they?

Margaret Dainty is an old friend. She frets about being lame, but has no reason to. She and I have been friends years. She occasionally lends me her husband's clothes if I've to go somewhere grand, like a wedding or funeral. She's an antiques dealer without much nous and barely scrapes a living. Her shadowy husband's always overseas mending fallen companies. Margaret and me occasionally make smiles. She said once she was my Out-Patients Department, which is not far from the truth. She blames herself for being lame, over forty-five, and too plump, as if any of that matters. See how daft women are? I wrote her a letter and a fax on the forms they provide at the Reception desk and handed them in.

It had been a rum sort of day. Worn out, I went to the quiet Horizon Lounge, upstairs at the front of the ship, to listen to the piano and see the distant lights of other ships moving out there in the darkness. I had a drink while I worked out what to say to Margaret on the phone. She isn't quite the SAS, but is willing. Green cards placed about the ship warned that the clocks were going to be changed during the night. I worked out that Margaret would be home by midnight, whatever she was doing. I'd phone on the stroke.

The lounge was fairly empty, everybody at late-night shows, dancing, and films. I'd assumed it would be peaceful while I worked things out.

The mistake found me when I'd almost made up my mind.

* * *

"I think that was a dreadful joke!" Lauren stood over me, seething with rage.

I sighed. The lounge was wide, muted colours, outside a tranquil sea with occasional lights, the night velvet royal blue and faintly starlit. The piano was playing softly, low armchairs and occasional tables dotted about, stewardesses wandering, occasional quiet laughter from passengers having a last slurp before turning in. It should have been the most placid of scenes. Instead, I get this bottle-eyed fury. She polished her specs furiously, working on a better glare.

"Joke? I never joke, miss."

"What you wrote on your card, about our rare Paul de Lamerie coffee silverware! Worth *nothing*?"

"You asked for a valuation."

"Everybody saw it! Some actually…" she closed her eyes and went for it "…*laughed* out *loud*! At Mr Semper! They *talked*! You are vicious!"

"I tried not to hand one in, but you insisted."

"Mr Henry was livid! You are despicable!"

"Look, love." I felt done for. "I don't want to be here. I don't like your nasty little boss and his nasty little antiques scam. I don't like you because you're helping him to defraud people who're too ignorant not to fall for his tricks."

Two ladies further along the lounge were listening. One was the one who'd cold-shouldered me and said about the shops having sales days.

"I shall complain to the captain, the purser, the ship's officers and the cruise director!" Lauren said, voice trembling. "I shall have you evicted at the very next port! You're an infidel. That silver piece was made by the hand of one of the greatest – "

"Ballocks, miss." I turned in my seat to look up at her. "Paul de Lamarie was a Huguenot refugee from the Continent who worked in London. He was a deeply religious man and entirely honest, unlike your slimy boss. Your illegal faked mark will stand up to ordinary scrutiny, but the coffee pot won't. It started life a couple of centuries after de Lamerie died – as a plain pub tankard. The handle Semper's faker stuck on it at right angles is an attempt to make it look old – servants poured sideways like that after coffee first came into fashion when Pasqua Rosee opened London's first coffee house in St Martin's Alley, off Cornhill, in 1652. The habit grew, so there's plenty of elegant silverware about. A real de Lamerie would be worth a mint, but your pot is naff. You've no right to defraud history, you rotten cow."

"The hallmarks – " She tried to get going, but strangled.

"Your forger bought an ordinary silver tankard, then added a spout and faked de Lamerie's marks. Tell him he forgot to add the fake marks on the spout and on the finial."

She gaped, her mouth opening like a fish working against the stream.

"I hate bad fakes, love. I don't mind good forgeries, because at least somebody's tried." She made a woman's exclamation, "Oh!", in anger and turned aside. I said after her, "I said it was worth nothing because it's illegal. It can't be bought or sold."

She spun, her face white. "I shall have you put ashore!" she rasped, and turned away to flounce off.

"One more thing, Lauren." For some reason I felt so sad, because now she seemed nothing more than an ignorant dupe – like the rest of us, I suppose.

"Haven't you said enough?" she spat.

"No, love. It's a *chocolate* pot, nothing to do with coffee."

She marched off. I relaxed, and saw the two women nearby looking hard at me, and that other people were finding their evening suddenly a little less mellow. Conversation slowly picked up, and the piano regained composure. The two ladies rose and crossed over to my group of three armchairs. I was going to get another wigging. Had the women on board the *Melissa* nothing better to do than ballock me, for God's sake?

"I do apologise."

"Eh?" This was new.

Her friend retreated to the exit, smiling. "You were trying to escape," the remaining lady said. "I didn't realise. In the shop."

When I'm not in the wrong my mind thromboses and I can't find anything to say, used to being useless I suppose. Speech is overrated, but sometimes it's worth giving it a go. This was the first time for weeks I'd not been savaged. Did she mean real escape? Then the penny dropped. She meant I looked furtive by the flowers and those tee-shirts. I groaned inside.

"I could have been kinder, and made it easier for you to avoid your friends."

"Yes, sir?" a stewardess said. The lady declined with a headshake, but sat in the next armchair.

"I'm Lovejoy. How do."

"Delia Oakley." She smiled, at ease. "Are you on a terrible table? You can always ask to be changed. Speak to the head waiter."

"No, they're fine. Friendly."

"Is that so," she said evenly. "We think you're a happy bunch. We're the next table, the one with only four on. Rather dull, I'm afraid."

"You can always ask to be changed. Speak to the head waiter."

She gave it a laugh, though it wasn't much of a quip. "Was that true about the silverware? Fern and I were really interested. No shame in eavesdropping."

"Sorry." I went red.

"How marvellous to be an expert on silver!"

"Wish I was. Dates are hard to remember."

"I wondered what you were doing, deliberately dropping your serviette then stooping to pick it up. Fern thought you were being amorous." And explained, "Lauren's legs."

"Dates should be stamped about the base, or lined up near the handle. It's illegal to fake up a silver tankard as a coffee pot then sell it as a true antique without marking the changes you've made." I shrugged. "So I wrote zero on her card."

"I'm one of Henry Semper's antiques group." She grimaced. "Groupies, you might call us."

"You run an antiques shop?"

"Not yet. I'm hoping to start a small antiques business now my husband's gone. Fern does antiques in Salford. People joke about cruise ships, don't they? Full of widows and all that. Fern is the real expert. We were friends at school. It was her idea to come. I'm new to cruising. It's lovely, isn't it, everything you could possibly want?" She waited for my story, but I said nothing. She told me about her husband's fatal car crash. I never know what to say. "Fern was wondering how you knew it was a chocolate pot, not for coffee. Aren't they the same thing?"

"No." I spoke with relief, on safer ground. "The finial on the silver cover – the projecting knob –

comes off, leaving a hole into which the lady of the house would insert a swizzle, to stir the chocolate lees. You didn't need do that for coffee. Making a new screw finial is always difficult. I've made similar mistakes. Mine wobble, like hers did." I coloured up, cursing myself for clumsiness. "Er, I mean I *suppose* that's what forgers do."

She did her woman's amused non-smile. "Why did you come, if you hate cruising?"

"I'm just desperate to get off."

"We saw you slip away from our Rijksmuseum group. You looked so desolate returning in that lady's motor. Quite like a prisoner."

"I hoped to make it back…" Back where, though? "Home," I completed lamely.

"You can leave any time, Lovejoy. Just tell the purser's office. The shipping lines have port agents at every landfall. It's a legal requirement."

"Sounds easy." She looked kind and ready to talk, even though it was getting on for midnight. Could she be trusted? Better not; I'd already opted for Margaret in East Anglia. "I'm sorry, er, Delia. I have things to do."

"Not at all. Perhaps I'll see you in Mr Semper's antiques lecture tomorrow? Or in Oslo."

"Oslo? Isn't that in the other direction?"

She laughed, shaking her head. We parted at the lifts. I avoid unneeded conversation by using stairs instead of elevators. A lift is hell on the nerves, especially if other people are full of boisterous snippets. Still, Delia Oakley might turn out to be someone neutral, if not exactly an ally. So far I'd unerringly picked out enemies, so maybe my luck was changing. I went to ring Margaret and beg for help. Oslo, though? There were ferries from our east coast – Newcastle, was it? – to Norway.

No reason for optimism. Optimism never did me any favours. I've found that.

Chapter Ten

Ringing home's easy. Press the ship-to-shore button, and a mechanical voice says the call will cost you an arm and a leg. Dial, and presto!

"Hello?" I almost screamed. "Margaret?"

"Lovejoy?"

"It's me! It's me!"

"Where are you? The police are looking for you, and Hackney louts are asking at every auction. Tinker's been arrested, and Belle's disappeared."

"Listen, love. I'm on a ship, and – "

"The line's funny, Lovejoy. Did you say ship?"

"Course I did, you stupid . . . er, sorry. Called *Melissa*, going to Russia. I want to get off." I halted. What did I want her to do?

"Doesn't it stop?"

I felt this was all her fault. "They're keeping me on it."

"Lovejoy." I heard doubt. Women are all suspicion. "Who is she? You've gone walkabout with some tart, want me to lie you out of it."

"Eh?"

She sounded bitter. "Like that American bitch from Wichita. Look, Lovejoy. I'll help you when you come home, but not when you're playing the fool. Incidentally, that David Buddy has hired Smarmy on North Hill as a scout. And my Norman's home."

"Don't ring off!" I could tell she was going to. Norman is her husband. Smarmy's an antiques dealer in a ruin he calls a shop. He'll do anything for a groat. "Please, Margaret. It's not a woman. They're going to top me."

The line burred in my ear. Gone. I looked at the receiver – how daft is that? – then tried to redial. The line was engaged. A third time, engaged. Ten minutes

later, engaged. She'd blanked me off, the cruel bitch.
See how women leave you in the lurch? I beg for help,
and she reminds me of some bird I'd forgotten?

The affair honestly had been really innocent. An
American dealer's wife came a-calling at my cottage
and stayed until next morning, honestly only to see
some antiques. They didn't arrive – honestly not my
fault – so she stayed another night. The antiques never
did turn up. Her husband cancelled a huge buy of seven
eighteenth-century gaming tables. Two of the seven
tables were genuine, the other five being forgeries
made by me and Balk Haythorn from Weeley. I had
sweated blood getting the ends of the folding-leaf
tables exactly right (the rounded corner projections are
for candlesticks, so card players would have enough
light). They were beautiful. We would have made a
king's ransom. Margaret forked out money for the
heart-wood, varnishes, certificates of provenance and
similar grey areas, so she lost heavily when the Yank
dealer had to be fobbed off with fables of where his
wife had stayed. Margaret placated him with white lies
– I begged, I begged – but the deal didn't go through.
Margaret and the others still blame me, which isn't fair.
I was honestly innocent.

The ship's calendar on my cabin TV said people
would still be wassailing on the Lido Deck at the
swimming pools, but I went to bed and thought.

My mind's a ragbag at the best of times. Like,
Finland leads Europe in drinking coffee, the Greeks
lead in bread consumption, and Russian women knot
their headscarves to state their observance of marriage
laws. India has 59% of the world's remaining tigers.
One in three of the world's leaders – from Napoleon
to the dimmest prime minister – lost a parent before
they reached the age of 15. Wellington was known as
the Iron Duke, not from military resolve, but because

his house had iron-framed windows. King Francis the First of France bought the *Mona Lisa* to hang in his bathroom, and our Henry the Eighth was a tallish slim bloke, not the gross nerk of the movies.

Concentrating, I rummaged for facts about ships, and realised I knew nothing. Except 171 ships had been attacked by pirates in the past six months; the place for it is the Malacca Straits and, just like ram-raiders who drive a lorry through an antique shop window and nick specific antiques, so modern sea-borne pirates capture ships to order. Of course, it's mostly massive cargoes – new cars, helicopter parts, aero engines, missiles and munitions, tankers carrying crude oil. No help there. Another datum: anybody aboard pegging out from natural causes is discreetly whisked off, or zoomed to hospital ashore by helicopter.

I'd already heard Millicent telling Ivy, "That's why they stopped posting passenger lists. So embarrassing having to cross people off."

Other facts? Oslo. I was stuck. And as if I hadn't enough enemies, I'd alienated Margaret, the one person I trust. My loyal barker Tinker was arrested, God knows why. I'd added to my foes on board by earning the undying hatred of Lauren and her mentor the great antiques TV expert Henry Semper for exposing his rotten little scheme. Who on earth were the Hackney louts? I felt sick. The Marquis of Gotham must have hired some tankers, violent GBH blokes usually from Leeds. I gulped. North London hoods are as bad, and never give up. I thought, Goodnight diary, and slept.

* * *

The lecture theatre was really the cinema between movies. Henry Semper came limping out to loud applause. I sat at the end of a row. The place was crammed. I saw Fern and her friend Delia Oakley in the centre chatting amicably with a mob who all seemed to know each other. The antiques coterie? Fern turned round to scan the audience. Her eyes locked on mine. My fellow-diners came. They seized the front row and waved to pals.

Semper began by accepting a card from Lauren, who had so far unbent as to wear a faint trace of lipstick. She peered around the audience as Semper read out the successful person's name.

"The value of the genuine silver Paul de Lamerie antique I showed round at dinner is . . ." He held the suspense, then stated a price that would buy a superb house in Dulwich, Hampstead Heath, or some other undesirable slum (joke). Amid scattered applause – nobody is pleased when somebody else wins – a gent went to get the prize, a Royal Copenhagen figure of lovers snogging on a rock above a faintly purple sea. Genuine, but less than twenty years old, so I scored it as pretty but yawnsome. Tip: Ignore anything antique dealers call "tomorrow's antiques" – we're all that, for heaven's sake.

He began his talk. Lauren operated slides. It was a mundane sequence of antiques sold at London and international auctions. Gracefully he skirted Sotheby's scandals, the price-fixing deals and the ghastly Impressionist fiasco that ripped off trusting buyers from Tokyo to Los Angeles. I almost dozed off from excitement. It grew especially dull when he talked of opportunities for investing in antiques. I shook myself alert. Money was really Semper's subject.

"Tomorrow's antiques are the thing to buy."

Hello, I thought, here we go. He had a knack of speaking to secret cravings, and judged his audience with cunning. It's the trick used by all con artists. I'd got his number.

"And why?" he intoned. "Because, dear friends, they are soaring in value! Inflation, deflation, the value of money, stocks and shares – all these things let you down. Antiques never will!"

He nodded to Lauren. She clicked. The screen showed a lovely Imari vase. This is a bulbous porcelain piece with a cover, a lovely style. The colours (remember them) are dark blue, a faint red, and slender black for outlines. The base rim had a faint greenish hue. On the picture it looked authentic, so I was pleased. He mentioned a value that set everybody gasping. I felt sure I'd seen its lookalike in the University of London's porcelain museum, near Betjeman's favourite church of Christ the King. (Easiest place to rob, incidentally, if you like Eastern porcelains – I mean the museum; the church has zilch.)

Then he uncovered a display stand, flinging the cloth aside with a magician's theatrical gesture.

"And now, the real thing! Isn't it exquisite?"

Heads bent as everybody talked animatedly of vases they had known, seen, just missed, turned down when they could have bought them for a penny. In the hubbub I saw Ivy, the quiet Wirral wife of Billy the showy ex-cop, her sad face illuminated in the glow. Her expression was woeful. You can always tell misery. She was three seats along my row. I shouldn't watch other people. I'm always at it. It gets me into trouble. She caught my look and gave a feeble smile. I nodded, went back to watching the great TV impressario.

"This is of a slightly different date, but is the genuine Imari…" and similar balderdash.

Imari wasn't a porcelain factory, though antique dealers pretend it was. It was simply the port through which Japanese porcelains were exported. The word porcelain's supposed to come from a resemblance to a Cowrie shell, which is similar to cured pork skin, but wordsmiths never tell the same tale twice so we'll never know. I listened to Semper wax eloquent.

The poor little fake pot stood there, its coloured slide projected up on the screen for all the world to sneer at. If it had feelings, as a genuine antique Imari has, it would have been ashamed. Semper was a demon for intangibles – the hallmark of a bamboozler getting into his stride. He kept saying things like, "The influence in a niello vanity case speaks of Russia's nineteenth century..." and "The flavour of the design justifies the eloquence with which..." It's all claptrap. It means you have to have seen a hundred genuine antiques before you can distinguish garbage from truth. Yet greedy people actually trust these charlatans, and spend their lives searching for china ware with a "hint of rococo" and pearls that feel "cooler than the average". My tip: if you're a beginner, learn to *measure*.

The expert was preaching about his vase. It was a brightish green. Tip: These modern Korean replicas are ten a penny in the Far East. Quite attractive, but two things give them away. Simply stand back, screw your eyes up so you can hardly see the leafy, curling design, and the pattern blurs into insignificance. Now do the same with the real thing and the pattern stays. It's never wrong.

My second tip is measurement. The diameter of the cover's outside rim is half of the width of the vase at its widest – so the cover's width divided by the width of the bell is 0.5, a sum anybody can work out, because one over two is a half, right? The Korean fake's ratio was 0.68, give or take a yard. There are other measures. I'm not knocking Korean replicas, note, because some from the 18th, 19th and early 20th centuries are crackers, really bonny. And of course the older ones count as antiques in themselves, so are worth finding. Koreans made them, as Chinese still tend to, in tributary devotion to ancient pottery masters. Fine. The only thing I don't like is people being sold one as the other for a thousand times the price.

I don't know what antique hunters have against measurement.

"Excuse me, sir," said an American in the next seat. "Would you please stop muttering?"

"Sorry, sorry." I keep doing that. It gets me into trouble.

"The expertise of a skilled antiques aficionado," said Semper, aheming modestly so the audience knew he meant himself, "is beyond price. The risk is yours!"

He repeated his catchphrase and went on to the next series of projector slides. I asked the Yank's pardon and edged out. I was fool enough to glance at the stage, and caught Lauren's venomous glare. From being a winsome mousey creature, so meek and prim, she was transformed into a death ray. Her face was contorted in a snarl of fury as her gaze followed me. I slid from the cinema. Semper tried to cover my departure by a glib wisecrack.

"Somebody wants to get back to the bar!"

I made my way down to a bar lounge and sat listening to the band and a gorgeous woman crooner while folk danced. Above, the shops were on the go, one of them announcing a sale. Across, on the balcony of the second floor, people were selecting hand-made chocolates and exclaiming at new flavours.

"I thought you'd be at the art sale," an American voice remarked. "It starts in thirty minutes."

He sat beside me, signalled for a stewardess and ordered a highball. I declined his offer of a drink. I was relieved he hadn't followed me out of Semper's talk to black my eye. He was a giant.

"Sorry I spoiled your lecture."

"Your grumbling was more interesting than Semper."

He was one of these urbane, ultra-groomed transatlantics with perfect teeth and luxuriant silver hair. I didn't doubt for one moment that he owned Nevada or somewhere and that he could buy the shipping line with pocket money. His patent leather shoes looked worth my cottage.

"Measure vases, though?"

That narked me. "I've already apologised. Sit somewhere else."

He laughed. Two women glanced across, captivated by his film-star looks. Women adore power, whereas men worship form. There's this theory, isn't there, that men are instinctively guided by clues to supposed fertility – shape, waist-to-hip ratio, smooth youthful skin and curvaceous breasts, undulating walk. It only goes to show what gunge medical research is, because there's a grace in older women you don't find anywhere else, and every woman has her own beauty. As for women going for the masterful millionaire, I'll never know.

"Pleased to meet you, sir." He reached and shook my hand. "Victor Lustig, New York."

"Lovejoy." Odd name, but I should talk. I'd heard it before somewhere. Maybe one of those folk on the front of *Time*?

"I'd be obliged if you'd write me those criteria you were muttering about. Measurement proves authenticity?"

"I don't know what people have against measurement. They want mystique, the idea of a sixth sense." I quite liked the bloke, so I kept going.

There are loads of measurements you can take that

might differentiate between a clear fake and a genuine antique. Like, acrylics weren't known two hundred years ago, but that didn't stop the forger Tom Keating from faking Samuel Palmer's watercolours in ten-year-old acrylic paint. I saw them sold for the price of a new saloon motor car in galleries off Piccadilly, London, before he got arrested. He was a neighbour of mine, and I used to watch him do them. Acrylics shine on the paper in a way different from watercolours. So while some elegant salesman talks gunge about "perceptual style interrogating the natural world's emotional stresses", just carry the painting to the door where you can see how it sheens (or doesn't!) in ordinary daylight.

Once I'd got going, sitting there while Lustig sipped his bourbon, I told him what beginner antiques hunters should carry with them.

"Assemble an antiques-buyer's kit, to start out. It only costs a few coppers. Buy a tape measure marked in metric and imperial. Get a X 10 loupe (a higher magnification's no use at all), and a little pair of old-fashioned brass weighing scales in a velvet case – complete with weights, it'll cost you the price of a cup of coffee, because India exports them as trinkets. Then nick your wife's eyebrow tweezers."

With a twinge of sorrow, I remembered I usually nick my tweezers from Margaret Dainty.

"Then a solar-powered calculator – you get them free in Christmas crackers; a colour chart – free from art shops; I like Daler-Rowney because it folds small and there's space to write the dates each colour came in. Then a midget plastic microscope for examining surfaces of furniture – also free in Christmas crackers; the battery is always dud. A pen-torch. A few carob seeds to remind you how heavy one 'carat' weighs.

"Make a small case for them all from the covers of

a hard-back book, small enough to go in your pocket. I include a midwife's spring balance. It's the size of a pencil stub – not because I'm likely to leap into action and start delivering neonates, but for weighing Old Masters, porcelains, jewellery, any of those antiques that keep on coming round time after time in country auctions. If, say, a familiar painting's suddenly twice as heavy as when you last saw it, it's a clue that it's a fake because age dries, right?"

He tried to interrupt but I was motoring.

"With that cheapo kit, you'll save yourself from a whole series of blunders. I also carry a couple of small wooden rulers made up of different slices of polished heart-woods, all named. Ecology groups give them out free in village fêtes. They're good for identifying woods when you're new to the game. I always get American and Japanese oak wrong, dunno why."

He listened, smiling. "You've been around antiques."

"More fakes." Especially on this voyage, I thought but did not say.

"I might market it! I'll call it the Antiques Hunter's Pack, price ten ninety-five!" His splendid evening suit expanded with his magnificent baritone chuckle. "Marketing's what I do. Selling, buying. Otherwise, I'm only good at poker. Fancy a game?"

Graciously he allowed me to say no, ta. I didn't tell him my job and didn't ask his, because asking about jobs is nosey. He told me anyway.

"Dry goods, bulk buys and imports – as long as the Almighty Dollar stays out of intensive care!" More mellifluous laughter. The two women at the bar smiled and exchanged more glances. "Incidentally, Lovejoy, I shouldn't ask that Lauren lady for the next dance! See the way she looked at you?"

"Didn't notice."

"Would you write me down those measurements for that Imari vase? I'd be obliged."

Another person on the make. I felt tired, and it was only getting on for noon. Was it anxiety? I said no, left him and went to the main desk, asking if any messages had come for me.

"You'll find them in your cabin, sir, or on your telephone." I went round behind the band, and saw an odd thing, only coincidence but I'd had too many to like yet another. I saw Ivy enter the Atrium, give a quick glance round, then step forward and sit with Victor Lustig. You can always tell, can't you, or have I already said that? I went to my cabin, to find one phone message.

"Lovejoy? Come to Suite 1133 immediately. It's time you earned your keep."

This, note, was the silly old bat I'd taken pity on in Benjo's Emporium, now sounding like Napoleon. And I'd paid for garden lights for her grandbaby's birthday, which was how I'd got myself into this mess. I made myself as presentable as I could, and headed for servitude. As I went, I thought of Napoleon, then France, then Paris. The train of thought helped me, because I suddenly remembered.

Victor Lustig was the name of a famous old conman, long since deceased. He'd once sold the Eiffel Tower.

Going upstairs, I thought well, well.

Chapter Eleven

That afternoon I wheeled Lady Veronica about the ship. I felt a right prat, but kept up the farce, her a cripple and me her serf. She played deck quoits, squealing when she got one of those little rope rings near the dot. She gambled on one-arm bandits in the casino and lost money hand over fist. She played blackjack, at which I learned you hadn't to touch your cards. I hadn't known that. For a whole hour she put tokens into slot machines, losing the lot and exclaiming, "Oh, all I needed was a seven for the jackpot!", the cry of the eternal gambler. She played roulette, sternly telling me, "Gambling's a mug's game, Lovejoy." From a phoney geriatric going to take on Russia?

Her grim nurse Inga was absent, thank God. When Lady Vee wanted to go to the loo I got a passing lady to take her. Then it was back to bingo, six cards every game and marking off the numbers like lightning. She called out audience responses ("Twenty-two, two little ducks!" to which the entire mob shouted, "Quack! Quack!"and so on) while I tried to keep awake. How did they know what to yell?

She didn't win there, either. Lord Montgomery, victor of El Alamein, used to play bingo on the *Queen Elizabeth* and was always shouting for the bingo caller to slow down. Lady Vee could have taught him about speed.

As I rolled her to the Conservatory for tea she said, "The ship takes a percentage. I've never won yet. Get me tea and three cakes, not those jam things. No egg-and-cress sandwiches, either. Egg binds you."

And the ship sailed gaily on.

Passengers discussed how far the ship had gone – you gambled on the distance and won yet another jackpot. Somebody said the *Melissa* had sailed 400 miles since leaving Amsterdam. The thought made me feel lonelier, Amsterdam a hell of a way off. We sat in the open air by the stern bar, where karaoke music played and eager Aussies – always the best – bawled into a microphone.

"Are you lot serious about St Petersburg?" I asked outright. Nobody could overhear in the din.

That extraordinary youthful look returned to her eyes, the coming thrill bringing it on.

"Nothing's certain, Lovejoy, except death, taxes, and the Hermitage."

"How?"

"Why, you'll do it for us, Lovejoy. It's why we chose you!"

I could have clocked the daft old bat, except she laughed, her complexion younger still. I marvelled. Women's faces are a miracle. No wonder they spend so much time staring at themselves in mirrors. I always fall head over heels when I paint a woman's portrait, can't help it.

"No, love. You've got that wrong." Time I told her the facts of robbery. "There's only four questions in any burglary – who, when, how, what. Four. You had me abducted from Benjo's, so I know I'm the who. And the *Melissa Today* says we'll spend two days in St Petersburg, so the whole world knows when. That leaves two questions: how and what."

"What a mistrustful person you are!" She whaled into her tea. I managed to grab a small sandwich, a tooth-filler, before she engulfed the lot. "I tell you it's all arranged! Think of the jolly celebrations we shall have homeward bound!"

She leant and whispered, "It will be the easiest thing imaginable. Russia is porous. You can bribe anyone to do anything! With your skill, the climbing will be simple!"

Okay, so she wouldn't say how. I pressed on.

"That leaves what. The loot." I felt unreal, like talking about some child's midnight feast in the dorm, such a spiffing jape, Hazel. "What do we steal?"

"You and your silly details!"

And she sent me for some more grub. There's supposed to be this newly discovered set of slimmer's hormones, isn't there, that stops you eating. Drug firms intend to synthesise them, so we can all be skeletal. She can't have produced any. I'd never seen an old bird scoff so much, yet she stayed miniature. She noshed like a stoker frantically raising steam.

We went to the art auction in the Harlequin, a lounge with the inevitable bar and stewardesses trolling for drinks orders. And in there I finally started thinking. One sudden question arose: how come she knew I could climb when doing a robbery? I remembered the crone looking out into the night carrying a Norfolk lantern, me clinging to the wall of a certain mansion house.

In the lounge thirty works of art lay about, two svelte girls wafting among us saying how marvellous the items were. The stuff was dross. Even the frames were gunge. The main lass, a Russian maiden called Irina, assured us she'd worked for impressive European auctioneers. She pointed out a Rembrandt etching, a Picasso engraving, Impressionist works, and prints by everybody. She used the term serigraph every second. Even as a con it was ridiculous. I didn't guffaw, just manoeuvred Lady Vee into position so she could see.

Somebody waved, Victor Lustig, placing himself across from us. Soon after, Ivy entered but didn't even glance Victor Lustig's way, simply sat consulting her catalogue.

Irina ("Everybody say hello to Irina!") began the

auction, describing each offering in saccharine detail. Lauren worked as her assistant, mounting the paintings on stands then replacing them when nobody bid. Irina was embarrassing. She actually muttered in some foreign tongue when the third item died unsold. Victor Lustig at that moment hid a smile. So he knew Russian.

I leant back, relieved I'd found at least one piece of the jigsaw. I'd been floundering, running scared until now, because some pieces were starting to fit. I watched Victor Lustig.

* * *

Every crook or copper who scribes his autobiography "reveals secrets" of how they functioned. It's an old game. They pretend they're saying something original. Very few are worth listening to. I always think that unless a crook – forger, thief, conman, trickster, footpad, counterfeiter – has actually pulled off some famous scam, he's whistling in the wind.

Once upon a time a long time ago, there was a fraudster so famous he was admired the world over. He formulated the infamous and widely published *Ten Commandments for Conmen*. He was a real bloke, in his day famous as any king.

Victor Lustig sold the Eiffel Tower for scrap. Unbelievably, he duped the gangster Al Capone. He awarded himself the title of Count Victor von Lustig, and swanned about the US in a Rolls driven by a Japanese chauffeur. Arrested forty-eight times, he became a great escaper, using everything from the traditional knotted sheets and drainpipes to threats, bribery and abject confession to get away. Fellow hoods said he was the greatest-ever passer of counterfeit money. A super linguist, our Victor spoke every European language including Russian. He started out by duping rich passengers on cruise liners (a clue here!) and specialised in works of art. He was an expert gambler, cards his speciality. The original Victor Lustig is sadly no more, yet is still famed in legend for his monocled persona and myriad monikers. I couldn't help thinking that the suave Yank smiling across the auction floor might be proof that heredity actually worked. Grandson, perhaps?

Maybe my expression revealed my thoughts, because he raised his eyebrows in derision when Irina made Lauren walk round showing the small Rembrandt etching. Victor didn't quite sneer, but came close. Like grandpa, like grandson? I reflected on the man opposite.

These are Lustig's *Ten Commandments for Conmen* (he really did call them that). I think they're a lot better and more explicit than Oscar Wilde's five rules for confidence tricksters, though Oscar's aren't bad. Whichever you prefer, statistics prove that over ninety per cent of us – you and me included – will sooner or later be duped, so they're worth a minute. Here's how we'll lose our shirt:

Listen with patience; no fast talking. Don't look bored.

Agree with the victim's politics and religious convictions.

Hint at sex, but be ready to drop it quick.

Never mention illness.

Never ferret personal details – the victim will offer plenty.

Never boast – just exude importance.

Be tidy; be sober.

Count them up, and they make ten. They are the same now as when Count Victor formulated them. He knew what he was talking about. Incidentally, the only significant one Oscar Wilde added was this: *smile*!

Even as I watched, I saw Ivy nod to a stewardess to bring her coffee, and I saw her gaze casually take in the audience and touch on Victor. She did that clever non-smiling smile I'm always on about. He smiled and looked away. Same as me, while Irina tried to talk us all into bidding for a "genuine serigraph" of some crud.

"What are you smiling at?" Lady Vee asked tetchily.

"Nothing," I told her, narked with myself. See? We can't do it.

"Yes, Lauren, I think it's lovely," she told the girl.

"I've seen better oil slicks, love," I said. Lady Vee tittered and gave Lauren an apology. The lass stalked away in fury.

Delia Oakley came in late with her friend Fern. They sat on lounge seats and sipped tea, making catalogue notes. Unbelievably, they actually bought a watercolour, of four horses approaching along a rainy boulevard, the sort you get by the truck load in Continental flea-markets for half a groat. Delia gave a pleased smile at her success, raising her eyebrows like they do. I wouldn't be visiting her new antiques business when she finally got it going, that's for sure. I dozed. Roll on Oslo.

And found myself thinking of strange Middle East tales. In the West we call them suffees, from the word sufi, a wise man. He's always called Nasruddin, in stories invented to teach students to think. One tale went round in my mind. Every month, Nasruddin crossed a particularly difficult border. Officials stopped him to examine the panniers on his donkeys, and found only three straws in each box. On Nasruddin's return, the boxes were empty. Next month same thing – three straws per box going in, empty coming back – yet each passing month Nasruddin grew richer. In time he became a wealthy man. The officials took the boxes apart, found nothing. They tested the donkeys' hooves for gold, found zilch. Years passed. Eventually the officials heard Nasruddin, now aged 100, was dying, and went to ask what on earth he had been smuggling.

Nasruddin, expiring with a smile, whispered, "Donkeys."

I dreamt of climbing into the Hermitage Museum, after landing from a ship that carried only a load of donkeys. By the time the stupid auction ended, I'd planned my escape by jumping ship in Oslo.

The best ideas come in daydreams.

That evening at dinner, Lauren brought round a Russian ikon. I noshed on, ignoring her prattle ("A genuine Muscovite ikon, completely authentic, fifteenth century…") She kept pausing, challenging me. I said nothing. It felt dud. No bongs in my chest, so it was fake.

"Well, Lovejoy?" Holly prompted, her gambler's eyes a-glow. "Aren't you going to tell us the value?"

I looked up. Quite a drama. The next tables had also fallen quiet, Fern and Delia Oakley trying to look casual with those directional ears women have perfected over aeons. Even the stewards slowed near us.

"No." A daubed plank has no value.

"He says no," I heard Ivy say. I was having a hard time with something called pan-fried orange roughy on mushy peas under sauce Robert. I'd not known it was a fish until they brought it.

Lauren exclaimed and flounced off. The table discussed the possible value, while Henry Semper glowered and limped, trying to exude confidence. A few people stopped as they left early for the first floor show, one bluntly asking me outright if the ikon was genuine.

"Never looked at it, wack," I said, which was true.

As I left, though, I thought what the hell, and pencilled in another zero for Lauren's stack of cards, and left.

Delia and Fern were in the corridor where Irina and Lauren had arranged easels and stands displaying their so-called antiques. I love a good laugh. They saw me coming.

"You hate ikons, then?" Delia said.

I wouldn't have bothered to give the wretched fake a look, except I'd taken to Delia. A woman is worth almost everything, even if she's only using you to learn, so I paused. Secretly, I didn't want her to start up yet another antiques shop. The reason our creaking old kingdom is creaking is that it's littered with dud antiques shops, most of them not worth crossing the road to visit.

"He didn't even look," Fern said, scathing. "He's just taken against Henry Semper the world expert. At least Henry knows what he's talking about."

That narked me. She was the antiques dealer, and obviously thought highly of the ikon. I was jumping ship Oslo next morning, leaving them all to it, so what the hell. I could see I'd need to find some reason to prove the ikon's phoniness.

"Please don't be annoyed, Lovejoy," Delia apologised. "Fern specialises in – "

"What did you say it was worth, Fern?" I asked.

"Eleven thousand." She was defiant. "That's the rule for a genuine ikon. Three thousand for each century before 1900. Henry said I was close."

For the first time I looked at the ikon, pathetic on its stand. It showed the Saviour, gaunt with those stencilled eyes. I saw red and went for it.

"They used cypress wood, a good point. Lime's as good, but cypress darkens with age. Reddish streaks, close grain, resists insects."

"See? It's lovely!" Fern said in triumph. Delia

looked wary.

"The sheen's good. Sniff the painting – no scent of oil, so it's older than three years. The halo's real gold. The blue is genuine lapis lazuli." I had to smile and went on as Fern preened, assuming success.

"This was made by a skilled faker. He probably ground his lapis and green malachite on granite with pig iron. Quite correct. Old Russian artists believed the stones they powdered, to mix the paints, were touched by sanctity. They thought the colours remembered the stones from which they came, and could resume the form of the original stones. God did it, so Russians who became blind in old age could touch the surface and still understand the sacred image."

"What a lovely thought!" Delia cried.

I went on, "The faker correctly used linen stretched on the wood with fish glue, covered in gesso in egg yolk. Then red clay and beeswax mixed with white of egg. It's a lovely forgery."

A small crowd had gathered. I went red.

"If everything about it is right, why is it wrong?" Fern almost shouted. She was itching to take a swing at me.

"The idiot's put gold tears on the ikon's face. The old genuine ikon painters wouldn't make that mistake, because all light must emanate from the image itself in dark Russian winters." I thought a second. "Go to Walsingham. There's a side chapel in total permanent shadow. The gold alone shows brilliance."

"You've just got it in for Henry Semper!" Fern raged.

"Think what you like, love."

Time to leave them to their discontent. I pushed away. I wish folk weren't so *against*. It's like they wake up and look about for things to hate. Imagine how an antique must feel, living with a sourpuss like that silly cow.

Is it any wonder that sometimes someone somewhere dreams of living with antiques, the only materials that can give ecstasy? I felt sorry for Delia Oakley. She seemed kind. I wish I had time to dissuade her. Opening an antiques shop is the road to rusty ruin.

A woman I knew once was bonny, married, and a classical linguist, whatever that is. She was bossy as hell, always finished her husband's sentences so he quickly learned to shut up. She had his answers ready whenever anybody spoke. Megan knew it all, decided their home, decorations, and ballocked poor Wilf without mercy. She drove him mad about the garden – plant this, don't touch that you fool, an endless tirade of denigration. Megan would ask him for an idea, then pour scorn on it, ridiculing him before anybody. It was embarrassing, and I stopped going. He bought a few handies off me – our name for small antiques you can conceal in a palm. Some folk collect nothing else, and some dealers specialise in them. Wilf paid me the odd groat for antique lessons. I'd take him round auctioneers' viewing days, boot fairs of a Sunday, street markets if I was going on to Bermondsey. He'd pay travel and nosh. Pretty dull bloke, really, and couldn't tell a chalice from a chip pan.

One day he won a small football pools thing. Not much. He came in while I was repairing an Art Deco dressing table. It was marked Liberty & Co and was genuine, but who cared? I wouldn't give Art Deco house room, even if I could afford it, because it's no excuse saying furniture serves a useful purpose if it's crud. And it's more or less modern, named after the 1925 Paris *Exposition Internationale des Arts Decoratifs et Industriels Modernes*, which set the fashion. I thought he'd come for another brief lesson, and immediately started up, "Wotcher, Wilf. See this rectangular pattern? Spot that, even on a Liberty piece as bright as this, and you can buy yourself a good used car – "

"No, Lovejoy," he said. His eyes were glowing. "Megan gave me an ultimatum this morning. Told me outright. I've to make something of myself, get membership of the golf club, extend the house, bring in more money with a better job, or she's going for a divorce."

"Don't tell me, Wilf," I said sadly. "You've decided to leave her to it?"

"Yes!"

"And you're going to become an antiques dealer." Sadder still.

"Yes! I can't think why I've taken so long to decide!"

"Wilf," I said with sorrow. "Take up duelling. Be a mercenary. Go after the Great White Shark in your nip. But don't ever do anything really risky, like becoming an antiques dealer."

The world's streets are littered with derelicts and mumpers living rough. They're all ex-hopefuls who thought that owning "a nice little antiques business" would be bliss. Like dreamers who think the same about "a lovely little country pub", they're doomed to fail. I told Wilf. He didn't hear a single word, just sailed out with the light of eagles in his eyes.

Now he lives rough in Lincoln's Inn, London, in a cardboard box. The Salvosh feed him most days, the church at St James's Thursdays and Saturdays. The usual cycle of beginners in the antiques trade. Others get abducted to Russia to rob the frigging Hermitage and never know why.

* * *

Ivy caught me as I went past the theatre and handed me a heavy book in a brown paper bag.

"I thought you would like to look at this, Lovejoy."

"Eh? Oh, ta."

"It's the Hermitage catalogue. Lovely pictures. Seeing you're so good at antiques."

"Very kind, Ivy."

She took a long time speaking her next words. "I'm so glad you're here, Lovejoy. And on the same table."

"Oh, right."

"No need to tell Billy I've lent it to you. He gets so . . ."

I gulped. "Right, love." Jealous? Of a frigging book? More maniacs. I went quickly on my way.

Chapter Twelve

The ship's berth in Oslo was almost a parking space on the quayside beside a mound topped by gardens. Touristy buildings sold cards, woollens, carvings and various liquors. I was delighted to see how easily you could walk into town, up the slope and soon among buildings and traffic. Clean place, Oslo, but they're not early starters. It was nine o'clock on a bright Sunday morning when we were freed. Nice, friendly, and a whole capital to vanish in.

Nobody minded when I made my way off the ship, though I was on edge. I was compelled to shove Lady Vee's wheelchair, the dreaded Inga drifting immensely along with cell phones dangling from her hip. The comedian Les Renown accompanied me, still cracking jokes ("There's this giraffe goes into a Tel Aviv brothel, and a crocodile says . . .") with Amy the dancer. They didn't look like police, Fraud Squad or not, but some never do. They were chatty and so-o-o friendly. I talked too much, nervy at the idea of lamming off as soon as I found a side street. I tried a few moves, including almost boarding a coach for a city tour, but no go. Les and Amy helpfully stood in the way while I consulted a city map and tried to point out places to Lady Vee.

Disembarking passengers complained darkly of Scandinavia's inordinate expense and Oslo's terrible credit-card charges, all above my head because I'm not credit-worthy. I could see it might matter to people who were. My chance came on the waterfront when Les and Amy stopped for a coffee in a small caff with coloured tables and chairs. Lady Vee wanted to go to the shops. I insisted on coffee, and ordered. Les and Amy wanted to sit apart, which was good, and Inga took the opportunity to go shopping in the godowns.

Kevin and Billy passed, Kevin yoo-hooing and wag-gling his fingers. That left me and Lady Vee.

"I suppose this is where you, what's the word, Lovejoy... scarper? Take it on the lam?"

"Me?" I said, all innocent. I'd been eyeing alleys.

"Your heart isn't in loyal friendships, is it, dear?"

"Truth is, Lady Vee, antiques invites nutters. Like you daft people. You dream of finding Old Masters on market stalls. Antiques bring greed. I hate it."

"But you're greedy, Lovejoy. Everybody is."

Narked, I gave her my bent eye.

"There's nothing wrong with finding treasure, you silly old sod. It happens even on Henry Semper's telly show. Like that Richard Dadd painting scrunged up for years in somebody's attic, that finally the British Museum collared for a king's ransom. Like that geezer's silver hoard in cardboard boxes under his bed. His folks sold it all for a fortune. And that teapot in Liverpool, sold for enough to buy the lady her own house. It's fair game."

"Then what isn't?" Her eyes took on that youthful dazzle. The sun trickled weakly from behind cloud just then, and I realised I'd been had. She only looked old because she wanted to appear so. Previously, I'd actually thought how young she talked, and how women change their appearance with a ton of cosmet-ics. "What?" she said again, and I realised even more. Her old age voice was put on. And it was more and more like that of the lady with the Norfolk lantern at Gotham's manor house, the night I'd robbed it of my fake painting with Belle.

"Eh?" My mind didn't go that fast.

"What isn't fair game?"

"Robbing somewhere I could get killed," I managed to say, staring at her face.

Psychiatrists say all kind of things about faces

nowadays. Asymmetrical faces imply jealousy, but symmetrical features show you're naturally trustworthy. This is why publishers always slide a hand mirror across publicity photos; the best photo is the one showing the same honest expression whichever side of the face the mirror conceals. Lady Vee's was even, trusting, symmetrical. But can women balance their faces up by rouge, lipstick, mascara, eye shadow? St Jerome, vitriolic master of women's vices, thought they were always up to something along those lines (sorry for the pun).

"Nonsense, Lovejoy! You'll be home safe and sound in a fortnight. Trust me. Why else do you think the police would let you board the *Melissa* with us, if it wasn't to help us catch the perps who're going to rob the Hermitage?"

Indeed. Why else?

"Honest?" I asked. My throat had gone dry. I badly wanted to know what I'd landed in, but escape called and I'm good on duty.

She looked away, gesturing at the peaceful waterfront. Tourists strolled, people off the ship waving to each other as if they'd not seen one another for weeks when they'd just left the same breakfast table, small ships berthing here and there, cars moving. Safe as houses. She hadn't answered.

"See, love?" I said sadly, and got up and walked away. She called a sorrowing, "Goodbye, Lovejoy."

Les and Amy were too engrossed to notice. I moved casually to the alley, then ran to the far end. Nobody was after me. I dodged into a multiple stores, up and down a few escalators and out by different doors, wheezing from the good life on the *Melissa*. I was in a street of slick shops, only one or two open, and walked towards a garden by the tram stop. I paid a few zlotniks for a cup of liquid, perched behind a fountain to hide and took stock.

"Oslo bad costing, yiss?" a familiar voice said.

"Aye."

Then I realised. The little swine was stirring spoon-fuls of sugar into his cup. I wondered how he'd got there. Amsterdam to Oslo isn't a million miles. A plane?

"Mr Moses Duploy, Lovejoy. Rememberings?"

Touts follow cruise ships from port to port, doing deals, arranging amnesia in Customs. The gelt game. Some such syndicates dealt only in antiques, I already knew, and the *Melissa* advertised Antique Treasures of the Baltic as her theme. He looked as dapper as the day he'd handed me over to elegant Mrs Van Rijn in Holland. It seemed weeks since.

"Okay, Moses, " I said, resigned. "Tell."

"Thirty per cent, Lovejoy?"

"Agreed," I said. This was his territory. Anyhow, promises are made to be broken, or they'd be facts, right? I keep saying that. We shook on it. "Tell all."

"I have a circle of friends," he said, coming to perch on the fountain rim. "We survived many pitfalls in the Balkans. Currency smuggling, drugs, the calamitous advent of the Euro, running guns for pals, fights over girl-slavery franchises in Moravia – still the best place to buy females, incidentally, if you need dozens…"

Suddenly his broken English was eloquent and idiomatic. He spoke it with assurance. I vowed to watch this bloke. The question was whether he was a copper, a hood, or someone between like a nark or paid informer. He might be paid as one while moon-lighting as another.

"Who are your friends?"

He spread his hands at such an impossible question, then stood. We walked through the garden.

"What does it matter? In your case we simply follow as your splendid cruise ship sails on. Each landfall brings you closer to St Petersburg in..." he didn't quite sneer, concluding, "Holy Mother Russia. There are enough of us, I assure you. I am merely eyes and ears. My job is to track you."

"Me? Look, wack, you've got things wrong. I'm just – "

"The only divvy." He smiled. "We used that Frog, the old man from Provence who died. Pulled off three fantastic scams. But life has moved on since then. You never met him?"

"No. Didn't he do the Duke of Wellington portrait rip-off? I heard he was doing some Impressionist scam when he popped off. And there's been rumours about the Amber Room since last autumn, but news of it dried up after his death." Moses said nothing. I didn't like his smile. "Here," I said uneasily. "You're not thinking I'm going to take over any of his scams?"

"We need a big one, Lovejoy." He seemed so sad. "The old Frog's linguistic ability was superb, a typical Francophone with every language except Hungarian – and who has that horrible garbage except the Finns? You are cast in the lead role."

I thought of the dinner arrangement, the people I'd gone aboard with, the team of coppers in Lady Vee's Suite 1133. Friends of his?

"I see you're finally realising." He gestured at the city. "Look about, Lovejoy. We have sufficient expertise to try any con trick, large and small. But think of the paltry return on such investment. Money is no longer simply money. Money is now pure expense."

"I don't do anything that risks me getting killed." If I said it often enough people might listen, except hope's as dud as optimism.

"We still call these places by their old names," he said, a little wistful. "Did you know Oslo only became

Oslo in 1925? We consters still call it Christiania. Think, Lovejoy. What could we do in a place like this, to keep up our vast payments to our shippers, abductors, thieves, greedy Customs people? Do you know we even bribe archbishops to alter religious holidays when need arises? And they're among the cheapest. The variety of payments!" He cursed elegantly in some lingo.

"Then get organised."

"Oh, we're organised all right, Lovejoy. Here in Oslo we could taxi east to Tøyen, rob the Munch Museum – where Munch's paintings are temporarily available for public view."

He chuckled at the crack. Munch's *The Scream*, since being stolen, had appeared in the form of fakes all over Europe, so somebody was still making money out of that famous theft.

"Did your lot do that?" I was impressed.

"Why bother asking?" I understood his bitterness. "One swallow does not a summer make, isn't that your English proverb? We could steal the statues of Gustav Vigeland from Frogner Park – have you ever seen anything so ghastly? But then what? Oslo has diamond technology almost equal to your Hatton Garden in London, so we could resort to serving Sloane Rangers, those ladies who want their dead pets to be changed by irradiation and heat into diamonds, to wear as pendants or rings in memoriam. It's all the rage. That would undercut Chicago's Life-Gem firm who is big in that trade," he said, "but how much trade is actually there? Who these days can afford mad money simply to wear their dead wife as a tie-pin, or their deceased Golden Labrador as an evening clasp? Such scams are mere trivia, Lovejoy. We call them tea-time trophies."

"With so many, er, friends, you can run a hundred scams."

"We do." It came out wistful. "You don't understand, Lovejoy. We go in groups. Haven't you read the United Nations reports on international fraud? Or some of your famous English tabloid exposes?"

"You have to compete with each other?" I guessed, trying to judge what he was asking.

"That's it. And we must achieve money targets. We've a team in South Africa – can you imagine the expense of *that*? They've been in Johannesburg ever since the UN Conference on World Poverty. It cost more than Jo'burg is worth. The tsotsis – African yakuza to you, Lovejoy – have all but cleaned them out." His eyes looked suddenly pale as he said bleakly, "What's their fate when they report back? Go on, guess."

I shook my head. I didn't want to.

"My team's been scratching around for a scam good enough to get us promoted, Lovejoy."

"Your mob is like in a league?" I was really interested.

"Exactly." His eyes went distant. I followed his gaze. Nothing. "I thought up a scheme to fix the Pan-Pacific Swimming Olympics, but it'd already been done. And the Moscow Formula One motor racing concession. And the Guatemalan Recovery Programme." He snorted a laugh. "See how desperate my team is?"

He tasted his coffee, grimaced, simply dropped it into the fountain. The gesture said a lot about this innocent-looking nerk. I'm the sort who looks for a waste bin. I'll carry rubbish for miles even in a country lane before I'll chuck litter. He didn't give a damn.

"We've tried all sorts, Lovejoy. Fake Mussolini diaries, secret paintings by Saint Bernadette, plagiarised *Psychic News* editions, even had a go at sunken treasure galleons off those tiresome Florida Keys. Emerald mines under Scafell Pike – "

"Eh?" I asked, coming awake. "Was that you?"

"Yes," he said with some pride, shrugging.

"It must have made almost half a million!" I said admiringly.

You have to admire class. The Scafell Emeralds took place about two years back, starting with an Edwardian necklace and suite of pendants, all said to be from a mythical emerald mine under the highest peak in England. Scafell's at the end of Wastwater in Cumbria. Rich people were sworn to secrecy when invited to invest. They only got a photocopy of a forged map – X marking the time-honoured spot of course. I thought it superb, especially as the dodge had exploited only insurance defaulters. Nobody gained a bawbee, except the conmen.

"That much!" He was a bitter man. "For the syndicates it wasn't worth the bother."

So much gelt, not worth the bother? I gaped. And thought I saw Margaret Dainty. A woman was walking slowly towards the waterfront. I could have sworn it was Margaret, limp and all. She always wears flowery dresses, wouldn't be seen dead without a hat and gloves. And she feels the cold, so is never without a jacket. I can make her shiver just by getting out of bed and peering through the curtains even in a heat wave and saying, "Brrr, looks chilly out there." She'll shiver all day after that.

The lady passed from sight into the leafy lane, a tram obscuring my view. I could have sworn...

"Not worth the bother?" Which raised more questions.

"Gun-running is the business, sewn up. Girls is already in hand; you've only to think of the state that business is in. Drugs is a mess – look at the simulant drugs pharmacologists turn out these days. Athletics is desperate – those Yank-European wankers have got that bound and gagged. Zurich and Marseilles won't budge on world athletics. Everybody wants a cut of them. There's nothing else."

"Antiques?" I'm ever helpful.

His eyes came back. "We read your police Fraud Squad article. The boss said the Lovejoy Factor was among the Big Four corrupting causes undermining civilisation today."

I'd written a silly book once on antiques. Not the Lindisfarne Gospels, it had somehow spawned the term and plagued me ever since.

"Look," I said, on edge. The floral lady had reappeared at the far end of the park, evidently on her way to the ship. I could see *Melissa* looming white and serene beyond the first row of buildings. It couldn't have been Margaret, could it? "God above, Moses, I was only three when I wrote the damned thing. You can't blame me."

He went on, "So when we heard of that inept group of incompetents clubbing together to take on St Petersburg, Lovejoy, we decided to take over."

Which group? Who? "And they agreed?"

For some reason I thought of Holly's dark eyes and her slick Kevin with his stiletto fingers, rather than Les Renown and Amy, June Milestone and Executive Purser Mangot. I didn't really like any of them, and that meant I couldn't trust a single one.

"Agreed?" He did that upturned palms gesture and smiled properly for the first time. "Ah, not quite *agreed*. They don't know they've been taken over, you see. You're not to tell them, or else."

The lady in the flowered skirt with the hat and gloves had gone now. I didn't ask or else what.

"Who can I trust, of those on board?"

"Me," he said. "I'm not exactly on board, but I am with you in spirit."

Who was his agent on the *Melissa*? I guessed

maybe Victor Lustig. Or Mangot, seeing he never looked directly at me, shifty sod?

"I have never fewer than three, ah, friends within call at any moment, Lovejoy." He glanced at his watch. "I rather think you'd better head back. Don't want you to be late for your next gargantuan meal, do we? Incidentally." He leant towards me. I leaned closer anxious to hear. "Tonight's dinner offers lumpfish caviar with capers and fromage frais for starter. Try it. I recommend the veal osso bucco milanaise on pearl barley for main course. One warning."

"What?" I bleated, worried out of my mind. I thought, he's going to tell me somebody had a gun.

"Steer clear of their Brandy Alexander. The chefs on the *Melissa* invariably drown it under Tia Maria sauce. I wouldn't feed it to my cat." He stood. "And you should see my hungry cat! I am so pleased we had this conversation, Lovejoy. *Bon voyage.*"

He strolled off. I rose to follow, but he just walked round a line of rhododendrons and was somehow gone. Nervously I scanned the park, but saw no one I'd think suspicious. I went slowly out, crossed the road, and found the lane where I'd run from Lady Vee. She was no longer in the coffee place, though Les and Amy were still gazing fondly into each other's eyes. I went straight past and caught up with Inga shoving Lady Vee's wheelchair. Without a word the baleful nurse surrendered control.

"Glad you could make it, Lovejoy," Lady Vee said, smiling up at me. I was getting sick of smiles. "You decided not to leave us?"

"Wouldn't dream of it, love," I said grimly, which set her off in peals of laughter all the way to the ship.

Chapter Thirteen

That night I fell in through my cabin door, worn out from shoving Lady Vee between shows, casinos, bingo sessions, and watching the stars in the night sky from the Horizon Lounge. I was half undressed before I saw the message light blinking on the phone. I vowed to leave the damned thing but temper got the better of me so I listened.

"Message from Sir John Fortescue," a familiar voice said, eerily calm. "Ancient law condemns your position, and the law is inflexible. We regret law cannot help individuals such as you. You will understand. Message ends."

I almost dropped the receiver. It went dead. Like a fool I said, "Hello? Hello? Who is this?" then tapped the repeat button. Margaret Dainty's voice, clear as a bell. Occasional clicks before and after her words warned me, so by a whisker I avoided saying her name. I sat and looked at the thing.

Definitely her voice. Clues and messages everywhere. I started to smile.

Once upon a time – six centuries ago, in fact – a bloke called Sir John Fortescue changed the whole world. And I do mean yours and mine. He's one of my heroes, being the only good honest lawyer Planet Earth has ever had. Trust me. I've seen plenty, and I know. This old geezer was born in 1385 in Somerset, and rose to teach law to Edward, the then Prince of Wales. It was Wars of the Roses time. Sir John stuck to the Lancastrian Henry the Sixth (hang on in here; it matters). Even after the Lancastrian defeat, Sir John stayed loyal.

Naughty historians mutter cruel asides nowadays about noble Sir John and Henry's Queen, Margaret of Anjou, at whose court he lived in exile. They hint

scandalous allegations about Sir John's affection for
Queen Margaret – the two definitely were friends, and
maybe even more. Yet even if they did make secret
smiles now and again in the lantern hours, so what? If
that's the worst we all got up to, the world wouldn't
be in such a wretched mess. Love is a rare commodity,
so I say let them be.

Time came when the Lancastrians made a last desperate sally at Tewkesbury in Gloucester. The bold Sir
John, by then a doddery 86 years old, rode out with
the army to total defeat. Feeling that time wasn't helping much, he chucked in the sponge.

Fini? Not a bit of it. Our hero wrote a treatise on law,
which still helps you, me, and everybody else. It begins
De Laudibus something or other. In it, he pronounces
the only worthwhile legal maxim. We all know it, and
every single day it saves our bacon from oppression. It's
this: You are innocent, until proven guilty. Out with
Roman Law, he wrote in stern Latin, and in with the
common law of England. Old Fortescue, wobbling out
on his warhorse to military disaster, was the first and
only lawyer who ever existed with enough nerve to state
that immortal and fair principle. And he pronounced it
loud and clear against all comers, and paid with his life.

So let's hear it for old Sir John F, because he insisted this essential principle: What does it matter if newspapers, gossip mongers, neighbours, the police, the
whole world and everybody else shout that you're
guilty as hell? If they can't prove it, you're innocent,
and you stay pure as the driven snow until they can.
It's in every worthwhile country's legal system. As
long as folk stick to Sir John's sensible law, innocent
duckeggs like me remain safe. It's all the doing of old
Sir John Fortescue, *requiescat in pace*.

The significance is this. Me and Margaret Dainty
met once in Ebrington, Gloucester, the night before a

small town auction. We made smiles there, our first time. She bought me a prezzie, a small pottery bust of Fortescue. I'd never heard of him. She laughed, and said, "That man might be your saviour one day, Lovejoy. Don't break it!" Course, I broke him one night a year later, but glued him together. He's still in my kitchen alcove. Sometimes I even say, "Wotcher, Sir John," to him, like a fool. Margaret smiles when she sees it, and sometimes says, "You still have him, I see." And goes a bit red, remembering.

Now, her phone message said that ancient law condemned my position, and was inflexible. Fortescue said exactly the opposite, that Roman Law had to be scrapped and Common Law should rule instead, for the sake of truth. Other nations followed, and common sense was still in with a chance. It didn't last, lawyers being lawyers, but brave old Sir John died still giving it a go.

Margaret must have believed me. *She was somewhere around*!

At last I had a pal. Not much of one, but one's more than none. Even I knew that.

For the first time since Southampton, I slept like a babe.

* * *

Next morning I was ordered to help Lauren with the evening quiz. It seemed Mr Henry Semper was ill.

"Why me?" I asked June Milestone, who caught me watching the line dancing.

"Mr Mangot says so."

"I won't do it."

"I'll tell him you said that, shall I?"

"Do what you like, love. No skin off my nose."

About ten o'clock there was a talk about our next

port of call, somewhere in Germany. I decided to escape there, a little more successfully than I had in Amsterdam and Oslo.

"Oh, Lovejoy." Les Renown caught up, Amy with him. "Got a sec? We'd like to show you the ropes."

"Oh. Ta."

They chatted amiably enough, me suspecting nothing, directing me to the Lido Deck. There, an open swimming pool had plenty of folk trying to get a tan and a bar, a combo playing, some entertainers fooling about getting laughs. Coco Chanel, she of Little Black Dress fame, started the craze for a tan. Before Coco, ladies strove for the pale and wan look of the refined aristo.

Through double doors, the Sidewalk Cafe was open.

"Anybody can just go and have yet another meal," Amy laughed. "If you're still starving!"

They were pleasant company. We went into a place full of exercise gadgets.

"This is one of our favourites," Amy said, squeezing my arm.

"Empty," Les said.

Mirrors on the walls, stacked exercise pallets on sprung floor, machines for weighing you and testing body fat. Graphs of weight against height against pulse rates, it would have trained a regiment. I glanced in without enthusiasm.

"This way."

I followed them across. We were between a tall row of static machines itching to make the most inept weakling superb at cycling, lifting, rowing. Nobody else was in. I could hear faint music of the let's-jog variety.

They stood smiling. I looked about. I was between the machines, my back to a wall full of charts. They stood beside each other facing me. Of a sudden I had a bad feeling. I couldn't get past them, and I wanted to be among friendly people, people who weren't smiling.

Les held a device that looked something like a cattle prod. I'd seen those horrible things before, in farms in East Anglia.

"What?" I said. It came out as a pathetic bleat.

"You've no right to buck us, Lovejoy."

"What?" A worse bleat, almost a begging letter.

Amy took the prod and came forward. I had nowhere to retreat. She touched it on me and the world went thump. I was flung to one side, head striking a cushioned seat and my arms tangled in some lifting thing suspended from chrome handles. I tried to stand, move away, run anywhere but my feet wouldn't shift. I heard myself groan. Les went to a wall switch and the music deafened me.

I managed to stand, and this time Les used the prod. I jolted over backwards, my ankles twisting round each other, but that might have been the squint I suddenly seemed to have. Everything was double. Amy laughed, clapping her hands.

"Let me, Les!" she cried. "Let me!"

They fought like lovers do over trinkets, affection written all over them. Les let her win and she prodded me so the world shot black and I found myself crawling under a cycling machine, the pedals hitting my head as I tried to scramble away.

"Mind the chrome," Les said in a fond voice to Amy. "It's a conductor of electricity. We daren't lose the bastard, or she'll finish us."

She who? Amy whimpered with delight as Les dragged me out from under the machines then prodded me. I rolled, slavering like a rabid animal, double vision and a terrible nausea not helping as I flicked and folded, my legs flailing against the chrome piping and the stanchions. I heard a faint moaning and recognised my voice. I'd heard my groans before. I was sick.

Some time later I felt water on my face. Amy was crouching over me and a man's voice was asking what was the matter.

"I was taking a short cut through to the hair-dressers," Amy said. "I heard him fall. Do you think he might be an epileptic?"

"Has he any chest pain?"

"He hasn't said."

I gibbered a bit and tried to edge away from the malevolent bitch, heels on the wooden flooring. My jacket was stained with saliva and morsels of food.

"Poor thing," Amy said. "Are you all right, sir?"

No sign of Les or of the cattle prod. A man I presumed was one of the passengers was trying to lift me.

"Bring one of those blue exercise pallets. I should call the doctor. Is he a friend of yours?"

"No." Amy was all concern. "I think he comes to the shows."

"Oh, right. You're one of the dancers?"

The man was an American, tall and lanky. He moved me about easily enough. Victor?

"I think I'd better stay," Amy said. "I've had a basic training in first aid."

"Good. Shall I go for the doctor?"

"Please."

I lay, trying to push myself up on one elbow, watching Amy. She saw the man hurry away and stood, cold as a frog.

"You can go now, Lovejoy. Any more disobedience, you'll have more antics for our amusement. Savvy?"

Les put his head round the door. "All right in here?"

"Yes, Les."

She walked away. She had a beautiful walk, but then

all dancers look stylish. They're trained, you see.

"Be gone before the doctor and that man come back," she warned me from the exit.

My hands were almost too weak to pull me erect. I tottered out, caught the lift just as I heard three people hurry by into the gymnasium, the Yank explaining about some passenger who looked like he'd had some kind of fit.

I pressed any button for any deck just to get away. Kind of that Yank to come and help. They're great, Yanks. Always too late, but kindly.

* * *

After cleaning myself up and changing, I called Lauren and we met in the Curzon Lounge. I said I'd help her with the evening antiques quiz, as I'd heard Mr Semper was poorly.

"Let's choose the antique now, then!" She was a pest. I still felt odd and creaky, bruises everywhere. Wisely, they'd spared my face.

"Later, love. I feel bit rough."

"Now, Lovejoy. We must make a list."

"We? I'm not running this cruise, love. You are."

"I'm only an assistant!" Lauren shrilled, then glanced about. Guilt kept her voice down. "The trouble is I've nobody to assist now Mr Semper's unwell."

"Assist June Milestone."

"She hates me. I've tried. And as for that Russian woman, I can't stand her and she can't stand me!"

"Pick out from where?"

"Mr Semper's store-room."

Weary from failure, I gave in. We went down several floors and emerged in a corridor. I heard voices, stewards, differing languages, a radio or two playing and somebody singing. Crews' quarters. There was a large store-room. Lauren had the key.

"These are all the antiques Mr Semper brought on board for his sessions. He took such pains with them, made notes on them all."

She stood to one side. I almost walked off in disgust. Not a chime in my chest. If even a single one had been genuine, I would have at least gone a bit clammy. Not a carrot. The store-room was crammed.

Ceramics, a couple of supposed Old Masters and several fake Regency watercolours, some temperas in phoney frames. Some silverware, a balloon-backed chair – it looked familiar, probably made in Kelvedon from its seat covering – several fake Roman and Egyptian glass pieces, a teddy bear, some replica mechanical tin toys, and a clock or two (hardest of all antiques to find genuine throughout, because bits are so easy to replace) with tribal artefacts, paperweights, vases, pressed glass ornaments, sugar casters, tobacciana, breweriana (sorry about the word; it's not made up, just the antiques trade at its usual naff terminology; it means things to do with named distilleries, breweries and alcohol; I suppose someone will invent the word alcoholiania next). And one or two small pieces of furniture, a fake wine cooler and a Victorian workbox…

"Lauren," I said, all sad. "I wouldn't buy this dross for a bent groat."

"What?" She rounded on me. "I shall have you know…" I sighed. There was nothing to do but exude pity and walk away. The lass followed me along the corridor hissing rage.

At the lift, safe in the passenger areas, I stopped and faced her. Nobody was about.

"It's all fake, love. Get June Milestone to appraise it. She'll be taken in by about twenty per cent, but she'll tell you the rest is dud, fake, sham, replicoid."

"You hadn't even the politeness to examine them!

Henry Semper selected them himself!"

"You've been conned, love. Telephone your beloved Henry and demand the truth. If all else fails, go ashore at our next port of call and hire a reputable antiques dealer – assuming there is such a thing. Get him to list the genuine antiques in Henry's store-room. If he's honest he'll run a mile."

"You've had it in for Mr Semper ever since you came aboard, Lovejoy! You're jealous because he knows more about antiques than you ever will!"

"Your precious Henry is charging the cruise line for genuine antiques, and bringing aboard cheap fakes. The oldest scam in the world."

"I hate you. You are vile!"

I chucked the towel in. "You're probably right. See you at dinner time."

Nimbly I joined an elderly couple going up to the golf on the sun deck and called a cheery so-long to Lauren.

"Have you had a row?" the lady asked in a stage whisper, glimpsing Lauren's face.

"No, love. She won't come dancing."

"What a pity!" the old couple carolled. "We do so enjoy the ballroom dances! Daniel here loves Latin-American!"

"Doesn't everybody!" I wittered, a perfect prat, poisonously full of bonhomie.

It was only when I escaped by the Photo Gallery that I felt a strange memory try to come back. It didn't quite make it. I wondered what set me frowning. That store-room was quite a size, full of supposed antiques. Hadn't Henry Semper given it a single thought? Surely it must have crossed his mind that somewhere on this ship, with music and antiques as its cruise theme for entertainment – leaving aside all the other thirty or forty shows, games, dances, films going on – there might possibly be a passenger who knew at least a little about antiques? He'd taken a hell of a risk bringing on that stock of duds trying to pass them off as genuine. It was as if the musicians – twenty-five on board, not counting bar pianists – brought soloists who couldn't play a tune.

Ever since I'd realised that antiques had as much voice as any human, and could speak across centuries if only people would listen, they'd been my life. Could anything be as beautiful or as loved as the antiques that once lived with our own ancestors centuries ago? And Henry Semper had the gall to think he could con everybody with his roomful of utter gunge. The more I thought about his arrogance the wilder I grew. As for Lauren, she obviously craved to be conned. She just adored fostering her hero's grandiose scheme.

She would hate me from now on, of course. Par for the course.

Temper made me careless, and I nearly got roped into doing the Conga, some celebrations in a private party. I narrowly escaped, developing a spectacular limp and ruefully shaking my head as they frugged past. Sometimes I wonder about people who do the Conga, singing and whooping. Those great snaking lines are a cruel mimicry of a Congo slave coffle. It's one of the few things I think should be forgotten. I once told our M.P. so. He thought I was off my trolley.

Chapter Fourteen

The captain, a suave man, sometimes held a cocktail party. I got ready to tackle him. I could hardly say I'd been shanghaied by an old dear in a wheelchair, so instead, I decided to make a simple, polite farewell. Hundreds of witnesses was what I wanted.

I got togged up, cleverly buying a static black tie from the shop, seeing Gloria had only bought me one I didn't know how to tie. The steward came to check me and passed me fit. People were the height of glamour, all of us done up like tuppenny rabbits, ladies in gowns and men in tuxedos, older ones with medals. We were photographed by the ship's camera girls, smiling at the lens. I'd seen this before. The snaps taken as we'd come aboard were mounted in the display panels on Deck Seven. We filed forward into lights, music, the throng in party mood.

Somebody said my name and I went forward with an ingratiating smile.

"Sorry I have to get off, Captain," I started glibly. "So – "

"Lovejoy is one of our antiques experts," Purser Mangot cut in, moving me speedily along as the camera clicked. "Passengers want to meet him."

The skipper's eyes were glazed. "Excellent! Carry on!"

"So if it's okay with you," I was saying when two of Mangot's serfs hustled me sideways. The captain was already shaking hands with a couple, his smile stencilled in place. He'd not heard a word I'd said.

"Don't try that again," Mangot said quietly through grinning teeth. "It's a long swim home."

"Er, I only meant..."

"Good to see you taking part in the festivities!" Amy the dancer took over as Mangot returned to his chaperone duties. "Where did you leave Lady Vee?"

"Here, Lovejoy," Les Renown the comedian said, already chuckling. "Heard the one about the parrot who wouldn't stop cursing? His owner shoves him in the fridge as punishment. The parrot is scared and shouts he'll be good. As he's released, he asks, 'What the fuck did that chicken do?' Get it, Lovejoy?"

People sloshing back the whisky roared laughing. I tried to smile, keeping up appearances.

"Yes, I get it," I said gravely. More than most.

"That's terrible, Les. Can't you can find some nice jokes?" Ivy slipped her arm through mine.

"Here's one." Amy drew breath. "A savage man-eating lion says to its little cub, 'I thought you said this shop was crowded at weekends!' Isn't it lovely?"

Ivy was pleased. "The best jokes are quite sweet, aren't they?"

"I don't get it," a lady was saying.

Les started to tell the joke voted the world's funniest ever. "This hunter sees his mate collapse out in the Rockies. Luckily he has his cell phone so he calls..."

I moved away, like the talkative parrot wondering what the chicken had done to be entombed in the freezer. Ivy caught my eye. I didn't stop, just left my wine glass and made my way out through the crowd.

* * *

Thoughts accumulate in the dark. I find that women are the only saviour of insomniacs like me, whereas antiques are sleep's ruination. But with the next port soon due outside the porthole I finally had to make a fist of escaping. Every passing day took me nearer to St Petersburg, and I knew I'd never come back. The ship was sheer bliss, if you liked rest, sun, entertainment, superb food, and a whale of a time. If you were a prisoner, it was different.

I *had* to get off.

* * *

That night I dreamt.

I'm never big on sleeping. It wears me out. At home in my cottage I have a radio – given free with a magazine subscription taken out by a friend, only she didn't like me listening to it in the lantern hours. She was a travel writer, never had anything published. I listen to my radio through the night. It tells the strangest things – or does it? A half-doze is as far as sleep ever takes me. I usually rouse before dawn with weirds floating in my mind. Like, Tanzania has the best goat races. Sir Isaac Newton invented the cat-flap. Women athletes and ballet dancers perform better if they've made love earlier that day (doctors say it's due to lower blood viscosity, but how do they know?). The Itelman tribe in far-flung Siberia is down to 350 native speakers. I can't understand why some things are missed out – or maybe I dozed through bits. Like, Frinton-on-Sea was once covered in orange ladybirds – I saw it, the whole place bright orange with the creatures so thick underfoot I was scared to walk for fear of crushing the little things – yet it wasn't even mentioned. The radio waxed eloquent, however, about red clouds of sand from the Sudan blowing over East Anglia after a storm, and frogs raining down on Wiltshire. See? People's minds just pick out what's odd *to them*.

What was odd to me on the *Melissa*?

I found myself sitting up in my cabin, with something stuck in my mind from a long time ago. I struggled to recapture what seemed so strange.

My dream had been about Belle, my robbery pal, she of the gabby cell phone. She once had this bloke.

He was an army corporal who loaded heavy guns. He was sailing away some war to, well, load guns I suppose. Belle was in tears lest he got killed. She knew how to make his departure memorable, and told the Marquis of Granby regulars en masse, "Fine. Easy. I'll just... well, you know?" The women regulars nodded understandingly, and we blokes nodded with what sagacity we could assume.

"I mean," she explained, standing beside the roaring log fire, "it's only right, yeah? And fair, yeah?"

"Yeah," everybody said, because it was.

"The only trouble is," she said, and paused.

We waited. Big Sadie, recently back from Hackney because her sister was playing up, put in, "When he comes home?"

"That's it." Belle started crying, tears flopping down on her blouse as she casually sipped her sherry, her expression unchanged. "What can I do? His wife's a bitch, y'know?"

The women dealers glanced. This time the blokes nodded.

"Where, er...?" I said. This is my tactic, prompt a sobbing woman to supply her own question because then she'll answer it, and that lets you off the hook.

"You mean where did we first get it together?" Belle pondered. "You're *right*, Lovejoy! In my garden shed! That's it!"

Everybody regarded me as a seer possessing the wisdom of the ancients and bought me a drink. Belle's idea was to make her garden shed a new love nest. Women dealers applauded.

Time passed. The distant war ended and Johnny came marching home again, hurrah, hurrah. We all took an interest in Belle's hookery nook. Belle's friends started bringing in miniature swatches of taffeta, plus those painter's charts that always get colours wrong, and making suggestions for mood music. I only ever learned Gregorian chant at school so I was useless. Belle wanted romantic melodies. Vera who runs the plant barrows in Coggeshall market was brilliant at tunes. We listened to her selection. It was really nice.

And it came to pass that the seduction shed worked like a charm. We were all pleased. Belle was back on track, until she or the corporal got fed up and they parted and life's rich pageant, dot, dot, dot.

Which was very strange to me. I don't mean Belle's fickle affections, or the response in the tavern, no. I mean the image of Belle's garden shed that I'd wakened with. People said it was quite sumptuous. I never saw it myself. The walls were done in a red flock velveteen, with coral window frames and two dozen orange pulsing candles made to look like Christmas tree lights even though it was Easter, pink balloons, and a purple ceiling Dandy Jack built for her in exchange for a fake Victorian Belgian mantel clock. It sounded real class. I could see why Belle had such appeal. Thick, but full of artistic talent.

What stuck in my mind, though, as I woke when it was almost day, was an odd word heard in my dream. A dealer called Poncer said it while we were talking over Belle's love nest the week before her corporal was due back. Poncer is a tall languid Oxford aristo whose family owns Hertfordshire or somewhere. He rides horses, shoots for England at the Bisley championships, golfs in plus-fours, and knows incomprehensible African dialects. We're proud of Poncer. He's a hopeless antiques dealer, though, and only took up with Martha when he left the diplomatic service because she owns a lavender field in Norwich.

"It sounds quite a boudoir," his Martha said. "Can I see it?"

"You'd hate it, dear. You only like muted colours. Belle's shed positively dazzles."

"I'm sure I'd think it lovely."

"Let's hope," Poncer said, casually raising an aloof digit so barmaids would hurtle to replenish his drink (serfs respond to Poncer's slightest whim; I have to brawl to get served) "that Belle's serdab proves effective, what, what?"

We all quickly agreed, pretending we knew what a serdab was. None of us did. I would have asked outright but Forelock arrived just then with news of Edwardian furniture due at Gimbert's auction rooms, so I forgot. I thought vaguely it was some kind of collar.

If you're fascist the ship stewards bring your gasp-awake tea on a tray. I pressed the miniature kettle's button unaided, wondering why I was dreaming of Belle's tryst. I'd never met her corporal, nor saw her shed. I actually knew little about her except for those incidental bits one antiques dealer knows of another, and that's only what you pick up trying to do auctioneers down.

The sea outside was fairly smooth. I sipped the tea – it was horrible – and saw a couple of distant vessels with their lights showing. We were slowly overtaking. Ships pass each other in the night. Like people. Like ideas? Like fleeting images prompted by an unfamiliar word like serdab? One thing's for sure, I told my ghastly reflection later in the tiny bathroom, serdab won't have anything to do with Belle's spectacular shed.

The enticing notion faded. I yawned and got ready to start the day.

*　*　*

As soon as the library opened, I was there among the books. The library was on the top balcony of the

Atrium facing the row of shops, boutiques, nooks for sitting and having your cocktails. The main staircase looked bright, with its waterfall tumbling three storeys to the well by the elegant sweeping staircase, the band softly playing. I got a book on St Petersburg and sat in a plush armchair. I felt a fraud. I should have been pushing Lady Vee to her bingo or the casinos, but decided this was urgent. Her casino could wait a bit; she'd save herself a mint.

History is simpler than historians make it. The area round St Petersburg was once nothing but marshland, until Peter the Great battled the Swedes from the River Neva in the Second North War, and decided to build a city. He used enslaved Swedish prisoners and his own peasants, and drained the marshes. He raised money by taxing beards, shoes, horses, cufflinks, food, coffins, and even dying. In 1712, this huge man moved his court from Moscow. You had to fetch your own wood (taxable), serfs (taxed), tents, bricks, nails, and your families. Everything was taxed. Workers and Swedish prisoners died. The splendid city rose.

Peter was "the Great" because he was a giant of a man. He loved getting sloshed in a pub among visiting merchants. He often wore tatty gear like a common man. Despite this, he got people to elect their own municipality complete with magistracy. As Tsar, he took his stick to idlers, even to ministers of the crown, and literally clobbered them until they got their act together. This hero also joined his own Tsarist army as a private. A boisterous seventeen, Peter got fed up being married and slung his lovely Eudoxia into a nunnery so he could slog at carpentry, gunnery, blacksmithing, and sailing an English sailboat he found mouldering in a boathouse. In short, he zoomed about Russia non-stop and changed everything. He even introduced his famous "Table of Ranks", whereby civil servants rose by merit – do nothing, you lost everything. Hard work got you promoted. A true revolutionary.

St Petersburg was his legacy. He started an art collection, the embryonic Hermitage.

Catherine the Great, a Polish lady famed for promiscuity (exaggerated actually, though nine lovers at one go does seem rather a lot) developed the museum into world leader. I can never really judge women. I mean, she'd win the Ten Word Woman Game hands down because, although she had her husband Peter the Third assassinated by her military lovers so she could rule, as it were, untrammelled, and so counts as a truly naughty lass, she was Voltaire's best pal and brought Russia into the Enlightenment. Who can balance that?

There was a small badly drawn map of St Petersburg. I located the Hermitage near the shore, and stared at it until my eyes grew gritty. I learned nothing. Except I looked up serdab. It's a room, a cellar, an ice-house, a secret chamber, and has been taken into our language like so many thousands of other words. I had to sit down, thinking.

Lots of rooms about.

Chapter Fifteen

Executive Purser Mangot had a hanging judge's face on him. I wasn't worried. Things seemed better than they had been since I'd come aboard, now I had a few clues of my own.

"Lovejoy. I sent for you to say you're to do two things."

He stood, coming round his desk. I realised how big he was. We were the only two people there. He fisted me in the belly with a swinging blow so I whoomphed double and fell. I found myself kneeling on the carpet when the room came back. I thought, what the hell have I done wrong? If they only told me, I'd stop it.

"You listening?" he said, quite conversational, and sat himself with his feet up on the desk. I hate people who do that. Another reason I hated Mangot: he never looked at me, only somewhere about my throat. I'd noticed he was the same with other folk. Some actresses do it too. There's one on that ITV soap. Makes you wonder what they're hiding, avoiding your eyes like that.

"Yes."

He tipped his fingers together, the way headmasters always did before they gave you a good belting. The threatener's gesture. I never get away unscathed when people do it. Real killers don't need to be quite so showy. I mean Big John, or Daffy from Liverpool who did that Midland paedophile who was released from prison, or Gerbil who does crispers – translated, means he burns houses of drug dealers and the like – for Glasgow and Liverpool folk, for a small fee. (Actually 1200 zlotniks; I'm always amazed they can do it so cheap; supply and demand, I suppose.)

He looked smug. I felt sick and slumped on the

only other chair. Sweat never comes when you want it, only when you start to recover. God made us wrong. That morning from the ship's rail I'd watched a shark, and wondered how come that God had told the Great White Shark only to eat warm-blooded creatures like mammals – like, in fact, me. Had God never heard of fish, for Christ's sake? I added inappropriate sweat to my life's grouses.

"You're causing trouble."

"Eh? I've done no such… " Did he mean Lauren's pathetic little scam with the antiques she brought round on Henry Semper's say-so? "The antique business?"

"Yes." He straightened, his heels thumping to the floor as he leaned threateningly over the desk. (Real killers don't do this either. They don't need histrionics, just an occasional glance.) "Trying to speak to the captain. And you've bubbled Henry's scam with the passengers, Lovejoy. Stop it."

"Stop it? But the stuff is utter crud. I wouldn't pay for their fakes in tap washers." I realised I was being too mouthy, and instantly stooped into my grovel. "If you say so."

"In future, Lovejoy, you'll say Henry Semper's antiques are genuine and great value for money. Understand?"

"Look," I managed to say.

He shook his head. "The word you're looking for is…?" He spelled it, "Y…E…S. Got it?"

I nodded.

"Say 'Yes, Purser.' Go on."

"Yes, Purser."

"If you don't, Lovejoy, you shall have to take the consequences when we reach St Petersburg."

He spoke briefly into a phone, just numbers, replaced the receiver. I knew I was to stay until dismissed. I tried to uncrouch but my belly doubled me up. Sweat started at last. I was soon drenched. Ta, God. Late but eventually good value. God must be a Yank. The pain faded.

"Hello, James."

"June."

She entered, taking in the scene. She'd once seen me battered by the Brummy circus – you'll have seen these, a team of antique dealers who go about the country mob-handed, taking over auctions by bullying. Auctioneers help them, of course, because otherwise the honest old public might have to be fairly treated. She knew the signs, and gave Mangot a quick glance. It lacked sympathy. Smart lass, June Milestone. They say there's no more desperate competitors than TV presenters on walk-talk shows. They've got to be fast on their feet to survive the cut-throat rivalry. Like, between June and Henry Semper?

"Lovejoy, sod off, you corrupt little pissant."

Holding my stomach, I left. Luckily, there wasn't a soul in the corridor. Out there I leant against the photo display of the ship's staff. The door didn't quite close. I stayed silent, and heard Mangot speak to June as if she were a minion.

"Time you earned your keep," he said. I heard his heels thump to the floor. Changing positions while giving orders seemed to be his thing.

"What do you mean?" Defensive. "James, I've done everything – "

"That pillock's causing ripples. We brought him aboard on your say-so. It's up to you to keep him quiet."

"Not just me, James! It was all agreed." No indignation there. Mere submission from the great June Milestone the TV darling?

"Do as you're told and we'll all get on. Do what you

have to to keep him in order. Understood?"

"Yes, James."

"Okay. Find Amy and her tame pillock, tell them I want them."

"Yes, James."

I just made it to the Atrium, where luckily only a few passengers frolicked, all too busy to notice me. I sat, feeling ashen. I badly wanted fluid, but didn't dare ask for a drink in case it made me worse. I tried to doze, hunched in the armchair, a picture of yet another idling passenger slumbering to music. One or two stewardesses paused to ask if I wanted some tipple or other, then smiled and went on, leaving me to recover.

Grudges, I find, are hard to keep up. However, Mangot would have to go. I can forgive anyone who acts on principle. Like, women scrap with supermarket managers, on a matter of principle. And, a bloke has to defend his righteousness, whatever it is based on. Mangot had to defend his ship's reputation. Just as I could forgive Lauren's ignorance – she was standing by her dishonest boss, duped by his dazzling popularity.

Another point of principle: if everybody else is allowed to have principles, then me too. Mangot had ordered me to betray my divvy gift. I simply don't do it. The pig had stepped over the line separating right from wrong. I'm no saint. But think of those wondrous inventors and artists like Josiah Wedgwood, who studied all their lives to get the right glaze on a humble pot, exactly the right look to a painting, the perfect setting for some gemstone, the most dazzling colours in an embroidery. How many hundreds of thousands across the centuries gave their lives for perfection? Now Mangot was making me betray every single one.

When I've had to, I've betrayed people. Everybody's done it. You, me, him, her, we deceive lovers, husbands, wives. Some are trained – I've already said how I appreciate lawyers in my own special way, and politicians never give a straight answer on anything. Other folk are forced into betrayal. Most of us assume we've a right to do a bit of treachery when we think it's fair. Like when somebody dies, and friends and families gather to pretend grief and eye up the spoils after the "ham butties and slow walk," as Lancashire folk call a funeral. Ever seen a contented heir? There's no such thing. Everybody thinks that Auntie Elsie snaffled those valuable Welsh dressers and Uncle Ernie's priceless collection of glass paperweights. It's just families doing their thing, and I can understand it and forgive.

Betray *all* the lovely people in history who ever stitched, drew, built, fashioned, shaped, carved, worked? I came to. My stomach felt sore. I kept burping, and there was June, smiling in the next armchair.

"Come on, Lovejoy," she said, raising me. "Time to go gambling. Nothing takes your mind off a silly argument like a really good gamble."

"Silly argument? Is that all it was?"

Slammed to my knees, threatened with… I hated to think that far. Experimenting, I slowly straightened. We started towards the casinos. They were two floors up. We went up in the lifts. Our progress was quite pleasant once I got moving. The sickly feeling began to fade. I was with a celebrity. Almost every passenger said hello to June. She moved among the people, saying hello and laughing at their quips. I felt a bit bad because I saw Ivy, wife of Billy the Kid ex-cop from my table, and had the distinct impression she wanted to speak. She withdrew and went quickly on when she saw I was with the great June Milestone, darting me a glance that shut me up. June was nodding affably to three blue-rinses, saying they could ask their questions at the tea-time lecture, because Henry Semper, poor darling, wasn't really very well.

"I shall have to do it instead," she said. They trilled laughs and said things like, "Splendid, June!" Crawlers. Worse than me.

We went to see people lose fortunes at roulette. I saw Holly playing blackjack with single-minded intensity. She won steadily. I saw no sign of Margaret Dainty. I wondered how not to snarl up Lauren's antique scam at nosh time.

"There!" June exclaimed when the roulette session had been won, lost, drawn, or all of the above. "Now a bite to eat!"

She led the way. I pointed out she was going in the wrong direction.

"I don't think so, Lovejoy," she said demurely. June can be demure, but surely this wasn't the time. There was something wrong. "Your cabin, I think?"

All cabins had electronic keys, plastic cards into a slot. Tea was laid on my small table. Who'd ordered that?

"There!" She kicked off her shoes and sat on the bed, curling her legs beneath her. If I try to sit like that I topple over. Women are different shapes. "I do hope the salmon has fresh cress." She looked, and purred with satisfaction. "Yes! It isn't fair to the salmon otherwise, don't you think?"

Something was still not right. We sat and talked. I asked after Henry Semper, said sorry he was poorly. She said it was nothing to worry about.

And, miracle of miracles, we made smiles. She was just the same as when we'd been friends – note the past tense – so I was in paradise. June was always good at staying silent afterwards, and gave me time to slowly come out of the faint death that invariably follows. I don't know why women don't keep quiet for a bit, but mostly they do what they've seen women, heroines to trollops, do in the movies, light a fag and predict the butler did it or solve the plot. I blame Hollywood. Producers think movies need perpetual motion and constant yak. They forget love needs silences. June pretended to wake only when I stirred, which only goes to show how good she'd have been if she'd turned to acting. I wish I'd remembered that.

Thinking this, I realised what was wrong. This was a plot. She was simply doing as Mangot had ordered: Do what you have to do. For me, ecstasy is a complete entity and always perfect. Otherwise it wouldn't be ecstasy, right? But I'd known June pretty well once. I roused, smiled, blessed her. We got ready.

"Mind if I come to your lecture?" I asked. I wouldn't have been surprised if she'd said no, leave it, some other time.

She said fine. And I went. The theatre was crowded by people with notebooks. As they waited, they were all talking about passing through the Kiel Canal then Warnemunde, where we'd dock. A lady next to me asked if I was going ashore. "Lovely place," she enthused, "but dreadfully expensive…" It seemed to be the passenger litany, that and staggering from one gargantuan nosh to the next.

I wondered if Margaret Dainty would be there. And if Mr Moses Duploy would make it. And if I might somehow get away.

June came on to warm applause. The talk started. It wasn't bad, but I noticed she slipped things in to nark me. Twice she called a single turkeywork chair of the seventeenth century (no arms, wide seat, low straight-line back) a farthingale chair. It was never called so, not at first. Me and June used to have words about this. The farthingale was a lady's dress with hooped whalebone used to spread petticoats and dress widely at the hips, creating a splendid impression as an elegant lady seated herself in a fashionable gathering. It became especially admired about James the First's time. By then, the chair had been a standard piece of furniture in affluent households for donkey's years. The "farthingale" chair's name only became an antiques dealer's term almost a century after the farthingale's appearance. I swear June hid a smile as she said it a second time, riling me. She loves Windsor chairs, and made a great thing of them, but in the nineteenth century they were regarded as humdrum and lacking in fashion, more a kitchen or coffee-house chair than anything.

Delia Oakley and her friend Fern chatted with me as we left afterwards. We went to see the ship enter through the Kiel Canal's massive sliding gates. This was Germany, so much nearer to St Petersburg. Secretly I decided if I was going to get thumped, bullied and enslaved, I wanted more details. They might be my only lifeline. I looked about hoping to catch June, but she was surrounded by admirers. I must have seemed surly to Delia because I didn't say much. The countryside looked beautiful. Astonishing to see the vast *Melissa* gliding through the terrain, people cycling alongside and waving from footpaths.

Somebody said Warnemunde was just a quiet fishing village. It proved not quite so tranquil.

Chapter Sixteen

Nervous at having to deputise for Henry Semper in his chat, I was relieved when only twenty or so passengers turned up. They'd never heard of me, and I wasn't famous June Milestone or good old TV star Henry Semper. I decided to speak on jewellery. The shops had some on sale. I recognised a few faces. Delia Oakley and her friend Fern, of course, with Lauren along presumably to suss out the opposition (me). One old lady came wearing every bauble she had.

The ship's newspaper listed seventeen different entertainments in competition. I was glad. A salesgirl came with trays of trinkets. She put pendants and rings out on velvet. For a few minutes I spoke about the problems of wearing baubles.

"Think what a jewel is," I said, once I'd got going. "It's only a bit of something we value. Like, when aluminium was purified by a Dane in 1825 it was the same price as gold, even though it's Planet Earth's commonest metal and the Ancient Babylonians used its compounds in medicines and dyes. See? Now, it's stacked in every rubbish tip. We'd laugh to see an emerald set in aluminium, but the Victorians thought that beautiful."

I asked the salesgirl to uncover her trays of jewellery.

"Hands up those who use spray perfumes, aftershaves and the like." They all did. "Everybody? Well, you want locking up. And who keeps their rings on when washing up? Everybody? You're under arrest. Even diamonds are affected by washing liquids supposedly gentle to your hands, as the advertising slogans say."

Somebody interrupted. "But a gemstone can't be destroyed, can it?"

"Untrue, missus. Want an example? Remember those bonny marcasite brooches? There have been instances when they've been left in an ordinary box. Years later, you find the box holds nothing but powder. It hasn't been stolen – the marcasite has simply oxidised to powder. And marcasite is pure crystalline iron sulphide."

"Diamonds are indestructible, though, aren't they? They're the hardest substance known."

"Almost true. In Australia and South Africa, old miners believed in the sledgehammer test. If they whacked a gemstone with a sledgehammer and it didn't break, they thought it proof the gem was a real diamond. Not necessarily true. They must have shattered hundreds of genuine diamonds, right from the moment little Erasmus Jacobs found his 'sparkling stone' in South Africa in 1866 and diamonds became everybody's darling. A diamond is more vulnerable than you might think. It has planes of cleavage."

"Which gemstones are most easily damaged?" That was Delia.

"Organic gemstones. Spray perfumes are a real risk, especially to pearls. The pearl's nacre – the shiny outer coat you pay for – gets dissolved at the pearl's equator. You can never get it back. It's the same with mother-of-pearl. I once was in a lady's … er, room. She had a beautiful mother-of-pearl inlaid box for her jewellery, eighteenth century, on her, er, coffee table. It was blotchy. She often used one of those spray perfumes, see?"

"Why did she have it on her coffee table and not in her bedroom?" a lady demanded.

I went on, red-faced, "It happens with all the natural gems. There are principally four: pearls, jet, amber, and ivory. Traditional jewellers add coral, making five."

"I have a coral necklace," said a lady, proudly showing

it off. "It's a gem*stone*. They said so when I bought it."

"That's true," said the shopgirl, immediately defensive.

"Lovely," I said feebly.

The lady's necklace was clumsily done, a sequence of coral pieces mismatched and made from waste fragments powdered and glued to simulate the real thing. The trade calls it resining, because you crush powdered coral (adding a pinkish dye to make your rubbishy fake even more gorgeous) and simply add resin adhesive. Let the thing set, in the shape you think will sell quick, and there you've made a perfectly good-looking piece of "original coral", if you stretch the truth a bit. Her necklace was mostly resined coral powder. I sighed. I hate having to tell a lady she's spent good money and bought only gunge.

"Coral is getting rare now, luv, because of pollution. It's actually the skeletons of small sea creatures in the *Cnidaria* phyllum. Its personal name is *Corallium*. It was highly prized even in the ancient world. When the creature dies, it leaves behind the red stone we call coral, sometimes white, pink. One species actually creates slatey-blue coral, but I don't like it."

"Are all gems really stone, then?"

"Come close and see."

The girl, Donna, had on display ivory and bone rings and bangles, amber earrings, one small jet piece, some coral, and various cultured pearls. The folk left their seats and crowded round.

"No. Some purists say amber is the only true organic gem, because it is a fossilised tree resin. The Baltic, where this ship's sailing, is sometimes called the Amber Sea, because of the amber they find along the littoral. It floats as far as England's east coast."

"Is this ivory?"

A lady passed me a brooch of pseudo-eastern

design. I could tell from the way she glanced with hard eyes at Donna that she'd bought it from the jewellery shop on Deck Seven in the Atrium. I borrowed the salesgirl's loupe and peered in the best light available. She carried a MacArthur microscope – basically a small illuminated tube. It focuses by a little ratchet wheel, and shows you the surface of any material in high magnification.

"Ivory is a chemical they call oxyapatite – calcium phosphate to you and me – and a bit of chalk, with a little organic material." I looked up. "This is nicely cut." I was being kind. It was horrible. "Ivory's elastic, in fact, and lovely to carve because it's not very hard. People who work in ivory praise its tenacity – that means it won't splinter easily."

"Isn't it banned?" asked a young woman, ready to crusade.

"Dunno. Some folk argue the African elephant is over-multiplying now it's protected, others the opposite. Stored ivory abounds, but it dries out and tends to crack."

"What about the elephants?" the belligerent bird said.

"They only live fifteen years in zoos, but live to over sixty in the wild. Why keep them in prison? I think we should let them go. More years of life is generally a plus."

"Is it real, though?" the brooch's owner asked.

"It's ivory." I passed it back. "Bone has a heterogeneous network structure – you see it by one of these tube things Donna has. Remember the density test we all did in school and thought a stupid waste of time? Loss of weight in water? Transparent resins can be used to trick the buyer by adding white oxyapatite and chalk mixtures, but they're more dense. Ordinary solid plastic is less dense. Do the simple test in your kitchen at home. It's easy and interesting."

Donna looked relieved. Well she might, because many of her "ivory" items in her shop were actually plastics, but there you go.

"One of the easiest tests – if the shopkeeper will allow you to try it – is to heat a paper clip. Press the tip into the ivory. It turns black and gives off a pungent burnt-meat smell. Plastic offers no resistance to the red-hot metal. Any questions?"

"Would you look at these pearls?"

A man passed me his wife's string of pearls.

"There's always one give-away with every gem," I told him, smiling. "These are synthetic. Look at them. Perfectly spherical, whatever their sizes. Natural pearls are eccentric, however slight the tendency. Jewellers pierce natural pearls so the axis along which he drills the string hole makes the thing like Planet Earth, which only seems a perfect sphere but really isn't. It's slightly flattened."

I looked through the loupe. "You can tell they're not frauds because the surfaces look like they're trying to appear ploughed, with miniature plecks. Beginners call it moon-surfaced."

"Write me a certificate saying all that," the man said, highly narked. "I bought them from a jeweller as natural pearls, not cultured. I'm going to sue them."

"Not me, mate," I said wearily. I always get this. I once got sued for not helping a couple to sue. Can you believe folk that daft? "You want to march on Rome, get on with it."

"You've got to!" The bloke got heated. His wife tried to pull him down. He stood glowering. "You're an employee of this company! I'm going to – "

"I'm a paying passenger," I lied. "I'm only filling in here because somebody's sick. Do your own lawsuit."

"Can I ask, please," Delia interrupted smoothly, saving me more lies, "about amber? It's the only one you've missed out. I've been wondering whether to buy some from the Mayfair shop upstairs."

"Ta." And I meant it. The bloke, silly sod, sat whispering angrily to his missus. "Actually, jet is an organic stuff too. No longer fashionable because it was used once for mourning brooches and pendants. I love amber."

Donna nervously passed me the tray. I picked up some earrings.

"Genuine amber. I've yet to find anybody who hates amber. The least dense of all organic gems. The loveliest-ever line of poetry in the world was inspired by amber. In Milton's *Comus*. Only a few words, but it's inspired a succession of Hollywood films about the lass called Sabrina."

"Say it!" some lady called.

I went red and said I'd a poor memory. I saw June Milestone smile, now standing at the back among more passengers. The meagre crowd had grown, probably thanks to the seething bloke and his frigging cultured pearls.

"Floats in ordinary salt water, which is why it's found on the seashore. Splinters when you slice it. Amber workers get spicules in their skin, causing what they call amber rash. The insects and spiders entombed in it are highly prized, but make me feel ill."

"They're proof it's genuine," Donna put in, proud of her displays.

"In a way, but remember that copal – that varnishy stuff portrait painters use – looks just like amber, and is also a natural resin. It's cheap, and you can immerse an insect in it as it hardens. Make a strong salt solution – ordinary kitchen salt – and your amber floats, but so does copal. Plastics sink, unless they're hollow – hold them up to the light and you see the space."

"Look," the man said, still wanting a war because he'd been stupid.

"Doesn't amber attract shreds of paper?"

Thanks, Delia. "So do many things, if you rub them. Proper alcohol – not methylated spirits – in a minute or two will soften copal, so you can rub a mark onto a white hankie. It's a good test. Amber's resistant."

"So this amber is genuine?" Donna, still batting for her shop.

"These earrings are, love, yes. The risk is buying amber fragments heated and pressed together. A terrible fraud. Amber carvers use this trick to save wasting amber bits. Always test amber in alcohol. In two minutes, you see the crazy-paving look on the surface if it's amberoid, meaning fragments pressed together."

I passed Donna the earrings. "No offence, but myself, I'd wait to buy in St Petersburg or elsewhere in the Baltic. They say people practically give it away, it's a quarter of what you'll pay back home. That's it, folks. Ta for listening."

A few gathered round to ask questions. This always happens, people too shy to blurt out their queries but wanting answers about this pendant or that antique.

Prompted by the kindly Delia, they pressed me how to buy amber. I was gasping for a cuppa.

"Pliny in the Ancient World knew about it. The Romans loved white amber, which they thought was a kind of sea wax. Red, transparent amber was thought to protect against evil, so was a special present for babies."

"Isn't there gold amber?" from Delia, kindly obstructing the irate bloke who wanted to force his way through.

"The Teutonic Knights were busy all along the Baltic," I said with gratitude. "They wanted the white amber, for making rosary beads, symbolising purity, see? Most of the Baltic amber's pale gold. I like the red Chinese amber most. Clear amber sells higher in Britain. An ancient amber cup workmen found under Hove railway station near Brighton is in the British Museum. I'd give anything to... er, hold it just once."

She smiled knowingly. "Have you ever worked amber, Lovejoy?" She segued sideways, still blocking the narked goon and his blinking pearls.

"I've had a few goes, with the small pieces I've gleaned from the East Anglian seaside. It's easily done. Any morning at low tide you'll find a couple of pieces an hour, average, with a bucket of salt water.

"You see all sorts of amber antiques. Candlesticks, bowls, meerschaum pipes, carved plaques, devotional religious carvings, snuffboxes, chess boards, chess pieces, amazing things."

I tried to drift away. They drifted with me. I tried to keep going on the subject, to prevent the man trapping me into conversation about his grievance.

"You either get amber alone, or as encrustation. Not a pleasant word for such beautiful material. It means using amber to embellish other stuffs, as in amber plaques round a chalice. There was even the famous Amber Room – a whole room!"

"Look. If I were to offer – "

"No, mate," I told him. I was getting as narked as he was. "I won't testify under any circumstances. Law never does anybody any good. Don't throw good money after bad."

"The Amber Room," Delia prompted quickly. I blessed her for sticking by me.

"Aye. Frederick the First of Prussia started it. He got a bloke called Wolffram, a famous Danish amber turner, to build a whole room of the stuff in Charlottenburg, but fell out with designers in 1707.

It's a famous tale. Other craftsmen came and went. It got finished about 1711 in time for Peter the Great to see it when he visited Berlin."

"Did he steal it?"

"Got it as a pressie, and took it to St Petersburg for his Winter Palace in St Petersburg. His daughter Elizabeth shifted it later. They called it the Wonder of the World." I smiled. "Now, *that's* an antique!"

"Is it there now? Can we see it?"

"It went missing in the war, love." I tried to make a joke, to escape. "If anybody finds it, let me know and we'll split the proceeds! Oh, Harry!" I pretended to see somebody beyond them and waved. "Just coming! Look, I'm sorry, but I'm late for an appointment. Ta for listening…"

And ran, with a grateful smile to Delia Oakley. Nice lady. The bloke trotted after me with his pearls, but I kept going. Honest to God, I thought, does he want blood?

And made it to the Raffles Lounge, where a concert pianist was playing, so nobody could talk to me for at least an hour. No wonder people go on voyages for their health. I wish I did.

Chapter Seventeen

The harbour was sunny with a river, tangles of shops, cafes, harbour steamers and yachts. A nautical fairground, all colours and on the go. In other circumstances I would have loved it. I was allowed ashore, which only meant Mangot could get me back on board any time.

Trying to make up for my surliness the previous night, I smiled at Delia and Fern as we made our way off. I was pleased they didn't seem offended. In a few paces we were among shops in a sunny seaside. Not many antiques places, and those pretty manky, but a holiday atmosphere lifts the spirit. I liked the place.

"It's the kind of port people call tacky," Delia said, laughing. Fern agreed, and went off all eager to find clothes. "Fern hunts presents," Delia explained. "So far she's only bought two prezzies, and she has seventeen on her list. It's all she comes for!"

A bridge spanned a river where estuary ferries glided and disgorged revellers.

"Don't worry about last night," Delia said. "I guess you don't like Lauren. Mind you," she added when I started a denial, "she frightens me too. Such intensity! She's devoted to Henry Semper. Must be very upsetting for her."

"Upsetting?"

"He's terribly ill. Didn't you hear?"

I watched a small boat disembarking passengers, families out for a day's revelling. Seaside holidays are among the best. Several arrivals set out with determination for the cafes. I saw a familiar figure, who looked up and made an economical gesture of recognition. I didn't wave back. He carried a camera and went towards a row of gaudy shops along one arm of the estuary. I'd go that way and see what he had to say this time.

Delia was looking at me. "Someone you know?"

"Eh? No. Coincidences don't happen to me."

"Come on. You can pick me out some amber. They say this place is good for amber."

"Don't you want to wait for Fern?"

"No. She's a shopaholic."

We started into the touristy shops. There was a range of amber, much of it moderate, with one or two good pieces. I had the feeling that most had been cleared out by wholesale merchants long before the holiday season.

"That's ambergris." I stayed her hand when she picked up a piece of greyish material. "Sperm whales produce it, to protect their intestines from hard bits of squid. It floats in the sea. It's a horrible black stuff and stinks. Then it mellows after a while, and looks ochre-grey, like that. It's used in perfumes. Charles the Second liked his eggs cooked with ambergris."

I dissuaded her from buying a small magnifying glass with an amber-coloured handle. It was only ambroid, those waste bits of amber pressed into shape. Block amber is real single pieces worth carving. I showed her how to look at amber in different lights, turning the piece as you go. You can see the planes where the fragments have been pressed together to make one large chunk. Dealers always pretend ambroid is genuine block amber because they can charge you five times more. Chemically it is genuine, but it's really only the sweepings from the floor after the amber-carver's gone home. Anybody can scoop up rubbish and press it. You only need a kettle.

"Don't be fooled. Daylight is your best friend when buying amber."

She squinted. "I can't see the different areas, Lovejoy."

"Look at the bubbles. If they're elongated, then most likely it has been made of spare bits. Old antique dealers say ambroid – the pressed amber – always looks 'frozen', but I never know what they mean."

"There are insects in this."

The thought of some poor insect struggling, looking at sixty million years of imprisonment until it gets a chance of hanging on some gentle lady's breast in a pendant … I winced.

"People fake amber. I mentioned copal varnish. They put pine pollen and insects in it. It's very convincing. The test is to touch the surface of copal with a dot of ether, and it will cloud. If it does, don't buy it. Glass lookalikes are heavier and sink in salt water. So does Bakelite."

Mr Moses Dulpoy was taking a photograph of the harbour up ahead. He wore a natty check suit with a straw boater, out for the day. He must have done another airport zoom to get here. An organised bloke.

"Tell me, Lovejoy. If you know so much about antiques, why are you broke?"

"I'm not!"

"I'm on the next table, remember. I overheard them laughing at your mistake about the meals that first dinner night. You looked like you'd suddenly lost your wallet." She was smiling. "I'm offering to help."

"I don't need help."

"Of course not," she said quickly. "What I mean is, you and I could come to an arrangement. You could teach me which antiques are genuine. Lauren and June Milestone are doing an antiques quiz after we sail tonight. There's a prize."

It was tempting. Delia was the only trustworthy person I'd met so far, someone who was neither policeman, crook, or a bent antiques dealer on the make. We stopped to watch children feeding ducks by the jetties. Amy and Les Renown were just boarding a small hired motorboat. They saw us and waved. We waved back. Les took the controls and moved the craft with expertise, very nautical. I just wished they weren't wherever I was.

"I want to learn, Lovejoy. I'm new at antiques. I'd pay."

"There are talks by experts. Go to those."

"I do." She glanced about. "You're on edge. What is it?"

"Nothing," I said innocently. "Why?"

She smiled. "You haven't arranged to meet some lady here, perhaps?"

"No. We've reached the end of the shops."

The last place was a small caff with wooden tables and benches set out on a verandah projecting above the edge of the riverbank. Hardly a soul, just a couple talking over some photographs and a babe in a pushchair slumbering with its feet in the air. Between the caff and the last shop was a narrow alley overgrown with weeds. It led down to the water where a small dinghy rocked. Beyond the balcony was a series of bushes. I could see a donkey staring at the water traffic on the river. Where had Mr Moses Duploy got to? The path petered out, from a firm metalled surface to a track, finally becoming a footpath onto a small peninsula. He'd vanished.

"Look," I said, suddenly nervous and wanting to find the little blighter. He'd made me an offer and I'd accepted. I could at least play along. "I think I'll maybe have a drink here for a minute. I'll see you back at the ship."

She looked blankly at me. "Shall I not come with you?"

"There's Fern," I said. "Don't miss her."

"Oh, right. See you later, perhaps."

We did that hesitation dance with which people

hope to avoid misunderstandings, then parted. I went onto the caff's verandah, certain that Moses would be lurking nearby, possibly down by the water. I ordered a coffee and paid as soon as it appeared so I could be off the moment he showed up. The couple were laughing at their holiday snaps. I saw two rowers heaving a skiff across the surface. A ferry glided beyond, raising a wake into a million glitters. Delia was walking back along the promenade. It was peace.

I saw figure moving by the dinghy. I could just make it out. A boatman maybe, or somebody trying to attract my attention? The couple were inside the cafe. I pretended I'd finished my scalding drink, and went down the alley among the weeds and tall grass, as if moving to the waterside to gape at the boats.

Moses was lying half in the water, bleeding onto the surface in great bursts of red. It floating with a curious sheen. I'd seen blood before but never quite such a colour. Blood goes brown once it's aged. They get it wrong in the movies, usually making it bright garish scarlet when that's only the hue of new blood. They use eosin. My mind snapped and went into a silent scream, *What the fuck am I saying?* He was bleeding, so it was a new injury. The side of his chest was heaving as if it was being punched then pulled, punched in and pulled out, by some invisible powerful hand.

And it stopped moving. Moses died. Just stopped everything and became still, except his lower half was in the water. Bloody froth gathered about his mouth. A trickle went down his chin, and he slipped further into the water. I backed away, turned and made my way back up the narrow alley.

On the path I looked at myself. No blood. Blood would have been all over me had I tried to pull the little bloke up out of the water. I was clean. No trace of anything incriminating. No sign that I'd tried to help the poor sod, nothing so honest or noble.

No, I'd simply turned and left him there dying, dead in the river. He might still be alive, waiting for me to lend him a hand, drag him up among the weeds and run for help.

But I've seen death before. I know it. There's no mistaking the moment when somebody's alive and with the rest of us on earth going about our business, and the next when it's all ended and there's no more of anything. I'd seen him.

I couldn't feel the ground. I noticed that as I started along the track back towards the bustle and activity of the harbour, following where Delia must have gone only moments before. It came to me, as I plodded on in a state of utter disorientation, that whoever had stabbed – had he been stabbed, coshed, or smashed somehow? – whoever had killed him must have been within a hand's reach. Perhaps the killer was there, hidden under the wooden pilings on which the projecting verandah stood? Or maybe he'd gone out on the dinghy. And now I couldn't even remember if the dinghy had still been there when I reached the water. Had I seen it leave, the killer moving upstream?

About then I began shaking, my knees and feet becoming uncontrollable. I found my teeth chattering – this on a warm sunny seaside day. I should have gone for help. They can do wonders these days, bring people back from... I mean restore people to life however dead they look, if you believe the newspapers. Except I'd come within a whisker of joining Moses Duploy. I'd no doubt. If I'd run screaming into the shops and raised the alarm, I'd have got one step and that would have been it.

The trouble was, I'd not even bothered. I could have pretended to walk back to the path, then ran and told the caff proprietor about some poor chap who looked like he might have fallen into the water. I might have said I couldn't quite see because I'd not got my glasses, could you please take a look. And then stood back while they called for the ambulance and police.

I'd not done that. I found myself sitting on a chair outside a small bar with a waiter asking me if I wanted anything. People were milling about and another boat was just moving away from the nearby jetty carrying a load of holidaymakers, music playing, people in and out of small stores. It was as pleasant a scene as you could wish to see. Further along, there was the bridge. I glimpsed Fern showing Delia what she'd bought, something in a coloured bag. Delia glanced my way, and just as quickly turned away. I'd offended her. I should have told her about Moses Duploy. She might have been with me when I'd seen him, and could have been a witness, proved my innocence. And allowed me to be safe while I helped the poor little geezer.

"A beer, please."

I sat and drank in the sunlight, safe and sound. Down the riverside path, I saw people start to gather when passengers on one of the yachts started to shout and point. Somebody a hundred yards back came running. A policeman on the bridge pedalled his bike, coming nearer, talking into a device on his shoulder, everybody getting out of his way.

He pedalled towards the caff where I'd sat during the last moments of Mr Moses Duploy. His scams had ended. It wasn't fair. I settled the bill, the waiter preoccupied by the disturbance. I heard a distant wah-wah, an ambulance coming. As casually as I could make myself move, my feet recovering their feeling, I walked slowly along the grass verge towards the bridge. I kept looking at my shoes, my trousers, and my cuffs for signs of blood. Not a one. Had I tried to help, I would have had at least a trace.

But I was pure and unsullied. Which is about as pathetic as you ever can be. I made the ship, half an hour's slow walk, stopping every now and then to go into a shop and examine their goods. I kept thinking. Had he fallen, perhaps cracked his head on the dinghy? But then why was his chest bubbling and stove in? And that red froth in his mouth? And was the dinghy still there when I reached him?

And I'd seen no sign of head injury. But had I looked?

I bought a tee-shirt with something on in German. Jolly, no doubt. Only when I was being sick in my cabin did I realise, as I wiped my mouth on the damned thing, that it had a picture of the harbour printed on it. I'd inadvertently bought a memento of my bravery where Mr Moses Duploy had died. It made me sick again. Like I say, pathetic.

Eventually I came out of it. For over an hour I sat on the bed staring at nothing. I had a shower, made sure I wasn't trembling. Then I went for a swim in the Crystal Pool in the sunshine. I thought of Amy the dancer and Les the comic. They would perform on stage with the troupe after dinner. I found a recorded phone message from Lady Vee saying to collect her for the show. She'd ended her message with a titter. "June sends her love!"

Aye, I told myself, we're all a load of inscrutable masks. I felt cold, and deliberately stayed wet after another shower in my cabin. I grew cold. The light began to fade outside, day drawing in. Time passed. I got colder. Still I stayed wet. My teeth began to chatter. I'd once had malaria, and knew it was quite like this. The image of Moses Duploy stayed with me and I shivered worse.

He was no angel, but who is? And was he any worse than, say, you or me? Time I stopped being a drogue and did something off my own bat.

I dried and dressed. The noise bonged for dinner. I went out calm and confident, saying hello to everybody, poisonously hearty to one and all.

Chapter Eighteen

"Poor Henry Semper," people were saying at the table.

Holly told me as we all took our places, "They fly sick people back."

"At least we'll be spared his *ghastly* shirts!" Kevin tittered, so witty.

"The ship's hospital can only do so much," Millicent remarked. "A lady once broke her ankle, line dancing…"

Ivy looked pale, but didn't she always? Billy her husband was telling jokes, "better than that comedian chap," he kept assuring us before each one. Jim Akehurst was explaining ring auctions in antiques – still illegal, the law unused these many decades, antique dealers still getting away with it. Kevin was having a fit of the vapours, Holly Sago trying to soothe him.

"Bad news, I heard," Millicent said. Ivy kept looking at me, God knows why. "Has Henry Semper a family, do you know?"

"You ill too, Kev?" I asked, changing the subject of bad news.

He recovered instantly and spat, "Kevin's the name, infidel."

"Kevin's had a mishap today." Holly held his hand. He looked about to burst into tears. "He bought the wrong eyeliner."

"And they haven't my brand in the shops here!"

"Does it matter?"

Kevin went white with rage.

"That's the sort of remark I'd expect from a buffoon like you, Lovejoy. First you make dear Henry sick as a parrot about his antiques, then you go ashore with that ghastly woman in bottle green, the one with the terrible legs."

Fern and Delia were seating themselves at the next table. They looked at each other and smiled, hearing Kevin's remark. I'm always surprised how women take people of Kevin's disposition, really tolerant.

"They're saying June Milestone's taking over all Henry Semper's talks and quizzes," Millicent said. Lauren was approaching. "It must be serious."

"Excuse me, please." Lauren stopped by us. "Lovejoy, could I have a word?"

That's what they always say on TV soaps, I thought, when they could just as easily say what they wanted without preamble. Back in the cabin, getting ready, I'd decided to be cool and direct. People were either good or bad.

"Yes." I waited.

"Lauren means in private," Kevin said roguishly. "Lovejoy's so *thick*, sweetie."

One day I'd clock Kev. I could see it coming.

"Go on, Miss Lauren." I didn't move.

She saw I wasn't going to budge. "Would you please do the dinner quiz with me? Mr Semper is unavailable, and Purser Mangot…"

"Certainly."

I was hungry, but easy come, easy go. I followed her to the entrance, people watching as we went. Lauren's colour was high. I was trying to be calm. I wondered if Henry Semper'd been ashore in the German port.

"This is what we do," Lauren said, stopping at the main doors where restaurant captains were welcoming late-comers. Lauren had her small table, stacks of cards, pencils and a tray on which stood a small Wedgwood style creamware jug.

She said quietly, interrupting herself to smile at couples entering, "You accompany me. I shall show the antique and give out the cards. Your task is to simply answer questions. Understood?"

Sharp rhetoric makes me fed up. It's always aimed at me. I swallowed and nodded. We set out, Lauren doing her spiel at each table. I was interested how people responded. One or two asked to see it, turned it over and said, impressed, "Wedgwood, see? There's a mark!" Some held it to the light. An occasional diner took out a loupe and tutted knowingly.

"The question is this," I said to the first table. "What's the give-away? Because it's a fake."

Lauren drew breath, quite a loud hiss. I beamed, ignored her, said it again. In the next hour I said this so often I began to get giddy, but it was plain hunger. Only when we'd nearly finished the entire restaurant did I realise I knew one of the ladies at Table 104.

"Can I pick it up?" Margaret Dainty looked up at me.

"Er, aye." When I'm flummoxed I stutter.

"Thank you." She inspected it. "It seems beautiful."

"Not new, lady, but a Sexton."

"Sexton Blake, Cockney rhyming slang, fake?"

"That's it, missus. Are you a dealer?"

She didn't crack a smile. "Hopeless in comparison," she said evenly. "Thank you for showing it to us."

She wrote a few words on her card, and blithely resumed the table conversation.

With Lauren I did the complete circuit, and went to stand by the exit while the nine hundred diners drifted out, dropping off answers.

"You chose a neat way of getting out of your moral dilemma," Lauren said quietly, smiling fixedly at everybody.

"Dilemma?"

"You think my antique Wedgwood is a forgery. You asked everyone to identify the forger's mistake. Against orders."

"Miss Lauren, I'm fed up with orders. From now on

I want details."

"Details of what?"

She looked so innocent I changed my mind. She wasn't in the know, just another dupe. Except she wasn't like me, who'd let someone die and not even bothered to raise a finger. I warmed to the lass, visualising her trying to hold Mr Moses Duploy free of the water as it lapped at his bubbling chest and flooded his glazed eyes...

"Sit down, Lovejoy," she said of a sudden, telling people, "He's not had his dinner yet, you see."

Somebody put me in the maitre d's chair between the banks of flowers. As I recovered, some passengers tried to coerce me into giving them the answer. They weren't above signalling the answer to friends who were still at the tables, to win the prize. I wouldn't be drawn, sat there all clammy. Women smile better than men. They almost always nearly sometimes manage to look possibly partly sincere.

Even Lauren was done for when the last of the diners had gone. We went to a staff restaurant on a different deck.

"Isn't it exhausting?" Lauren said.

We sat at a table near three of the ship's officers. I saw Mangot holding court at the far end. He didn't look. I didn't look at him either, so take that, fascist.

We sifted through the cards as we had our meal.

"There'll be one right," I told her. "Table 104."

Margaret's answer read: *Didn't Wedgwood's name lack the central letter E?*

We hadn't got the creamware piece, still up there for the second sitting of the evening. Lauren looked at me.

"I saw her write something," I said lamely. "Good for her."

"Does it?" She went a little pale. "Have I spelt it wrongly all this time?"

"Lots do, love. Even famous galleries. As did J. Smith & Co in 1848, of Stockton Potteries, who made your creamware piece. Nice old antique in the meaning of the word, but still a forgery."

We talked of the meaning of a forgery. I told her it was a problem, because Chinese two centuries agone made replicas of Chien Lung style porcelain, in homage to the old great potters. They didn't intend to fake as such, just to emulate and thereby confer honour on their ancestors.

"I suppose old Smithy in Stockton meant to do the same thing, and make a decent living at the same time. And Michelangelo faked older sculptors, with his *Sleeping Cupid*."

She was shocked. I told her Van Gogh had copied Corot, Delacroix, Gaugin, Rembrandt. And Rubens faked Caravaggio, Leonardo, Michelangelo, Rembrandt, Titian, and a couple of dozen others. I could have gone on.

"It was a business, like your Henry Semper. He can only tout words and a few opinions, none of them very good. Painters, artists, motor car makers, everybody simply makes something they can call brand new – while nicking ideas from everybody else. They put together what they hope will sell."

"It's so cynical," she said, distressed.

"I'm not knocking it, love. Just saying it's how the world is." To appease her, I asked after Henry Semper.

"He didn't even say goodbye," she said, eyes filling. I never know what to do when women cry. I wanted to leave. "Not even a note."

"He's gone?"

"Yes. The executive purser said he needed to go to a hospital. He should be there by now." She sniffed over her pudding. "You never got to know him like I did. He's such a splendid person. Everybody admires him."

Except me. He was a wart in creep's clothing.

"You'll have to help Mrs Milestone to cope."

A bit sudden, Henry's leaving like that. I tried to remember if Henry had been unwell before we docked last time, or whether he'd simply not come back from a trip ashore.

We did the second restaurant sitting with our tray, Lauren putting on a show of bright friendliness to one and all. Two more people got the give-away, answering that Wedgwood was spelled wrongly.

Lauren sent each winner a year's free subscriptions to *The Antiques Trade Gazette* and free tickets to all of England's antiques fairs. I wish I'd won, because they can be expensive if you've no gelt. I usually cadge my way in, except the Chelsea and Kensington Fairs are a sod for security. When I asked Lauren if I could try for the prize she said stop it, keep smiling at the passengers, don't give the ship a bad name. I said to her, "Me?"

*   *   *

"Your Secretum sold, Lovejoy."

For a moment I wondered what Margaret was saying. The word didn't make sense. Secretum? Then it came like from an ancient mist.

Several months before, I'd been really desperate. A lass, Anya, took me to the cleaners. She talked me into paying for a set of opaline chalices from Dandy Jack, a rival dealer. I was broke, so snowed paper IOUs for a day or two. I was sure I could make the money. Opaline is very beautiful stuff. Think of glass trying to become porcelain, and there you have it. The very best is mid-Victorian English, though pieces were made in France and passed off as London or Birmingham. The trick is to do a simple specific gravity test (the same old weight business on cotton threads). English pieces are almost all lead crystal, so very heavy, and virtually opaque or at best translucent. Decoration is usually floral, improbable blooms in yellows and browns. I love them. If uncracked, each one will net you a week's holiday.

The set Anya bought consisted of eight, plus a small opaline tray to carry four. I fell for Anya's passion for it, mainly because I'd fallen for Anya's passion. Together, nine pieces, complete. (Note: If one antique costs X zlotniks, then a complete pair will cost four to eight times X. It's not just twice the price of one. Sometimes, the price will go as high as 16 times the price of a single one, depending on rarity.) So I was confident. We celebrated by making smiles that night.

Anya wasn't there when I woke. The opaline chalices were gone. I've never heard of her since.

Which left me paying off the IOUs with a terrible headache caused by Wilco, Big John Sheehan's assistant, who kicked me silly when I said I'd no means to pay until I could run some antiques across Gimbert's auction on East Hill. Big John is one of those quiet smiling Ulstermen you don't cross in case they stop smiling. He ordered me knocked around. I was allowed one day to come up with the gelt, and went to Margaret Dainty to lend me space in her flat while I worked a scam up.

It was the Secretum, and how secret is that for heaven's sake?

There's only one Secretum, and it's multo famous. It is the erotic museum of mid-Victorian Dr Witt, Mayor of Bedford. Well, dear George Witt became a rich banker – some doctors have a sideline – and developed a healthy, maybe not-so-healthy – interest in the occult erotic. He amassed antiques, all to do with erotic pastimes of the Ancient World. So, the God Pan's erotic doings, sordid bestial frolics in porcelain, mosaic, wax paintings, and sculpture, he collected avidly. Then in 1857 Parliament poured cold water on the private glees of Dr Witt, by passing a stern corrective called the Obscene Publications Act.

The government's notion was simple: erotic art is important, yeah verily, but seeing most working classes were just learning to understand culture it was vital to protect them from sordid sexual fetishes. Only the affluent educated should be exposed to such dark passions. Dr Witt thought his duty clearly lay in donating his collection to the British Museum, a very proper going concern established long before in 1753.

They called it the Secretum, and stuck it in a sort of closet thing called Suite Fifty-Five. It's kept under lock and key to keep shifty-eyed gloaters out. You have to beg on an official form to reach it. Only a couple of dozen (mostly females, incidentally) crave to ogle it every calendar year, and though a few books have been written about erotic arts as seen in the Secretum, it was simply asking to be forged up. In a frantic afternoon of phoning round and offering money as wildly as if I actually had some, I managed to acquire thirty erotic items. After my pasting from Wilco, I was in no fit state to forge letters from Dr Witt, so I had to resort to Geordie – mercifully sober and for once not in some religious crusade (he sings hymns to trees) – I managed to make my phoney collection look authentic. I got Bernice from Coggeshall to mock up some earthenware phalluses, and used some rusted mattress springs to devise a chastity belt. Phosphoric acid's the stuff for making the fastest rust, and I had two chastity belts (nails from Wickes Builders Merchants on the by-pass, locks from an old Utility cupboard vintage 1940, holes by Black and Decker power drill) mocked up in less than two hours.

Pottery is easy, because Parsonage sells those near

Southwold, and he brought two down, lately done. I coloured them in acrylic, and while Margaret went out for some nosh microwaved them after chipping the edges to give them age. (Don't heat them on High setting, or they crack asunder.) I knew a lady who owns a trout farm beyond Arlesford who'd bought from me a replica homoerotic scene – only in a job lot from holidaymakers just back from Corfu, where they're on sale everywhere. I bought those back for an unmentionable promise. I had phalluses of various kinds, with two dozen small tokens – flat coin-like coppers and bronzes made in Hong Kong in the 1970s, penny a ton and worthless now. Yet if mounted on red velveteen cards and labelled with various legends in gibberish they look convincing. ("The artistic links with the reign of Yang Sher Peng, 1311-1517, will be apparent to those familiar with the poems of Tsu Shing" and the like, all made up.)

In spite of aches and my splitting head, I did three swift paintings in wax using egg yolk and a sort of mad gouache I make up myself on occasions requiring speed. I use Gum Arabica. They depicted matrons being ravished by men or other formless beasts. One was so good it nearly broke my heart having to age it up by fragging the edges of the board. I had no cypress wood, so used pine from Margaret's wardrobe; lucky she was out. I sawed it into small pieces and submerged it in hot water for an hour then heated the little panels in a dry oven before giving them a coat of rabbit-skin size – all dealers have it – and chalk. It stank the place out. Margaret played hell when she came home, but what can you do? Women lack priorities and lose a sense of what's important. I've always found that.

Later than day I fixed up an appointment with two buyers from Apaloosa. (Where's Apaloosa? Margaret said in the USA. I think the Yanks make these names up.) I cut out after leaving Margaret to do the deal, and scarpered. It was that night that I was made to do the robbery at Gotham with Belle. And the rest, as they say, is...

"It sold? The Secretum?"

"It sold, Lovejoy. And you didn't come back for the money."

She looked lovely sitting there, telling me this. And the more I thought of what she was telling me, the lovelier she looked. I think women have a really sound sense of what's important.

"Sold? Did – ?"

"I got the money to Wilco. It was more than enough."

Odd how relief makes you shaky but it does so I shook for a bit. Margaret watched and finally said, "You hadn't heard?"

"If I'd heard I wouldn't be so scared, would I?" Women always miss the obvious.

"Belle went missing."

"Eh?" No wonder I couldn't reach her. "What for? Where to?"

"Nobody knows. I spoke to her, her, ah, gentleman friend."

The man she was crackpot about. Margaret shrugged. "He was worried. He went to the police. They passed it off, said she was a grown woman and told him not to worry, seeing he isn't her husband."

"That'll be old George."

He's our village policeman, a real dead-leg. He couldn't catch a cold. He's got bad feet. The village lads painted his police car pink one night for a laugh. His list of suspects named forty-nine people, all wrong.

"Is she okay?" I meant safe. Margaret said she wasn't sure, somebody said they'd seen her in Sheffield. With every question, each reply, she judged me for honesty. I could tell.

"Which raises the question what are you doing here, Lovejoy?"

I told her almost virtually nearly practically everything, sincerely and in truth. Almost. I tried hard to reveal all, but it goes against the grain. We made smiles that evening instead of going to the show. I was glad. I didn't phone apologies to Lady Vee. I ought to have reported and shoved her about, so presume the mighty Inga did it, with her usual grace.

Lady Vee said nothing about my absence when I turned up and took her to the antiques talk next morning.

Margaret also attended, in a wheelchair pushed by a stewardess. She didn't even glance my way. Women can be really cunning. I was a bit put out, and thought she might have just given me a faint nod or some token of recognition. Instead she talked to some nerk next to her. I heard her laugh. I sometimes think women don't have feelings like us. They can be hard as nails. June Milestone gave the lecture, on how to select household antique silver for investment. It should have been Henry Semper, who was down to do the talk on "Porcelain Collectibles".

June knows I hate people who buy antiques "for investment". You don't court a lovely woman "for investment". Or go to see a wonderful film "for investment". So why must you buy beauteous antiques for the sake of loot? People who do that deserve to make mistakes. I wished, though, that she'd mentioned how to spot altered silver. She showed a photo of a lovely Hester Bateman silver tray with a gadrooned edge. It should cost the price of a new car, but wouldn't ever reach that price because it had been altered.

Good silver – and it's a rare piece that's better than Hester Bateman's stuff – shouldn't be altered. Like, a tray will usually have an armorial, meaning some sort of crest or coat-of-arms engraved in its centre. Because retainers sometimes were given items as farewell presents – or, worse, because they often nicked them – they tend to come to auction with the central area slightly ground down lower than the rest of the tray's surface. Dealers call it "dishing". You'll often see antique dealers examine silver by holding it up to the light, to see if the sheen reflected from the middle is different from its periphery. You can also tell by breathing on it and looking at the mist on the surface. It shows up rougher. You can even feel the slight depression where the armorial has been ground away by a wheel polisher. June didn't even mention these things.

Otherwise, I enjoyed the talk.

With Margaret aboard I felt I could face anything. I decided I liked cruising, and told Lady Vee I was glad to be aboard. She celebrated our new companionship by losing a fortune at poker, and at the one-arm bandits and blackjack.

Chapter Nineteen

When Delia Oakley met me by the Playhouse Theatre for the lesson I'd promised her, I was surprised she was alone. No ubiquitous Fern? Delia looked bright.

"Fern's having a heart-to-heart with a gentleman friend. Will I do?"

I shrugged. "Please yourself. This display's as good a start as any."

The ship's antiques experts had arranged exhibitions in glass cases about the ship. The wide corridor led past the theatre, the photograph gallery, then on past the Cafe Bordeaux. This one was of ladies' Edwardian and Victorian dresses in tableaux, and the next of miniature furniture.

"The dresses are genuine," I told her. "The furniture's reproduction."

"How do you know?"

"Er, I think I saw them earlier." I moved on quickly. "The little furniture's wrongly called apprentice pieces. They were made by real craftsmen for salesmen to take to grand households and retailers. A mere catalogue didn't do. Nowadays, antique dealers label them Doll Furnishings. It's a neglected field. Collectors have only lately woken up, and new forgers are moving in. Soon we'll be flooded with the damned things."

"And the dresses? Just look at the work!"

Genuine old things are honest company. I felt myself relax. Women also do this.

"You're looking at the most profitable area of collecting," I told her, feeling a smile come. "But troublesome. Storing dresses and uniforms is a problem – space, moths, mould, ventilation, decay, sunlight causing fading. They're a real slog."

"Profitable how?"

"You can get them virtually for nothing. A few

pence would buy all of these. Every village amateur drama society has scores of them, donated over the years. Every junk shop has stocks of handbags, purses, brooches, hatpins, jewellery."

"I'm going to become the greatest antiques dealer ever, Lovejoy! What else do I look for?"

"English watercolours after 1851, up to the 1920s. The date alone is a good enough criterion. You can honestly forget names and quality. Some dealers vacuum them up sight unseen."

She rummaged for a pencil. "Can I take notes?"

"And treen. That's wooden household implements, farmhouse devices, kitchen measures, anything wood. Look out for any locally carved."

Women write slower than men, but with a more rounded hand.

"Always feel in the pockets of old clothes for Edwardian jewellery, especially loopy designs that look too slender for the gems they carry. They might even include some of the early Australian coloured diamonds that are now so costly. In Victorian times the Aussies thought them a waste of time. Now, yellows and blues and even browns bring a fortune. They saw them as simply discoloured diamonds. As recently as 1950 they could hardly give them away."

"Anything else?"

"Modern small potteries," I said, grimacing, "if you accept modern. And ephemera. Those things I call mere trinketry, not antiques."

"You're going too fast."

"And kiddyana. That's dealers' slang for toys, mechanised or otherwise, dolls – I always think them gruesome – tin ships, early cars, miniature fairground carousels, lead soldiers. And automatons."

Her pen was flying. "Promise you won't tell Fern this, Lovejoy."

Now I really did smile. "You're starting to talk like a real antiques dealer. Don't go bad, though, Mrs Oakley."

"Bad?" She paused, head tilted, her gaze quizzical.

"Who can't recognise dealer fraud."

She led the way to seats placed at intervals for corridor chatting. I thought, here comes the cheap psychiatry.

"Fraud? Is it so big in antiques?"

"It's like barometric pressure, everywhere, unavoidable, and invisible."

"That's too cynical."

Who else had just said that? "Call it what you like."

We sat. I can't help wondering why women always seem distracted. I suppose it's me. I was lucky to be with her, because she was really smart and I'm a scruff.

"What is fraud, though?" She bristled, combative.

"What is truth? Answer: Whatever you can make the buyer believe. That's antiques in a nutshell, love. Magazine adverts brag about watches that are correct to within one second every million years – so ask the salesman why is there only a one-year guarantee? Is that fraud?"

"Don't get upset."

"I'm worried, not upset. Nobody knows any longer where honesty ends and fraud begins. None of us knows what to believe about anything or anybody, not even nice folk we meet on the *Melissa*."

"You *are* a cynic."

"Judge three things, then. I think all three are unbelievable. Last Michaelmas in Dublin, the home of an Irish collector was robbed of four paintings, including two by Rubens – *the fourth time his house was hit*. Okay?"

"Then he was careless," she said, spirited. "He should have – "

"Hang on. That's only the first. In the same week, a bank robber in Spain grabs a bag of money. He dashes out, stuffs his gun into his belt – and it goes off, wounds him. He drops the gun, runs into the road, and gets run over by a van. Bystanders drag him out, help him to a nearby car. It's actually his getaway vehicle, which then zooms off. He gets away, loot and all. Okay?"

"Why on earth did the people – ?"

"Hold it. Third problem? Some African nations are too poor to buy AIDS drugs. So a vast American pharmaceutical firm sends the medication to Africa, cheap. Good news? Not quite, because the drugs are being sold in Holland and Germany at an enormous mark-up, so the dying Africans can rot. Is any fraud sicker than that?"

"Why are you telling me all this?"

"Because of a Christmas card. It's your fourth problem." I gestured her to shut up, let me speak on. "Tell me what you'll do. Your first customer in your brand new shop is an old lady. Her husband's sick, and she's brought in a few treasured belongings. They're all rubbish, except for one perfectly preserved Christmas card, early Victorian. It's marked *Christmas, 1843*. Do you buy it?"

"I suppose so."

"How much for?"

"Well, an honest price, of course."

"Remember truth, that old thing? Do you give her enough for the fare home and a meal? Remember, her beloved husband of fifty years is sick at home, and it is midwinter, snow outside."

"Weather is hardly my fault, Lovejoy!"

"Ah, but this Christmas card is signed by Sir Henry Cole in 1843. It measures a little over five inches by three. It shows a happy family wassailing it up at

Christmas, with the words 'A Merry Christmas and a Happy New Year to You'. Nothing special, just a crude lithograph on stiffened cardboard. Incidentally, I think Victorian umber sepia looks ugly, don't you?"

"You're tricking me."

"Honestly not. I want to see how deep your honesty goes. This card, you see, is hand-coloured – you can always tell from the margins. How much do you give the old lady?"

"Well, I suppose a few – "

"No numbers, please. In terms of what she could buy with the money that an honest antique dealer like you would give for her old Christmas card." Delia had gone silent. "Would you give her enough to buy her sick husband food and heating the long cold winter through?"

"Hardly that," she said, indignant. "Perhaps – "

"No perhaps, no buts. How much, for the first-ever Christmas card, that twenty-six year old John Callcott Horsley designed and lithographed for his august friend Sir Henry Cole in the winter of 1843?"

She was close to a sulk and wanting to hit somebody. I got ready to sprint, being the only one within reach.

"He wasn't much of an artist, wasn't young John Horsley Callcott." I tried to ease her distress. "He hated having to paint nudes. His fellow students at the Royal Academy scoffed at his prudery and called him J. *Clothes* Horsley. He didn't quite drop out, but the poor chap didn't really become famous for anything except inventing the Christmas card."

Embarrassed at the silence, I said, "Sorry, love. My mind's a ragbag. Like, the moonstone is Florida's official state gem. What on earth's the use of facts like that?" Even my laugh was unconvincing. "Antiques are never easy. One J.C. Horsley Christmas card would buy you a thoroughbred racehorse, plus a complete world cruise. There's said to be only twelve Horsley cards still extant. The problem in antiques is always the same: what is a fair price? Like, if the card was brought in by a millionaire Sloane Ranger, would you offer her the same price as you would offer the sad old lady I described?"

"You needn't go on, Lovejoy."

"Truth can break your heart. It does mine."

I was full of pity, mainly for myself of course. I stood.

"Can't waste time chatting to bonny women," I told her with false bonhomie. "I've got to shove Lady Vee to the Trivia Quiz in that lounge. Bye."

"Bye, Lovejoy."

Talking to people sometimes does damage. I'd probably ruined a promising career and an enterprising business there, with any luck.

* * *

Instead, I went through to the Conservatory. The familiar scatter of passengers was snacking away, a catering officer walking about supervising the buffet counters. I'd noticed the smart uniformed lass knocking about.

"Excuse me, please." I soothed her instant anxiety by, "No complaints, just a question."

She looked relieved, and was willing to explain the refrigeration facilities in the galleys – kitchens, for us landlubbers – deep down in the ship. She didn't say, and I was reluctant to ask, if the freezers were on Deck Three, very low in a structure with fourteen decks to its massive hull. I said how enthralled I was, having been in catering myself, or so I lied with a glibness that surprised even me.

When I casually mentioned the volumes needed for cold storage, she was delighted I was amazed by the ship's capacity. I heard her out without interruption, told her ta and left the place really glad to have pleased her by giving her the chance to boast about *Melissa*, especially to a passenger with such an enquiring mind.

You could store things that needed to be kept very, very cold down there.

Chapter Twenty

"Lose another hour?" I was indignant. Those rotten cards had come again. Every blinking time we had to put the clocks forward an hour during the night.

"We'll get it back when we sail home, Lovejoy. Don't be such a child!"

That stopped me. Outside, the wharf announced GDYNIA. Poland, I guessed.

My throat went thick. Next stop after Poland would be Russia and the Hermitage Museum. That building loomed vast and brooding in my mind, and I'd never even seen it.

"We can go ashore, Lovejoy!" Margaret had dressed. I emerged from the shower, monster from the Black Lagoon, towelling. I'm always embarrassed because a naked woman's lovely but a bare bloke looks like a bushel of spuds. "I've heard it's a charming city."

"Not together." I still hoped my watchers thought Margaret and I were strangers. They mustn't know she was my ally. I would soon need her even more.

She was at the mirror doing her make-up. I love seeing women do it, but can't help wondering why it doesn't hurt. She did that gruesome thing with curved tongs to curl her eyelashes. It makes me cringe. My knees itch while I watch yet I can't look away. She'd restored her hair from the night. It was five-thirty, the ship hardly awake. On the harbourside, stalls were being established, silver, amber, woollens, some textiles and trinkets and little dolls, put out by girls in Polish national costume getting ready to welcome visitors. I liked the lace many wore, so much bulkier than Coggeshall lace back in East Anglia. My heart cramped with homesickness.

I'd told her how I came to be on board, Gloria, Benjo, wanting to escape. She said she'd seen me wheeling Lady Vee.

"I think they're setting up some robbery. It'll be the famous exhibition, Impressionists and the Old Masters. It's advertised everywhere."

"And you'll divvy them?"

"I suppose so. I'll be a visitor."

"Then what?" She wouldn't look away, pressing for an answer. "Stealing a whole exhibition, Lovejoy? Even you have never done that before."

I stood at her window watching the little market on the wharf. The vans and cars looked pretty grotty, like it was lucky they'd managed to start this morning, but how else can a vehicle look? It can't put on airs.

During the night, here in Margaret's cabin, safe from being bugged, my mind had gone into free fall. I'd thought all sorts of dross. Like, Romania – so said the International Cartoonists on the BBC – is the only country in the world ever to arrest a cartoon (not a cartoonist, note; they'd arrested the actual drawing). It had committed the offence of depicting some mayor as a swine. Another: a football team in Dar-es-Salaam in Tanzania had been accused of witchcraft. They'd hired a Ju-Ju man to sprinkle magic powder in the goal-mouth, so rendering the team's goal invisible. (The proof? Simla kept winning.) True crazy tales.

Plain simple factual news, not fiction, is the real horror. Like, a 13-year-old kid kills a pizza delivery man stone dead – wasn't it in staid New Zealand? – and all the kids in the neighbourhood queue admiringly for the killer's autograph. And collectors of antique erotica bid dementedly whenever the most popular erotic antique turns up. It's an oddly shaped carving that ladies in past ages called St Cosmo's Toe. This phallic plaything was fashioned for maidens, who recited a special prayer as they dwelled, so to speak, on its possible uses.

And a frightened dapper little man in a straw boater, dogging the progress of an enormous luxury cruise ship along the Baltic Sea, gets slain down by the water's edge and floats among plastic bottles, orange peel and other flotsam, because he hoped to pick up crumbs from a scam he'd heard about.

To focus, I did a pencil sketch of Margaret seated against her mirror. I'd painted her portrait a year since, Gainsborough style. I intended to keep the sketch, take it back to my cabin and maybe frame it.

"They say Warsaw has a World Gang-Bang Championship." I felt so grateful to Margaret, coming all this way to help save me. "In public on TV. Last year a Polish girl called Klaudia won it, made love to 646 men."

"Your mind's like a ragbag, Lovejoy. Can't you remember useful things?" She knew not to move when I sketched because it changes the light, which is death to a portrait.

"Each man's allowed one minute. It's not much, is it? A Brazilian girl called Magda came second."

"Thinking of going?" she asked drily, still as a hunting heron.

"The previous world record was only 251." The sketch finished, I rolled it up and stuck the edge down. It made me start to think. There was something horribly wrong about my table companions, the planned robbery, even Margaret's arrival.

"Come back, Lovejoy."

"Help me, Margaret." Once pathetic, always. She looked stricken. I'm never this frank. "They're going to top me."

She pulled my head to her as I sat on the edge of the bed.

"I've never seen you like this, Lovejoy. Tell me everything you know. How long before we reach St

Petersburg?"

"The day after tomorrow. Maybe they'll let me off here today. Will you get me home, please?"

With Moses dead, I might be able to make the airport, if Gdynia had one. Or a train. Or just some cheap bed-and-breakfast where I could hide until the ship sailed, then make a run for it.

The day began with a casual summons from Amy the dancer, and her comic pal Les Renown.

* * *

They were doing a racing game in one of the lounges, dice and cardboard horses on squares. It was quite hot weather on the Promenade Deck. People had come into the cool, settling about bars and lounges to be entertained.

Shows of all kinds began about ten o'clock, with demonstrations, talks, films in the cinema, dance lessons, fitness club, chats over coffee with the ship's officers, lectures about the next port of call from experts eager to tell you where to shop. You could tour the ship's engines, or listen to chefs talking about favourite recipes, or visit the galleys. The contract bridge club thronged, dancing lessons began, it was all happening on the *Melissa*.

Lady Vee collared me. She told me Amy and Les Renown were looking for me. I pushed her to the nearest casino, and found them in the Horizon lounge talking to passengers. I waited and they drifted my way.

"Morning, Lovejoy."

"Morning."

They looked so smart, pleasant. I could see why people admired the golden couple. Amy looked about. Nobody within earshot, so she leant closer.

"You're badly indebted, Lovejoy. A warning."

"Eh?" I fumbled for my plastic card. Les put out a hand and stopped me.

Amy grimaced. "You've spent a fortune in the casinos. It's totting up, Lovejoy. As long as you can pay it off."

I was stricken. "I thought it was all free."

"Everything on board is, Lovejoy." They greeted somebody coming in with an officer and returned their attention to me. "Except shops and gambling."

"I don't gamble. And I've bought nothing."

"The casino manageress says otherwise." Amy's expression would madden a saint. I stayed cool. Good Queen Bess once said anger makes you witty but keeps you poor. She was always right about everything, except who she slept with in Islington. I gulped and nodded.

"I'll watch it, then. Ta for telling me."

They looked at each other, hesitating as if they expected more of a panic, then went on circulating, Amy being charming and Les cracking jokes. I sat watching Gdynia though the panorama windows.

They wanted me to protest, run scared at their threatening news, and I hadn't done anything of the kind. I heard Les start his patter, people near the bar already chuckling. "There's this actor, see…" I didn't look round. I knew Amy would be staring at me, wondering why I hadn't gone berserk at their falsehood.

You *can't* be overdrawn on a cruise ship. Your Cruise Club plastic is for boozing, for trips ashore, garments you might buy, gambling you might get up to. All else is free – meals, the shows, cinemas, lectures, snacks. So I was being needled, provoked into fright. I was being made to jump, take off, use every desperate means to escape. And I didn't know why.

Except…

No Yanks or Dutch slaving over the hot stoves in the galleys, so my coffee was undrinkable.

In antiques, you learn to think *except*. Like, you might see a Victorian card table, say 1842. It looks fine – walnut, very ornate carving, sturdy, lovely job, make any dealer's mouth water. And the vendor says, with tears in his eyes, "I'm short of cash, something urgent's come up." And offers it to you, this lovely rarity. Before you reach for your cheque book, say, "Great, sure, yes – *except*…" Then inwardly ask yourself "Except for what?" And it's only then that something odd hits you. That lovely walnut surface looks just a fraction smaller than it should be, a little out of proportion. You realise the dealer had bought it with straight edges, a plain rectangular top. It's still a genuine antique, but he couldn't resist getting a carpenter to make the table's edges wavy. Presto! He's converted it into a serpentine-topped card table – worth four times the value of the plainer straight-edged sort. And you're the mug he wants to pay four times more than he deserves? No, ta.

So from habit I thought *except for*…?

And it dawned on me. I must be thick as a brick not to have seen it before.

Since we sailed, I had had maybe a score of chances to escape – Oslo and Amsterdam especially. And on board I'd tried phones, facsimiles, e-mail, everything except a message in a bottle lobbed into the briny. I'd seduced as best I could, trying to gain allies. I had done a deal with poor Mr Moses Duploy, chiseller and crook. I'd contacted dealers ashore. In fact done everything I could. Used them all up, played every card in my hand.

In fact, it had been so easy I had crowed with delight at my cleverness. Stupid. And still I was trapped, no nearer escape. I'd been had. It came to me in a wash of relief. They – never mind for the minute who – had let me go ashore, then hauled me back aboard like anglers reeling in a silly gudgeon.

They knew I'd become increasingly desperate, and that by the time the *Melissa* berthed in St Petersburg I would have used up all my feeble escape notions. No wonder they were confident. And now they were putting on the screws, telling me I was in some fearsome debt. It was one more jab of their goad.

Suddenly, though, they were unsure why I was docile and obedient. It was Margaret's presence on board. I knew that, but they didn't. It wasn't much, but I felt one up. They were rattling my cage.

I asked a stewardess for today's entertainments list. Thirty-seven events, with WELCOME TO GDYNIA across the top. I smiled a good morning to some passengers I didn't know and went to find Lady Vee. As soon as the ship left Poland, I'd take her gambling again, and hope she lost a lot more. She was still in bed, her stewardess Marie told me when I knocked on Suite 1133.

Making a last-minute booking, I happened to meet Delia Oakley and Fern at the Deck Four gangway, and had the luck to spot Millicent and Ivy joining a coach party touring the city centre. I went too. The Ghurkas on the gangways didn't turn a hair, checked me through unquestioned. Ivy was silent as ever, Millicent talking enough for us all.

Gdynia was really pleasant, completely restored after terrible historical events. The Poles are a fine lot, affable to a fault, full of music and colour. We all enjoyed it. I even began to think, roll on St Petersburg. I spent a few zlotniks on a silver pencil I knew I'd lose the minute I put it down because I always do. We heard street musicians, and I argued with the women about varieties of lace. We watched locals making bobbin lace.

Lots of people moved about among tangled alleys where a felon could escape, if he had been so inclined. I made a couple of sallies, but turned up among the main gaggle of passengers within moments, just to nark whoever was watching. It made me happier. Our courier was an entertainments girl from the ship. I recognised her. A dazzlingly blonde Polish girl carried a small flag on a stick, our guide. We had to follow it so as not to get ourselves lost. It had almost happened in Oslo to two old duffers who'd forgotten the time.

Impeccably obedient, I kept reminding people of the time and making sure we all knew the way back to the coach. Didn't want anybody to go missing, you see. I wouldn't want that, would I? I was a right poisonous ray of sunshine. Margaret was on a different coach. I happened to glimpse her, talking away to passengers who'd spent heavily in some jewellery shops. I saw her speaking to James Mangot, but didn't worry.

Start as you mean to go on, I always say. I was one big hello. On the way back to the ship, I dozed contentedly. I remembered another of Queen Elizabeth the First's remarks. She likened some people – courtiers she mistrusted – to "Strawberry wives, that laid two or three large strawberries at the mouth of their pot, and all the rest were little ones." It made my smile broader still. Shrewd lass, Bess One.

Back on board, I hurried to find Lady Vee and wheeled her down to nosh. I chatted of the lovely city, explained how everybody else got Polish lace designs wrong except me. She could hardly get a word in edgeways. I insisted on shoving her to the casino, and complained when I found the casinos closed.

"They only open when the ship sails, Lovejoy," Lady Vee said. "I keep telling you."

"Just when I'm enjoying myself," I groused.

"Are you all right?" she asked me several times.

"You're different."

"Got my sea legs. Where next?"

"What on earth's got into you?"

We went to watch Latin-American dancing. I even had a dance, with Ivy, who kept going quiet. The floor was admittedly a bit crowded. I was beginning to see how folk liked cruising. If you were going to survive, that is. I pushed Lady Vee to her tea and didn't bring the wrong cakes or sandwiches. She too was quieter than usual, and kept eyeing me. I was obnoxiously talkative, recounting anecdotes from the jaunt ashore. Most of my stories about Gdynia were invented, but one or two brought a feeble smile to her face. I told her to cheer up, this cruise couldn't last for ever. She asked me if I'd had a word with Amy and Les Renown. I said yes, just a little moan about money, and said what a nice couple they were.

"Think they'll get married?" I asked innocently. "They're well-suited, don't you think?"

I was repellently cheery, and determined to keep it up.

※ ※ ※

The last hour before we sailed, I went down to the wharf where the folksy Polish market had been set up. Few antiques, but attractive silver, new porcelain, old amber. I particularly like the gedanite amber, even though it had only been named in 1878. Odd how the Baltic states still love the whitish amber. The Chinese like their native red, red symbolising money. English dealers, as I, love the gold colour. Sad, though, to see only newly carved pieces. Strange how my mind kept telling me the same things about amber. This was the Amber Sea, right?

"Beg pardon?" Ivy said. She was standing nearby.

"Sorry. Talking to myself." I'd have to stop that, the

plight I was in.

There were only a few passengers about now the daylight was dying and the stall holders starting to pack up. Ghurkas were putting out the sign saying *Melissa* was to sail in thirty minutes. They had a blackboard clock.

"Are you looking for anything in particular, Lovejoy? A present?"

"I'd like to see a set of amber candlesticks, inset with ivory, carved in 1695," I said. "They did these in Danzig. And facetted amber bead necklaces for Russian courtesans. And North German amber carvings, minutely detailed, of the Crucifixion or the Judgement of Paris. You'll never see more skilled carvings, except maybe those limewood tableaux, centuries old. Brilliant."

I drifted along the line of stalls. I thought I was quite content, but Ivy smiled a proper smile and said I sounded wistful.

"Once you've seen the genuine things, all else is sham. Including people."

She seemed so sad I asked what was up. "You're the only one who isn't," she astonished me by saying.

"Eh?" I'd never been called genuine before. "Sorry, love. Back home I'm the typical phoney."

"Not at our table."

To brighten her mood I showed her what to look for in amber, the faint flecks of gold leaf some fakers put in to make the copal fakes look priceless.

"Amber's a beautiful material."

Ivy bent over a stall to peer at a small brooch in silver, grapes against vine leaves. Two Polish girls were busy wrapping their trays up and stowing them into their dad's van.

And she whispered quietly, "Lovejoy, can I see you?"

"Eh?"

"Somewhere. Anywhere. Billy will be gambling tonight. I'll slip out of the casino."

"Eh?" I'm slow most of the time, and I'd no idea what she wanted to see me for. I mean, we were here talking now, yet she was peering over trays of brooches and rings. She intended secrecy.

"Please," she said.

I was so confused I bought her the stupid grape brooch – actually it wasn't all that bad – not even haggling about the price. She accepted it with that non-smile, and went towards the gangway. I drifted on, taking my last look at Poland before returning to the ship alone.

Passengers emerged onto the decks as we cast off, waving at the market people. Down at the quayside I noticed a woman in a fawn overcoat limp to a smart limousine waiting by the harbourmaster's building. Limp? She looked familiar. I almost called out her name, and stifled the impulse. She smiled, said something to the driver inside. I couldn't see him for windscreen reflection.

The door opened and she got in. A ship steward loaded three leather suitcases into the boot. The car pulled away. She didn't even give the ship a last glance. I'd been so grateful to her. Like a fool, I'd assumed she'd come to help rescue me. As they say on TV, reasons apparent but unforgivable.

If I'd had half the sense I was born with, I'd have stowed away in one of the market vans and gone into orbit. When I got back to my cabin Margaret's sketch was gone. I'd rolled it up and hidden it behind the top drawer. In its place was a piece of ship's notepaper.

"Dear Lovejoy,
    Mr Mangot has told me all about your real rea-

sons for being on this cruise, and the three women with whom you are in partnership. You are despicable. Please do not contact me again.

   M. Dainty (Mrs)."

She'd listened to the gaolers, not the prisoner. I was now seriously alone, and leaving Gdynia bound for St Petersburg.

Chapter Twenty-One

That evening, now even more determined to be obnoxious, I radiated good humour, cheerily greeting everybody until Lady Vee snapped at me to stop it for God's sake. Beaming fondly, I told passengers she hadn't been herself all day but what can you do? Some said I was a saint, which is true but isn't often detected by others. I was heartbroken over Margaret's defection.

Lauren called for me to do the endless antiques quiz round the dinner tables. The antique was a French bisque doll, for once genuine. Only 1878, but so highly sought nowadays that one will buy you a little flat in Harlem. I don't like them (dolls, not Harlem flats). Bisque is sort of raw unglazed porcelain. Usually, the expensive dolls have closed red lips, fixed blue eyes and a cork scalp onto which a little wig is stuck, usually blonde mohair. The clothes are often sumptuous, on a kid leather body. They make me feel queasy, even though you can admire the tiny stitching of the separate fingers. It's real craftsmanship. Lauren was relieved and pleased when I told a lady yes, the doll's stockings were real silk and the dress hand-embroidered. Gaultier wasn't the first of these French makers, though the best. He started trading about 1866, I mentally told the absent Margaret Dainty in silent defiance. See? I *could* remember useful details, M. Dainty (Mrs), so there.

Lauren closed on me and whispered, "Smile, Lovejoy. You've started frowning." Obedient, I grinned like an ape. We had a quick nosh and did the second sitting. God, it seemed interminable.

"How come you fetched a genuine one?" I had the sense to ask Lauren.

"What do you mean?" she snapped.

"You never have before."

Head bowed, she finished sorting the stack of answers and picked out the one coming nearest the price I'd decided.

"Because it's mine, Lovejoy."

"Your antique doll? Then you're rich, love." She looked stricken so I tried made a joke of it. "Lend us a fiver, eh?"

"You don't understand. I fetched her with me on the voyage, for company. My grandma's christening present. It's the only antique I didn't take from Henry's stock."

That sobered me. We said so-long to the restaurant folk and told the purser girls in Reception who'd won. It was some lady in a private suite. To them that hath, and all that. The winner's cabin number would be flashed on the ship's TV.

"You were testing me? What a nerve."

"Not really." We sat in the Atrium. The bars were thronged, as ever when the ship sailed, and dancers were trotting the light whatever. "I was just sick of the deception."

"Me too," I said glumly. "Sorry about Henry, incidentally. I won't grumble any more."

"Thank you." She hesitated. "Lovejoy? Are you and… and anybody, well, together?"

What now? "Me? No. I just came on the cruise to help Lady Vee." Lie, when all else fails.

"Then…" She couldn't finish, just dithered, sitting there with her beautiful spooky doll in its basket. "Perhaps, may I invite you for a drink, perhaps, one evening? If you're not too busy, perhaps."

So many perhaps. "Ta." I waited for her to explain what she wanted to see me for, then gave up. "I'd better find Lady Vee."

"Yes, of course."

"See you, Lauren. Ta for, er, perhaps…?"

"Perhaps tomorrow?" she said.

We separated, me thinking folk are definitely odd and Lauren probably thinking the same. People never say what they mean. I think they should be open and honest, like me.

In a lifetime of close scrutiny, I've only learned one thing about women: don't ever buy them anything clockwork, electrical, or a pet, because within 48 hours it will fail and be the cause of endless requests to fix it, take it back, or rid it of worms or the dhobie itch. Like a duckegg, I shelved Lauren's offer.

Lady Vee and June Milestone were talking in the Raffles Bar. I put a stop to all that, gave June a beam of utmost sincerity and whisked Lady Vee off to the Monte Carlo Club, the biggest and most dedicated of the ship's casinos.

"You know you're desperate to lose even more, you daft old bat," I lectured her, making passing passengers smile. "Never change the habit of a lifetime."

"I don't want to gamble tonight, Lovejoy!" she was giving it, but I drew out a fortune on my plastic, and told her to get going.

She was into it instantly with hardly a glance. That's the trouble with gamblers; their addiction ousts all others. I watched her slam into roulette. She lost steadily, hunched forward in her wheelchair and staring across at Victor Lustig, Billy the Kid – his Ivy standing behind him, without a glance my way; she must have forgotten – and sundry others. Jim and Millicent Akehurst were playing the slot machines, calling out to each other how they were doing.

"If they only had better decor, luvvie!" I heard Kevin say loudly, making a glittering entrance with Holly in tow. He had tinsel on his eyelashes so his face sparkled when he blinked, and each fingernail was differently coloured.

"The casinos are quite tasteful, dárling," Holly was giving back.

"Which," Kevin shrilled over the din, "is a perfect *hoot* from someone who thinks sap green is a *perfect* co-ordinate for magenta and opal!"

Billy the Kid grinned and beckoned the odd couple. Kevin glided past us, head in the air. I often wonder if it's just an act. Do they need to perform constantly? I mean, do they act even to a mirror? Attention is their addiction. Kevin changed his mind and swept out with, "I can't stand mandarin orange against chrome!" or some such. Once departed, there wasn't even a fragment of him anywhere in the memory. Was that simply his trick, though, to make himself forgettable? Holly remained.

"Money, Lovejoy."

More, and so soon? I drew more money from the cashier behind her grille. The croupier exchanged it for coloured discs. I dropped two together on a square, and to my surprise won. Money actually coming in, from a bet? I dropped another two on a different square, and it came up. Lady Vee grew really excited.

She made me choose a third, which lost, then a fourth which won an even bigger stack of coloured discs. I was bored sick. Lady Vee was delirious with excitement.

"Keep on, Lovejoy!" she shrilled when I turned to go. I noticed Ivy had left. Time for me to join her outside in secret. I suppose I was in for another ballocking, God knows what about.

"No, love. Give us a shout when you're done. I'll be in the bar."

"You can't stop now! You're on a roll!" Several people yelled the same thing, frantic.

"You have to gamble, Lovejoy!" Billy the Kid said

earnestly across the roulette table. "You've discovered you're lucky!"

"Billy, I'd sooner watch fog." I looked round at them. They'd gone quiet, like I'd ridiculed patriotism, motherhood and the Holy Grail. "Just look at the lot of you madmen. You put a coin in a slot and you either win or you don't. Big deal. Or you put a token on a card and either win or you don't... See what I mean? It's stupid. I just don't get it."

Apart from the racket of the lines of one-arm bandits, the place was silent.

"He's mental," Billy told the others.

Holly spoke for them all, harsh and determined. "Everybody *must* gamble, Lovejoy! Look at Grudon." They all nodded, looking at me. I felt on trial.

"Grudon? What's that?"

"Grand National winner in 1901, Lovejoy." They looked so earnest, in prayer. Lady Vee even bowed her head in reverence.

"A horse is a horse is a horse, love."

"Grudon proves why everybody *has* to gamble." And spoke over their chorus of agreement. "Arthur Nightingall rode it in a terrible snowstorm. First of March. You know what he did? He smeared pounds of butter on Grudon's hooves, so the snow couldn't ball and weigh its legs down."

"And won?" I saw how deadly serious they all were. I got the odd feeling I was arguing against robbery in St Petersburg.

"By four lengths, Lovejoy. Don't you see?" Holly was in anguish at my blasphemy.

"No, love, I don't. You lunatics would bet Elvis is still alive."

"She already has!" Lady Vee said with admiration. "Thousand to one!"

"You silly cow." I honestly think gamblers are

insane. "Last month Elvis was seen directing traffic. And in a hurry-curry nosh caff in Palmers Green – he ordered chicken masala, with onion bhaji for starters. And at a Cumbria sheep-dog trial; his collie came second. All true sightings! Now." I stared round at them. "How many bets got paid off? None!"

"Nobody had a camera!" Lady Vee cried with anguish. "The proof is out there!"

"If Elvis came back nobody would believe him. Didn't he enter an Elvis lookalike competition in real life? And he *lost*!"

A few passengers were strolling and chatting on the Promenade Deck in the slight evening breeze, having a smoke. No sign of Ivy. Well, it couldn't have been important, just another telling off for something I'd done, nearly done, not done, ought to have done. My spirits quailed at being here without Margaret. I wondered about Amy. She might prove the safest. Then I remembered her eyes, so manic and hard with that electric prod thing...

"Lovejoy?" Ivy was at the rail. She shivered. "Can we go in? It's chilly."

"Okay." Women and chills. I thought it was really pleasant, the Baltic calm and the night warm. "Look, love," I started, as we strolled towards an entrance, "if I've been a bit offhand, it's just I've a lot on my mind, see?"

"I know, Lovejoy," she said. We walked like strangers, at arm's length so we wouldn't bump. "It must be hard."

"Hard?"

"For you. Being the only one not in the camarilla."

"What's a camarilla?" I already knew. Plotters everywhere, politicians included, have them. The Junkers had been one, and the Inquisition. They are the elites, cliques in control. They're always evil. The

Olympic Committee, the World Bank and the UN are full of camarillas. Q.E.D.

"People in the game." Bitterness is a woman's art, and all the more alarming. Did she mean gambling, or something worse?

We went into the bright lights. The Atrium combo was playing. The shops were still open and the library across the intervening balcony was on the go. The chocolate bar had a cluster laughing and comparing tastes. "Don't give me sympathy. I'm never in the know. It's just the way I am."

"It's not sympathy, Lovejoy."

Then what? I was more or less letting her lead the way. I'd assumed she would pause in some lounge, I'd procure her a drink and it would be back to the casino or maybe listening to a bar piano in the Horizon. Instead, she had us in a lift, then along a corridor I'd never been down. Canberra Deck?

"I get lost," I told her lamely. "We okay here?"

We said hello to an elderly couple emerging from their cabin, togged up for some late entertainment. She paused at a cabin door and did the plastic key. More spacious than mine, but then Billy the Kid was an affluent copper, with hard-earned money to burn. You can tell the grade of cabin from the space and the window sizes. Not as grand as Lady Vee's, but not a cupboard.

She stood by the window looking out. I felt a lemon, wondering what I'd been brought here for.

"I'm sorry, Lovejoy, for the plight you're in."

What did she know? I wasn't in any plight, as far as the rest of the world was concerned. I said so.

"It's safe to talk here," she said, head turned slightly like they do when they're all attention and supposedly looking elsewhere. "One of the few places on this ship."

Safe? Why weren't other places safe? I remembered Margaret and me making smiles, my sketch, and Margaret's departure, which made Ivy seem more important than a minute ago.

"Billy isn't often here. And I'm too much of a mouse to do anything rash like inviting a friend in. Don't you see?"

She was in tears. I never know what to do when a woman cries. Some blokes say it's a trick to make you agree, but to what?

"No."

"We're all in it, Lovejoy. I mean them, not me. I'm only the pathetic mask Billy brings along for appearance's sake. They're the backers."

She moved away from the window. I could see into the dark, a light flashing ever few seconds, probably some headland. I didn't really like watching the sea. Some passengers stared at it endlessly when there was nothing in sight, like a fascination.

I was surprised to find her walk into me, not bumping, just coming against me, her head almost under my chin.

We stood there like bookends with no books between. I felt daft, trying to find foothold behind me so I wouldn't stumble back.

"It's been so long."

I recognised quiet desperation, but what was I expected to do? We stood there, me slowly overbalancing because she'd pressed me back so there was nowhere to put my feet. I toppled slowly onto a chair. She took my hands and pulled me to my feet.

"Look," I said, more desperate than she could ever be. "If your bloke comes in..."

"Another beating, like from Les and Amy?" She did that bitter smile and suddenly sounded so tired. "I don't think so, Lovejoy. I've locked the door."

Sometimes I've made smiles in less ideal places, in less of a party mood, and at times which were definitely lacking in rejoicing. I'm not proud of the episode with Ivy, who seemed readier to mourn than frolic with a bloke like me who was no more than a shabby stranger.

One odd thing. When you think oh dear, this is a real mistake, a force takes over. Before you know it you're in heaven with paradisical choirs and waves on the seashore and you wonder how on earth you could be so wrong. I've heard it's different for women. I've no way of knowing, because with us making smiles is always bliss and ecstasy and mind-blowing wonderment.

Only later, rousing from that terrible semi-dying limbo in a tussle of limbs, did realisation come. How the hell did Ivy, meek quiet little Ivy, wife of the rumbustious Billy who'd bossed the Wirral's tough cops, know I'd been beaten senseless by the odious pair? I tried not to move, and stared at her. She was asleep. Women are all awake after making smiles, wanting a fag and talk about emotions. We want to slumber and slowly climb out of that sombre pit into wakefulness. She must have understood. My respect for her soared. Less than one in a hundred women know this. If one actually understands, makes allowances and gives you time, she's the one in a million. I wondered if I should apply my Ten Word Game, get Ivy straight in my mind.

The time, though? I looked. Ivy stirred, came to. She said was I all right.

"Fine, ta." Please, not the litany again, was she as good as others, was I disappointed. "Look at the time."

We agreed on time passing and other platitudes. Better get back because folk would notice.

"It's been so long," she said again.

"Thanks, love." A lucky interlude, probably no more. "How did you know about Amy and Les doing me over?"

"They're Billy's people. It was to make you conform."

"Who're the others?"

"Everybody, Lovejoy. Except you."

"Millicent and Jim? Kevin and Holly too?"

"Especially Kevin." She almost spat the name. I stood up, and looked down as she started to find her clothes.

"Kevin?" Why was she mad at Kevin? The image came of Billy beckoning Kevin in the casino. I used to believe I could always tell, but sometimes I'm too bone-headed.

"Billy and Kevin – what is it people say? – catch a different tram."

"Oh. Thank you, love," I added lamely, not knowing what to say.

"Thank you, Lovejoy." She wept, doing that complicated wrist movement to fasten her bra. "You just don't know how tormenting it has been, or how degrading. I was afraid you'd run a mile from me."

Narked, I almost exploded at that. I was the one going to get topped in Russia the day after tomorrow, and I didn't know torment?

I left first, going the wrong way down the corridor and emerging near a laundrette where passengers can do their own laundry. I went up in the lift and found a score of people eating ice-creams.

"Come to the midnight buffet!" one or two urged. "We're just going. It's the chocolate evening!"

"Right!" I told them. "See you there!"

And went to the casino where Lady Vee had lost a fortune, all on my card. Her friends were holding an autopsy on the vagaries of Lady Luck and blaming me. If only I'd heeded the signs/portents/runes/astrological fluxes, or none or all of the above, she'd have won a king's ransom.

"Time for the midnight buffet, Vee." I commandeered her wheelchair. "Chocaholic night."

"If you'd only stayed, Lovejoy," she said over her shoulder as we barreled down the corridor, "we'd be up a fortune."

"The bookie always wins, you daft old sod."

She cackled a laugh at that and said slyly, "Who was she, Lovejoy? Don't tell me you've just been having a quiet drink. A woman can always tell."

"I watched the contract bridge lesson," I lied. "A lady there had an infallible betting system."

"What is it? What?"

"Not telling you." I pressed the button for the lift. "I don't deal with losers."

She said nothing after that, just eyed me calculatingly as we went to assimilate yet more kilo-joules in chocolate. I maintained my grins for the rest of the evening. I thought of Ivy, and whether she, like June Milestone, had accepted me on orders of the camarilla. If not, the odds were narrowing. If yes, I was in it worse than ever.

Chapter Twenty-Two

Very late, somebody knocked at my cabin door. I'd just got in, well knackered. Lady Vee's hairstyle was burned in my brain, my only view when pushing the old goat. I liked her.

"Yes?" I called. The laundry delivered at all odd hours.

The ship's laundry was terrific. Put any clothes in their big paper bag, list what you were sending, and next day suits, shirts, linen all arrived back pristine. Fantastic. I'd not had service like that since Mazie, who came one winter and showed her husband what's what by hibernating at my cottage. Came the first thaw, she left rejoicing in the harmony of marital reunion. I was heartbroken, because she took the two suits, eight pairs of socks, nine shirts (with ties), and even singlets and underpants she'd bought for me as a Yuletide gift. I saw her husband around town the week after, wearing my (that's *my*, note) best worsted salt-and-pepper suit. I'd only worn it once. I was glad in a way because he looked a prat in it. But then so had I. Easy come, as they say. Mazie was blonde and had a gold toothpick, as far as I remember. I truly loved her, and was heartbroken for almost a whole afternoon. Women are fickle. They manipulate.

Nobody there when I opened the cabin door. No plastic-covered shirts hanging on the door, no parcels of wrapped linen. To the side of each cabin door there is a slot for notices, ship's newspapers, messages, purser's bills from indefatigable accountants and the like. Mechanically I looked, saw a small note and picked it up. I glanced down the corridor, and saw somebody – stewardess, maybe? – slip from sight, as if she'd been peering round to make sure I'd taken the message.

It was a scribble: *L, Please. Hospital, 1-30 am, ward 3*. Quiet.

Hospital? On board? I'd heard dinner talk about people going to see the doctor. I'd seen signs. All passengers carried a ship's plan with their plastic card, though that didn't stop us from getting lost. I checked. Deck Four at the front, a lot lower down than the passenger cabins. The time now was an hour after midnight. Five minutes at the most to get down there. I sat on the bed. Why does it always seem worthwhile to read notes twice, three times? The words don't grow another sentence or sprout extra adjectives full of meaningful import. Yet I do it every time. If the thing had been an epistle from some lovely lady and was packed with hints of assignations and coloured with enticing promises, sure, another perusal and a longer think would be wise. But this scrap? Come to the hospital at an impossible hour, with no reason or identifiable sender? Not likely. I shelled my jacket. Whoever it was could hang on until morning, and I might not even go then.

Don't go judging me. I still fumed from being mauled by smiling Amy and chuckling Les. I didn't want more. Basically, I'm scared of hospitals. Doctors and nurses are armed with syringes and phlebotomes, and you're naked as a grape. Think of those odds. I go queasy visiting pals in clinics. I just know that every nurse is eyeing me up, working out how she's going to inflict maximum pain. There's no future in hospitals.

It wasn't a woman's writing, smooth and looped where the letter a and t are hard to read. It looked like a bloke's hand. Henry Semper? Purser Mangot or one of his ghouls?

I donned my jacket and went.

This late, there was nothing audible except the distant hum of the ship's engines. Corridors were empty. I heard a lift creak as I went downstairs. Somebody came out on a higher floor, a lady explaining how she'd misunderstood somebody in the Conservatory about the next whist club match. Fading laughter.

The medical centre sign indicated a waiting room, chairs laid out, Riviera pictures on the walls, notices about clinics and who to ring if you were taken poorly. It was surprisingly large, three corridors leading off the waiting area. A hatch saying Pharmacy was closed. I went in and stood, wondering if I should PRESS FOR ATTENTION. The note could have told me to phone if somebody wanted a chat, right? The late hour was a clue, and the warning to be quiet.

Which wasn't odd. Hospitals always have signs asking for quiet, though they make incredible rackets with trolleys, bleeps, doors slamming. No din here. One corridor was signed for doctors' consulting rooms. Another, unlabelled, led to paired operating theatres.

I heard voices, a nurse with a smile in her voice, a man answering, "If one more passenger demands chlordiazepoxide, I'll resign back into the NHS."

"Or forgets their beta-blockers."

"Yesterday was all varicose veins."

The door was not quite ajar. The carpet underfoot ran out where the sign pointed to wards 1,2,3, presumably so nurses' heels could click noisily and wake patients. A window panel would have allowed me to see into the office. I ducked and slipped silently past. Ward 1 and 2 were empty, doors gaping. Ward 3 was shut, a hooded light filtering through the curtained window. The white card for the patient's name was blank. So why the light? I opened the door – pull it towards you, makes less sound that way – and slipped in. The wall clock said 1.29 a.m.

The bloke in the bed raised a finger, shush, watching as I shut the door. I didn't make a sound. Henry Semper, no less. He looked gaunt, with an infusion dripping into his arm under swathed bandages. He looked at death's door. He gestured to the right side of the bed, indicating a gadget on the bedside table. I nodded, got the point. Some listening device? Frankly, I was scared. Fright's an odd thing. You don't need to know who you're scared of, or what the scarers might do. It simply freezes conscious thought. You can't work out a plan of action or decide where you're going while you're terrified. I stepped closer, whispered into his ear.

"You okay?" I put my mouth to his ear for this routine idiocy of the hospital visitor. Like, certainly, great, which is why I'm having a transfusion.

"Lovejoy. The antiques thing."

"Yes?"

"Tell them wrong when you get there."

"Eh?"

He sighed, winced trying to move. I honestly felt his pain. He tried to say more. I stooped to hear.

"You're the divvy. They're depending on being told right. Tell them wrong."

"Wrong with what?"

"The room's the thing."

Somebody went down the corridor. I froze, because in darkness it's movement alarms vigilantes, not sizes or shapes.

"Look," I said, nervous as hell. It had been a man's footfall. Henry seemed to drift into some kind of delirium. He was sweating, his hand trembling, breathing in rasps.

"Right, Henry. I'll do that. Okay?"

He tried to say something more. I didn't catch it, became scared and went to stand by the door and opened it slowly. The corridor to the waiting area was clear, the nurse and the doctor still talking. I scented cigarette smoke and thought, Aha, so much for the fitness crud you keep giving us, huh?

"Tara, Henry," I mouthed. "Er, get better."

He didn't answer, just beckoned me back. I waved feebly and stepped out, closed the door slid out to safety. Unseen! I felt like Raffles, the great night-stealing burglar, or Spring-Heeled Jack, the ancient prison escaper. I was drenched with sweat as I eeled out to the stairs and went out onto the Promenade Deck to cool off. I was so relieved. A few couples were still out there, even at this late hour. I wondered if I needed an alibi, and looked for somebody I knew. No luck. As soon as I was safe, I regretted not having turned back to hear the extra he'd wanted to tell me.

I stood there, leaning on the rail like in some cruise advert.

Good of Henry to give me a warning. About what, though? Tell who wrong, about what? I guessed in St Petersburg, but where there exactly? And who were they? The room's the thing, he'd said. But everything's in one sort of room or another. Or were some St Petersburg antiques in the gardens? I felt narked. I could have been arrested or worse, down in the hospital. The ship's security people could have accused me of nicking drugs. All to see somebody delirious. I felt I'd been really brave, going to visit a sick bloke I didn't even like. I was quite noble. I almost filled up at the thought of how courageous I'd been, going to minister to the sick at enormous risk to myself. Selfless.

Wishing I still smoked, I finally went in. I had another dream, luckily not about Belle's love-tryst shed. It was about Ivy on the wharf at Gdynia, looking at the silverware and the gedanites and the mother-of-pearl, and her sad distant face after we'd made smiles. I woke quite refreshed in the morning, my usual time, sixish, and thought I'd had a really good rest.

* * *

Lounging by the Crystal Pool, I was sent for by the Purser. Not Executive Purser Mangot, but Mr Lessing. He was a rotund bloke who could hardly tear his eyes from Internet screens between which he sat like some demi-god. Standing there, as irate as when I'd last seen him, stood a bloke I hardly recognised without his string of pearls. His wife stood beside him. She was beautiful, her eyes on me.

"Lovejoy, I hear you've been less than helpful to this gentleman."

I stayed silent.

"What's your answer?"

"What's your question?"

"Will you assist Mr Bannerman? I believe you have specialised knowledge that would help this passenger in the matter of his wife's, ah, jewellery."

"I paid a fortune for those pearls." Bannerman was choking with rage. Was he ever anything else? "Lovejoy says they're false."

"I don't. I merely say they're cultivated."

"Will you testify for him if he brings a lawsuit?" Mr Lessing asked. "It would mean a lot to the ship, if you would."

"No. You have jewellers shops. Get them. If," I said in a sudden brainwave, test the water, "you want to sanction me, send me home at the next port."

A flicker crossed his expression. You had to be watching closely to see it because it was so fleeting. A sudden shadow of doubt definitely whizzed through his eyes, then was gone. I thought, aha. He was in with the mob.

"Very well," he said evenly. "I can't force you. But I think it's rather a poor show, Lovejoy. That is all."

So I was a bounder and a cad. Dear me. I left his office, Bannerman going on about lack of co-operation, that he'd sue the Line for not making me obey their orders, et yawnsville cetera. Burkes, I thought, and went to see the dancers rehearsing a new number for the evening show.

* * *

The Promenade Deck was quieter than the ruckus on the Pennant Bar at the stern, where there was a karaoke session. For once I didn't fancy a swim in the Crystal Pool among such suave elegance. Despite the luxury, I wanted to be home. I'd felt safer being hunted than among this mass of ephemerals.

"Over there," Ivy said, coming to lean on the rail, "is the first bit of Russia we see. We pass it soon. It's called Kaliningrad now."

"Lovely," I said. A distant smudge was on the horizon.

"It is a beautiful country. They are suspicious of foreigners."

I was pleased to hear it. Instead, I said, "Don't blame them. *Homo sapiens* is a rotten species."

"Did you like the Hermitage book?"

"Yes. Ta."

She smiled. "I was in love with a Russian poet once. Pushkin. You've heard of him?"

Was it sarcasm? "Sorry, love. I'm uneducated. Barely heard of Shakespeare."

"I think you're fibbing, Lovejoy."

"What was Pushkin like?"

"Socially, he was everything wrong. Chased women, got in trouble, challenged people to crazy duels, gambled with a compulsion to lose. But you have to put him in heaven as a poet."

"Okay by me." What else could I say? And why was she telling me this?

"I hope you like St Petersburg, Lovejoy. Perhaps we

will be on the same coach."

Who'd said I was going ashore? I looked at her. I often wonder about people. I mean, flamboyant Billy "the Kid", as he announced himself, with his cowboy heels and tooled-leather boots, his cheroots and black string tie and his Mexican moustache. And here comes his wife Ivy, mousy despite her bonny face, definitely muted apparel, careful shoes, her hair done into a bun as if striving for dowdiness when she had a brilliant figure. They were an essay in comparisons.

"That'd be nice."

"I could show round one or two places, if you get a visa."

"Doesn't the ship take care of that?"

"They say so. And you can always get round rules in Russia."

She smiled. It was a warm, friendly smile that pleased me. I'd have said open and honest, if I wasn't heading for perdition.

"Ta. I'd be pleased. If it's okay with your Billy."

No harm to be cautious. After all, he was a retired cop, and wives can report back to husbands. I've heard that.

We stayed talking, mostly of nothing. To my relief, she didn't press me about my background as most women do. I admitted a few things, told her of my cottage. She told me very little about herself, simply likes and dislikes. She was so pleased to be speaking, I mostly listened. We parted saying how much we'd enjoyed each other's company. Mentally I added a qualification: an exquisite woman, if she really was neutral.

A note waited in the letter slot by my cabin. Warily I opened the envelope.

Lovejoy,

With your help we can clean up on this pearl

business. *I've seen the way you operate with those antiques. I'll fund the lawsuit. You get 20% of the net – repeat net – profit. Okay? Ring us.*

Josh Bannerman.

I chucked the letter away, relieved it was only another maniac.

Chapter Twenty-Three

The head chef was speaking to us in the main theatre. It was thronged, standing room only. I was at the back because I came in late. Ivy was there, and June Milestone. Lauren was next to me. I'd just finished a talk on buying antiques – auctions, how not to get done in street markets, the pitfalls of antiques collectors' clubs, glad it had gone well. I'd come for a rest.

The stage was occupied by chefs and caterers. Each had a go, bragging about the efforts they made to stuff us to the gills so we'd all be fatter still.

"Over 20,000 bottles of wine are served every cruise," the chef said, to gasps of adulation. "Beef is the most popular dish."

Somebody called out, "What's the most popular desert?"

"Sponge pudding!"

Laughter.

"Coffee and tea served every day, 146 gallons."

The restaurant manager rose to put his bit in. "Some 120,000 main meals are served on an average cruise, for which we use fifteen tons of beef and twenty-eight tons of fresh vegetables and fruit."

"Including," a chef popped up, "51,000 fresh eggs, and over 10,000 litres of milk and cream, with 70,000 bread rolls and half a ton of chickens every single day!"

People applauded at the scale of it. In the gloaming, I saw Lauren's eyes. I thought, well, I too feel sorry for all those chickens and fishes, but don't take on. Nothing we can do about it.

"Every cruise, a waiter walks ninety-one miles, the laundry washes 14,000 table cloths and 88,000 serviettes!"

I whispered to Lauren, "Meet you outside in half an

hour, okay?"

Women and weeping. I had a lass once who cried every time somebody ate vegetables because carrots had feelings. She kept asking how would I like it if I was a turnip and somebody chewed me to bits. I was glad when she left. She wrote books about amino-acids in nuts. Insensitive fascist that I was, I asked if filberts were unemotional beasts. We parted.

Free, I went to Reception, and told the lass I wanted to see Mr Henry Semper. She conducted me to Executive Purser Mangot.

"What about?" He glared at my throat.

"The antiques in the store room. I want to know what Mr Semper's scheme is for the evening quizzes." I paused. "It's just," I explained lamely, "I'm doing his talks, see? When will he be back on duty?"

"I thought you couldn't be in doubt about antiques."

"Look. If he wants me to follow the same order, I should know, see?"

His brow cleared. "Do it any way you like." Then he chilled my spine by saying, "The thing is, Henry had to leave. He's having a serious operation in Copenhagen this very minute."

"Poor bloke," I said. I meant me, not Henry. We'd long since passed Copenhagen, unless my geography was wrong again. "Wish him well from me, eh?"

"Get out."

"Er, ta."

The Lido Deck was thronged, the day bright. A rock band was rocking, teenagers were jigging – or does that term mean something else now? People were lounging, swimming in the pools, drinking the morning sunshine, a scene worth at least a postcard. Somewhere at the ship's back, abaft the beam or whatever, anyway behind the funnel, I knew there was a flat space marked out for a helicopter to land. It was usually covered in nets, for cricket, golf, and some kind of shuffle game using long handles. I'd gone up there the day before, to look for whales or dolphins from a vantage point.

The nets were still in place. Passengers were hard at games, one man showing his wife how to use a nine iron, aiming the ball at a screen countryside. Her ball missed the whole landscape. She laughed as friends cheered. I saw Fern and Delia Oakley waiting their turn.

The whole area looked exactly as it had the previous day. Therefore no helicopters. Yet ships the size of *Melissa* have little boats. I walked round the lifeboats and tenders. They're usually all wrapped up, so you forget they're waiting there for catastrophe in life's mad gaiety. These too looked undisturbed. A crewman painting the davits was halfway along, another day's brushwork to finish.

And Henry Semper, too sick to rise from his bed earlier the same morning, was now in Copenhagen under the surgeon's knife, was he? I tried to recapture the glimpse of the lass who'd delivered the message to my cabin, and failed. Female, I'd been sure, but was she a stewardess, or a passenger? A woman would have spotted the difference in dress; we blokes can't tell. And Lauren wept at the thought of all those poor lobsters the galleys cooked for our supper. Maybe, but was it likely?

"What's next, Lovejoy?"

"You made me jump, Mrs Oakely. Next?"

"I saw you getting bored in there, like me and Fern. We came out to play golf."

"Next what?"

She was a bonny woman, never looked shivery the way others did. She could do that knowing smile women use to hide guffaws, but just friendly, not to put people down.

"Antiques. Give me a clue about the answer. You're doing the afternoon session with June Milestone. Isn't she brilliant?"

"I'll make it up as I go along."

"Are you serious friends with Mrs Milestone, Lovejoy?" She was offhand, which meant deadly curious.

"Me? No. She's rich and famous, I'm hoi-polloi."

"Then why does she have you followed?" She laughed at my expression. "Her friend – the big American man – never takes his eyes off her, then acts on her signals. Fern jokes about it." She gave me a mischievous glance. "Haven't you noticed?"

Did she mean Victor Lustig? My head ached. I don't get migraines, just a throb twice as bad. It saves itself for moments like this.

"Fern says you're a true divvy."

Good old Fern. I looked across. Delia's pal was just swinging her golf club. The screen's computer registered the ball's thud and said she'd sent it 109 yards near a bunker. The landscape changed. I wonder about golfers. I think it's a terrible ailment. Fern had seemed pretty normal until now.

"Not me," Mrs Oakley said quickly. "Golf's so obsessional, isn't it? Fern saw you once in Wimbledon at an antiques auction. We were wondering if you were free for lunch at the Boulevard, Deck Eight."

The Boulevard was an ultra-smart restaurant and you needed to book. It never closed, had special wines and was for late owls wanting quiet.

"Er, I'm pushed for time."

"Please try." She smiled. I weakened. "We shan't talk golf."

"Noon, then?"

I finished my trudge and came on Lauren looking for me on the Promenade Deck. Her eyes were red and bulbous. I told her Mangot's news.

"I heard, Lovejoy. Poor Mr Semper."

"How big's that store room?"

After all, it had to be emptied, presumably to house the stolen art treasures of the Hermitage, right? Or something had. Mind you, a ship is a massive place.

She looked at me. I thought, do women who wear specs cry less than those who don't? She kept trying to slide a tissue up underneath the rims to blot her tears.

"Henry wanted more space, to bring furniture aboard. Mr Mangot did the arranging. Henry was so cross. He had to send most of the antiques back *in the same van*. It was outrageous. They were lucky to get Henry to agree to... to everything. He's not appreciated."

"Why didn't you go with him?" And explained, "To hospital."

"He wanted me to stay and complete the contract. He isn't a rich man, Lovejoy."

Lauren and Henry. Lovers, or disciple and teacher?

"When did he go?"

She wept then. An elderly couple strolling arm in arm looked daggers at me, wanting to ask what kind of a sick swine did I think I was. I smiled weakly.

"I'm so frightened, Lovejoy." She stared out at a distant freighter heading past towards civilisation. "Henry tried to get us off in Warnemunde but Mr Mangot wouldn't give permission."

"Frightened of what?"

"Henry said he would forego his fees if we could be allowed to fly home. They said no. I would have gone with him, Lovejoy." She eyed me, worried I would be cut to the quick at the revelation. "He and I were ... He's never had a really good woman, you see. Women take advantage of him. I would rescue him. He needs me. The money from this cruise was going to be our nest-egg, to make a new start."

"And Mr Mangot?"

"Henry said we should escape before we reach Russia."

"Escape?" I made out I was gormless. "From this cruising paradise?"

"He told me something horrid would happen in St Petersburg."

"Did he say what?"

"No. They wouldn't let me see him when he became ill. I tried phoning, but the Danish hospitals say he's not there."

"Look, Lauren. Can I be excused this evening's dinner quiz? I'll ask Mrs Milestone to do it with you." I thought of Henry Semper alone in his ward.

"Why? What are you going to do?"

"I'll try to find out how he's getting on. I'll be in to dinner same as usual. I can speak Danish, you see," I lied with dazzling inventiveness. "Don't tell anybody."

We parted. She had to get ready for the Antique Collectors' Club. I needed to think with whatever logic I could scrape up. I went for coffee in the Horizon lounge. No officers, just Ivy joining me as soon as I sat.

"Your bag, Lovejoy. You left it in the chefs' session. You don't want to be taken by surprise, do you?"

I hadn't seen the bag before and drew breath to tell her so. It was one of those open canvas things with some stamped logo *Antiques For Yonks*, whatever that meant. I took it. She walked off. I didn't look inside, just dropped it beside my chair as if it was unimportant. I saw her shoes as she turned away, and saw they were dark crocodile, false or real skin I didn't know. And remembered the dappled sheen on the message woman's heel as she'd slipped from Corridor F. Ivy, passing me that note to see Henry Semper in the hospital?

The headache really swung in. I tried to reach oblivion in case it was an all-day banger. I might have made it, but Les came round the lounge doing card tricks. He was really good. He insisted on including me, and a crowd gathered. Imagine how pleased I was to see his sleight-of-hand pulling the Jack of Diamonds from some lady's earring, if only my flickering vision would have let me see the damned thing.

An hour later I tottered to an armchair in the ship's library and looked in Ivy's bag. It contained yet another catalogue, this time of the Hermitage's latest exhibition. I could hardly read the title, so bad was my migraine by then: *Hidden Treasures Revealed*. I find some colours terrible to read at the best of times, but almost impossible in blue capitals on Van Gogh's ochre and browns. I sat on the bag and tried to doze. Ivy, though? And on whose side? I wanted some Flash Gordon to zoom in, tell me who was Ming from Planet Mongo and, better still, who wasn't.

I came to with my side aching from a hopeless slumped posture, too late to join June Milestone at the next Antiques Clubber Talk. She'd give me hell for letting her down again. My head was almost back on, though, so I didn't feel too bad about it. I looked about. Only two people clicking away in the nook reserved for Internet folk, and the occasional book browser along the shelves. I opened the catalogue of the State Hermitage Museum, and read.

* * *

Another note from that lunatic Bannerman was under my cabin door.

Lovejoy,

> *Okay, 30% of the gross. That's as high as I can go. My wife Cynthia agrees. You write the script, and she'll say*

exactly what you tell her to. We've watched you, and reckon you can do it good. Deal?
    Josh Bannerman
    I ditched it. One less complication.

Chapter Twenty-Four

"Lovejoy?"

Blearily I came to. Bannerman stood next to my recliner. I'd just had a coffee by the Riviera Pool reading *David Copperfield*. I always feel so sorry for the poor little blighter. I used to fill up, reading the story to my gran, and so did Gran.

A beautiful woman stood beside him. I'd seen her before, at my talk and in the Purser's Office. His wife?

"Eh?"

"This is Cynthia. Look." He crouched down. "Final offer. We go halves, and I fund the legal business. Won't cost you a penny. Cynthia's taken a real shine to the idea. We'll make a killing. You simply say your piece in court. How about it?"

The loonies had taken over. When that happens, pretend to be one. I glanced about in mute warning.

"Right. Say nothing more here. Give me your address when we leave the ship, okay? I'll meet you in Southampton, fix the details."

"Thank Christ for that. I thought I'd lost my touch." He grinned at Cynthia. "This gooner drives a hard bargain. I like that in a man."

"So do I," said Cynthia, cool.

She smiled down. I peered up. Height gives a woman a distinct advantage, but they're always unfair because they start at their legs and go on up.

"Any time you want to rehearse me, Lovejoy," she said calmly, "just call."

"Right." I meant no.

They left. I went back to *David Copperfield*. He was in a worse state than me, but he gets out of his mess and wins through. Only in the story, though, only in the story.

✳   ✳   ✳

As I came out of the swimming pool, I collected my towel and bag from my deck recliner, and found a note from Cynthia. I shrugged and thought oh, well. No harm done just to go and say hello. An hour later I was at the deck quoits match.

The excitement was out of all proportion to what was happening. People were shoving rope rings into marked squares. A breathless crowd of three had assembled to witness the gaiety.

Sports and me don't mix. Frankly I think they're dull. Ice hockey is beyond me. Rugby variants are as dire as each other, ever since that daft so-and-so William Webb Ellis in 1823 picked the ball up and ran with it at Rugby School and so started the game. Horse riding is fascist – those poor nags – and I'd sooner bottle smog than see a Formula One race. Good antiques abound, though, with sports themes, if you can get hold of any. Golfiana (sorry) has gone mad, up 200% in a year, item on item.

Cynthia Bannerman's note said to meet at the Deck Quoits, so here I was. She was playing. Gripped by the tempestuous action, I went to a deck chair to nod off.

"Lovejoy? I won!"

I stirred. "Yippee."

"Walk?" I stood, stretched, and we strolled the deck. People were reclining on loungers, having a smoke, sending for drinks.

"Your heart isn't in the deception Josh suggests, is it?"

"No."

"Why not?"

"It's hard for me."

"Don't be silly. You do it all the time."

"Look, love. In a lifetime I've heard of hundreds of

so-say divvies. Every cheap TV junk-stall presenter claims to have the knack, the gift. Antiques Road-Show experts all hint they posses the magic seventh sense for antiques. Every corner-street dealer says he has the divvy factor. Know the truth?"

"I'm sure you'll tell me."

"I've only ever been sure of one other divvy bloke besides me."

"One? Then it is rare!" She slipped her arm through mine. It felt marvellous, walking with a lovely svelte woman on my arm, and me a scruff. "You'll be all the more convincing! It is so easy to pretend!"

"Ever seen anybody pretend to have the divvy shakes? They are so embarrassing it's ridiculous. It's a laugh. Even the phoney divvies know they look absurd. Pathetic."

"You won't do it?" She halted us.

"In court would be worse."

"Not for me?" She fluttered her eyes.

"Look, love. Your bloke . . ."

"Not if I persuaded to the uttermost?"

I had already decided not to lie for Bannerman's gain, so what difference would it make if I let myself be persuaded? It's so easy to pretend. She'd said it. And my gran said it's polite to agree with a lady.

"Very well," I agreed, politely. "Where shall we go to talk it over?"

"I'll think of somewhere," she said, and we walked on.

The day passed in a blur. In a trice I was saying goodnight, wishing people wouldn't leave the show and go to bed. Crowds thinned, the decks cleared as the black horizon showed more lights of Russia's shoreline. Ships passed more frequently. I wanted to shout for everyone to stay awake. Nobody stays loyal when you need them – look at Margaret Dainty, my lifelong pal. I almost broke down as I realised the barman and two stewardesses were the only folk left in the Horizon Lounge. I felt sick, though I'd only had one glass of wine after supper. Lauren had gone, saying she'd try the ship-to-shore phone link, see if she could raise (her unfortunate phrase) Mr Semper. Some hopes. We used to say that as children, when games got forlorn, some hopes. The parrot in Les Renown's joke knew about freezers.

The cabin seemed a small box when finally I turned in. I made tea, stared out of the porthole at the gathering lights, trying to visualise the captain and his officers looking into the night, their instruments telling them exactly where the ship was. Holly told me they had ways of knowing how many people were aboard. Did that include dead? I shut the curtain on Russia, and lay there. I only had *Pride and Prejudice*, so I lay back and thought of Ivy's Hermitage catalogue. It had had no map, just prints of the Impressionist paintings. I supposed these were the ones we – meaning I – was to spot, then to snatch.

* * *

One thing about Russians, they know where they stand. Okay, ideologically they move about a lot and say they don't, but they know whose side they're on. In England, justice is a trick that possibly almost virtually nearly occasionally sometimes constantly must be seen to be done. In Russia, justice is in the eye of the beholder; it simply depends on whose eye is doing the looking.

Russia is there very like the USA. Not similar, but vast and impenetrable. They're the same in one special way: if neither existed, the rest of us would have to invent both, just as we invent God and Satan. Which is which is up to the individual.

I knew little about Russia except the usual exotic fragments in my ragbag mind. Catherine the Great locked her hairdresser in an iron cage for three years, so he couldn't reveal the ghastly truth that she'd contracted dandruff. Which country has most USA 100 dollar notes in circulation? Answer: Russia, outstripping America by a mile. What drug is used to abduct Russian moguls for ransom? Answer: heroin (the kidnappers inject it). And what Russian magnates get abducted most often? Oil tycoons. Russian jokes have made the satirical magazines in the West with quips like, How do they congratulate new deputy mayors in Novosibirsk? By giving him a new Kevlar vest (bulletproof, see?). And, how can you tell when a Duma deputy's salary rises by one dollar? Answer: he buys another Rolls Royce. Yet isn't politics the same the world over? My dad and uncles once played against the famed football team Moscow Dynamo yonks ago, and said how they'd suffered in wartime.

What else did I know? Nothing. I wondered what Ivy had given me that catalogue for. I'd scanned it, to no avail. I started *Pride and Prejudice* all over again. My trouble is I do exactly as women tell me. It didn't work, so I tried to sleep.

A room is a room, nothing more. That cabin storing Lauren's stock of antiques kept coming to mind. Lauren said Henry Semper wanted a bigger space, for maybe some genuine antique furniture for the passengers' entertainment. Had June Milestone advised him? This room kept coming back, worrying me.

There's my game. Ten Words Everything. Like I said earlier, I invented it, to teach myself clearer thinking. You have to describe anything in ten words. For instance, I knew a man who was wealthy. He bought a small French 1870s clock off me, good value. I ate for a week on the proceeds, really posh meals at my cottage, with a new sauce bottle and everything. I even brought out my saucer and bread-and-butter plate. You'd never seen such elegance. Guy met a woman who stayed with him and spent his money like a drunken sailor, then she met a richer bloke and took off. Guy went to pieces. In my Ten Word Game: She moved in, spent up, met another, moved on, desolation! That's ten, and it says everything. Poor Guy has never been the same since.

How would I describe my plight? My ten words would be: Shanghaied, Russian robbery planned, two dead, frightened I'm next . . . That's nine. But then what? Dead? Gaoled? Arrested? Missing? There was one decent word at the end, though. Escape. That would do me.

My mind flipped pages. Ivy's book had talked of where the seventy-four priceless Impressionist paintings in the Hermitage *Hidden Treasures* exhibition came from, and their value to the world. Only two had ever been seen in public before. This means they'd be simple to sell, once nicked by enterprising thieves – say like an organised gang sailing in by cruise ship, and consisting of reliable officers, antiques experts, policemen.

My dozing mind went sideways. *Hidden Treasures Revealed* had a subtitle: *Impressionist Masterpieces preserved by the State Hermitage Museum, St Petersburg*. I get narked. Is there anything more useless than a prologue, a preface, a foreword, or an introduction? If they've anything to say, I always think, get on with it and stop annoying us. The masterworks weren't in doubt. Painted between 1827 and 1927, they appeared from the rubble at the end of the 1939-45 war, mostly undocumented. Earliest was Camille Corot's *Rocks*, the latest Matisse's *Ballerina*, a creative spread of 100 years.

You could dramatise the arrival of such master-pieces (actually in railway trucks) in the poverty and heartbreak of post-war Europe, as they were sent to the Pushkin State Museum of Fine Arts in Moscow or the Hermitage in St Petersburg, and simply stored there. Rights and wrongs seemed clearer back then. The Western and Eastern Bloc nations took up pejorative attitudes, name-calling the other. I ignore political terms and even words like Impressionist, Post-Impressionism, and Expressionist, because they interrupt my view of paintings by Vincent, Monet, Gaugin, and the rest. They're for writers of prologues.

To me, it's simple. The paintings were protected by good old Russia when destruction threatened, and were now brought out for everybody to see. Enough.

Or for people to sail into St Petersburg's lovely harbour, in order to steal by arrangement, let's say?

※　※　※

I thought I was sleeping soundly, having dismissed the Hermitage book Ivy lent me. Yet something lingered. Once the Introduction began, there were only three photographs. Black and white. All three were of rooms, small grainy snapshots showing old-fashioned … well, just rooms with carpets, pelmets, and careful furnishings. Oh, and paintings hung about the walls. Some you could identify, by Renoir, Courbet. Others weren't so easy.

Underneath each blurry photo were the names of collectors who'd bought the paintings. The superb collection had been owned by three main buyers. Their names weren't important to me, but are famous. I mean, Joseph Otto Krebs matters, not because he ran a steam-boiler factory, but because he liked artistic beginners known as Vincent Van Gogh, Cézanne,

Gaugin and suchlike, and stuffed his house in Holzdorf with their art. He snapped up young Picasso's works as well. Top marks to Joe, then, for perception.

Another German industrialist collector was Bernhard Koehler, who subsidised young artists like my favourite, poor August Macke – his 1913 charmer *Zwei Frauen vor dem Hutladen* has just gone for four million zlotniks in Sotheby's even as I write, giving an idea of the gelt we're tilting at here. Everything in modern art you see nowadays leads back to Bernhard of the big bucks. The story of what happened to the collections is fraught, leading through the carnage of the July Plot on Hitler's life and subsequent executions, the bombings and ruination, and thence to the Hermitage.

The final major collection, Otto Gerstenberg's, eventually joined the others in St Petersburg. He was a mathematician who turned to running an insurance company (the only blight on his life) in Berlin, and loved everybody from Constable, Reynolds, Goya, and the other famous names everybody knows.

The French masterpieces of these rich aficionados were the *Hidden Treasures* exhibition we were going to nick. Yeah, right, I thought in my doze. My mind saw rooms turning and shifting shapes and colours. Even asleep I found myself thinking about rooms, but why?

I woke, and it was bright daylight, half-seven. I looked out through the porthole. We were gliding up an enormous waterway towards a beautiful city. St Petersburg, golden amber in the morning sun. The steward knocked, summoned me to Suite 1133 in thirty minutes.

The faces were excited, enthralled like children before a seaside outing. I sat. They'd laid on breakfast, Lady Vee's stewardess Marie providing an enormous buffet. I helped to scoff most of it, so she didn't feel she'd wasted her time getting it ready. The others seemed too excited to bother with food.

"The Hermitage in St Petersburg," Mangot said, doing his Napoleon-before- Waterloo. "Doubts, anxieties anyone?"

"St Petersburg!" Lady Vee exclaimed, eyes aglow. "Where Catherine the Great founded the Bolshoi! City of Pushkin, the dancers Nijinsky and Pavlova! Most of all, Dostoevsky!"

"*Crime and Punishment*?" I asked, lamely keeping up.

"His scribbles are incidental," she cried in contempt. "Such a brilliant gambler! His infallible gambling system went missing after his death. Legend says a foreign lady will sail in one day and rediscover it! Don't you see? The fable means me!"

"Aye, right," I told the loony bint.

Mangot showed some sense by ignoring her, but less by ignoring me.

"This is the war council, everybody, so listen. The Hermitage is five immense linked buildings along the waterside, starting at the Winter Palace and ending in the Hermitage Theatre."

He must have seen my expression change and said wearily, "What, Lovejoy?"

"Look," I said through a mouthful of nosh. "It doesn't sound much if you say it quick, except the Winter Palace alone houses over a thousand rooms and 117 magnificent staircases. And they know we're coming."

Mangot sounded strangled. "What's that supposed to mean?"

"Put the Crown Jewels in a tower, everybody knows *everybody* is coming. The world and his wife wants to nick them. Bound to be the same at the Hermitage. Armed guards. Dogs. Electronics. Every minute of every day, they'll expect robbers."

"We aren't the robbers," he said in exasperation. "It's laid on. We are the good folk. We're safe."

"It won't work. Somebody will get hurt." I meant me, and I think they understood because they all turned to look at him, even June and Lady Vee. "If you're bent on nicking the great Manchester clock in the Wyndham Franklin in Philadelphia, America, you'd need an army, not just a few dead-legs like us. Why? Because the bloody thing's twenty-six feet tall and six feet wide. Victorians built things big in 1869."

"And your point is…?"

"We should chose what we're nicking."

"We're not nicking anything, Lovejoy," now with ill-suppressed anger. "We're doing a let's-pretend."

"Honest?"

The room held silence. I saw the golden sheen come off the sea through the balcony window. Quite like amber, I'd thought earlier in my own cabin. Our faces were golden. I wondered anew why Ivy had slipped me the book of the treasures we were going to steal. Then I wondered how on earth she'd known that fact. She wasn't one of our group, never had been.

"You think we're going to all this trouble for no reason, Lovejoy?"

"No." And I didn't.

"We *pretend* to thieve the Impressionist paintings in the Hermitage. How many times do I have to tell you? Seventy-four paintings." He looked round the others. "Lovejoy will authenticate them on a routine visit, in the company of a hundred other passengers. Then we go for it."

"How?" I asked Marie for some more toast. She looked at her table in disbelief, amazed it had all gone. I thought, for God's sake, woman, eating is what toast is for. Toast isn't a proposition by Wittgenstein.

"That isn't your business. When the exhibition went on show, the whole world shrieked one question: Are they genuine? You're here to tell us yes or no. Got it?"

"What if – ?"

"You just go in," he shouted, losing his rag, "make sure they're genuine masterpieces, and tell us. Then we set things in motion."

"What things?"

"I have arranged that with the Russians." He leant back. "Safe enough, Lovejoy?"

"Still no facts, though."

"There!" Lady Vee said brightly. "We've all got to be in special places at the right time, haven't we James?"

"Yes, Lady Vee." He brought out a map of the Hermitage, several layers of the damned thing. They were marked with red crosses, each cross with a single letter in scarlet. "L is for Lovejoy," he said, all sarcasm. "He simply goes into the Exhibition, picks out the duds, if any. Lady Vee is V, okay?"

"It's really thrilling!"

He went over the list. Stairs were going to be awkward, because the lifts were sacrosanct and might be out of service.

"It's the way things are here. We're two days in St Petersburg," he finished. "I've arranged excursions for us."

Us? I didn't like the thought of being on a trip with him. The less I saw of the murdering swine the better.

"We must stick to the times marked on the charts, follow the guides at the proper times, and all will be well."

"Must I see every single painting in the collection we're, er, not going to steal?" My heart was thumping. Marie brought a mingy three pieces of toast. I asked for more. She stumped out. See? Nothing to do all day except make a manky plate of toast, and she goes to pieces.

"Yes. Timing is critical. If you detect a fake among them, keep a list. They're numbered and named."

"Who gets my list afterwards?"

He looked exasperated. "For Christ's sake, Lovejoy, shut the fuck up. It's simple. Sensible questions, anyone?"

"Not me," I said, wondering where his excursions were going to. I vowed not to be there when the trip went carousing off. I'd heard of folk who'd been there before. "No questions. Ta for the nosh."

"Thank God," he said, sinking back in relief. "Somebody open the door and let the cretin out." As I made off he said, "Ten o'clock at the gangway, Deck Four. Be there."

"Right, right." I went for a proper breakfast, kippers, poached eggs and a decent stack of toast with proper marmalade. I don't know what some women have against food. Marie should get a grip.

* * *

Estate agents – those who sell houses for extortionate prices and horrendous commission fees – have this saying: Three things decide price: location, location, and location. It's similar in antiques: there's three things decide what an antique is worth: provenance, provenance, and provenance. Everybody (including me) forever quotes the mythical Anglo-Saxon axe, that has only had three new heads and two new hafts since it was dug up. When somebody reminds you of that old crack, you're supposed to smile knowingly and pretend you've never been taken in. Better, though, to think of some antique where provenance was authentic and the world of antiques is stunned by the mega-wealth involved. Think, for example, of Lord Nelson's sword.

In 2002, this bloke wanders up to an ordinary antiques valuation counter, bringing a brooch. It happens to be diamond, authentic Georgian, anchor-shaped, with H and N giving clues to its long-dead possessor. The owner was a descendant of Horatio Nelson's personal assistant. The man's family also had a box containing scores of letters, account books, a blood-stained purse still holding Nelson's twenty-one golden coins ... and the great hero's personal sword, actually his famed Turkish sabre. The scabbard was in the Greenwich Hospital. Amid excitement, the Turkish sabre was tried in the scabbard. Like Cinderella's shoe, it fitted! A portrait of Nelson's assistant painted by Arthur Devis in 1808 shows the same sabre in detail. Provenance reigned.

"The collection," recorded the newspapers just before the 21st October, 2002, sale in London's New Bond Street (anniversary of Trafalgar, incidentally, save having to look it up) "is totally new to the market *and with a provenance that is second to none.*" Everybody I know, including me, groaned with unrequited lust at the thought of all that beautiful provenance going to undeserving (meaning other) buyers. Needless to say, the Sotheby's Sale Catalogue is now a collector's item in its own right. See? To them that hath provenance shall be given. It's in the Bible, or should be if it isn't.

Now, I define antiques as the commerce of old items where lies are only rarely encountered but falsehood is the natural means of expression. Here on board the *Melissa*, St Petersburg clamouring for me to go ashore and gaze breathless upon the zillions of priceless antiques in the Hermitage, the reverse seemed the case; lies were endemic, and falsity merely there as background music in the plush lounges and luxurious trappings of day-to-day ship-board life. For instance, I didn't know who Mangot's famous team was, or who would pull off the robbery. Did he seriously think I'd believe this mob of duds was a swashbuckling league of Raffles lookalikes, who could even pretend to take on the entire Russian army?

Worse, I'd read about modern Russia. Oppose the tide of graft and corruption, you got lobbed from a roof or abducted and deliberately suicided in, or off, some hotel. They had an expression that's been grafted into English: krisha is the word for roof, meaning a safety factor protecting you from adverse forces. So their politicians are merchants who provide a krisha to protect the criminals. The forces of law and order can likewise be a krisha if you bribe the right people with the right amount of zlotniks. They say it was worst of all in the free-for-all 1990s, but others say things are a hell of a sight worse now. It was into this mayhem that, this bright morning, I was going to step ashore and divvy a priceless collection of masterpieces.

Now, Germany, France, and other assorted nations with multo political and diplomatic clout, had tried to wangle the paintings back. It had been in the papers for half a century. They got nowhere. The Russian government itself was said to have displaced the old Russian mafia, using the time-honoured nudge-splash of the sailor's elbow technique and usurping their street power. Law has evaporated, says rumour, and local authorities are merely the first layer of krishas. There's a resistance, like in any occupation of any country; you can pay to have your opponents eliminated. Simple.

And if, say, somebody decided on an automobile accident as the means of choice, why, what could be simpler than bribing the authorities to delay/prevent/avoid/ignore investigations? Life has to go on, and by life is meant the level of corruption you can afford. Crime must flourish because it's essential. Ask any government.

Mind you, I should talk. In our own country justice is a miscarriage; law is simply the description of how justice fails.

I tried thinking over the events of the cruise: Southampton, the Baltic, my attempts to escape. And the two deaths, Mister Moses and – probable, but unconfirmed as yet – Henry Semper. It had been good of Ivy, though, to give me the massive beautifully-produced catalogue of the Hermitage's special exhibition. Good guess, Ivy.

Ten o'clock, I went to sit in the Atrium near the gangway exit on Deck Four, hoping I'd not be spotted. Amy and Les Renown caught me and hauled me off the ship, laughing.

"Here, Lovejoy," Les said, choking with laughter. "Two psychiatrists meet. One says, 'Morning Joe. You're fine today. How am I?' Get it? See, they're psychiatrists!"

"Hilarious, Les," I said gravely. Down the gangplank, into Russia.

Chapter Twenty-Five

An assortment of coaches assembled on the wharf. The couriers were all beautiful ponytail blondes with polished nails, decor on wheels. They made us look shabby. I was glad I'd given my teeth a special go, to confront the fabled State Hermitage Museum of Russia. I was clean, done up in my – well, Gloria's imaginary brother Cal's – gear. The crew gave us bright yellow lapel stickers saying D4.

Millicent and Jim Akehurst came along, she glittering with diamonds, he as sober as any conveyancing lawyer. Billy the Kid and Ivy were with us, the former looking like a fifty-year-old cowboy in riding heels and shimmering waistcoat. It's a wonder he didn't have a green eyeshade, but he had the cheroot. Kevin came, pouting over some restriction imposed by Holly Sago, both so tasteful in black as to create suspicion. Amy the dancer and Les Renown sat at the front of our coach with the courier. Mangot I saw on the quayside chatting with June Milestone. He was in mufti, but wore an imposing badge and emblems on his arm.

"I am Natasha," the guide announced in her microphone. "Can everyone hear me?"

On the drive to the city we were treated to a summary of Russia's efforts in the Great Patriotic War and her subsequent development.

"She'll elide over the attempted Christmas Coup of 1991," Ivy said. She'd somehow landed next to me. I was by the window. I can't resist looking out, especially at a place I've never been. Natasha was prattling on, statistics mingled with history.

"Coup?"

"Pathetic," Ivy said. Her voice had a wistful quality, but then most women have that. It makes them worth listening to, especially when you think of my gender's most popular representative on the cruise, Les

"Chuckles" Renown.

"I didn't know they'd had one. Don't you mean 1905, or 1917?"

"The Winter Palace march was on Bloody Sunday in 1905, the Potyomkin business the same year. Then the siege, 1941 to 1944. Those are what foreigners remember about St Petersburg. I meant the hopeless business in 1991. It dissolved the Soviet Union within minutes."

She spoke without bitterness but with an odd resignation I hadn't heard before. Natasha was still rabbiting on. Ivy looked across the river at the imposing buildings, the onion-topped churches. They looked glorious.

"They're coloured!" I exclaimed. The exteriors were beautiful with pastels, the pillars and facades down to the waterlines. It seemed utterly innocent, as if beyond harm. I said as much.

She smiled, better word. "Yes. Colour is a custom here."

"Painting the buildings?"

"That, and the ability to convince everyone how innocent St Petersburg is." Only, she didn't say St Petersburg, like she hadn't said Potemkin, the name of the famous film *Battleship Potemkin*. She pronounced it Sankt Pieter Burkh in a slithery guttural.

It made me look at her anew. Mousy, sure, but she had depths. And that book of the Hermitage's prize exhibition had been well handled. Some passages had been underlined.

"You've been here before, Ivy?"

"Yes. It has not always been so beautiful."

She listened to Natasha answering passenger queries. Millicent was annoying everybody with questions about money, Russian wages, price of furs, income tax, bargains, jewellery shops and other vital essentials. Holly asked about casinos, was it true Russians all knew how to rig faro in only eighteen cards. Billy was laughing with Kevin and ignoring everything else, including the superb city.

"You will know straight away which of the antiques is a forgery, Lovejoy. Am I right?"

"In the Hermitage? Probably."

"Not for sure?"

"I never know."

Ivy glanced at her husband and Kevin. They were immersed in their own happy chat. From what the lass was recounting, the Russians seemed to have had a hell of a lot of wars. I saw Ivy's lips move as if in mute answer when the guide stumbled over translating a word

"The *cruiser*," the lovely guide managed at last, remembering with relief, "is called *Aurora*. You can see her there. She fired her gun in 1917, signalling the October Revolution. She is famous. She is painted very bright colours for general admiration."

Ivy therefore spoke Russian, and she'd been here before. If Natasha was in on our scam, as Purser Mangot had implied, was Ivy?

"Please keep together when we arrive at the Winter Palace, ladies and gentlemen. I shall carry this umbrella. Remember we are Coach D4. Please follow my umbrella at all times."

I found myself smiling, and was caught by Ivy watching me. I went a bit red and shrugged.

"Well, she's bonny," I said lamely.

"That lady who left the ship at Gdynia, Lovejoy. She too was bonny, in her older way. Had you been friends long?"

"Margaret? I forget." I sound crass.

"Forget deliberately?"

"I don't disclose a lady's confidences, love. Ask her.

Don't ask me. Gossip is women's work, not mine."

"I'm glad you think like that, Lovejoy."

What can you say? Usually women are narked if they catch you admiring another woman, and here was one actually pleased I thought the courier gorgeous? I gave up and looked out at the passing canals, the buildings, the coloured facades of the architecture. The guide promised we'd arrive in ten minutes and warned us again about her blinking umbrella.

"I never believed there was such a thing as a divvy, until I saw your disagreement at the dinner quizzes with Mr Semper. Do you wish you weren't?"

"Sometimes I keel over. It feels rotten."

"Poor thing," she said, and meant it. I thought she was joking until she touched my arm. "Tell me, Lovejoy. Aren't you ever tempted to get it wrong deliberately? Fool people, I mean."

Who'd said something like that, not too long ago, from his hospital bed? I muttered, "Dunno."

"Can I go in with you?"

"We're together anyway," I pointed out. "A school crocodile. Only we don't have labels on a string round our necks."

"I mean for the pleasure of your company."

My company, a pleasure? I stared at her. She was obviously off her trolley. Since making smiles there had been a strange distance between us. I shrugged and agreed. "If you like, but I hate people pointing things out. I get shirty. You'll have to put up with me."

"I'll last out, Lovejoy," she said quietly. "Don't you fret."

I wasn't fretting at all, not that I knew. I said nothing as we arrived, last of four coaches in line within a stone's throw of the dazzling Winter Palace. I was almost starting to shake, probably from excitement or, worse, fright, as if I could feel the dangerous vibes up ahead.

* * *

Ivy took my arm as we assembled, the whole coachload. We were alongside the river. Nervous, I glanced at Billy, but he just gave me a grin of approval and continued his waggish conversation with Kevin. I saw Lady Vee wave from her wheelchair, pushed by unsmiling Inga. Les Renown and Amy were alighting from Coach D1, Amy tapping her watch to me as a reminder about time. Holly Sago was striding angrily among some beggars, ignoring everybody. I thought, we're a rotten species.

We trailed after the guide's gaudy umbrella. I breathed in some strange scent. It was Ivy, puffing at me from a small spray can.

"Repellent? You'd only to say."

"Mosquitoes, Lovejoy. You just don't know their ferocity here."

Whereas she, on the other hand, did? I tried not to gaze quizzically at her, just noticed how she turned to the right towards the entrance before even the courier's umbrella swayed that way. Ivy knew St Petersburg in a way strangers never would.

"Admission fees are included, Lovejoy." She had felt me reach for my pocket as we got to the entrance. "Russians pay less than one-twentieth what foreigners do, and have separate entrances. There's a close security. You're not carrying a weapon, or anything with wires and batteries, I hope?"

"Next time, maybe."

My feeble joke made her stiffen slightly. She relaxed as we shuffled inchwise into the entrance hall. Two beefy women at tables near immense pillars began a long exchange with our courier. Natasha hadn't even glanced at me. Fine, but if she was secretly one of Mangot's lot, and I was as valuable as he said, shouldn't she at least have counted us to make sure I hadn't slipped away among the Russian families thronging the place? The noise was of a subdued pandemonium. Natasha's conversation with the two ticket women seemed heated, became friendly, went back to anger, then full of dismissive merriment. I saw Ivy suppress smiles as the verbal brawl went on.

"Can't we get in?" I asked her. Almost too nervous to speak, I was desperate to see the rarest collection on earth.

"Of course. It is already decided. They see each other every day. St Petersburg people can't resist gossip."

We were let in after more delay. No tickets seemed to be handed over despite our numbers. I asked Ivy why. She gave an enigmatic smile. Another mystery? It was quarter to eleven.

Natasha assembled us round her coloured umbrella and racked her delivery up another load of decibels to tell us of the history of the Hermitage. I switched off. Like everybody else, I already knew of Catherine the Great. That empress was a true con artist, playing off every other national leader for gain – and any gain would do. She chiselled away at Walpole to con him out of over a dozen Van Dykes, in exchange for a grotty portrait of herself. (He was our start-up prime minister, so was easily twisted.) Her famous Ten Commandments is in every schoolkid's essays these days; I like her Seventh, *Do not sigh or yawn*, but hate the thought of her Eighth, *Agree to join in any suggested game*, without saying what the games would be. Her best was her First Commandment, *Leave your rank at the door with your hat and sword*.

"Why are you smiling, Lovejoy?"

"Her and Prince Potemkin. Didn't he amble through her rooms when she was holding court with influential foreign ambassadors?"

"Yes. But of course, she wasn't Russian. He was."

"Dynamite, though. Got things done, eh?"

"Stay together!" cried Natasha up in front.

"I never admired him," Ivy confided, "not as I admire Pushkin. Though all brilliant Russians have flaws. Dostoevsky had epilepsy. Prince Yusupov had been to Oxford." Ivy smiled mischievously at her quip. I quivered as our lot edged forward en masse. "Keep calm, Lovejoy. They will still be there when we reach Rooms 143 to 146 on the second floor. Nobody could possibly remove them, could they?"

That tone again. Some private grief, from a former visit perhaps? I didn't quiz her about it.

I'd not done so well with my attempts to sound educated in Lady Vee's meeting, so I kept off Russian writers.

"I did my dissertation on Pushkin, Lovejoy. Hopeless."

Natasha shrilled, "On this tour we pass the first floor! It has all manner of prehistorical Russian items, Transcaucasian and Egyptian and Greco-Roman artefacts. We ignore these! We move to the second floor by staircases."

"Excuse me," said an anxious gentleman, who always looked so scholarly in the ship's library. "I had hoped – "

"First floor not on our D4 ticket specification! This way!"

We climbed the stairs, the man expostulating to anyone who would listen, "I've come all this way to see the Black Sea Greek colonies of the Seventh Century BC. I wish to draw the Siberian jasper Kolyvanskaya Vase." His voice receded as we draw ahead in the crowd. Ivy had an enviable knack of somehow overtaking people without effort. Left to myself, I'd have been trailing the entire throng within a few paces.

"Another gambler, except he had enormously long yellow fingernails?" That exhausted my knowledge of literature.

"Please don't criticise Aleksandr Pushkin, Lovejoy," Ivy told me. We were still climbing, with the scholarly bloke still wittering below. "Here, it's seen as treachery. A tiny man, given to womanising and fighting duels. His grandad was an Ethiopian slave, they say. Couldn't keep still."

Nice to see Ivy smile. Years fell off her as we got to the top of the narrow staircase. I began to feel queasy and thought, here we go.

"I've some water, Lovejoy." She brought out a small plastic bottle and broke the seal. I took a swig, patted my forehead with a glug. "Put your arm through mine. Do I have to watch you for anything?"

"I can totter on my own, ta," I said, gracious to the last, pulling away and returning her bottle.

"Here!" cried Natasha. "We now pause to see the Malachite Hall!" And led us into a tall green room. That is *green* green, so intense and swirly I almost recoiled. I closed my eyes and grabbed for Ivy's arm. She clutched my hand and that's how I made it out of that place, clinging. The room was so frigging green it was claustrophobic. Malachite's a green rock, once used in making paint or green sculptures, clock pedestals and the like. It's gone out of fashion now, thank God. I find green a problem even in emeralds and other green gemstones, and women can never match the damned colour with anything else except tan, so why the hell do we bother? As a little lad I used to be spectacularly sick seeing red and green together, a sensitivity that made me dynamite at Christmas. We edged along.

"We're out, Lovejoy," Ivy said quietly, and I let daylight seep back into my brain.

The crowds had thinned but people were still about in numbers. I glimpsed another mob from our ship passing across one of the grand doorways in the distance. I'd never met such space in a building before. It dwarfed anything I'd seen. And gloriously, beautifully restored.

I even recovered enough to ask a question as Natasha passed by. It was about a chandelier, and proved Natasha's mettle.

"Excuse me, please," I got out. "Is that papier-mache chandelier made by hand modelling or by – ?"

"No! By the compression process of machine-emulsified material," she replied briskly. "You require the chemical composition of the glue, or the length of incorporated fibres?"

"Er, no, ta, Natasha."

"This way, D4!" she shrieked, and we were off like another marathon start.

"She's great," I said. Too good, in fact. I noticed she kept acknowledging the stout ladies who invigilated in every doorway of the numbered rooms, and once I saw her slip a cell phone into her handbag. She also seemed occasionally to mutter into her umbrella's handle, her eyes everywhere. Nobody would get lost on Natasha's watch, that was for sure.

We emerged on a wide landing. The air stifled me. I had to go slower, Ivy hanging back to stay with me. I had another swig of water and felt no better.

"We ignore the two Leonardo paintings!" Natasha called over her shoulder, "beyond the Council Staircase. And the Michelangelo statue of *Crouching Boy* that is in glass-encased but repays intensive study on another visit! Quickly, please!"

No wonder I felt definitely odd. My hands were clammy, my muscle masses aching, my breath rasping. I was drenched with sweat. Ivy got worried.

"Look, Lovejoy. I think we should try to find somewhere to sit a minute."

"No." I knew I wouldn't be better until I was out of the place. Another guide, this time a man in uniform, tagged along in the rear, shepherding us after Natasha. "I'll keep going, love." I'd my job to do.

"The Hanging Gardens of the Little Hermitage visible through the windows!" cried our beautiful guide at ramming speed. "Across is Dutch works of art, including many Rembrandts! You can photograph if you have paid for special star on special ticket, $3.60 in American moneys! Using camcorders extra!"

The windows were easy. I couldn't help noticing how simple they were, like the old Crittal designs. I know lads in East Anglian pubs who wouldn't even break step as they strolled in through windows like that, any height. And a canal seemed to come off the wide River Neva at exact right-angles and run underneath the Hermitage. Unless they surrounded the entire place with tanks and a battalion or two, an average robber could have the Hermitage's contents away before dawn, given enough transport. My sense of misgiving got much, much worse, the sicker I felt.

"Is it the antiques, Lovejoy?" Ivy whispered. "You're sure it isn't something you ate, or maybe the flu?"

"No, love. It's always like this." My chest griped, my shoulders creaking like rusty machinery.

"Across is Hall of St George!" Natasha trilled, her voice a bandsaw through my brain. "Here is *Hidden Treasures Revealed* exhibition! Enter in order! Fifteen minutes, please!" She added darkly, "I ... am ... *wait-*

ing!"

The rooms were frankly badly lit. I tottered in, glad to lean on Ivy. She was only slight, but kept me propped up as vibes shot through me. I could hardly see. The paintings were brilliant.

It's hard to realise how much our own famous works of art have changed even over so short a time as a century or even less. The paint alters, as the oil vehicle in which the pigments were applied become set over time. They grow less lustrous from pollution, from changing air temperature, barometric pressures, humidity, light. Worst of all, the exhaled breath of thousands upon thousands of visitors, the faint shaking of the human voice, and the microorganisms we carry about, does damage. The average human sheds a teaspoonful of skin scales a day, not to mention threads from our clothes, our hair – we lose sixty-three hairs on average a day, some scientist slogging to earn his money claimed.

These paintings, though, simply glowed. They had remained in unchanging conditions for half a century. Okay, I would have hung them differently, had more control over the light, kept visitors down to a few every hour, but the Russians had done a superb job conserving these. They were just as they left the artists' hands. Ten out of ten for Russia.

I gaped at the Cézannes. Who'd have thought his *Mont Sainte-Victoire* actually shimmered in its original condition? Every other version I'd seen looks flat from a yard away, from deterioration of the surface. Or that Vincent's *Landscape with House and Ploughman* was so clamorous to the eye that its colours almost yelled? I reeled from one canvas to another, Ivy apologising to passengers as I blundered through the press.

Minutes later I was propped on the wall by the great

staircase looking out at the Neva, shaking. Ivy spoke quietly to a Russian guardian lady, and I was given her chair. Ivy seemed to be explaining that I wasn't drunk, just unwell. The woman didn't believe her. I asked for tea, which seems understood in every language. We went downstairs, Ivy grunting and gasping a little unnecessarily I thought, but she got me into a small caff near the computer room. I got served mint tea. I hadn't known mint tea tasted so good.

The vibes receded slightly once Ivy got me mobile and among the crowds. We seemed to be the only ones buying anything. Ivy was adept at making herself understood. Natasha's gloomy trailing bloke followed us all the time, which I didn't mind. He glowered when we failed to offer him some tea, so I beckoned him over and he accepted a glass of the stuff. Ivy ignored him, but he chattered a lot and seemed to be telling me about football. He was called Ilya. He looked a born killer, steady eyes, Slav chin and upturned nose, but hands that had strangled.

"The Golden Rooms, Lovejoy?" Ivy asked. She spoke to the man in Russian and notes changed hands. I tried counting the dollars in case I'd have to owe her, but gave up. Nobody absorbs notes slicker than a security man on the take.

"Ilya will let us in to the Golden Rooms, Lovejoy. Come. Can you stand? We have eleven minutes only."

I made it, exhorted by Ivy. She proved a tower of strength. Like many women who looked puny, she had disproportionate power.

"Here. By the Secondary Entrance." She opened her hands like a Palladium showman. "The Hermitage's famous Special Collection!"

It cost. Ivy had to do the verbals, with Ilya along to lend baritone and subdue the stout female guardians. More dollars? I thought, God Almighty, I'd be paying this free visit off until I was ninety, the way Ivy was spending. She'd already bought me four great tomes, each an arm and a leg. Once inside, over I went and came to myself on a stool being lectured to by a security lady in uniform and three stray ladies who'd come to see the gold – pure ancient gold – artefacts but found a dizzy male stranger much more interesting. Like all females, they delightedly seized the chance of ballocking a man for being ill in the first place, sternly admonishing Ivy in various languages for not living up to her woman's job of keeping me fit. That gave them all the opportunity of bringing up ailments they themselves had suffered, to great satisfaction, then recovered from. That dealt with, they then argued different remedies. I suppose that's all it was.

Meanwhile the rooms ramjam packed with gold from the Crimea, Ukraine, and the Caucasus, shimmered and blinded. I apologised, pretended to recover, got no further in than my stool by the door, thanked everybody profusely, and let Ivy lead me out of Special Collection Rooms 41 et seq.

"I'm sorry, Lovejoy," she said from a great distance. "I thought it would bring you round."

"Okay." We went through the security check to escape, and I got a chance of a cool breath of non-antique air at the entrance.

Within minutes Natasha's bandsaw voice pierced the halls of the Winter Palace and we were on the move. The security man Ilya sheepdogged us to the exit and wistfully waved us off as we disgorged by the Neva. It isn't often streets look truly glamorous, but Russia manages it. Or maybe it was just that I was relieved to be feeling better? I think it was the glamour.

My muscles stopped aching, my hands dried themselves spontaneously, and my face no longer dripped with sweat. I began to walk fairly upright like a late-order primate, getting as far as, say, Neanderthal.

"Sorry, Ivy," I said in the cold fresh air of the waterfront. "It was stuffy in there."

"Real, were they?"

"Well," I began, then realised.

"I was joking, Lovejoy. Your collapse was too convincing. Is it always like that?"

"Yes. A headache will be along soon. It will be bad."

"I'll see to you."

"Look, love, I'm spoiling your outing. There's really no need."

"I'm enjoying myself," she said, sounding really honest. "Best morning I've had in years."

"Shouldn't we find your Billy?" I didn't want to be accused of anything devious, him such a macho bloke.

"Don't worry. I know exactly where he is."

We moved to the coach the instant the driver came. A few Russian children pestered us, begging. I reached for some money. Ivy stayed my hand and bustled me away. She was cross.

"That was a bit harsh, love," I remonstrated. "She was only eleven, and carrying an infant."

"Lovejoy." She was so exasperated she said my name like teachers did at school, making two enormous syllables – Love… *joy* – and rolling her eyes. "Didn't you notice? Her hair was streaked and tinted. Do you know how much that costs? And she wore designer slacks and handmade London shoes. Have you no sense?"

She went on and on, how the girl had gold caps to two teeth, the infant wore two valuable jade necklets and the girl three gold bangles and a custom watch.

"Begging is an industry here," she lectured me quietly on the coach as Natasha started up hope-you-all-enjoyed prattle. "You have to learn."

From the coach window I watched the little girl, who nonchalantly took out a gold cigarette case. She extracted a cigarette and lit it with a gold lighter, staring insolently up at the coach as we drove off.

"You aren't really streetwise, are you?" Ivy said.

This narked me, because nobody is more streetwise. I told her so, adding, "No need to keep on, just because you can yap a few words of their lingo."

"I was born here, Lovejoy." She affected not to notice as Billy and Kevin looked round at us, said something to each other and roared with laughter. "I really think it's time I took you in hand, at least for the rest of your visit. What are you doing this afternoon?"

"Having a headache. You?" It was already starting, slamming down my right side and making my vision fizzle. No longer the flu feeling, just the cerebral stunner.

She smiled. "I'll help, Lovejoy. Close your eyes and I'll tell you about Russia."

Chapter Twenty-Six

I slept for an hour in my cabin, crawled upright with a stunning migraine, went for a feeble nosh, then swam even more feebly in one of the ship's pools. The passengers had mostly gone ashore on trips – all of them sounding exotic, this palace, that monastery. I felt filleted, climbed out of the pool and flopped onto the tiles. My head was splitting.

Ivy leant over from her promenade recliner and handed me a towel. No Billy the Kid.

"Any better?"

"I'm done for."

"Can you be ready in ten minutes? A banya will cure you."

"Not thirsty, love, but ta."

She did the non-smile, making me feel idiotic. "It's not a drink, darling. It will restore you."

"What is it?" I asked with suspicion, remembering the women at the Hermitage and their competing remedies. "Something Russian?"

"Oh, yes, Lovejoy." A real smile lit her features. She was lovely. "Very Russian. Everyone should visit the banya at least once. It never fails."

"Honest?" I couldn't go on like this. I'd once had a really bad divvy experience meeting a gold Ancient British torc found in East Anglia near Mildenhall, and fondly imagined my divvy-induced migraines couldn't come any worse, but this one was ruinous and I had to report to Purser Mangot at six o'clock. I'd be lucky to reach his office in this state. "Okay, then."

Uneasily, still mistrustful, I disembarked, making sure I didn't let my thumping head whack me over into the water as I reached the quayside. I made sure the Ghurka knew I was leaving, had my plastic cards bleeped on their machines. I chatted determinedly to a few other passengers, telling them I was going to a banya with Mrs Ivy Sands, just so they could tell our consul if I got abducted.

We got into a taxi, the driver voluble in Russian. He tried German, a bit of Swedish I think, then went back to Russian with Ivy, seeming amused. Twice his eyes lit on mine in the rear-view. He shook his head, chuckling, saying, "Banya."

"I didn't say so-long or ta to Natasha," I remembered as the taxi swerved and hooted and accelerated.

"I did. We tip a small amount after each tour."

The driver's eyes lit up. He knew the word tip. Still he chuckled. And stopped outside a squarishly dull building. We were about two miles from the ship. He opened our door with a flourish, and even a stranger as raw as me knew this courtesy was an all-time first. He said something to me, grinning.

"In, Lovejoy," Ivy said, paying him.

"Will you be here when I come out?" Translation: Was this the abduction and assassination I'd darkly imagined, finally here now I'd done my stint divvying the Exhibition?

"I'm coming with you, silly."

She sounded exasperated, which was good. Exasperation was safe. I let her go first, ever courteous, in case there was a gunman behind the transparent glass doors, and slowly followed, ready to run. We went in to a changing room, after Ivy paid more fees to yet more guardians. Russia, I began to see, was composed of two kinds of people: uniformed security folk, and the rest. They came in more or less equal proportions. You pay one lot whenever they look expectant, and can safely ignore the latter.

"Men that way, Lovejoy. See you later."

"Eh?"

The admissions lady said something to me, Ivy the

same thing. I nodded with a weak smile, and entered a changing room. Blokes, including Ilya I was surprised to see, were stripping off. I looked for what we were all to change into. Nothing? Everybody stripped down to their nip, like after a football match.

"Parilka," Ilya said to me, nodding and smiling.

"Parilka," I said, hoping it meant yes I'm fine. I could hardly see, my temples thudding. I couldn't make out what he said after that, but it sounded the same thing the taxi driver, Ivy and the wardress had told me.

We entered a room so hot I felt my skin try to peel itself off. Everybody stood around, some doing exercises, others posing or patting themselves. Sweat started but evaporated as soon as it reached the torrid atmosphere. Breathing was actually painful. I could hear my breath rasping as it went into my lungs. I thought, this is madness, and they're all off their blinking rails, quite barmy. What the hell is all this hot air for, for God's sake? Ilya tapped my shoulder and beckoned. I followed, anything to get out of the terrible heat.

We entered a room so thick with steam I couldn't see a damned thing. There were rocks. The heat was stifling. Breathing was like inhaling gravel, and my head thumped worse. Everybody was starkers. Some loon ladled water onto heaped rocks so we could be steamed worse. More steam hissed and filled the air. I scented eucalyptus. I thought my skin was coming off. It was unbelievably hot. Somebody said something in Russian. Others laughed. I heard swishing. Then Ilya, who looked hell of a sight more of a bruiser naked than when clothed, took up a bessom thing and shoved me onto a vacant plank.

Others were reclining, to be beaten by the twigs. The first swish drove the remaining breath from me.

That was the steady hiss-hiss sound I'd heard ever since we'd arrived. I heard women's voices somewhere close. The broom slashed at my skin. I noticed others swapping places and lashing out. My skin felt raw. I felt I hadn't breathed properly for a week.

Ilya finally stopped and I was given a switch of small branches. I lashed out at the blighter, thinking take that, you swine. Other blokes poured fresh water on the rocks to sizzle more steam. It was hellish.

A few minutes, with me spent and sagging, Ilya rose and beckoned. I followed out of that steamy hell into a freezing cold tiled room where an icy pool shimmered.

"Basseyni," Ilya said proudly, and leapt into it. He shrieked, "Colt! Colt!"

Basin? Cold? Wincing, I tiptoed slowly down the small ladder into the freezing cold pool, gasping and puffing as the ice – there was actually floating frigging ice on the surface that some lunatic had put there, for Christ's sake – as the ice rose up my legs. I shrivelled, the blokes splashing in the pool roaring laughing and trying to make waves so I would be engulfed. I made it, for the sake of national honour, and tried swimming about a bit, gasping and huffing.

Ilya, the sadistic swine, was already climbing out and beckoning.

"Parilka," he said, guffawing.

I'd hated parilka last time and wanted to go back to the ship. He hauled me out and dragged me into the steam for a second go. I was definitely on the blink by then, my circulation having given up and my brain beeping its last goodbye synapse.

The steam slammed me almost moribund. I got beaten stuporous by different twigs, floppy fir bessoms this time, in hot clouds that were surely lethal. I was too weak to switch Ilya, who was killing himself laughing by this time and explaining to his mates I was a weak-kneed visitor, which set them all roaring laughing.

The cold pool experience was almost natural by the time I followed dully for the re-run. Naked as a grape, I floundered in. My skin had given up trying to make sense of all the sensations. I couldn't feel heat or cold.

Three goes, and I was shoved unceremoniously through a doorway into ordinary climate, where some bulky woman slapped a sheet at me. I was asked for money, but Ivy was already there, draped in a toga and seated on wooden slats. Women and men were arguing about something quite passionately. I wrapped myself in my sheet and flopped exhausted by Ivy.

"You rotten cow."

"There, there, darling." She was laughing. "Would you have come if I'd told you what it was?"

"Well, no."

"And how's the headache?"

I tried to feel something, anything, in my head or anywhere else. It felt light, things at a distance but no pain between my temples.

"Gone." It was a guess.

"I can't hear, darling," she said, her pound of flesh.

I cleared my throat. "Gone."

"There!" She waited. "Thank you, Ivy darling, would be super."

"Ta," I said ungraciously.

"Not at all, Lovejoy."

She unscrewed the cap from a thermos flask and poured a little of the fluid for me to taste. It was unbelievably sweet.

"Tea, with mint, jam and honey and molasses sugar," she said. "It's traditional. Different parts of Russia people swear by various recipes. In Novgorod, where the banya started, they favour honey and a distilled juice they make from various berries."

It was good. Feeling crept back into my shoulders.

I could actually sense a breeze on my face. Maybe I wasn't dead after all. I returned her cup. She decanted some for herself. Cautiously I glanced round at the twenty or so people sitting round the room.

"How does your skin feel?"

"Smarting, like it's sore."

"That's good. The toxins are leaving."

"I haven't got any toxins," I said, narked.

"Not now." She was all smiles. "We rid ourselves of impurities by coming to the banya. In the West, people don't bother. This is more sensible, don't you agree? And you get to like it."

"Did they thrash you with those twig things?" I asked, curious.

"Of course. They don't do it elsewhere. Southern Russians think it's ludicrous. St Petersburg folk repeat the hot-steam-cold process twelve times in a fixed ritual, some saying favourite poems with each bath. Especially Pushkin. This banya doesn't have a hot open-air pool, but many banyas do. Russians favour those. You can gaze at the moon while floating in the warmth, even in the snows. Luxury, with friends drifting along to argue politics and poetry! Could anything be more Russian, or more wonderful?"

She gave me some more of her strange tea. I liked it.

"Alternative to toxins, eh?"

"Much better, darling." She smiled. "And you kept your key!" They'd given me a locker key on a string round my neck.

"Time to return to the *Melissa*?"

"In a few minutes. We can just listen to people."

So we listened, doing nothing except sit there. I couldn't understand a word. There wasn't a toxin in sight. I thought, God Almighty, do I actually love this woman? I thought of her in my Ten Word Game, and lost.

*   *   *

The ship was quiet. We were the only ones returning, and the Atrium into which we stepped was tranquil. Apart from a couple or two seated round the lounges and a stewardess serving a lone bar-fly, there was nobody to listen to the tinkling piano. The three balconies soaring above showed people reading or talking. It was so peaceful.

"Do come, Lovejoy."

"Look, love. Ta for the banya. How much do I owe you?"

"Not a thing. It was my pleasure."

"Are you sure?"

We went to her cabin. I hesitated when she opened the door and invited me in.

"Er, is this all right with your Billy? Only, I wouldn't want – "

"For heaven's sake!"

She pulled me and I entered. It was much larger than mine. Twin beds, a proper bathroom instead of just a shower, and a sitting alcove. Not quite on the scale of Lady Vee's, but getting there.

"Would you like a drink?" She had a fridge, and took out some wine. I demurred, but accepted some water. I was thirsty. She had two armchairs and a desk. I sat when she ordered.

"Peter the Great used a banya near the river. He used to run along the riverbanks naked after a good steaming." She laughed. "The phrase they all say, that you asked about, is 'Hope your steaming goes easily.' And afterwards they say, 'Hope it was easy.' It's a custom."

"Do you and Billy come back to Russia all the time?"

"This is the first. We've been married ten years."

A silence started. I find that silences don't just extend lengthwise, getting sort of longer. They actually spread out, covering everything you can see and touch. I was nervy for some reason. This was odd, because there'd been scores of mixed people in that banya place.

"Look," I said, on edge, putting my glass down. "I'd best go. I've to see somebody later. I don't want to be late."

"Stay, Lovejoy," she said, not looking. Her voice had almost extinguished itself.

"I'm in such a mess, love," I heard myself say, sounding even more pathetic than usual. "I durstn't make matters worse by – "

"Please," she said, and did a kind of brave smile. "And I'll tell you more about Russia?"

I tried to say it was a deal, but could only croak.

∗ ∗ ∗

We lay in the cramped single bed. I'd almost fallen off while we made smiles. She was lovely. I'd never seen any woman with such long hair, not since Norma from Swansea, only hers turned out to be a gruesome hairpiece she'd won in a raffle and couldn't bear to part with. She'd woken me (Ivy, not Norma) because I was crushing her leg and she'd got pins and needles. I came to grudgingly, hoping she'd given me enough time to sail out of the small death. I felt around inside my brain. Peace was in there. I smiled.

"Wotcher."

"Was I all right?"

See? Always that doubtful litany. I said she was stupendous, I'd been in paradise. I think poets should get their acts together and educate women to believe in ecstasy, tell them there's no need for doubt because making smiles is never anything less than superb. She squinted at me, probably wondering how many of her imaginary defects she could muster to convince me she was poor quality.

"I'm such a mouse, though. And I'm hardly a stunning looker." This from a woman who'd given me sheer bliss.

"Do I seem unhappy?" Ball in her court.

"No." She went shy. "You seemed … transported."

"Possibly because I was." There's no way to convince them, though I always try. "Then we're quits."

"Once before, I fell for another man," Ivy said softly.

"Did Billy see him off?"

"Billy?" She laughed a laugh with a snarl. "He wouldn't know if I'd written it in letters a foot high. It was Potemkin, the Prince of Princes."

Potemkin was dead. "Isn't he, er…?"

"I still worship him. He ruled Russia. Tall, a born ruler, a superb man any woman would go crazy for." This made me, a shiftless antiques dealer heading for doom, feel really confident. "Catherine the Great's lover."

"One of them."

"Don't believe rumour. She only ever took a dozen serious lovers. And always Potemkin. She married him in secret, and called him 'My marble beauty', saying 'better than any king!'" She giggled. "His old dressing gown kept flapping open, but he didn't care!"

The pillow was fluffed up. I pressed it down to see her better.

"I thought you were all for Pushkin, that poet bloke?"

"Oh, I was!" She drew patterns on my skin with a finger. "Pushkin sent me demented."

"Potemkin too?"

She gave my shoulder a sharp bite. I grunted. "Before that it was Byron. Every woman's dream lover. And Shelley. The things I did when I was on my own, thinking of poor Doctor Keats!"

"When was this?" I asked uneasily.

I'm no Sherlock Holmes, but even I could see something was seriously wrong. Fine to admire heroes, but Ivy's voice contained something near lust. Uneasily I wondered if she was slightly barmy. Now, I'm all for love. There's not enough of it about. But it has to be there, here, sort of somewhere, not a vague abstract fondness.

Take Marilyn Monroe, for instance. I'd give a lot to have known her, and history says Cleopatra was dynamite between her sheets. But I've more sense than sob in my ale because I can't make smiles with them in the car park. No chance of a swift snog and grope there, because sadly they are no longer with us. So I must face my deprivation with fortitude. Mind you, dreamery can be an innocent game played by educated people with truly brilliant minds. Like, the wholly imaginary Sherlock Holmes has a real London address, to please tourists asking for directions in Baker Street. And in October 2002 he was made a Fellow of some prestigious English Royal Society. Quite daft but harmless, people having a laugh. Ivy's cravings after dead lovers? It was beginning to sound like a weird career.

"After I was married, I never thought of Russia much. I was a little girl when we left. Bilingual, of course. At home we spoke Russian. Billy was always busy, so I did a degree in the language, and kept going."

"Expert, eh?"

"Grandpa was a poet here, in the great siege of Leningrad. Did you know that poets kept the city

going? When everybody was dying from shells and
hunger, the radio kept broadcasting poetry. Then one
by one even the poets died from starvation or the
guns. The radio had nobody left, and simply broadcast
the clock ticking, ticking, so the defenders knew that
they were not alone. Somewhere in the snow among
the ruins, others too were standing to arms."

She shivered. I held her. We all have too many
ghosts, and Ivy had more than most. I felt like saying
it, but I have a habit of getting things wrong.

"Sorry there's only me here, love." It was a joke, but
fell flat like jokes do.

"Thank goodness." She reached for me and I quivered. "I'm so grateful. Can I be on my side this time,
please? Only, you overlaid my leg and it's still sore."

"Oh, right." Still, whose fault was that? You can't
think of everything, when paradise is on offer.

✻ ✻ ✻

Despite what she said, I roused enough to leave before
half-four. Ivy said to stay a minute longer, but I was in
enough trouble. A barney with Billy was out of the
question.

Dressed and ready to go, I found her between me
and the door. Her face was streaming with tears.

"Did I say summert wrong, love?"

"No, Lovejoy. You've been lovely." She slowly
recovered. "Will you go to the evening show after dinner?"

"Dunno. I've to see Mangot."

"Please don't fob me off." Her arms came round
me. "I want to help you. Promise me one thing." And
when I nodded, "The tours tomorrow. Whichever you
are sent on, make sure I am on the same one. Promise?
Cross your heart and hope to die?"

I wouldn't go that far, so said, "Hand on my heart."

"Thank you for today. You're what I wanted."

"Me and Potemkin?"

She gave a shy smile and let me go. Nobody in the corridor, by a fluke. I left thinking, she wants to help me? How, exactly, and why? Why was it so vital to be on the same tour? Worst of all, why did I feel her gift of love had been in farewell? In Old London Town they used to stop the tumbrils at St Giles Church to give condemned criminals one last drink before they reached the hangman at Tyburn. Making smiles with Ivy was better than any swig, but I wanted the rest of the cruise to be safe. I went to find Mangot.

Chapter Twenty-Seven

Purser Mangot was in the Mayfair Lounge, openly seated near the bar in an armchair and smoking a cigar. He couldn't have been less smug. I expected him to clobber me in private. He beckoned, booming, "Hey, Lovejoy! Have a drink!"

"No, ta."

Mangot was in full fig, attracting two ladies to join him.

"You liked the Hermitage exhibition, then? I heard you went today."

As secret as rain. What *was* this? Until now, all contact had been sub rosa, and here he was bandstanding in public. A steward brought him a brandy.

"Aye, great."

"You with your divvy skill." He winked at the two women, who simpered at his wit. "Any of them duds?"

"They seemed okay. I had to go out. It got stuffy. There'd been some surface restoration on – "

"Don't blind us with technicalities," he boomed. Everybody laughed. Such a popular bloke, our Executive Purser. "Going ashore tomorrow?"

"Dunno. I was waiting for you to tell me."

"What?" He did a theatrical start, guffawing. "Passengers needing to be told where to visit? You chose this cruise, or have you forgotten?"

"You said – "

"Seven guided tours tomorrow, and all excellent value. You'll like the Rasputin one."

"Do you mean that's the one I've to go on?" I wanted it spelled out before witnesses.

"Up to you. Glad you liked the Hermitage."

"Right." For a second I stood like a lemon, but that seemed to be it. I left, mystified, and went to find Lauren to get ready for the antiques quiz. I wasn't deceived.

By talking to me in the Atrium, Mangot was making sure everybody knew I'd been to suss out the Hidden Treasures Exhibition. He was setting me up. I can scent the trick a mile off.

Okay, those old-style windows in the Hermitage wouldn't give any self-respecting thief heartburn. Even I could get in with a rope and a putty knife. There'd be guards, and detectors. I'd seen no cameras, no CCTVs, felt no sticky-mats, seen no red-eye beamer lenses, but that didn't mean they weren't there. Security people hide their gadgets in walls nowadays, safe from fiddling fingers. And a canal running underneath the Hermitage was God's gift to grabbers. But stealing is one thing and escaping with the loot is another. Until tomorrow, I was presumably safe on the ship.

Lauren was in her cabin. She let me in, looking bleary and dishevelled. I'd been nervous coming to meet her. I always find it's difficult saying hello to someone you've made smiles with not long before. It must be easy for women because they're always in control, having the moral ascendancy. I never know whether to be cheery and extrovert or meek. It's a bit creepy. Women have it so easy. I always finish up getting narked with myself.

It's even more unsettling when you haven't made any smiles at all but you feel it's soon on its way.

"Wotcher, love. I came to see if you've picked something out for tonight's quiz."

"I can't get through to the hospital, Lovjeoy."

"For Mr Semper? Shall we ask the captain?" was all I could think of.

"I've faxed the consul in Copenhagen."

"Good idea. Who gave you the message about his operation?"

"Purser Mangot. He is in charge of us guest speakers,

you see."

He would be. "Look, Lauren. How about you hire some lost-person searcher? You can do it by phone. Tell you what I'll do." I realised by now the cabins must be bugged, or at least the phones tapped, but played along. "Tomorrow we'll raise the Salvation Army. Don't they have them in Denmark too? They're good at finding missing people. Then you can fly out. You'll be in his hospital room by noon, bet you a quid."

"You're such a help, Lovejoy."

I couldn't take any more tears, so grabbed the three antiques she'd picked out of Henry Semper's collection of gunge and took them to the light.

They were ladies' fans. One had sandalwood radii with patterned silk leafing, a copy of an 1820 or so. The next was in ivory and silk, the kind people call "mandarin fans" now, but modern crud. The last was a filigree ivory fan, the radiate blades without silken leafing and made from ivory throughout. It had a coat-of-arms engraved on the decoration. It was genuine, 1860 or so. I was surprised.

"We'll ask the diners which is the genuine one, okay? And they must guess its price. The winner gets the honest fan."

She sat dolefully on the bed. "Lovejoy? Henry is all right, isn't he?"

"Of course he is!" I said, faking enthusiasm. "Danish hospitals are famous. They're stiff with surgeons." I babbled on, making it up. "They practically invented surgery of the, er, gastro-fundicular. Good heavens, Lauren, you can't lose heart now. He couldn't be in better hands."

"Please don't be upset, Lovejoy."

"Upset?" I wasn't upset, except about getting killed in the morning or gaoled in the Gulag.

"You see, when we, you and I ... y'know? I feel I

am being disloyal to Henry, being drawn to you. There! I've said it. I shouldn't be. It is betrayal."

"Betrayal?" God, how I wanted to leave. "Look, Lauren. You're distraught with worry. Like me." I mentally crossed my fingers and fibbed on. "What are friends for? We're his friends, together working out how to help him. That's all we do. Nothing bad. He'll be glad his friends are teamed up."

"Do you think so?"

"Of course, Lauren!"

"You see, Lovejoy, Henry and I were never *really* really one, meaning together in the sense that we..." and so on.

There was half an hour more of it. I finally reeled out and had to dash to get ready for dinner. It wasn't a black tie-and-tux evening, seeing we were in port. Posh occasions were for sea days only.

✻ ✻ ✻

The talk was all of St Petersburg. Billy and Kevin laughed – he roaring, Kevin tittering – about local customs. I got the unhappy feeling that Billy's cracks, all derogatory, were aimed at Ivy. She smiled and said little. Millicent had had a marvellous time among the tourist shops, but found nothing much except silver. Holly Sago was replete, her eyes glinting still, occasionally snapping some Churchillian imperative to keep Kevin from showing off too much. Kevin had had a failed day, having tried to buy some antiques to ship to London and finding nobody able to make decisions.

"How the hell they manage their stupid commerce, God alone knows," he kept grousing. "They kept telling me I'd to see somebody else..."

Ivy said nothing. She was playing her allotted role. I began to get the drift. She was the simple uncompre-

hending wife who wasn't worth asking. I looked more
and more at Billy's extrovert performance with Kevin.

The dinner-time antiques quiz was better organised
now. After the main course, I'd get up and go to the
restaurant manager's table, check the "antiques", then
give the nod. Lauren and I would simply walk them
slowly past the tables, on which stacks of the blank
cards were placed by stewards. No delay, no hesitation, no pausing to explain or answer questions. If I
noshed fast, and Lauren got on with her meal, we were
be back at our seats in time for pudding. Then it was
only a matter of collecting the cards with the answers
as folk left, and we'd be in time for the evening floor
show, the theatre or the latest film. We'd simply take
the first correct answer. Fini.

That evening I reported to Lady Vee, took her to
see the exquisite dancers – Amy to the fore – and
found myself laughing edgily at Les's full-on routine.
Lady Vee admired the dresses, the band, the music.
Then a quiet drink in the Monte Carlo Club, where
Lady Vee tried to outdo Holly Sago in losing at poker
and blackjack, then roulette, then the fruit machines.
I finally took her to her suite and said goodnight. She
demanded I take her on an outing in the morning – to
guess where – the palace where Rasputin got killed.

"I've booked our tickets, Lovejoy, dear!" she carolled. "Won't you stay for another drink?"

"Ta, love. Night." I was knackered, and left. I made
my cabin just as I slumped into oblivion.

Or I would have, if I didn't come from the shower
to hear my cabin door click shut. I sprang to open it,
and saw the familiar heel just disappear at the end of
the corridor. I could hardly chase after her in my nip,
whoever she might have been, so I went back inside to
check what was missing. Answer: nothing. On the
bed, turned down with tomorrow's newspaper

"Welcome To St Petersburg – Second Day!!" – and the usual three chocolates on the pillow, was a large parcel.

Expecting a bomb, I undid it, head averted in case it exploded. It was a set of clothes. I put all the lights on to see. Clothes? Dark corduroy trousers my exact size, and a black rather worn leather jacket, with one pocket slightly torn. I sat on the bed and looked at them. Dark socks, and grubby shoes? I quickly took the shoes off the bed – it's a prophesy of death in Lancashire and still gives me the willies. A piece of paper read: *Darling, please don't spruce up tomorrow. Love, I XXX.* If it hadn't been so late I'd have rung Ivy and asked what the hell I was supposed to do with this load of tat, except her Billy would be there.

There's a fascist in each of us. I had become institutionalised, living like a lord on this grand cruise with its luxury service. And here was Ivy providing me with dross. To wear this gear, I'd have had to shed my clean snazzy clobber, and go about looking like a scruff. That made me think. I found an envelope in the jacket pocket. It held photocopies of my passport, driving licence, boarding card, and two visa cards. I scanned them. I found a small fold of American dollars, ones and fives. Were these clues? If so, in what game?

She wanted me to carry these things, but why? To report me to the St Petersburg police and have me arrested for false pretences? I'd heard stories about people getting slammed in the pokey for not being able to produce passports and boarding cards on demand.

I slept, with my new – okay, old and grubby – clothes folded on the chair waiting for the dawn. They were good enough for me. I made a vow to escape – how many was that? Eight? Nine? In the morning, I'd finally make a run for it, not stop until I reached some border, and never come back. This time I'd keep going whatever happened.

Chapter Twenty-Eight

"I lost over seven hundred!"

"Give up, love. You're worse than Holly."

"Holly Sago won last night, the bitch," Lady Vee said, with all the caring compassion of a gambler who hears her friend has won.

"She's better than you," I said.

"Right!" Lady Vee shrieked, causing heads to turn in the lounge. "I'll challenge her! Tonight!"

"Go on, waste your money, silly cow," I said, off-hand. "Serve you right."

"It's my reputation…" etc, etc.

She kept on. We were assembling to disembark. I got a small bottle of water. My gear caused smiles. Les Renown and Amy were whispering at the far end, looking at me. Les, always a scream, pulled his lapels to show he found my worn jacket a laugh.

Ivy entered with that Victor bloke. I felt jealous. She sat without a glance, reading some catalogue. I saw with relief she had the same colour of sticker on as we, for the Yusupov Palace tour. The tickets were handed me by Lady Vee's maid as I wheeled Diamond Lil to the Atrium. In one sock I had extra dollars. My mouth was dry. I felt full of panic, curt with the world, but ready to go.

"You're not usually surly, Lovejoy," her ladyship said.

"I put up with you, so I'm a frigging saint."

She fell quiet, waiting for the exodus. Half of me wanted to leap to the quayside and sprint to the airport, assuming there was one. I had Ivy's little fold of money and photocopies in my trouser pocket. The other half of me was curious to see what the scam really was. Bannerman and Cynthia were just getting their stickers. He gave me a wink. Cynthia's stare was compelling but I glanced away.

Millicent and Jim waved at us as they joined Billy and Kevin who arrived together, surprise surprise. Delia Oakley came over and said hello. Her pal Fern was going to a palace fifteen miles away, she told us.

"Fern hates all that Rasputin business."

"He was assassinated in the Yusupov Palace," Lady Vee announced with glee. "Will we see the bloodstains?"

"Can I help with the wheelchair, Lovejoy?" Delia offered.

"Ta."

Tour B2 was called. We shuffled down the corridor and through the security bleeps. I felt a pang when passing the Ghurka checkpoint, as if it was farewell. They were slick with Lady Vee's chair, slotting it into some lifting device on the coach's side.

"Pass this note to Holly, Lovejoy," Lady Vee said with sly malice, "seeing you're silly about her."

"Shut your teeth, you owd crab."

Delia looked sideways at that. Maybe it was my tone. Ivy and Victor Lustig boarded last, just as I was getting worried. I had the passengers pass the note along. Holly read it and beamed at Lady Vee, thumbs up. The gambling challenge was on. I noticed Natasha – lo and behold, our courier for the day, summery in a daffodil-yellow suit – pause and read the note, laughing with Holly. Nothing escaped Natasha's notice.

I couldn't help asking, "What's the bet?"

"All debts. Shops, casino, incidental expenses."

"Don't come crying to me."

"You're our antiques man, Lovejoy." She plucked my sleeve. "Will you get me Hoyle's famous book?"

"Edmund Hoyle's *A Short Treatise on the Game of Whist* came out in 1742, love, and is as rare as unicorn horn. It'll cost you a world cruise."

"That's ridiculous! It's so small! I saw one in a library." And on she whinged, the grumble of a collector wanting priceless antiques for a farthing.

Natasha meanwhile was deafening us through her microphone about Rasputin and his baleful influence on the Tzar and the Tzarina. I didn't want to hear about killing today, ta very much, so I just looked out at beautiful St Petersburg, where the giant Peter the Great ran naked along the banks of the Neva through the snows after his banya. I was still smarting from my own banya. Perhaps that was the idea, but I'd rather have the toxins.

"The Yusupov Palace," Natasha thundered through her echoey microphone, "was where Prince Yusupov, the husband of the Tzar's niece, killed Rasputin. A Flagellant monk, Rasputin taught that holiness comes only through sexual exhaustion. His name means He-who-is-debauched…"

Eventually we passed a market, the next street the Moskovsky. Even I could make that out by saying the letters over to myself. It was at a wide junction with shops on every corner, a smart part of town.

Almost immediately our coach turned off into gardens with a small lake dotted with islands. It looked rural. My spirits rose. The canal beyond was within running distance, say for a fleeing man. From the busy square to the Yusupov Palace on the canal was no more than a couple of hundred paces. I could do that.

And no Amy on our coach, no Purser Mangot, no Les Renown with his tiresome ten-liners. We alighted, my spirits wondering if it was safe now to peer out. I got hold of Lady Vee's wheelchair, all but shoving Delia Oakley away in my eagerness. Gallant to the last, I realised I could use Lady Vee as a shield if somebody tried to gun me down.

The Palace was exquisite. I wondered about Ivy, but

I couldn't see her or Victor. I couldn't swallow, my throat gone dry. I tried to gulp a little water.

"Are you all right, Lovejoy?" Holly said, closing in to arrange tonight's gambling match.

"Yes, ta. Just admiring the, er, gargoyles and that."

"He's in a temper because I tell him home truths," Lady Vee said.

"What about?"

"He's crazy for you, that's what."

Holly Sago laughed. "Better not tell Kevin that," she said evenly. I wondered what was going on, and between whom.

"Let me, Lovejoy," Delia said, taking the old lady over. She was good at coming to my rescue. She'd done it when Josh Bannerman went berserk over those pearls. I really liked her. "You're probably tired from all your exertions," she added sweetly.

See what I mean about women? I couldn't stand her. She meant she believed Lady Vee about me and Holly. Here was I in danger of death, and they concentrate on pecking order, when there can't be any such thing among women, who are all as brilliant as each other. I hung close as we were mustered by Natasha. We trailed after her bright umbrella into the Yusupov Palace. My heart was going like a Maxim. I found it difficult to inhale. No clamminess, though, so it was plain fear and nothing to do with antiques.

The place was tranquil. No Russians about, except for two ladies at a stall near the hallway selling tourist trinkets and brochures. Nice amber, mostly the white amber so favoured in the Baltic States. For a moment I delayed, wondering if some small antique on the stall had caused me to dawdle. The lady became quite animated, offering me this and that. I smiled weakly, said my thanks and hurried after the B2 passengers. We looked a right motley throng. I've been in better retreats. Still, I felt safer in a crowd, so I eeled to the middle and trudged along as Natasha explained about the restoration of the Palace.

"The steps are very narrow!" she cried through her microphone. "We proceed one by one."

Here it comes, I thought, checking the exits. No sign of Purser Mangot, nor his aides. Where was June Milestone? With her boyfriend Mangot, that's where, drinking white Ukranian wine on the lawns of the Summer Palace, knowing I was for it anyway.

"No turning back!" Natasha screeched. My ears rang. "In sequence please!"

The rooms we entered looked as if they were deliberately left in a state of dinginess. It was a series of tableaux. Wax figures in authentic costume were disposed about behind glass. Prince Yusupov was there with the gun, and Rasputin seated, legs asplay, at the table where he was actually shot.

It was a bungled affair, Delia explained as I edged along down the narrow wooden stairs, peering in the weak light.

"They poisoned him first. He didn't die. So Prince Yusupov – this is his palace – shot him. He still didn't die. So they dragged him out across the snow and shoved him into the river where he drowned. Rumour says he *still* didn't die, crawled out of the river and back up these very stairs … are you all right?"

"Fine!" I said, perversely determined to appear the opposite of what I felt. Maybe it was a dim memory of what Henry Semper told me, to tell everybody wrong. I'd not done it so far. I'd been as honest as I could be. From now on, I would appear and say the opposite of everything I felt and thought. "I'm choking laughing." They sounded nearly as efficient as me.

We emerged into an open hall with a grand sweep of staircase. One thing, you have to give it to St

Petersburg. When they set out to restore a place, they do a perfect job. The stairs, carpets, gilt chairs, banisters, walls, mirrors, chandeliers, everything was spectacular. It was hard to imagine the place shelled to rubble, or whatever happened to it in the Great Blockade. If this was an instance of Russian restoration, they are masters of the art.

"Now to the Yusupov Theatre!" Natasha boomed. We were standing next to her. I think she saw herself as stage performer aiming for Number One in the video charts. I wondered if there was a way to fuse her microphone to shut her up.

"Did you see the blood?" Lady Vee hadn't been able to manage the narrow stairs, pretending in her wheelchair.

"Buckets," I told her. "Blood everywhere."

"And poison?"

"Buckets of it."

"I wish I'd seen it," she said wistfully.

"I'll buy you the film. It's gory."

"Is it?" Her eyes shone.

"This is the Yusupov Theatre!" Natasha bellowed. Gold and white doors were flung open onto the most stunning auditorium I'd ever seen.

The walls were spectacular. Velvet seats, all bearing the Prince Yusupov crest, were arranged for an audience. The carpet was plush and deep. Overcome, we tiptoed in and meekly took seats in turn along the front row. Natasha had the usual slanging match with some cuboidal lady guardian who insisted on counting us over and over. The whole theatre was brilliantly restored. We needed these Russian workmen to do our Tate Modern, the new gallery Londoners call The Tat Modern.

"This theatre was the scene of many performances by Russian performers for the Prince's invited audiences."

She signalled, and the splendid curtains swished back to reveal the stage. Instantly I felt rough, yet the scenery was only crude modern village mock-ups, the sort you'd see in any amateur drama company's pantomime season for Christmas revelries. They're what am-dram folk thespians call flats, daubed canvas and hardboard on plain wooden supports, with scenery poster-painted on. I'd done scores myself, for our village's mid-winter pantomimes. This scenery was Jack-And-The-Beanstalk tat. The glue and size has to be poured on hot, and stinks to high heaven. I could detect the aroma from where I sat gaping up at the proscenium.

It was hell of a size, the stage having two royal boxes, all gilt, gold leaf and yellow and white and red decoration around the "fourth wall", as actors all call the proscenium arch opening.

"This practice scenery is for students from ballet and acting schools for rehearsals," Natasha yelled. "Of course, to be thrown away when the actual performances begin later this week. A minister of culture will attend!"

She paused. We looked at her. Did she expect applause? She resumed.

"This theatre is restored in every particular. It is an example of Russian skill, and is admired by everyone from overseas."

"It looks great, Miss Natasha," I chipped in.

"Yes!" she said evenly.

"Is that it?" somebody grumbled in the seats behind me. I think Tour B2 expected some sort of show, perhaps the Bolshoi to come on doing *Swan Lake*.

"How long did it take?" I asked, trying to look calm and interested. My head was already pounding. I felt the theatre swimming round me. Giddiness started, but I stuck to my resolution. Sweat trickled, and the terrible muscle ache began. Gamely I started an enthusiastic beam.

"Four years, three months and two days," Natasha said. "Now we have admired the expertise of restoring skills, we move to the lovely courtyard where a glass of Russian champagne which is better than that of France is offered to you our kind guests, with St Petersburg cake which is tastier than that of the Dutch…"

"That's more like it," said Josh Bannerman.

I could hardly move. My hands were clammy but I forced myself to stretch and yawn as our courier led the way to the exit.

"Come on, Lovejoy," Lady Vee groused. "We'll miss everything."

"Go on, then," I said, giving myself time to get moving. "I'll race you."

"He's a case," Lady Vee said, less than happy at my tardiness.

I wasn't the last to leave, but nearly. I saw how I'd been hoodwinked, and why I was so necessary for the scam. I also saw what the scam was. I'd known all along, just been too thick to see. I must have the brains of a pot dog. I'd been mesmerised by the wine, women, shows, manipulated every single minute of the voyage. I've always known I'm stupid. This was my dimmest achievement.

"I do scenery like that for our village," I said, grinning and looking full of enjoyment, trundling Lady Vee into the garden. I should have said, "The robbery is nothing to do with the Impressionists, is it? Nothing even to do with the Hermitage, either." Except I didn't. I was too scared, still waiting for somebody to come and arrest me.

The gardens were so perfect they were distressingly neat. Not a blade of grass out of place, not a plant on show but was blooming vigorously. People exclaimed, while they got their mouths round the cake and gulped the champagne.

I could see the lake, the small artificial islands studded with blossom. It was a glimpse of paradise. Natasha boomed information about this garden designer, that architect.

"Marvellous, wasn't it, Lovejoy?"

"No," I answered Kevin. "A bit dull, after the Hermitage." Billy offered me a glass of the wine.

"We thought it superbissimo, didn't we, Billy?" Kevin insisted.

"I do better scenery than that in our village." I could hardly breathe, let alone swallow, but I forced a mouthful of the crumbly cake down and had a swig of the champagne. "They were obviously done in a hurry. Only students, though, Natasha told us. I use poster paints. Emulsion colours are a pig on canvas. It cracks like hell under stage lights."

"You weren't impressed?" Kevin looked alarmed and about to cry.

"Oh, the restoration was brilliant! I told Natasha that." I laughed heartily, I'd show the bastards. "I thought you meant the tatty stage scenery! Even Lady Vee could do better!"

"I'll have you know I once acted in a Strindberg's *Miss Julie* in the Liverpool Playhouse!" Lady Vee chirped up.

"That the one where she says she can't act?" I said, laughing.

"Don't be rude!"

"Any more of that cake?" I looked about. "I'm famished."

Billy and Kevin were looking at each other. Ivy and Victor came over to speak to Lady Vee, Ivy bringing her another glass of champagne. You'd think every-body hadn't seen food or drink for a fortnight.

"I was extremely good," her ladyship was telling anybody who would listen. "I was always applauded. They said my Ophelia was second to none in Oldham."

"Ophelia only floats on the river," I argued loudly. "Any actress can do that."

My throat wouldn't work and my breath was hard to shove in and out after the experience in the theatre. No wonder Henry Semper had wanted a bigger room for his fake antiques. I could practically hear my muscles screeching as I moved.

"Much you know!" Lady Vee shot back, scathing. "Lovejoy daubs a few pieces of canvas on amateur-drama sets and thinks he's Olivier."

"Never met a dud thespian who isn't the world's greatest," I said, chuckling. I was almost falling, but I kept going so the swine wouldn't have the satisfaction. "Did you hear Les Renown's joke about actors? Why does an actor not open the curtains in the morning? Answer: To give himself something to do in the after-noon!"

And I laughed and laughed. I deserved a medal for my performance.

Natasha started rounding us up on the terrace to take us to the tourist shops. I looked around casually for the loos and handed the wheelchair over to Delia. I strolled off, idly thanking the ladies who'd provided us with the nosh, and slowly followed the M and WC sign. I heard the voices recede. I stood for a count of ten, then eeled into the bushes.

Move slow, stand and look, take a few even slower paces as if your attention is caught by something, then take a few more paces. Make sure you follow the direction you originally planned, minimise the sight lines from the house, and keep obstacles – bushes, trees, sheds and shade if any – between possible viewers and you.

Then move fast, once you're unseen. Astonished, I stepped out into the street a few minutes later. I wore my tat with a swagger, like the rest of the blokes, trying to look cool – or is that slang obsolete? Once among people walking to the market, I went slower, hands in pockets, conscious I had no real plan.

The thing was to stay away from the ship, where I'd be done for. After, I wasn't really sure of who, only how and what. The only chance seemed to try for the airport or a later ship. The Line had shore agents in each port visited, but I couldn't trust those, and Mangot and his mob might have people waiting for me.

I entered the market near the large square, and strolled in among the stalls away from the main street. Our Coach B2 would soon be roaring past, passengers at every window. I roamed among the barrows. I was still shaking, but recovering. I'd done brilliantly, showed them all that the Yusupov Palace and its theatre hadn't affected me one bit. I'd looked completely unaffected. I proved to the bastards that I knew nothing, that their exquisite Wonder of the World might actually be dud. And I'd escaped. I offered a prayer of thanks to Henry Semper and his death-bed warning.

For one American dollar I bought some tea and unlimited sugar. Looking cocky and know-all, I stood and sipped. Some thirty minutes later I saw our coaches roll by, and felt the world had finally got back on its orbit.

Chapter Twenty-Nine

The next couple of hours I loitered, as only a lowly antiques dealer can loiter in a pretty average market. I grew sick of Russian grandma dolls – one inside the other inside the other. I strolled among the crowd, saw one or two cackhanded pickpockets hard at it. They worked in threes, like in the Middle East. In London they go in pairs, more efficient I suppose. I felt sorry for a German couple who got done, as we say, the lady's handbag being lifted. (The strap was sliced by scissors – new technique to me; usually it's a knife – by No.1, the bag grabbed by No.2 and cast to the third accomplice, who legged it. Pretty slick.)

The shoppers were mostly Russian. Tourists, identifiable by coloured stickers, drifted in baffled groups. I ditched my own B2 sticker. I saw more roubles here than I'd seen anywhere so far, visitors using dollars. A flock of children trailed foreigners, importuning and sometimes tempted to do a little subtle-mongering of their own. I tried to look bored. I judged time by the daylight, having no watch.

It doesn't take long to spot local customs. From the safety of the market I kept an eye on the traffic. I recognised taxis, with their chequerboard stripe and peridot-green windscreen light, but intending passengers seemed to have to dialogue his way in, but they sometimes gave up and walked away.

There seemed another technique to collar a motor: Stand with your arm doing a slow flapping motion, as if patting a non-existent child on the head. A car stops. Usually they're those noisy sewing-machine Lada things. The driver converses, you argue back, and the Lada drives off in disgust. Or, praise be, the driver raises a hand, still disgusted, and you get in. I had no way of knowing, but supposed they were fixing a price. Since I couldn't name my destination, I was immobile.

Another local custom seemed to be highly skilled spitting. Men were adept, hawking up and expectorating with accuracy. I wished I could do it. I saw one bloke spit at, and hit, a flowering weed from a distance of several paces. I took warning from this: don't duel in St Petersburg. Pushkin should have heeded. They also did a certain amount of expelling nasal mucus by pressing one nostril ... I'll not go on.

The thought occurred that I should leave the market, get some distance between me and the locality where I'd hoofed it. I decided against it. Police might pick me up and demand what I, a gungy stranger, was doing roaming near elegant houses of the rich. I'd be for it, or, at worst, put back on the *Melissa*. I had no illusions, now I knew what the scam was and what part I was to have played in its finale.

For what seemed hours I drifted, avoiding butchers' stalls because they make me queasy. As I went, trying to look unemployed, I did that truculent look most Russian blokes my age seemed to adopt. One or two came up and, holding up a droopy fag, muttered in Russian, presumably for a match. I moved off as if annoyed; I wasn't to be bothered by riff-raff. One bloke even tried to pick my pocket. I harrumphed as if to say what a pillock he was, trying it on with me and nodding amiably at where I knew his accomplices would be. He raised a hand in mute apology and edged away, probably assuming I was just another subtle-monger.

When I was faint from hunger – must have been well into the afternoon by then – I scented familiar fried food. I was too scared to try any of the small stand-up nosh bars in case I gave myself away, but was getting close to despair. At the northern edge of the market, where the Metro station was and the Moskovsky prospekt ran into the big open place, I saw a sign familiar the globe over, instantly recognisable. No cutlery, but the fastest food on the planet. I hadn't known they had them in Russia too. My heart warmed.

If possible I avoid meat. These days they say chips must be a foot thick or they kill you with saturated fat. Thin chips are death. Worse, quick nosh corrupts and is infected and stifles Planet Earth. What choice had I, though? I forgot all the health warnings. Here was a grub place I might understand. International cuisine, however badly it is talked down by posh chefs, became my instant hero. It had saved my life once before, in the USA late at night when there was simply nowhere else to eat. I'd had a long journey, and was starving, just like now.

A queue snaked onto the pavement. I was willing to wait. I saw a few tourist-looking people inside, and heard American accents. Some looked non-Russian, meaning they didn't wear the same sombre colours as I, and one or two exhibited coloured lapel stickers. Refugees from some coach mob, I supposed, off cruise ships – there were two others in the harbour. I'd had them pointed out. I wondered about talking to them, perhaps claim I too was a true-blue tourist. I was saved this risk by seeing some Russian youth, in similar drossy gear as I, try his luck engaging Americans in conversation. They shucked him off sharpish, even though he'd acquired a sticker. Maybe their couriers warned them?

My turn. The menu was in English and Russian. I asked for a load of everything, paid in dollars, and sat and gorged myself on chips with everything. The tomato sauce was bliss. Reckless with the salt, I wakened taste buds dormant for decades. I love bread, and had everything in a bap. Tea-logged from the market, I couldn't face yet more Russian tea, and thoughts of coffee were too daunting. I settled for cola and milk shakes. A long time afterwards, I went to the loo and then went round the nosh a second time.

It was pretty crowded. Time had gone faster than I'd supposed. When did *Melissa* sail? I was unsure, too het up to remember mundanities. If she cast her mooring in, what, eight hours, Mangot and his mob would somehow have to invade the Yusupov place, remove all that scenery, and somehow transport it to the wharves and load it into the ship's hold, all with the approval of the captain and port authorities.

Except, port authorities would be compliant, because of the bribery hereabouts. And the captain might control the ship, but what went on aboard her was in the hands of others. Like, the Cruise Director ruled show-business and entertainment. The Hotel Manager controlled catering and nosh. The Purser and Executive Purser ran the money, and money was paramount. So if they shipped some cargo, it would be done without question as long as it was legal and the right papers were signed.

Especially if the stuff looked like innocent designs for some manky stage production, and the sections were properly crated. Easy to handle. If, I guessed roughly, there were forty or fifty crates, so what? A ship of 75,000 tons could accept that without a wobble. She took on 2,000 passengers in three hours without batting an eyelid, and another 700 crew. What was a box or two?

Weakening, I went to the counter to justify my staying there. They'd given me change in roubles, and that went on fluid. The late afternoon sky lost its edge, the weather turning cold. A smattering of rain speckled the window panes, and still the St Petersburg folk crowded in. Odd, seeing their own nosh stands were brilliant from what I'd seen, but maybe this nosh was in fashion.

With wistfulness, I saw the last of the Americans leave, calling out to each other that their ship sailed at seven, or the hotel coaches would be leaving soon from the Bolshoi Theatre. Evidently an anti-culture brigade.

My choices were two. I could get a taxi to the airport, mill about there pretending I was early, or late, for some flight somewhere if anybody asked. Or I could loiter until dawn, then go to the Embassy ... but then what, claim political asylum? Or was that the other way round, what strangers did if they wanted to stay forever in a country? Or, probably safest of all, turn up at the Embassy and say I'd lost my way (this was it) and strayed from my coach. Then, what, fell asleep somewhere? Or say I'd been mugged, been unable to find my way back to the quaysides knowing no Russian? Not bad. I'd only to lurk in the shadows. With luck, I could stay safe until the morning.

Watching the sky turn grey, then dusk, then night with the lights of St Petersburg coming slowly on here and there, I felt a certain magic.

Cruelly the nosh bar closed. It was down to me and Russia's old capital city. Survival of the fittest.

* * *

If I'd got *Melissa's* midnight departure right, Mangot's thieves would have only a few hours of darkness to lift the stage scenery from the Yusupov Palace theatre. That meant they couldn't simply pack it into some boxes then lorry it across the city, crane it aboard and batten it down or whatever they did to cargo before setting sail, at least not until the city slept. Say, nine o'clock to midnight? Three hours.

So they'd be too busy to search for me, once they realised I'd gone missing. Still, they could blacken my name. I'd just not be there to get arrested for whatever they'd frame me for. Easy enough. I'd done similar things.

I reminisced in the dying market, thinking how to bubble Purser Mangot. Bubbling is our word for landing somebody in trouble while you look innocent. This is an example of a classic bubble: A lass called Devvie stole money from a children's hospice, a place for sick children. It was the usual fraud. Devvie was a bonny antiques dealer in Crouch Street, facing the Capitol cinema. She bought some worthless drinking glasses and had them engraved with grapes and vines, less than a penny a glass, and sold them "In Aid Of The Children's Hospice" for a fortune. She did other scams. Of course, her pure motives touched our hearts.

Devvie's Fund Raisers became a feature of the landscape, because people dig deep for ailing babbies. Her antiques shop burgeoned. Such a charitable lady, you see. She began to live the life of Riley, holidays, toured Europe, bought a pad in the Costa Brava, got one of those long cars that are all engine and nowhere to sit.

Then one day a genuine hospice collector – standing in the Arcade selling paper flags at fivepence a time – asked for help. A ward would have to close, see, if money couldn't be found. The government, so pure were they, told the Hospice to get stuffed. He asked me if I would sell a few nick-nacks. I said sure, and asked should I combine it with Devvie's next sale. He asked a terrible question. "Who is Devvie?"

"That antiques dealer in Crouch Street who supports your hospice," I said, gormless.

He thought. "There's a gypsy in Rowhedge who helps us with bric-a-brac. Don't you mean him?"

No, I didn't. The penny dropped. Devvie had kept

the entire proceeds. We'd simply helped the bitch
feather her own nest. She'd taken us all for idiots, me
most of all because I'd divvied multo things and
brought the money in. That year had been one long
headache. She simply made away with the gelt. She had
to be bubbled.

Word spread, and Big John took over. He had St
Albansbury's mayoral silver nicked on the sly (it was
only in a cabinet, never used) and sold cheap to the
uncomprehending Devvie. She gleefully flogged it to a
stranger, one of Big John's goons, who politely reported it to London's Lemon Street police station, who
arrested Devvie. The case against Devvie was cast iron.
The public fumed. The girls in gaol, where Devvie was
consigned for two years by an irate judiciary, sharpened their spoons. (Female prisoners stab their foes in
the showers with spoons sharpened against the walls
of their cells; just so you'll know.) The real reason the
authorities seethed most, though, was that pretty
Devvie had omitted to file tax returns, and kept the
Value Added Tax due to Customs and Excise.

That's a classic bubble. It'll be worse for her when
she gets out because the lads never forget that kind of
evil. Restoring the Hospice's finances cost us the earth,
and me any chance of getting back on the electricity.

Dark now. In the gloaming I saw two or three
layabouts buy a swig of hooch from some barrow.
Better if I too stank of booze, if I was going to sleep
rough, then the police might leave me be. I shuffled
up, watched some dosser buy his bottle, and when it
was my turn proffered the same notes, giving an irate
gesture to indicate the same stuff. It was colourless.
I'd never tasted vodka, but tossed it back merrily in
one go – and felt I'd been slugged with a brick. I actually staggered, gasped, croaked, almost fell. My head
gave one thump, a reminder not to drink it again.

Lights were on in the Moskovsky prospekt. I turned towards the main square, then left past the caff opposite and passed the station. From there it was less than a hundred yards back to the rear of the Yusupov Gardens, where I'd escaped from Natasha's eagle eyes and my B2 passenger crocodile.

A bloke staggered into the gardens, pausing every now and then to bawl a ditty, presumably aiming to slumber away his booze. I ambled along among the shrubbery. I found a place behind a shed. It wasn't warm, just out of the drizzle. I huddled down.

Sleep doesn't do much for me. I've always thought it a waste of time. I think God was a real beginner. I mean, what's sleep actually for? You get through the days as best you can, then are forced to lie horizontal gazing at the ceiling until it gets daylight when you can safely rise and shine. If you don't snooze you feel terrible. If you do manage to doze, you can get up and go about your business, knowing you'll have to waste another eight hours tonight, and so it goes. I think God didn't know his onions. He should have worked us out beforehand, saved us a load of grief. Still, I tried to kip knowing I was destined to knock on the ambassador's door in the morning complaining that my ship had sailed without me.

Except nodding off in the lamp hours brings thoughts you don't want. I find that. My mind wears itself out when it should be asleep instead of delving in its burrows, scouring for facts, piecing together bits of a story that finally I understood.

* * *

The greatest amber carver of all time was a Dane, Gottfried Wolffram, the one I'd mentioned, who was sent to work in Charlottenburg for the King of

Prussia. He became heated when people disagreed – not an all-time first for an artist. In 1707 he flounced off when Goethe (no, not that Goethe; a far humbler architect) thought the amber wall Wolffram had made should have been designed different. Other amber craftsmen were drafted in, took up the work, and eventually, unbelievably, finished a whole room made of amber. Like I told Delia Oakley and others when doing that talk on the ship, the Amber Room was called a new Wonder of the World when it was installed in Berlin. The "most glorious work of amber artistry in all history," it's always called nowadays when folk bother to remember its transitory existence. Tzar Peter the Great, who got around, received it as a gift. Packed into special crates, slab by precious slab, the stupendous Amber Room went off to Russia.

It landed up in the Summer Palace in 1763. Courtiers who saw it have left feeble descriptions – all agreeing that the fabled Amber Room was a dream of such beauty that it was beyond reality. Roman landscapes, flowers, bouquets of blossoms, trees, wandering figures, were carved so brilliantly that courtiers needed magnifying glasses to see the detail. And everything was amber, pure priceless amber of yellow, white, brown, golden colour, with occasional scenes in red. Not one inch was stained or artificial. Later designers tried to copy it in amberina glass – but that stuff only came in when the New England Glass Co. introduced their reheating technique to colour mere ordinary glass to an amber hue in the 1880s.

Mirrors increased the Amber Room's dazzling gold effect. Amber chandeliers with hundreds of amber droplets amplified the light of the golden amber walls and doors and windows.

Then came war. And in 1941 – so rumour told – Russia decided to hide her treasures and took it to vaulted tunnels near Sverdlovsk in the Urals. And guess what, the Amber Room vanished. A German officer, a prisoner in 1944, vaguely recalled orders that the Amber Room be taken to Koenigsberg in old Prussia, in the care of Alfred Rohde, that museum's curator. The Amber Room mysteriously disappeared, and so did Dr Rohde. After the war ended things sort of got back to sort of normal.

Except for one thing. The Amber Room was no more, and Dr Rohde – another mystery here – reappeared from the mist one morning to resume his job, and couldn't remember a thing. More mysteries followed, for when intensive questioning began Dr Rohde fell ill and died, poor chap. And a mysterious doctor who signed his death certificate, one Dr Erdmann, was mysteriously untraceable because he too vanished, if indeed he had ever existed. Odderer and odderer, right?

One unsolvable mystery is bad enough. Two is chance. Three is really a bit much. Four? Four mysteries occurring together is the stuff of mythology, or there are gremlins in the works. And the Amber Room's fate contains far more than four mysterious events. Like, just what was that mystery ship carrying, 23 nautical miles into the Baltic when it was supposedly torpedoed by a Soviet sub…? And *what* submarine, exactly? Wasn't the nearest submarine 200 miles away?

Every so often, magazine articles about the fate of the Amber Room turn up, mere copied copy churned by stringer reporters desperately worried for their pay. People exult about mysteries, and speculate how the Room must have looked, with that splendiferous and unmatched golden glow.

For me, shivering and dozing in the lee of that gardener's tool-shed in the Yusupov Gardens, the lights of nearby streets shining through the dank trees, I was

seeing the problem more mundanely. I like measurements, for reasons I explained to Victor Lustig. The
Amber Room is said to have weighed, when on its
travels in World War Two, some six-and-a-half tons.
The panels each measured five metres in height, brilliantly mosaicked in coloured ambers to show royal
coat-of-arms of different monarchies. Over 110,000
pieces were incrusted with the combined techniques
of the world's best amber craftsmen. No wonder
courtiers used to assemble to see the Amber Room's
dazzling radiance in the setting sun. Amber itself is
said to be magic, an aphrodisiac, health-giving, a substance that could even turn old age back to youth, the
cure-all in an age of miracles and wonder.

Valuable, no? Russian presidents as recently as Mr
Yeltsin harboured dark suspicions: it's still concealed
in German hands – where else? – or, even better, it was
stolen by American gangsters. Others gloomily say
the RAF bombed the great fortress of Koenigsberg to
extinction and so destroyed it as the Red Army
advanced. Still others say it's in the hands of private
collectors, wealthy souls gloating over it in the rays of
the setting sun...

Me? I was certain the worst bout of divvy sickness
I'd ever experienced, as we sat in the theatre to admire
the workmanship of St Petersburg's restorers, gave its
location away. The only single antique in the world
that looked like a room, was shaped like a room, and
was the size of a room, could only be, well, a room, the
panels concealed in the mundane painted flats on that
stage. And who would kill one poor bloke, maybe two,
for a set of canvas-and-strut splurges tacked together
as stage scenery? Nobody. But if that ordinary scenery
was lined with wall panels of priceless antique amber
carved by the greatest carvers in history, somebody
was being tempted. Speculators in antiques have reck-

oned its value close to half a billion zlotniks, but that was a decade since. Now? The Amber Room was worth killing for.

Teeth chattering in the cold, I stirred. Water had seeped under me, running from some trickle down the slope. I'd not had the sense to find shelter on higher ground. I'm hopeless outdoors, and indoors even worse.

Shame, I thought, that a pig like Purser Mangot and his motley thieves should purloin the fabled amber treasure from St Petersburg, which had endured so much tribulation since the days of Peter the Great. I rose, trying not to groan or make any noise.

They'd need lorries, transport of sorts. And two, maybe three, wagon drivers, plus blokes to crate up the amber panels and somehow get them down to the quayside. Once the passengers were at supper – about now? – would be a good time. It happened at every port, boxes and supplies coming aboard with the next few tons of caviar and wine.

The shine of the sky-glow showed me the lake. It lay between where I had rested and the Yusupov Palace. I walked towards the distant building, guided by the slender string of lamps along the canal and the three solitary floodlights up ahead through the trees.

Chapter Thirty

Back home, I always envied the night-stealers, those who poach in silence. I hate meeting them in the lanes to Seven Arches or Friday Wood. Walk down by the navigation limit, where Caesar's barges tied up bringing weapons, bricks, or wine for the Roman garrison in our town, you often see one of an early morning, their long coats heavy with dead birds or rabbits. Usually they have a dog, the slinking kind you never see. "Morning, George. Lost Rover today?" I say, and get back, "Morning, Lovejoy. No, he's close by." It's only luck if you glimpse the shadowy creature flitting among the hedgerows.

It must be pleasant being able to move through countryside, nobody knowing you're there. I once nearly stood on a poacher when I was setting up my easel to paint by the River Colne. It was snowing, and a low snowdrift said quietly, "Move off a bloody yard, eh, Lovejoy?" frightening me to death.

In countryside I sound like popcorn even when I'm hiding. Going slow hardly helps because every crackling twig, every crunchy leaf, makes sure it gets a spot underneath my next footfall. Bonfires are quieter. In the Yusupov Gardens I really tried, fondly imagining I was ghostly but probably creating a din worse than a cavalry charge. My idea was to come at the Yusupov building on the terrace from which I'd legged it.

As I got nearer I could see the great palace – not as huge as I'm making it sound, but still a size – in silhouette against the floodlights that shone where it faced the Fontanka road and the canal bridge. No lights on the garden side – or had Mangot's complicitors dowsed them? I saw only darkness until I was within fifty paces. Then I made out the vague shapes of three lorries, saw a flickering headlight and heard engine noise. They were loading something. Why weren't they being secret? I heard blokes calling instructions to the loader-arm vehicle. They sounded confident, and legitimate.

On my hands and knees I reached the last bushes. No animals, thank God. Three men angled a crate from a loader and waved it down. It dropped with a thump that made me almost cry out in grief. I thought, for God's sake don't damage the Amber Room now, not after these centuries. They levered it. Heavier than I would have thought. I could hear the Russian voices calling, probably the usual "Left side down a bit" that all lorry blokes shout. The loader rattled away to the rear entrance where more men showed, wheeling out another long flat crate.

Long and flat with black Gothic lettering. I was in darkness, but they worked under light inside their lorries and small headlights on the loader-arm vehicle. I saw the driver's cigarette glow as he called his warnings to the men. They kept the next box still while he backed his loader onto the terrace and turned it towards the lorries. His helpers vanished back inside, pulling their trolley.

Two choices, plus the coward's. That's what my gran used to say, "There's always two choices in everything, plus the coward's, making three." Assuming I was right, that they'd somehow found the priceless Amber Room and hit on a way of not only stealing it but simultaneously smuggling it out of the country, I could rush out and bring the police. Or, second choice, I could race back to the ship and find the captain, accuse the suspects, demand to see the ambassador, all that.

Then, as the crate was lobbed unceremoniously into the lorry, I saw something that automatically cancelled out my first choice. A uniformed policeman strolled into the light in full uniform, touching a match to his cigarette. The police were here, and in on it. Ivy had said something like, "You can arrange anything in Russia."

Second choice, then?

Well, on board they had something ready and lurking there for me. Why else had they buttered me up, given me an expensive cruise, sent women to lull me to obedience, and killed? And what ambassador would believe a tatty bloke like me?

Neither choice, then. I was left with the coward's. The trouble was, Gran never said what the coward's choice was. The question was to find out, and do it properly.

The policeman strolled to the rear of the last lorry and spoke to the men inside. I'd seen three. You didn't need more than that to manhandle a flat crate, even if it was nearly two metres in length. Amber isn't heavy. The first two lorries were open but unlit, their headlights off. It would have to be them. The coward's way, hoping Gran wasn't tut-tutting on some cloud, was do nothing brave and get away scotage free. I worked it out. The two nearest lorries were either loaded, or empty and waiting. Whichever I tackled, Number Three wagon would be in the light from the doorway.

When the loader-arm truck had gone back, I went slowly to the first lorry, crouching low. Movement catches the eye. Even if you make the most fleeting of shadows, somebody'll see swiftness. Go slow, you're in with a chance. I crawled under the first lorry, stayed a minute beneath the giant rear wheels, then rose slowly to peer inside over the dropped tailgate.

Empty. I climbed on, and felt around. There are always ropes, chains, crowbars. I came on an iron crow by almost knocking myself out on the damned thing. Three were hooked on struts fixed along the length of the lorry. I nicked two and a length of chain, dropped down and scurried underneath.

Until you've been there, you've no idea how massive a wheel is. Each vehicle seemed to have two couples of back wheels. I'd seen my trick done at the M18 motorway service station, where jealousies run strong because antiques thieves congregate there of a Saturday to sell what they've nicked while people are out watching football. It's quite simple.

Lacking a knife to cut the tyres, I propped the short arm of the crowbar underneath one tyre, so that when the lorry moved it would dig into the rubber. The long arm I lodged against the adjacent tyre.

It's very effective. The tyre rotates as the lorry advances, so the short arm, being the divided end, impales itself into the tyre. The other end rips into the next tyre. It was exactly the same action on Queen Boadicea's chariots, which had scythes projecting from their hubs to slice enemies' legs. Progress, you might say. The lorry I'd once seen nobbled like this hadn't got a few yards before it slewed to a halt. The extra advantage is that the wheel is damaged beyond repair. It isn't a matter of simply changing the tyre and driving on.

Making sure, I fixed the other crowbar on the other two massive wheels. If one didn't work – I couldn't see how it would fail – the other would.

That left the chain. I wrapped it round me and went dog-like to the second lorry. I had some notion of tying the axle to a railing, but it was too far off. Between loadings, I scouted for something, anything, to fix the chain to. I began to despair, even thought of going back for another crowbar, but that was too pathetic even for the coward's choice. It was only when I began to get scared they would soon move to the middle lorry that I realised I was kneeling on a huge grid. The chain wouldn't quite reach, so I left it and eeled back for more.

If I'd been more of a workman, it would have taken

me only a few seconds, but I'm all thumbs. Sweating, on my side, trying to tie two chains together, I began to make mistakes and had to do it three times before the thing got itself linked. Best I could do, tie the chain to what I hoped was an axle then onto the grid. I had the sense to loop it under the foremost grille so the lorry's forward motion might lift the grid up. I imagined it trailing noisily behind the big vehicle. It would be halted by police, something like that.

They slammed the tailgate on the last lorry. I heard the men walking, calling. I snuck away, staying under the lorries until I was within reach of the shrubbery, then went slowly into the shadow. I was tempted to wait, but we cowards have standards. I worked my way back, using the sky-glow to avoid falling too often. I was a wreck by the time I'd gone a hundred paces.

The rain had almost stopped. I found shelter under some dense foliage and sat on a low branch, hunching up and trying to doze. I could hardly hear the men or the loader-arm vehicle. Nothing more I could do. Wander the streets, I'd get nabbed by the plod and be worse off than I already was? Try to nig into the Yusupov Palace? Not a bad idea, except somebody would find me and blame me for theft, trespass, God-knows-what. Stay here, I could emerge in the morning and find the embassy and turn myself in. Or not?

Worn out, my exhausted brain abandoned logic and tried for oblivion.

* * *

Engines starting up woke me. I heaved myself onto a higher branch. I'm not so good at that either, only managed to lodge myself in the first crook of the stubby tree and couldn't go up any more. From there, though, I could see vague movement in the shadows.

The building's door was closed, its light gone. Presumably the loading was done. Hard to imagine a king's ransom in antique amber in those hulks. I prayed my sabotage would work as the first lorry's side lights came on. It revved, and moved.

The other two vehicles started up. I saw a couple of figures walk in the lights. Heart in my mouth, I waited for the leading lorry to stall, do something, but the damned thing simply kept going, slowly drawing away. It had gone two vehicle's lengths when it stopped. I couldn't distinguish its shape well enough to make out what was happening, but it revved, engine growling, then seemed to quieten. Its nose just edged into the light from the street lamps before it stopped altogether and somebody called out. Other voices answered, a door slammed, more figures moving into the headlights.

The next lorry started off. I saw its headlights, then the vehicles seemed to slew crosswise, coming against the side of the building with a crash, though it hadn't been going at any speed, just trying to move past the leading wagon. Its engine cut and more voices began.

The third came forward but there were urgent warning yells as it slumped down and tilted massively. Its engine whirred as if caught fast, and stopped. Maybe the grid had been lifted by my chains and the wheel had gone into the gap? Then voices went low. I couldn't hear anything. They must be working out that somebody had damaged their lorries. And it looked like I'd got all three, the first two by my improvised traps and the third because the grid had acted like a tank trap. The loader-arm vehicle was too small to lift or pull such large vehicles. Unless it unloaded them, they were immobilised.

It was then that I heard the noise. Men, not caring if they were detected, called. I saw flashlights stabbing the shrubbery, and like a fool I thought, what are they looking for?

My chest griped. Looking for me, hunting whoever had ruined their theft. There was only one place the saboteur could hide, and that was in the gardens where I was. I scrabbled down to the ground and started to run.

In daylight, scarpering through undergrowth is almost impossible. In the dark it's hopeless. Branches cut me, twigs poked and blinded me and roots brought me down. I headed for the road, thinking of the square with the metro stations and the caffs. Nothing had been open when I'd cut into the gardens, so unless they opened early...

I almost slammed into the shed. I ran round it, gasping for breath and whimpering. They'd do for me if I got caught. Flashlights flickered among the trees ahead, between me and the road. With hunters' instincts, the bastards had sent people round to trap me. I heard them coming, and hauled myself up onto the roof of the little building. It had a ridge, and I spread out on it, on the slope away from the Yusupov building. I heard them come and tried to quieten my breathing. They thrashed about, shouting. Their flash-lights sliced the dark sky. If they shone their torches ahead they'd see a bare roof, so unless they came round the other side and raised their beams, I might not be seen.

They came and milled about below. One or two went past, calling to the men nearer the road. I stayed put.

Then I heard them pause, stand and talk, a little breathless. One or two lit fags, everything in Russian.

Except one voice was familiar. Fluent, in Russian? It had never spoken Russian before. And then anoth-er, also familiar. Recriminations, possibly, and no love lost. Tempers flew, there were arguments. Then frank bawling. I heard a thump and more shouts. Somebody from nearer the gate, in the direction I'd been heading, came walking back, their beams on the ground so as not to trip, lighting the inevitable cigarettes, talking, calling ahead in those flat voices announcing no luck.

The group assembled while arguments raged. Some went back to the lorries, no need to avoid noise now. I could hear them reach the wagons and distant arguments begin round the vehicles. I guessed they were trying to work out what to do. Surely they must have had vehicles in reserve for a scam of this magnitude?

And the row near the shed went on, with those two familiar voices beginning to shout in Russian, others yelling back, and then a series of slaps. Slaps, like hands on faces? And somebody screeching what could only be abuse, then the whole pack starting to mutter, sullen and resigned.

A voice yelled from the direction of the lorries. An engine started, and the low revving of the loader joined in. Another engine, and somebody calling, I supposed wanting assistance. Maybe they were trying to pull the lorry forward so its wheels would come clear of the hole left by the grille? Except a laden lorry's wheel would surely buckle under the stress of a fall like that.

I heard one lorry creak, creak some more then fall with a stunning crash, maybe on its side. Music to my ears. With any luck it would be the first lorry, then the others would be hemmed in. Could a damaged lorry reverse? I wasn't sure.

One of the familiar voices mentioned a woman's name. I stilled. It was the last name I could ever have imagined having anything to do with a scam like this. I caught another name I knew, but surely that couldn't have been right. I was disorientated. It was then that a blunt snapping sound came, just when I'd thought tempers had cooled.

The sharp report dinned in my ears, so quick and severe I actually thought something tapped the side of my head. I almost looked round in fright. Somebody grunted once, twice, kept on until a second slapping sound caused one last severe exhalation. The sounds ceased. And the grunting, and the breaths.

"Bastard," a familiar voice remarked, nonchalantly as if winning a trick at cards. I'd heard other gamblers say things like that, almost affectionate, with a hint of oh-well-bad-luck. I almost exclaimed aloud.

More Russian, then the voices receded as the men went towards the lorries. I waited, trying to hear if anybody was lurking down there for me to drop into a trap. Five minutes or so, the revving engines still hard at it and the shouts uncaring now, as if everybody had given up trying for secrecy.

I dropped to the ground. I didn't risk going round to the other side of the shed, where some corpse was lying shot to death. I know what a gun sounds like close to, and didn't want my footprints all over a crime scene, nor did I want bloodstains on me. For a second I dithered, guilt telling me I should see if they were still alive. Except people who shot people like that were unlikely to leave loose ends. Good reasoning, for a coward.

Taking care, I went near the house, and saw a real mess. One lorry was on its side – my crowbar trick coming good. The rear wheels of the second lorry were splayed as if it had actually been broken and the truck bed split. The third looked driven into the ground, two of its near-side back wheels in the hole and its front wheels almost off the terracing. I was thrilled. The Amber Room wasn't going anywhere.

Time I looked after myself. I retreated to the shrubbery. I needed to get past the stricken vehicles. The men started to unload the crates, handling them so roughly I winced. The loader wasn't much use, until they could manhandle each crate off the bed of each truck. Only then could the loader remove the crates one by one and stack them on the edge of the terrace.

They finally started in earnest, and after about half-an-hour I got past. They must have sent for more trucks. I saw a faint sky-glow and guessed morning was on the way. About time too, but they must think they were still within a shout of success. It was odd stepping into the light of the corridor through the double rear doors of the building.

How long ago since I'd come through here, talking and smiling, having a glass of champagne with Tour B2 from the *Melissa*, Natasha rounding us all up and Lady Vee eager for cake? I went quietly to the main office, just feeling my way along the walls and taking my time, until I reached the main desk by the front entrance.

The doors seemed intact. There was adequate orange light coming in through the windows. It showed the desk where the information ladies had been seated when we'd arrived. I left a trail of mud from my shoes, but there you go. I took a good thirty minutes trying to make sense of the phone, until I saw a list of numbers in non-Cyrillic script stuck on the wall beside the desk. I cursed, cheated out of valuable time.

Keeping an ear out for the men – I was too far away now to hear them unloading – I dialled the numbers we'd been told on the coach trips. St Petersburg is easier than our own cities. You dial zero-1 for fire engines, zero-2 for police and zero-3 for ambulances. Before I called them, though, I rang a series of embassies. I did our own, then Germany's, France's, then the American, Canadian, Ukrainian, Danish – in honour of Wolffram the amber carver – then Poland's. I only got one who was awake and on the ball, guess whose. All the rest were recorded voices, so taxpayers could get stuffed and ambassadors could slumber their alcoholic stupors in peace and not be disturbed by the hoi-polloi.

Then I called the 01, 02, 03 and said, "Yusupov, fire, fire!" The police and ambulances just got the name of the place, nothing more. A master of disguise, I did one voice falsetto, one bass, and one a stuttery Italianate with every word ending in a vowel. I did it all a few times in attempted film-star impressions with my sleeve over the mouthpiece like I'd seen in bad movies. Then I wiped the phone free of dabs and let myself out by the front door. I had the courtesy to switch the lights on and leave the doors ajar.

I walked to the market and hunched down near a bare stall to wait for the dawn.

Chapter Thirty-One

Russian words were spoken by the same familiar voice, the one that had been raised in anger before somebody got shot. Strangely, I could understand what he was saying and knew who he was. He thought somebody had betrayed him. Ivy's name was mentioned over and over. I knew I was dreaming. Somebody threw water on my face. I came to, spluttering in the cold.

Three men in dark garb stood over me. It was nearly day. I was cold and damp in the street market. A few Ladas and Volgas and some gungy old Zhigulis were already whining about the streets, and the odd Mercedes. I knew none of the men.

"Up, Lovejoy." Purser Mangot pushed into view. He was in full uniform, wearing a hat crammed with insignia. I'd have saluted if I'd remembered how.

"I got lost," I stammered. "I got mugged, er, lost my memory."

"You're pathetic."

"These five blokes jumped out and – "

"It's no good, Lovejoy."

The Russians bundled me into a police motor. At a grim police station I was put into a room and watched over by some bloke in the uniform of those traffic cops who stand on every corner. I had evaded them until now.

The guard ignored me when I asked for water. Time passed. I was interrogated by a uniformed bloke accompanied by an interpreter. I told my story. They tested my coat, my trousers, my skin and hands with chemicals and took skin scrapings and pared my finger nails and took the residues away in containers. A Russian lawyer speaking an occasional word in English came and asked how did I manage to have some American dollars in my sock and pockets if I was mugged. I said I'd run like hell.

They asked how I'd become separated from the B2 Tour of the Yusupov Palace. I said I'd gone to the loo, and when I came out everybody had gone and I tried to catch them up and guess what but they'd already left so I started walking but missed my way...

"Pathetic," Purser Mangot said with that snarl, putting his head round the door. I asked him for some water.

"Don't be pathetic." He sounded disgusted, and went.

For a whole morning and most of the afternoon they asked me questions. I was glad Mangot was around, though I heard another voice speaking English. I was interviewed over and over by a new lawyerish geezer who sounded tired out and from Liverpool. I was never so glad to hear a familiar accent in all my life. They let me go to the loo, where I drank some water.

Later, I asked if I could phone the embassy. They told me to shut up. I asked to be allowed a phone call. They said no.

Another hour, another interview, same questions. They asked if I'd made phone calls to the fire, police and ambulance departments. I said I hadn't. They asked if I'd gone back to the Yusupov Palace and I said no. They took my finger prints. They made me read English sentences and recorded my speech. They photographed me with a card round my neck and measured my ears. I thought, ears? What the hell had my ears been up to? They snipped a lock of hair and washed the inside of my cheek and took the saliva away in a container. They labelled everything. They even had a container for blank labels.

As it was getting on for evening, I was taken to the door and a Russian man came. A grubby embassy official in a bad temper arrived with Mangot and signed forms. I asked if he was a lawyer. He glared. His suit didn't quite fit. I suppose he was one of the embassy people I'd roused by the phone calls I had denied. He hurried off to get ready for the next cocktail party. My taxes were some use, then. Purser Mangot said they were letting me go. We boarded a taxi. It took us to the airport.

There, I was handed into the charge of a man from the shipping agent's office. He wore a shipping line badge and spoke fluent Russian, but not to me. At the gate I asked Purser Mangot where I was going. He did his snarl. I told him thanks for getting me out of the Russian gaol. He said his bit about my being pathetic and turned on his heel.

My pal said nothing even when I asked questions so I shut up. I felt handcuffed, though he didn't even glance my way. I obeyed his beckoning finger without question. He directed me by gestures and tilts of the head, stay there, come this way, stand still. He signed forms at the airways desks. I wasn't a prisoner but made sure I was a model prisoner, if you follow.

Purser Mangot was visible on the spectator's gallery when I boarded the plane, watching me leave. The man came with me, sat behind my seat and still said nothing. After the shortest flight on record we touched down in Helsinki. It was already dark. With my silent warder I travelled in a taxi to a quayside, where a huge cruise liner was about to dock. It was the *Melissa*. Christ, she was a giant of a thing. I vaguely remembered the ship was due to reach Helsinki in Finland the day after leaving St Petersburg, so there had been no question of my escaping, not for real. My heart sank.

The quayside clock said nine o'clock. The passengers would be either at dinner or in the evening show or films, or grumbling because the casinos were closing on account of being in a foreign port. I was taken to the gangway and walked on board alone, the silent warder standing watching until I was taken in hand by the Ghurkas and the gangway door closed. I felt entombed by the air conditioning. I was put in my cabin, rather glad to be there in a strange way. I locked the door, had a shower and changed. I shaved, did my teeth and felt really quite good.

At the Bordeaux I had a meal, then sat in the lounge in solitude. I saw photographs by the ship's photographers among hundreds on display. The girls were just taking them down. I asked for the one showing me trying to grin over the side of the gangway as we'd left the previous morning on Tour B2. A memento, but silly to waste the money. I sat in a bar until my eyelids drooped. Distantly I could hear the riotous laughter of the celebrations of a great show, flags, everybody singing, the ship one big party.

Unbelievably, I decided this wasn't for me. I know I ought to have reported to Lady Vee, shown her friends I was still around and maybe build myself some security. Instead, like a duckegg I went to bed. No sign of any of my fellow diners, ladies I knew, or antiques experts. I didn't call June Milestone, Delia Oakley, or Lauren to ask how she'd got on doing the dinner-time antiques quiz. Maybe I was just done for.

Someone had once told me to tell everybody wrong. I'd done that, all right. I was getting more and more narked as the lamp hours ticked away. Thinking about it, I'd been really obedient, mostly. Even when that benign little bloke Mr Moses had been killed in that attractive harbour in North Germany, I'd kept myself meek and mild like in the children's hymn. I was so angry I could hardly think. I wondered how far an official protest would get, on board a ship like this.

Once, I'd heard passenger gossip about two families leaving Durban on this cruise liner. They'd fought, and been so obnoxious to everyone aboard that the crew told the captain. He'd simply put them ashore, to fly home at their own expense. Captain's word is law, they say. Can't hang anyone these days, but still law.

Making sure my cabin door was locked, I fell into bed.

＊ ＊ ＊

The steward arrived like a tornado, grinning and bringing a breakfast I hadn't ordered.

"You like Helsinki today!" he prophesied.

"Ta, Emil, but I didn't order breakfast."

"You eat! Good breakfast start the day!"

I noshed my way through, feeling better. I searched the cabin thoroughly before the stewards came to make the beds and vacuum. Nothing had been planted. I felt around every ledge, up-ended every drawer. Not a single thing.

A swim, then I had coffee when the morning passed a bit, watched Helsinki tours leave the ship on coaches parked along the quays. I even strolled ashore, to say I'd been there, saw a Greek Orthodox cathedral of all things and walked through a market – lots of flowers – and sat listening to a brass band competition in a little park. Good leather things, woollens, carved ornaments, in Helsinki. The ship, notices said along the harbour wall, would sail at the end of the afternoon, for Sweden. It was fine, dry and warm. The ship sailed on time.

Nice place, Helsinki. No trouble.

＊ ＊ ＊

Late that day, before dinner, I was getting ready to find Lauren, select some antiques for the evening quiz. My name was missing from the ship's newspaper, so presumably I wasn't needed to give and help to June Milestone or deputise for Mr Semper. I was pretty calm, even knowing it was close to my arrest over something trumped up. It came at quarter to six. I was dressed. No tuxedo tonight, since we had just left port.

They came in without knocking. I stared at them. Executive Purser Mangot was in a striped shirt, wearing an imitation straw boater and bow tie with a Pearly King waistcoat and string round his knees, a Cockney sparrow image as convincing as a promise. June Milestone was his Pearly Queen, with red, white and blue skirt and bolero in the national colours, a jaunty Eliza Doolittle bonnet on her head. Amy the dancer was even more floral, with Les Renown done up like John Bull, a shiny black topper and artificially rotund belly popping his waistcoat, gleaming black George boots.

There was somebody else with them. I stared, and drew breath to ask a searching and meaningful question, like what the hell. I stayed silent.

"Carnival time, Lovejoy. Come and identify someone."

"Who?" I got out.

"He's an old spoil-sport," Amy said, grinning mischievously.

"Deess away," Ilya said in his strange Russian accent. "Pliss, Loof-yoy."

They all laughed and pulled me into the corridor, enjoying some joke. Several passengers were already making their way from the cabins to the party. Maybe it was Honour To Sweden time? Or was their flag different colours?

"You'll like this, Lovejoy," Mangot said grimly. He looked a bit pale. I thought, who's the one at risk here, you or me?

We went to the front end of the ship, passing through the Atrium where passengers were assembling, all similarly bedecked with ribbons and boaters and floral hats in patriotic hues. I tried looking for Ivy, Fern even, Delia Oakley, Cynthia and Josh Bannerman, or Lady Vee at a pinch, anybody who might suggest normality.

We went to the elevators and descended to the medical centre. There, we turned to the side opposite Out-Patients, and went through an unmarked door covered in dark green beige, some kind of thoroughfare lit by strip lights. I heard a thick lock slam. I'd heard that sort of sound before and my chest griped.

"He'll like this," Amy was telling Les, punching him playfully.

"So will we!"

More laughter. We turned right after about twenty paces, into a bare room lined in stainless steel walling. Doors were set in the steel surfaces. At the far end was a double door, all steel. The air was cold. Ilya undid the bolt, slid it aside and pulled the door for us.

We entered a mortuary. I tried to hang back but was shoved none too gently and stumbled in with the rest. Purser Mangot was looking decidedly pale by then. Amy and Les were being as amused as ever at less than usual as usual, if you follow. I stood there. A medical technician, I suppose, in a green gown was standing beside the central table, everything stainless steel and freezing. Nervous, I glanced back towards the entrance door but they kept me there.

On the table was a covered figure. I saw heeled shoes projecting from the green sheet covering the deceased. I thought, why me to identify Henry Semper, when he came on board with his lass Lauren and a hoard of TV admirers? I drew breath to complain about this absurdity when Purser Mangot gestured to the technician. He removed the green sheet.

Billy? I stared from one person to the next and the next. My mind went ??? so I asked what had happened.

No blood, but Billy had been cleaned up. I saw another person had joined us, Kevin, incongruously dressed in striped patriotic colours and bishop sleeves and pearly waistcoat and straw boater. He was staring past me at Billy. A hole was in Billy's right orbit, a mess of staining on his chest.

"Lovejoy?" Purser Mangot said. "Can you identify this person as Mr William Sands from the Wirral? Your fellow diner on Table 154 in the Pacific Restaurant on this cruise?"

"Yes," I managed at second go.

"Are you in a position to say when you heard, saw or encountered the deceased last?"

"Yes." I looked round at Kevin.

"On what occasion?"

"I was on a shed in the Yusupov Gardens in St Petersburg. I heard him talking."

"Talking to whom?"

"To Kevin," I said. "Kevin spoke Russian."

"That's not true!" Kevin said, "you vicious bitch." He spoke in a voice that barely got beyond a hiss. "You're making it up."

"I didn't see who shot Billy, just heard two shots."

"I never left Tour B2!"

"Oh, aye you did, mate," Ilya said in perfect English. "I was within yards when you sloped off, you bastard."

He got my stare. I asked who he was.

"Ta for the evidence, Lovejoy," he told me, smiling. "We are recorded and certified."

He called out in Russian, and Natasha appeared at the door with two uniformed blokes.

"Time to go, folks." He nodded thanks to the technician, and led the way out. Purser Mangot, I noticed, was first through the exit and into the lifts, returning to the dementia of the ship party.

"Who are you?" I asked Ilya, one eye on Natasha.

"Just a humble member of the plod," he said back. Emerging from the lifts into the corridor by the Atrium he nudged Amy and said, "Hey, Amy. Loof-yoy! What about that?"

They laughed all the way back to sanity. I asked to sit down in Mangot's office while Kevin was taken away.

Purser Mangot recovered his poise as colour crept back into his face. He must have been unsettled by the mortuary. "This is your statement, typed up. Sign it."

"My statement? I can't give evidence."

"You already have, sufficient for our purposes. The St Petersburg authorities need it, not us."

"Right," I said, working things out, going back over the traces and trying to remember who'd said what to whom.

"You will be called upon to identify the painting."

He pointed. On the wall my painting was hanging, now expertly framed. Van Gogh's *Spinning Woman*, that I'd nicked from the Marquis of Gotham's mansion.

"It's my painting," I said stupidly. I went close and peered. "How'd it get here?"

"You swear it's yours?"

"Course it is."

He was smiling, his old authority returning. "You're under arrest, Lovejoy."

"For what?"

"Theft of Old Masters from the Marquis of Gotham. And forgery. And complicity to steal."

"Are you a copper, or crew?"

"I'm neither, Lovejoy. I'm David Buddy the bounty hunter. I know sod all about ships, but I know all about you."

By then I'd got there and said his name with him, nodding.

"You looked different on TV."

"That's my cousin's husband. A decoy. Otherwise crooks like you would see me coming and clear off, right?"

"Right." I said. Well, I would.

"I'll send for you early," he said, shuffling his notes. "We're going on a long journey, you and me."

"Want to come for supper with me, Lovejoy?" June Milestone asked. "You've tried the Bordeaux. We could do something less fashionable. Maybe the Al Fresco? I know you like the Lido Deck. It shouldn't get too crowded until after the late show. By then we should be quite tired. It's been quite a day."

She smiled at Purser Mangot, aka David Buddy, bounty hunter. Kevin and his guards were gone, Natasha with them, and Ilya staying to chat up two girls on Reception.

"Promise you won't ask any questions," June said, gracefully leading the way. "We have antiques to talk about. What did you think of the Exhibition in the Hermitage? Wasn't it brilliant? I have figures from Sotheby's recent antiques toys auction – the Great Teddy Bear Sale. You'll be interested. And I've had faxes of the Ince and Mayhew furniture auction. Just think what you've been missing!"

*   *   *

About four o'clock the next morning the *Melissa* was sailing slowly among a scatter of small islands, the grey dawn turning blue. Small boats, a myriad harbours, coloured houses, the approach to Stockholm looked idyllic.

June wakened me and told me we had to go on deck to see a special sight.

"You'll love it," she said, excitement in her eyes.

We dressed and I tottered after her. At the end of the corridor Purser Mangot was waiting with two crewmen. June handed me over with, "Goodbye, Lovejoy. It's been fun." And left me.

"Downstairs, Lovejoy."

Mangot led the way. The crewmen shoved me. We went down a ladder to the embarkation point. A small boat was travelling alongside flying the Swedish flag. Shaking, I got aboard, Mangot following. I kept away from him. The power boat accelerated away from *Melissa*. I saw June at the Promenade Deck railing. She blew a kiss. I turned away.

An hour later we were on a plane to London.

Chapter Thirty-Two

Back home I was allowed to return to my cottage after three days of statements, more statements, repeated statements. It only confirmed my view of lawyers – they're people in some private gold field beset with mines, the location of which they alone are trained to avoid.

My garden was even more overgrown, my Austin Ruby dwindling audibly among rust. My cottage had a broken window – who'd done that? Nobody usually bothers – but cardboard is in everybody's dustbin so I patched it. Water, electricity, phone, were all cut off. Council bills and final demands were fallen leaves by the door. Robins and blue-tits came shouting for nuts, cheese, crumbs. I shouted back for them to give me a frigging chance for Christ's sake, and rummaged for some grub. Not a carrot.

At the small Co-op shop, new to the village now with serving ladies who had a computerised till, I received a frigid refusal when I tried to cadge. A lady I baby-sit for down the lane gave me half a loaf and some margarine and jam, and I filched somebody's semi-skimmed milk from a doorstep. Well, they were church-goers and should feed the hungry. They were always on about good causes, and I was their sheep like the Good Book says. I wanted an egg because I'm quite good at cooking eggs, except they're hard to boil and I can't stand runny white. Same with frying, that rim of soft white round the yolk is a swine to get rid of. Another thing God got wrong.

A note in a lavender envelope persuaded me to open it.

Dear Lovejoy,

I was so afraid. That police officer Mr Mangot sent me off the ship. He said you would be safe. I am so

sorry if I let you down. Please call.
      Love,
                  Margaret   XXX

Aye, right, I thought. I wiped the table down with some old paper and sat to eat my bread and jam. No tea, which is always death, but I had a cup of water from my garden well and put it there as if I had a full tea set. I was the height of elegance, really impressive with a clean knife and everything. All I needed now was a gorgeous lady to come in and say the words I hungered for, namely

"Anything you want, sir?"

"Wotcher, love. You're just in time for tea."

She put two shopping bags of provisions down on the flagged floor, looking round.

"You make a pretty picture, Lovejoy."

"I maintain standards. My gran told me to."

"I'm pleased to hear it." She shed her coat, was unable to find a place to hang it, finally draped it on the divan bed. I'd pulled it down ready to sleep alone. "I called in the village shop to ask where you lived. They said you'd just been in trying to, ah, shop. I bought these, because I owe you. Think repayment."

Nobody ever owes me. I sometimes wished they did, but they never do. Wisely I didn't say these words, though they're part of my grievance litany.

"What'll you have?"

"Sorry, Ivy. I've just finished. Couldn't eat another thing."

"You've never tried my cooking, very Russian. I am magnificent. Sit there." She tried the stove, the phone, the water taps, grimaced and went out saying she'd be back. I lay down, worn out, and slept.

Long later she woke me. The place looked neat. Two blokes were in the garden. I detected food, fried this and steaming that. The table was laid. They'd rigged up some kind of trestle table out there, their

stove hissing flames from propane gas. Ivy was decorative in a floral pinafore. She called thanks and they
left, grinning, in a van that was more logos than vehicle.

"The proposition is this, Lovejoy," she said, combing
my hair. I wondered if that's what Russian women do.
She'd combed my hair after we'd made smiles in the
cabin on the *Melissa*. Was it a custom? "You dine with
me, then ravish me. Or, if you're far too exhausted, I
shall ravish you with techniques I am re-learning. That's
my final offer. Take it or leave it."

Beggars can't, can they?

✼ ✼ ✼

She slept beside me, and I thought, is she the one?

Years ago I invented the Ten Word Game. It's simple: put any problem into ten words. No extras. You
can describe the Olympics, America, or the whole universe, in ten words. It shows you what's what.

You can also describe the perfect woman. I'm not
saying it's easy, just that it teaches you. It makes you see
things about a person you never suspected, and it can
scare you. It can explain death.

I wanted to play it now, and get an answer. Was she
the one?

Ivy slept soundly. I often think life must be easy for
women, because they've got it all. They can, with virtually a flick of a wrist, soar a man to heaven in a way
he remembers all his life, put themselves right up there
on a pedestal along with the Virgin Mary or Mae West
or any gorgeous starlette. Or they can charm a bloke
with a fluttering eyelash, false or not, and synthesise a
shape that stays in your memory for ever and ever.

Was she the one? I could see myself wanting her to
stay for life. I would ask her when she woke.

Then I wondered what had roused me. I'd imagined I'd heard an engine, and somebody trying the door. Like I say, I've not much time for sleep, unless it's in that umbra time after making smiles, when a man has to be allowed moments to climb back to life. I imagined – heard? – some familiar voice say quietly, "Lovejoy? I've come to…" And cut to silence. Then some woman's footfalls receding.

Ivy moved, coughed slightly, raised herself to look. I drew breath to propose. No time like the present.

"Ivy, love?" I said, ready to go for it.

"Lovejoy, darling." She stretched, one of the loveliest sights, looking flour-dusted from slumber. She hunched closer. "That was my goodbye."

Goodbye? "Er, right."

She took my response in. Our heads were like bookends on the pillow.

"I'm returning to St Petersburg."

"Okay."

"I have to, darling."

"Course you have."

"Billy took up with Kevin so completely that I had no proper life. Kevin being an emigre, they hatched the plan to loot St Petersburg even more than the Arch-Looter himself."

No wonder Billy condoned my friendship with Ivy. "The Arch-Looter?"

"Boris Berezevsky, among other pseudonyms, was Kevin's relative. Poor Russia came unstitched in the Great Mob War of 1993. It lasted two years and Berezevsky led the looting. Everything went, even street lamps carted away for sale. It was dreadful. Kevin arranged the shipments. They always get off scot free, don't they?"

"Do they?" I never do, and I don't loot anything.

"And Billy being in the police…"

"Then why go back?" was the best I could manage. "They've collared Kevin for killing Billy in the garden after I stopped their theft. It's finished."

"And poor Henry Semper."

I didn't want to think about Henry because of my guilt, or how Kevin had done it. That Ilya copper guessed poison, but they were still looking for the body. My fault. I could have turned back that night and...

"You don't understand what Russia's gone through. I can at least lend a hand, show tourists a better side of the loveliest country."

What chance had I, against love for a whole country, including Pushkin and that lot?

"Victor thinks the same." She went quiet, then said, "We shall go together."

Ivy and Victor? We rose, and I thanked her for the nosh and making smiles. I walked her through the brambles to the broken gate. She kissed me. Little Elizabeth with Olly from down the lane came by just then and went, "Ooooh, Lovejoy!" and went pink. I wagged a finger at her. "Don't tell on me!" and she said, "I promise!" but didn't spit and cross her heart so I knew Radio Elizabeth would broadcast round the village within minutes.

Ivy had summoned a car on her cell phone by then. I waved her off. She looked back through the rear window until the car went beyond the hedgerows. I went in and started to stack up the messages and letters, discarding the red final-demand notices. They'd already done their worst. Two were from magistrates.

"Alone at last?" Delia Oakley said, knocking on the jamb.

"Not now."

"Need help with those?"

"I can guess most contents. These are summonses,

those others superfluous."

"Four or five look personal. One's from me."

"Saying what?"

She tut-tutted. "The cream of the correspondence is usually inside the envelope. Isn't that Goldsmith's crack?"

"Almost."

"I've leased a shop on North Hill next to the tea shop."

"You and Fern?"

She avoided my eye. "Our partnership dissolved. I'm hoping to be your assistant."

"To learn the antiques trade?"

"There's a flat above the premises. Deal, Lovejoy?"

Somebody once said, "Small-small fee deal?" I winced at the memory.

"I work alone, love. And I can't pay."

She smiled. "Bargain at the price. You can lodge with me until you get straight."

I was surprised she said that. The cottage was tidier than it had ever been.

If you're unsure, postpone. If you're absolutely sure, postpone absolutely. It's my rule. She was bonny and appealing, yet I didn't know how I now stood with local dealers. I needed to see them first.

"Right. I'll be down tonight, then."

She came and put her arms round me. "I'm so pleased, Lovejoy. Eight o'clock?"

"Ta, love."

I waved her off in her Toyota as a motor came up from Seven Arches. It must have gone past while Delia was here, because there is no way through beyond the river. Cynthia Bannerman alighted. I stood aside and she went in. I like the way women assume they've a right to go anywhere, which of course they have. I followed.

"Josh has spoken to Mr Sheehan, Lovejoy." For a

second I wondered who she meant, then remembered that was Big John's surname, Sheehan. He ran the Mighty Sheehans of Ulster Import-Export business, a euphemism for charging anybody for whatever he wanted for whatever he said he supplied.

"He spoke to Big John?" I went weak. "What have I to do?"

"Nothing, Lovejoy. Josh straightened things out. They hit it off."

If Sheehan said everything was okay, it had better be. Off the hook! I sighed with relief.

"As long as you do a few services for Josh. And me."

"Right. What services?"

She looked about. "No perjury, nothing nasty. Just occasional consultations about antiques. The first, this coming Thursday. I'll send my car. Be ready at ten."

"Right." Gelt by association?

Turning on her heel, she walked to her waiting motor. Some women can move as if the ground is making all the effort of gliding them while they just stay still. I guess it's breeding or something.

That left me thinking of Ivy. I'd been head over heels. Now I'd be heartbroken for life. Or until at least eight o'clock tonight on North Hill, and thereafter Thursday morning. I heard a tapping on the unbroken pane.

"I'm coming, I'm coming," I called in a temper, and went to the door with the birds' crumbs. "Oh. Wotcher."

"Lovejoy?" Lauren was standing there.

She wore a summery dress and high heels and looked totally different from the dowdy assistant on the ship. She carried a small suitcase.

"Lauren!" I tried to sound really eager. "How, er, great."

"I came to help." She set her case down, her eyes round the cottage. "After the way I behaved."

"After…?" I couldn't remember her doing anything wrong. It was me.

It came out with a rush in prepared phrases. "I was overbearing. You got into trouble helping me. I've come to repay you." She glanced around. "I shall stay. I don't necessarily mean … you know? But it would be irresponsible of me to leave a payment unmet. When do we resume your work?"

"Er, immediately. Always best to get back in the saddle … " An unfortunate metaphor. "Quickest is wisest."

"Indeed it is, Lovejoy." She took a breath, sizing up tasks ahead. "I am no shirker, Lovejoy. Whatever the task, I shall apply myself to the uttermost. You'll see."

"Er, good." I glanced out. "I need to catch the bus. See you later?"

She gave me her keys. "Use my car. Why is it so dark in here?"

I explained about the electricity, water, gas, phone. She nodded. "I shall see to those. I have funds."

"Ta, love. I'll be back about, er … Sorry about the state of the place."

"I like a challenge, Lovejoy."

Thank God for that. I bussed her quickly and left. As I turned right at the chapel and headed for the distant town I saw Margaret Dainty's motor coming into the village.

I kept going, trying to fit the mess into the Ten Word Game, so I could say I'd won something for a change.